FINDING US

J. L. Perry

FINDING US

Cover Design by - The Book Cover Boutique
Edited by - Evermore Editing
Paperback ISBN – 978-0-6486828-7-5
Hardback ISBN – 978-0-6486828-8-2

Books by J. L. Perry

Finding Love Series

Finding Him

Finding Forever

Finding Us

Finding Forgiveness

Finding Love

Finding Her

Bastard Series

Bastard

Luckiest Bastard

Jax

Cocky Hero World Series

Bossy Bastard

Sexy Bastard

Standalone Books

One Night Only

The Boss

Saviour

Nineteen Letters

This book is dedicated to my mum ...
You're not only my mother, you're my best friend.
You have always ... and I mean always been there for me
whenever I've needed you.
We have laughed together and cried together.
You have loved me unconditionally throughout the good
times and the bad.
I'm so blessed to have you.
You're my rock and I'd be lost without you.

A life lived in fear, is a life half lived.

When I decided to follow my stepbrother and move interstate, I still carried the scars from my past. Due to my violent upbringing, at my father's hands, my trust in men is limited. So much so that I'm twenty years old and I've never had a boyfriend.

My best friend Cassie convinced me to have a one-night stand—with a hot, tattooed, Harley-riding stranger—on my twenty-first birthday, and it changed everything. Even though I snuck out of his house while he was sleeping, I had zero regrets. Not only did *he* rock my world *multiple* times, he woke up something inside me, a part of me that I never knew existed.

I'll treasure those memories because they're all I'll ever have. I'm far too damaged for a serious relationship.

I've never been a commitment kind of guy; some may even call me a player. That's probably how I found myself in the situation I'm now in—a single dad to a sweet kid who has a severe case of mummy issues.

When that poor excuse for a human dumped him on my doorstep, it didn't take me long to become attached. That's when I decided it was time to stop living the party life and get my act together. This broken little boy deserved at least one decent parent, and since that would never be his mother, that job was left up to me.

I was content doing life with just the two of us ... until I hooked up with *her*. She was different to all the others; sweet and innocent, with a sassy mouth that turned me on. For the first time *ever,* I contemplated more—that is until she did a runner in the dead of night.

I didn't even know her real name, so I had no way of tracking her down, or so I thought. I had no idea that little temptress was actually my best friend's baby sister.

Chapter 1

Prologue

I follow my mum through the front door, she's just collected me from school, and I love this time of day—it's my calm before the storm, you could say. These few hours in the afternoon that I spend with her are my favourite moments. This is when I feel safe, and it's the only time me and my mum are free to be ourselves. Everything changes around 6 pm; because that's the time my father gets home from work.

I'm sitting at the table doing my homework, chatting and laughing with my mum while she cooks dinner. It's one of the few times I see her smile. She's a different person when my father's not around. She's always jumpy and anxious but it escalates when he's home.

My father acts as if he hates us, and I can assure you—as far as I'm concerned—the feeling is mutual. I've never understood why he doesn't love us. I try my best to be a good girl, but nothing I do is ever good enough for him.

There have been times I've prayed for something to happen to him, which sounds terrible, I know, but I've truly wished for that. My father is cruel, and he's always hurting my mum.

A sudden loud *bang* echoes through the house, as the front door slams closed. My mother and I both jump because we know what's coming. My eyes dart up to the clock hanging on the wall; *he's early*. I hate this dreaded feeling I get in the pit of my stomach when he gets home. That carefree feeling I experienced only moments ago is now replaced with fear.

I look up at my mum from where I'm sitting. Her hands are now violently shaking as she stirs the sauce on the stove. The look on her face breaks my heart; she looks terrified. I wish I could protect her from *him*, but she never lets me. She's scared that he will hurt me again. He's lashed out at me a few times in the past when I've tried to come to her aid.

My stomach churns as I hear his heavy footsteps approaching. When I glance over at my mum, she quickly motions with her eyes for me to leave the room; that's our secret code. It means that shit's about to go down. She told me years ago whenever she gives me that signal, I'm to go straight to my bedroom and lock myself inside. I'm not allowed to come out under any circumstances. No matter what I hear, or how scared I am. I have to stay there until she comes to collect me.

The waiting is torture.

This has been my life for as long as I can remember, and I truly hate living here with that man. *I hate all men.* I may only be twelve years old, but I've seen enough in my short life to know that men are horrible and mean. I don't trust them—at all!

I'm never, ever getting married. I'm not even gonna have a boyfriend.

Once I'm in the safety of my room, I make my way over to the corner beside my bed. I always go to the same place because it's the furthest position from the door. I sit down, and like so many times before, I bend my legs up against my chest. Wrapping my arms tightly around my knees and dropping my head, I start rocking back and forth.

I hear what sounds like someone being slapped. He's hit Mum so many times before the sound is firmly embedded in my brain. The sound of metal clanging on the tiled floor quickly follows; it's probably the spoon she was holding. I want to put my hands over my ears, so I can't hear them, but I don't. *I never do.* It would make it so much easier for me if I didn't have to hear him hitting her. But I have to listen. I don't have a choice.

What if my mum calls out to me? What if she needs me to save her?

"You fucking stupid, lazy, good-for-nothing bitch!" he screams. "You can't even cut the grass properly, you useless piece of shit." My breath hitches in my throat as I clamp my eyes closed. *Slap ... Slap.*

"Please don't hurt me," my mum cries. "I'm sorry." It breaks my heart when she begs like that. I wish I was stronger; I want to hurt him like he hurts her.

The trouble for my mum began yesterday afternoon when she was mowing the lawns and the mower stopped working.

"Please no," I heard her plead as she desperately tried to get it to start again, but to no avail. When her shoulders sagged, I knew she was petrified at the thought of going inside to tell him.

My eyes followed her as she hesitantly walked across the backyard. Her body trembled violently as she slowly climbed the stairs before disappearing into the house to receive her fate.

I ran towards the back door and came to a stop when I entered the kitchen. I watched on in horror as she lowered

3

her head before speaking. She always does this. I don't know if it's because she's scared to look him in the eye or because she doesn't want to see what we both know is coming.

"I can't get the mower to start," she whispered.

Whack. It earnt her a backhand across the face, followed by another hit to the side of her head. The hatred in his eyes as he towered over her made my stomach churn. It wasn't her fault the lawn mower broke down, but logic never mattered to him.

When we sat down to dinner, the silence was deafening. Neither of us game enough to speak. My mother was now sporting a swollen eye and a fat lip that I knew from experience would be black by the morning. They've almost become a permanent fixture on her pretty face, hence why she's always hiding behind those ridiculously large sunglasses when we're in public.

When I side-eyed my dad, I saw his face was red with anger, and the way his nostrils kept flaring told me he was still fuming. I knew this wasn't the end of it.

A short time later, he snapped again while my mum was doing the dishes. He'd been outside trying to fix the lawn mower, and when he couldn't, he came back inside to take his frustration out on her.

He grabbed a pair of scissors out of the drawer in the kitchen before stalking over to my mum. He fisted a chunk of her long blonde hair in his hand and tugged on it hard. She stumbled as she was dragged back towards the door. Aside from a tiny whimper, she remained quiet. I could tell she was scared by her large terrified eyes, but she'd learnt a long time ago not to fight back. Never! It only makes him rage more.

The fear on her face made my heart hurt. The tears were already streaming down her cheeks, and as she passed

4

me, the signal was clear. *Go to your room, and stay safe.* But I couldn't move. The panic running through my tiny body kept me planted on my chair. My eyes were drawn to the scissors in my father's hand. *Will today be the day? The day he finally goes too far and actually kills her?*

She stumbled again as he dragged her down the back steps, her legs grazing the wooden treads. She tried to regain her footing and stand, but he didn't give her a chance. He continued to pull her across the yard by her hair. I willed my body to move, and when it eventually responded, I didn't go to my room; I needed to know mum was going to be okay. I was petrified he was going to use the scissors to stab her.

My body shook and I protectively wrapped my arms around my waist, watching on in horror through the kitchen window.

He threw her to the ground before kicking her in the stomach. She instinctively put her hands up to protect her face. It was the only thing she could do. His next kick was a vicious one to her leg before he threw the scissors down beside her.

"Cut the grass by hand, you dumb, fucking whore," he yelled. He struck again with his boot, and mum yelped, screwing up her face. She'd been hurt, bad.

He stood, hands on hips, legs spread apart. He was intimidating her. She folded herself into a ball on the ground because his intimidation always worked. *He's a bully and knows we're both petrified of him. The sick, perverse monster that he is seems to revel in the fact he can terrify us both. I can always tell by the sadistic smile plastered on his evil face as he hurts her.*

Mum unfolded herself and with shaky hands reached for the scissors. They shook so much she couldn't grasp them, so he stomped on her hand. I gasped as a tortured cry

5

of pain escaped her lips. With tears flowing freely down my cheeks, I watched on, and I felt immediate relief when she finally managed to pick them up.

I hate him so much!

My mum wiped away the blood from her nose with the back of her hand, pulled herself onto her knees, and began cutting the grass by hand. Blade by blade. It was going to take her forever. He stood there, a cruel smile curling his lips, before turning around and heading back towards the house. I dashed to my room and locked the door before he made it back inside.

I desperately wanted to go outside and help her but I knew she wouldn't want that. It would have sparked his anger, seeing me help. She's often told me she can take the beatings as long as he leaves me alone. Sometimes though, I wish my father would hit me instead, just so she could have a break from it.

I lay awake in bed for hours, listening and waiting for her to come inside. I finally heard that familiar click, and my mum's footsteps padding down the hall towards her bedroom. I glanced at the clock on my bedside table. It was almost two in the morning. My poor mum had been cutting the grass, with scissors, for nearly eight hours.

"I love you, Mummy," I whispered into the dark. I knew she couldn't hear me, but I felt compelled to say it. I needed her to know that someone loved her, that somebody cared.

What happened last night must be why Mum's receiving another beating now. My father's obviously unhappy with the way she cut the grass. He'll justify his behaviour in any way he can. She'd been forced to use scissors and it had been dark outside. How can you possibly cut the lawn perfectly with a pair of scissors in the damn dark?

In his mind, there is always an excuse for his psychotic behaviour. "My dinner is too hot." *Whack.* "My dinner is not hot enough." *Whack.* "What did you put in the gravy? It tastes like shit." *Whack.* "Did you buy a different washing powder? My shirt smells like fucking flowers." *Whack.* "I had a bad day at work, and it's all your fault." *Whack.* I could go on forever.

No matter what she does, he always finds something to complain about. She tries so hard to ensure everything's perfect, to keep him happy. It's a waste of time; nothing she does is ever good enough in his eyes.

I rock back and forth in my bedroom. Things are smashing as my father screams at her. The only sounds from mum are cries of pain. This beating is bad; they don't usually last this long. The sound of things shattering filters into my room. That monster must be throwing her around the house.

I can't bear it any longer. I turn my head and glance at my wardrobe. It's where I hid my phone, the one Brooke, my dance teacher, gave me to use in case of an emergency. Standing, I open the double doors and stare up at the shelf, but I can't reach it without a chair.

Suddenly everything goes quiet. I listen harder, but there's nothing but silence. I tiptoe towards my bedroom door and place my ear against the wood. When I hear the front door slam, relief floods through my body.

Finally, it's over. I begin to relax.

He always slams the front door as he leaves the house. He's usually gone for a few hours, but unfortunately, he always returns, reeking of alcohol and full of remorse that never lasts long. I asked my mum once where he went after he hit her. She thinks he goes to the pub to have a few drinks and calm down.

I wish he'd drink so much that it killed him.

I wait quietly. Mum will come and get me any minute. But as time passes, I grow anxious again. Every part of me desperately wants to go to her, but she's told me over and over, *never leave until I come for you*. She will only retrieve me once it's safe.

I'm pacing back and forth by the door and when the minutes tick by and she still doesn't come, my mind starts to race. All sorts of images flash through my imagination. What if she can't come to me? Maybe *this time* my father killed her. Without thinking, I unlock the door and fling it open.

"Mummy," I'm so scared, my voice comes out like a whisper.

My hands shake as I step into the hallway and freeze for a few seconds, listening intently, but there is still no sound. Panic sets in as I run down the hall, rounding the corner that leads to the front room. The destruction I see has me stopping in my tracks. It's completely trashed and my heart drops when I see blood smears on the wall.

"Mum," I scream. Turning, I start running back down the hallway. "Mummy, where are you?"

As soon as I enter the kitchen, I see her crumpled on the floor. *She's not moving.* Blood flows down her face and into her beautiful blonde hair. I can hear the erratic beating of my heart in my ears as I step tentatively towards her. My body is trembling with fear.

"Mummy," I whisper, dropping to my knees beside her. *Nothing.* Why isn't she moving? Why won't she answer? Tears burn my eyes.

Blood flows from her nose and mouth. Her beautiful face is already swollen and the bruises are starting to show. I shake her softly.

"Mummy, wake up," I cry as I hesitantly reach out and place my hand on her arm. I'm desperate to know she isn't dead. "Please wake up," I beg as I lightly shake her. "Please, Mummy, don't leave me here by myself, I need you." I'm crying hysterically now. "Please open your eyes."

Jumping to my feet, I grab one of the kitchen chairs and drag it towards my bedroom. I have to get my phone and call Brooke; I don't know what else to do, but I need to do something.

I hear a male's voice calling my name, but it sounds far away. When a hand grasps my arm, panic sets in, and I begin thrashing my body around.

"Jaz ... Jaz, wake up. You're having another nightmare."

I recognise the voice immediately and know I'm safe —only then do I open my eyes.

Chapter 2

Jacinta

When my eyelids flutter open, I find Connor standing over me with concern etched all over his handsome face. "You okay, Jaz?" he asks.

Sitting up, I rub my eyes with my shaky hands. "Yeah," I lie.

"Fuck, I hate seeing you like this," he says, taking a seat on the side of the mattress and reaching out to run his fingers over my long blonde hair. "Have you been having many nightmares since I've been gone?"

"A few," I reply, dipping my face. They've actually become more vivid over the past year ... flashbacks of all the abuse my mother faced at the hands of that monster. Stuff I'd managed to block from my memory until recently.

Unfortunately, my father has always played a starring role in my nightmares, but when we moved to Melbourne after his arrest, they usually centred around him finding us. As traumatising as they were, my most recent ones are far worse, because they're actual re-enactments of the horrors Mum and I faced while living with that man.

"This one seemed a lot worse than the others, Jaz."

I lift one shoulder instead of answering. My eyes flicker back to Connor, and I see the deep frown lines marring his forehead as his gaze scans over my face. It may be the middle of the night, and dark outside, but not in my room. *I hate the dark.* I'm a grown woman and still sleep with a night-light beside my bed.

When I don't give Connor anything more than a shrug, he abruptly stands and reaches for one of the pillows behind me before scooping the throw rug from the foot of my bed.

Dropping them to the floor, he lies down on the rug, just like he's done so many times over the years. It was a common occurrence until he moved away. I've forgotten how comforting my big brother can be at times like this. Well, technically he's my stepbrother, but our bond is strong. We love each other like full-blooded siblings.

It's been over a year since he's lived with us. When Connor moved to Sydney, I was left to face my night-mares alone. He struggled to leave me behind, but he was following his dream ... I wasn't about to stand in his way.

He's a lawyer like our dad, but not a regular one ... he's a police prosecutor and was offered a position with the Sydney Police Department after he graduated. As much as I miss him, I'm extremely proud ... he's doing what he loves, and I can't fault him for that.

My mum and I moved in with Connor and his dad seven years ago, and I've loved living here. It's the first real home I've had where I truly felt safe. Our first week here was when my brother discovered my nightmares, he woke to my screaming.

That night I opened my eyes to find him standing over my bed. It scared the crap out of me. When a stran-gled sob ripped from my throat and I tried to scramble

11

away, Connor reached out and wrapped his arms around my waist, anchoring me in place.

"It's me, Jaz," he whispered in a soothing tone. "I didn't mean to frighten you ... I'm sorry. I wasn't thinking when I rushed in here. I could hear you screaming from down the hall. I thought someone had broken in and was attacking you."

As soon as I realised it was him, I sat down on the side of my bed and buried my face in my hands—I was so embarrassed. That's when he reached for one of my pillows and lay down on the floor. I remember asking him, "What are you doing?"

"Sleeping in here so you can feel safe," was his answer.

Needless to say, Connor Maloney became the first man I ever loved ... his dad, Jim, was the second. The damage I received at the hands of my birth father—when I was a child—has robbed me of so much. I have severe trust issues as a result. I'm twenty years old and I've never had a boyfriend. Like ever. I've kissed a few guys in my time, but that's as far as it ever went. Growing up with a violent abuser means my distrust for the opposite sex runs deep—my stepbrother and stepfather being my only exceptions.

I'm not sure if Connor knows the full extent of what my mother and I endured in our previous life, but he knows enough, because from the very beginning, he's been protective of me. We don't talk about my past, and he never pries or asks questions, which I appreciate. It's something that I'm deeply ashamed of. I know I shouldn't be. None of it was my fault, but it's how I feel. I worry I'll never be free of my father mentally—will he always haunt me? Do my scars run too deep for my nightmares to ever stop?

Lying back down, I stare up at the ceiling, trying to

get my racing heart under control. I'm scared to close my eyes in case I start dreaming again.

"Jaz," Connor says, reaching up and feeling around on the mattress for my hand. As soon as I notice what he's doing, I wrap my fingers around his.

"Yeah?"

"Come back to Sydney with me next week." Connor is only home for the Christmas break.

I roll onto my side and glance down at him. "For a holiday?"

"No, permanently. The apartment Dad bought has three bedrooms, there's plenty of room for you."

"What about my job?"

"You can get another one in Sydney. I'm sure Brooke would snap you up if she knew you were moving back. You're an amazing dancer, any studio would be lucky to have you."

"As wonderful as that sounds, I couldn't intrude on your life. Aren't you glad to be finally rid of your *little shadow*?"

"You wouldn't be intruding," he says, ignoring my question. The first time one of his friends referred to me as his little shadow, Connor gave him a fat lip. "I've missed having you around, Jaz."

A smile tugs at my lips, because despite the constant ribbing he got from his mates when we were kids, he's never made me feel like a burden. I remember one of them asking him why he let his little sister hang around all the time. He simply replied, *"I waited fifteen years to get her, so I have a lot of time to make up for."* He's always said sweet things like that. He never cared what anyone thought of him.

My grip on his hand tightens. "I've missed you too, Con." *I've missed him so much.*

13

"Then come back with me. Mum and Dad are talking about going on that cruise, and I hate the thought of you being here alone."

"I still have Cassie here."

He rolls his eyes, because he's not a fan of my best friend. He thinks her lifestyle is a bad influence on me.

"All the more reason to come with me." Letting go of my hand, he punches his pillow a few times—fluffing it—before rolling onto his side and giving me his back. "Think about it, okay?"

I'm grinning to myself as I lie back down. As much as I'll miss my parents, it's time to set them free and let them enjoy the rest of their lives. I'll be turning twenty-one in a few weeks and I can't live with them forever. It's time I stood on my own two feet. And the thought of being able to see Brooke and her kids more often, makes me happy. I owe that woman everything.

A nervous kind of excitement bubbles inside me as I lie here. I don't need to think about it, my mind is already made up. *I'm moving to Sydney.*

The next few days are a whirlwind as I break the news to my parents and start packing up my things. My mum cried; it will be the first time I've ever been away from her, but she knows my brother will look out for me, he always has. And I know she'll be fine here. My dad worships the ground she walks on ... this marriage is a stark contrast to her first one. She's now loved, cared for, and *happy* ... she is finally free to be the woman she was always meant to be. I couldn't ask for more than that.

Connor has cancelled his flight home; he's going to drive my car back to Sydney.

As we load the last of my boxes onto the back seat, I see a red flash zoom past out the corner of my eye. The red, convertible Mercedes proceeds to pull into the driveway with a screech.

Cassie, my best friend.

"You better not be leaving without saying goodbye," she says as she gets out of the car. Connor groans as he shakes his head and disappears inside.

"I thought we said our goodbyes last night," I reply as I cross the lawn to greet her.

"Well, I am missing you already," she says, pouting as she pulls me into her arms. "I still can't believe you're leaving me."

"I'm sorry, Cass," I whisper, hugging her waist. "We'll be together in a few weeks, when you come to Sydney for a visit. I promise to ring and text you every day. We can even FaceTime."

"It's not the same, bitch, and you know it," she snaps, grasping my ponytail and giving it a light tug. I laugh; she is so fiery sometimes.

I met her when I first moved to Melbourne. She was in my dance class, and it turned out I was enrolled at the same school as her. We've been BFFs ever since. I love her dearly. She's so much fun to be around. We are like chalk and cheese, but in other ways, kindred spirits.

Our personalities are total opposite. I'm quiet and shy and Cass is wild and loud. I am a twenty-year-old virgin and my best friend is a total hussy; a female version of Connor. She once told me she's slept with so many men she's lost count. I don't judge her though ... *I feel sorry for her*. I know she's only trying to make up for the love she isn't receiving at home. Cassandra's parents are arseholes!

15

The Cassie everyone sees on the outside is totally different from the person she is inside. I think that's why we click so well. Internally, she's just as damaged and fragile as I am.

Her parents are stupid rich ... old money. Her dad is a politician and her mother is a top-notch surgeon at some fancy private hospital. Their careers come first, even before their own daughter. They've never made time for her, and I mean *never*. Financially, they give her everything, but what she craves more than anything is their attention.

When we were younger, Cass would stay at our house for days on end. Not once did they call her to see if she was okay. As long as she stayed out of trouble and wasn't doing anything to embarrass the family name, they didn't give a shit.

I draw back so I can see her pretty face. "Are you sure you're going to be okay here on your own, Cass?" Because leaving her here all alone scares me.

"No," she says as tears rise to her eyes. "I've been slowly dying inside ever since you told me you were leaving; I feel like my life is coming to an end. How am I going to get by without you?"

"Oh, babe. You're breaking my heart. Why don't you think about coming to Sydney full-time?"

She rolls her eyes. "As if my parents would ever allow that."

"You're an adult now, they don't have a say in what you do."

"If I want them to keep funding my lifestyle they do."

"You could get a job and earn your own money."

She tilts her head back and groans. "Working is for peasants."

"Hey, I work."

"I rest my case."

"If my heart wasn't hurting so much, I'd totally bitch-slap you."

She laughs, bringing her face forward to rest her forehead against mine, cupping my face with her hands. "I love you, Jacinta Maloney, don't ever forget that. Thank you for being the bestest friend a girl could ever ask for. You've made the last eight years of my life so much brighter."

"Shit, Cass," I whisper as a few tears leak from my eyes. "You are talking like this is the end."

"It is, I just told you I'm slowly dying inside ... weren't you listening?"

"I always listen to you."

She draws back and narrows her eyes. "That is the biggest lie you've ever told. For years I've been telling you that you need to let your poor dusty vagina see some action ... do you listen? No! You are destined to become an old maid with a hundred cats."

"My vagina isn't dusty," I say, playfully shoving her shoulder.

"Maybe not, I've seen you bathe, but I can guarantee there's a cobweb or two lodged up inside your hoo-ha."

We both burst out laughing, which then somehow transforms into more tears until we are openly crying. I'm going to miss her so much.

I eventually release my hold on her and take a step back. "I'm worried about leaving you."

"Don't be," she says, flicking her hand. "I've been through worse and survived. Besides, I met this French hottie named Phillippe when I stopped to get coffee on my way over. I'm going to his place later to ride his gorgeous face until my brain is so fried, I'll completely forget all about you."

"You better not forget me!"

A smile tugs at her lips. "Never. You are my ride-or-die for life."

"Always and forever." I step forward and wrap her in my arms again, squeezing tight. "I love you, Cassie. Don't ever forget that."

"I love you too, Jazzie ... so friggin' much."

With one heartbreaking goodbye out of the way, it's time for another. As hard as this is, I'm confident I'm doing the right thing *for me*, but leaving the people I love behind is tearing me up inside.

"I'm going to miss you, sweet girl," my dad says, wrapping me in his arms and placing a soft kiss on the top of my head.

"I'm going to miss you too, Dad."

"I know Connor will look after you."

"He will," I say.

By the time our parents made it official, Connor and I were already becoming close. Connor said that the day his father told him he was going to ask my mother to marry him, he was so happy. He was finally going to get what he always wanted—a sibling.

Growing up for him had been lonely. His mother had been in and out of hospital before she passed, so Connor spent the majority of his childhood at his grandmother's house. His father worked long hours running Cavanagh and Associates in Melbourne. As a result of him losing his mum at such a young age, Connor bonded with mine instantly—she showered him with all the love and attention he was craving.

When Dad releases me from his hug, he slides his hand into his pocket and pulls out a credit card. "I got you this in case you need it."

"I'm good, Dad," I say, pushing his hand back. "I have some savings and hopefully it won't take me long to find a new job."

"Take it please. I'll feel better knowing you have it."

"What am I, chopped liver?" Connor questions.

Dad chuckles. "She may be your sister, son, but she's *my* daughter ... it's my job as her father to look after her." This is what I love about these two. From the very beginning we felt like a real family.

I reluctantly take the card from my dad's hand and slip it into my pocket. I know he won't let me leave without it. "I love you," I say, giving him one last hug. I can already feel the tears stinging the back of my eyes, and I haven't even said goodbye to my mum yet.

"I love you too. Your mum and I will fly down in a couple of weeks to celebrate your birthday with you."

"Okay."

The tears are already streaming down my mother's face as I move to her. "Don't cry, Mum," I say, choking on my words. "You and dad are going to have a wonderful time travelling the world. You deserve this ... you've dedicated your life to raising us, it's your turn to live yours now."

"It's just ..." she sobs, holding me tighter, "it was hard enough losing Connor last year, I'm not ready to lose you too."

"You haven't lost either of us, Mum," Connor says, wrapping his arms around us both, making it a group hug. "We are only a short plane ride away. We'll come visit and promise to be back for all the holidays."

My mum raises her face and looks up at Connor. "Look after your little sister."

"Always, Mum, always."

By some grace of God, I manage to keep it together, but the moment we pull away from the house, I bury my head in my hands and openly weep.

"Hey," Connor says, reaching over the centre console to place his hand on my knee. "Don't cry, Jaz, you know I can't stand it when you do. We're going to have the best time in Sydney ... and since Cassandra thinks you're destined to become an old maid, I might even let you get a cat."

"You heard that did you?"

"Yes," he answers with a chuckle.

Chapter 3

Jacinta

It's dark by the time we pull into the underground parking garage at the apartment complex. *I'm beat.* The drive between Sydney and Melbourne is eight hours, but with food stops and bathroom breaks, it took us over ten.

Connor did most of the driving, only letting me take over for a small amount of time on the straight open road. He was just being his usual protective self, but I've been driving myself around for almost three years now. The traffic in Melbourne's city centre, with the trams and those stupid hook turns, is a nightmare. If I can survive that without incident, I must be doing all right.

When I graduated high school, my parents bought me a sleek, black convertible BMW—I love my car. There's nothing like driving around on a hot summer's day with the top down and the wind in your hair.

My life is such a contrast to the one I once lived with my real father. My stepfather was born into money, and he not only spoils me, but he makes sure my mum never goes without. She has all the beautiful things she deserves, and I love that for her.

We live in a huge house situated on two acres of perfectly manicured land on the outskirts of the city. The home has eight bedrooms and nine bathrooms. My walk-in closet alone is larger than my childhood bedroom, and it's full of designer clothes and shoes, not hand-me-downs like I once wore. We eat out all the time at posh restaurants and I have a generous allowance, but I'm sensible with money. I'm nothing like Cassie. She blows through her allowance like there's no tomorrow. Her reckless ways are geared more towards lashing out at her parents for their neglect, rather than anything else.

My sperm donor never gave Mum money to put towards clothes, and eating out was something we didn't do. The first time I had MacDonald's was when Brooke bought it for me—I was twelve years old. Our old place was a small, run-down two-bedroom house in the suburbs. The furniture was all second-hand, but Mum did her best to keep it looking nice, making the most of what we had, but I know it was hard for her.

My father had a decent job, but drank a lot. I presume that's where most of his wages went. Even the house-keeping allowance he gave her was only enough to buy the bare essentials. She used to have to show him the receipts so he could account for every cent she spent. *Such an arsehole!*

I'm glad Mum's life is better now. After everything she endured at the hands of that man, she deserves every ounce of happiness. The privileged lifestyle she lives with her new husband isn't what's important—the love and respect he showers her with is all she's ever wanted.

"Why don't you head upstairs and have a shower, I'll unpack the car?" Connor says, popping the boot.

"Nice try ... I'm helping, I'll shower once we're done."

His lips thin. "Fine."

I nudge his shoulder with mine when I meet him at the rear of the vehicle. "Stop sulking, I'm more than capable of helping."

"Take the light stuff then," he says, picking up one of the smaller boxes and handing it to me.

I love how he looks after me, but there's no way I'm letting him do this on his own. "Put the other one on top, I can carry two."

He rolls his eyes, but does as I ask.

Connor is balancing two boxes with one arm and rolling my large suitcase with his other hand as we head towards the lift.

"You can take my bed tonight, and tomorrow we'll go out and get all the furniture you need to set up your room," he says. "I'll sleep on the couch."

"I'm happy to take the couch."

"Humour me, Jaz."

I screw up my face, because I know my brother is a man-whore. "How many women have you had in that bed?"

"None. I don't bring anyone back here. What's that saying? Don't shit where you sleep?"

"Umm, I'm pretty sure it's don't shit where you eat," I say, laughing.

He lifts one shoulder. "Same thing."

"Not even close."

Today was my first full day in Sydney. It started out uneventful because I got up early and cleaned. Connor's always been pretty tidy for a guy, but this place definitely needed a good dust and vacuum. I also did an online shop because his fridge and cupboards were sparse. I couldn't even make myself a cup of coffee, which sucked. I don't function that well until I'm loaded up with caffeine.

My brother doesn't cook much, choosing to eat out most days. That'll change now I'm living here ... I love to cook, and I'm looking forward to taking care of him like he's always done for me.

It was late morning by the time we hit the stores, and I ended up choosing all white furniture for my bedroom suite, similar to what I have back home in Melbourne. It's too early to be feeling homesick, but I thought having the same setup here, might help when that time comes. We ordered a bedroom suite for the spare room as well, so there's somewhere for my parents and Cassie to stay when they visit.

Once we were finished shopping, Connor took me out for a late lunch, and on our drive home, we made a detour through the city centre so he could show me the building where he works and the gym he goes to. That's basically what his life consists of—work, women, and weights.

The gym's where he met his best friend, Mason. Connor talks about him often, so I'm looking forward to meeting him. He's a single dad, who only recently found out he was a father. From the little I do know, the child was neglected by his mother and wasn't in the best shape when he came to live with his father—which breaks my heart—but I admire him for stepping up and taking care of his son.

I'm FaceTiming Cassie as I unpack my clothes and hang them in my walk-in robe. My new bed arrived late this afternoon and Connor and I put it together, but the rest of my suite won't be here until later in the week. At least I have somewhere to sleep, and Connor can have his bed back.

"Life just sucks now that you're gone," Cassie says, bringing her face closer to the screen and pouting her bottom lip.

"Ten more days and I'll get to see you again."

"Ugh. That seems like a lifetime away."

"It will fly by. How did things go with your French hottie?"

She flops back onto her bed and groans. "French hotties are so overrated. I practically had to draw him a map to my clit, and when it came to the sex part ... let's just say I'm pretty sure he almost perforated my skin when he tried to penetrate my inner thigh."

"Oh, no!" I bite my bottom lip to stifle my laugh. "That bad, huh?"

I have no clue when it comes to things like that, I'm almost twenty-one and still holding my 'V' card, as Cassie calls it.

"It was the worst. Anyway, I've been looking online for places to go for your birthday ... I'm so excited. It's going to be epic, and I'm thinking you should find a guy to have a one-night stand with while I'm visiting."

"Cassie! Please not this again." This has been her personal mission since she first discovered the opposite sex.

"Hear me out ... I understand why you don't want to have a relationship—even though I can assure you not all men are like your piece of shit father—but you have to let go of your 'V' card eventually. It's the natural progression of life, Jaz. This way you'll get a firsthand account of what you're missing out on, and the best part, you'll never have to see him again."

"Connor will freak if I bring someone back here."

"We'll get a hotel room for the night. He doesn't have to know."

"I'm not sure about this, Cass."

"Just think about it. Don't worry, I'll thoroughly vet him first ... I'm a good judge of character."

"Right, says the girl who picked up a guy who tried to penetrate her inner thigh."

"Hah! On that note," she says, standing, "I'm going to have to love you and leave you, I've got a pole dancing class to attend ... *solo.*"

"I'm sorry I'm not there to go with you."

"Hmm," she hums, straightening her shoulders and lifting her chin. "I might look for a new BFF while I'm there."

"You better not," I snap.

"Fine, but be warned, if I meet someone who, let's just say ... doesn't live almost nine hundred kilometres away—"

"You wouldn't dare."

"Ugh. You know you're irreplaceable."

"And don't you forget it."

I pull up Brooke's number on my phone and press call. It only rings twice before the sweetest little voice answers with a "Hello."

"Angel?"

"Aunty Jaz," she squeals.

"How are you, sweet girl?"

"When are you coming to visit us again? I miss you."

Brooke and I have remained close over the years; she's like family to me. Whenever they're down in Melbourne we always get together, and same if we're in Sydney. We even stayed with them in their new house while Dad and

Connor were looking for the apartment where we now live.

"I miss you too. That's why I'm calling, I wanted to see when your mum was free. I'm in Sydney."

"Mummy," Angel screams into the phone. "Aunty Jaz is in Sydney."

I hear Brooke in the background. "Don't scream into the phone, you'll damage Aunty Jaz's hearing."

"Sorry, Aunty Jaz," Angel whispers down the line. "Did I make you deaf?"

"No, sweet girl."

"There is a new girl in my class at school who is deaf, so daddy bought me a book on sign language so I can communicate with her."

"Wow. That is so cool."

"I know, here's Mummy."

"Jaz, you're in Sydney?"

"Yes. I'm living here now."

"What?! Since when?"

"I've only been here a few days, but I decided to come back with Connor after the Christmas break."

"Wow ... I can't believe I'm going to have you close by, what about your job?"

"I'll find another."

"With me, I hope."

"Well ... I'd love to come work for you, but please don't feel obligated to hire me."

"Are you kidding me, I'd love to have you. You'd be an asset at the studio."

"Thank you. I miss that place; going there all those years ago and meeting you ... it was the best thing to ever happen to me."

"I love how far you've come since then, that little girl you once were, broke my heart."

I clear my throat because it's still hard to talk about those times. "I have a great life now."

"I know. Do you have any plans today? I'd love to see you."

"No, I'm free."

"Great, do you want to come here? You can stay for dinner."

"I'd like that."

"Perfect, I can't wait to see you."

"Me either."

When I end the call, I pull up Connor's number.

> Jacinta: I'm going to head to Brooke's ... I'm staying for dinner so I won't be home until later.

> Connor: I didn't take my keys with me to the gym, I thought you'd be there when I got home. Do you think you could drop them off on your way?

> Jacinta: No problem. I'm just going to change ... I should be there in about twenty minutes. x

> Connor: Do you remember where it is? Do you want me to send you the co-ordinates?

> Jacinta: Vaguely, so send them just in case.

When he sends me a pin of his location, I open it in my maps.

> Connor: Drive safe, it looks like it might rain.

After changing into a pair of skinny jeans, a fitted black top, and my red vans, I slide my red hoodie off the hanger in my wardrobe just in case. It may be summer here in Australia, but if it's going to rain it could get cold, especially at Brooke's, since they live by the water.

I grab Connor's house keys off the hall table on my way out the door.

By the time I pull up at the gym, the heavens have opened up. I have an umbrella in my car, but it's in the boot. I'll be drenched by the time I get it, so I decide to slide on my hoodie instead. I was lucky enough to pull into a parking spot as someone was leaving, a few shops down from the gym. If I run, I hopefully won't get too wet.

I grab Connor's keys and my phone off the passenger seat and pull the hood over my head, tucking my long blonde hair inside it before opening the door. My face is cast downwards as I make a run for it, dashing towards the gym.

Chapter 4

Mason

My day has been an absolute shitshow; so much so, I wish I could wind back the clock and start again. It began with a flat tyre; I hit a pot hole after dropping my son, Blake, at day care this morning. I spent over an hour and a half on the side of the road waiting for a tow truck to take me to the closest Harley dealership. The damn hole in the road fucked up both the tyre and my custom rim, which I now have to replace. On the positive side, I was lucky I managed to stay on the bike and wasn't flipped over the handlebars.

It was almost eleven o'clock by the time I arrived at the office, only to receive a call ten minutes later that Blake had a fall while playing and injured his wrist. So, off I was again to collect him and take him to emergency to have an X-ray. Thankfully, it was only badly sprained, and not broken.

The doctor did mention two old fractures in his arm that showed up on the scan. When he gave me a look like I was an irresponsible parent, my blood boiled. *I would never harm my child* ... or any child for that matter. Getting confirmation that he'd been mistreated, on top of the neglect—from that good for nothing mother of his— makes me thankful he's with me now. At least I can protect him. It breaks my heart to know his formative years were hell.

Poor fucking kid.

Blake's been through so much in his short life, and has only been living with me for just over eleven months. He'll be turning six later this year, and it makes me angry that I missed the first five. I also feel guilty I wasn't around to protect him back then. Even though I didn't know he existed until recently, I can't shake the fact I've let him down somehow.

His mother turned up on my doorstep with him without warning, demanding money. She looked strung out, like she was on drugs. The little boy beside her, with the cute face and large, frightened brown eyes, was dressed in filthy clothes that looked two sizes too small ... my heart immediately went out to him.

The woman was pretty enough, and looked like someone I may have gone for in the past ... the sober version obviously, I don't get mixed up in that other shit. I saw the effects of substance abuse when I was a teenager living on the streets. For that reason alone, I was never tempted to dabble. Life for me back then was hard enough without adding an addiction to my list of woes.

Blake's mother wasn't familiar to me, and when she said her name was Annalise, that didn't even ring a bell. I've been with too many women over the years to remember them all, and I've never been in a serious relationship. I've always preferred the no-strings attached kind of lifestyle, and not for the reasons you may think. Witnessing the toxicity in my parents' marriage growing up was enough to turn me off ever wanting anything long term.

Instead of settling down, I chose to have sex with random women, often. The majority of the time I didn't even know their names. If they didn't offer it up, I didn't ask. So, it was no surprise I didn't remember this woman.

My old lifestyle is now a thing of the past; Blake's arrival saw to that. I want to be a good father to him, and to set an example. God only knows what he's seen growing up with an addict. He deserves to know what it feels like to be loved and cherished. I never got that from my old man, so I'm determined to give that to my son. I know firsthand how important it is to feel wanted.

In the beginning, I wasn't even sure if Blake was mine, but his brown hair and brown eyes told me there was a possibility. I had no pictures of my younger self to compare him to. When I'd left my childhood home at the tender age of thirteen, my only possessions were the clothes on my back.

Blake's mother's hair was bleached blonde, so I couldn't say for sure what her natural colour was. Her eyes were a pretty shade of green and she had huge, fake tits—just my type—so the possibility that I'd in fact slept with her were high. Although, I've never had unprotected sex ... I always wrap it. *Always*. So, there was also that.

Despite my uncertainty I gave her two hundred and fifty dollars, all the cash I had on me at the time, and off she went. *She left her son with a complete stranger.* Someone she'd possibly spent a couple of hours with years earlier. She had no idea what kind of person I was, which told me everything I needed to know. After informing me she'd be back for him later, she walked away without a backward glance. Whether this kid was mine or not, he deserved better than her. She didn't return for four days and had zero contact with me in the time she'd been gone.

My concern for this little boy only grew when I took

him into the house and gave him something to eat. There was nothing to him; he was practically skin and bones. The way he gobbled down his food, I knew it had been a while since he'd eaten.

I immediately called my friend Connor. I hadn't known him long at that stage, but he worked for the police department, as a prosecutor, so at the very least, I knew he'd be able to put me in contact with the right people. He turned out to be a godsend and helped me through every step of the process. I owe that guy so much.

Despite my reservations about the entire situation, the first thing we did was take a paternity test. When the results came back that Blake was in fact my son, my life changed in an instant. It was my chance to be the kind of father I wished I'd had growing up.

I've been working for the same company since I was fourteen years old and saved every cent I could. My boss, Rob, is a billionaire who dabbles in the stock market, and with his help, I've made some great investments over the years. I've always been good with numbers, so I picked things up pretty quickly. At twenty-eight years old, I'm financially secure. I had to cash in a lot of my investments to buy the house we are currently living in, and although my childhood hadn't been the greatest, I wanted my son to have all the positive aspects of the life I'd had growing up. A beautiful home and nice things. *Stability*. Material wise, I had wanted for nothing, apart from a new father that is.

The one I had was the devil reincarnated. My mother was the complete opposite, sweet and loving, and had the kindest heart. But over the years, my old man had beaten her down so much she was only a shell of her former self. She did her best for me under trying circumstances, and I can't blame her for leaving. My father was an absolute cunt to her ... a tyrant, abuser, and in my eyes a coward.

Thankfully, my nature is geared more towards my mothers, so I knew my son would be safe with me. I'd make sure he got the life he deserved going forward.

Connor advised me to fight for full custody via the traditional route, and despite his reassurance I'd win, I wasn't taking any chances. That kid was staying with me and I was prepared to do whatever it took to see it happen. I ended up offering Annalise a large sum of cash to sign over all her rights. Money talked, and I needed the transaction to be swift, and as stress free for Blake as possible. I wasn't surprised when the bitch didn't even hesitate, after all, the reason she had come looking for me in the first place was a financial one. What sort of mother would sell her own son?

We ended up settling on two-hundred-grand, all the money I had left in the bank after buying the house. My son is worth every penny, and I'd pay it again in a heart-beat. I have absolutely no regrets.

She didn't even shed a tear as she walked away from him for the final time. She looked like she was in too much of a hurry to go and score a fix.

Blake found it hard at first. It broke my heart to hear him cry for that woman. Even though I could clearly see she'd neglected him, she was all he knew. Time has helped because he doesn't even mention her anymore. He's a quiet kid but is flourishing with his new living arrangements. His fear around other females though, hasn't changed. I have no clue what his fucked-up mother put him through to make him so frightened? I tried to get him into therapy, but he just clammed up and refused to speak.

"You okay, buddy?" I ask as we leave the hospital.

"Yeah," he answers. "Are you taking me back to day care?"

When I first got Blake, I used to take him to work with me, but he was bored out of his brain there, and I knew it was important he be around other kids. That's when I searched high and low for the perfect place for him. It would also help with his transition into big school, which he'll be starting this year.

"No, I think we'll head home. I can set you up on the lounge with a movie."

"But I wanna go back ... I want to show Max and Braydon my arm."

The doctor bandaged his wrist and put his arm in a sling, which for a kid is probably cool. I can understand him wanting to show it off to his mates. It's Friday, so it'll probably be gone by Monday.

"I don't know mate." This new side of me—the over-protective father side—wants to bundle him up in cotton wool and take him home where I know he'll be safe.

"Please, Dad."

Hearing him call me that has a smile tugging at my lips. I can't say no to this kid, especially when he looks at me with those big brown, hopeful eyes ... I'm like putty in his tiny hands.

"Okay. How about we swing past McDonalds and get some lunch first?"

"Yes," he says, punching his good arm in the air, making me laugh.

This kid never stops eating. It's like every meal could be his last, which given the state he was in when he came to me, I get it. His mother probably chose to buy drugs over food for her son. His state of dress the day she dropped him off told me his needs weren't a priority to her. He'll never want for anything again ... I'll make sure of that.

As we walk down the path to where my bike is parked, an elderly lady and what I presume is her middle-age daughter are heading towards us, and the first thing Blake does is move to the other side of me, creating distance. To me they look harmless, sweet even; to my son, not so much. I could throttle his mother for the damage she's inflicted on him.

When we reach my bike, I grab his helmet out of the side saddlebag, placing it on his head and squatting down to secure the strap. Once mine is on, I straddle the bike and reach down for him, lifting him up and placing him in between my legs. With one arm out of action, I'm not going to take any chances with him riding on the back.

I had absolutely no desire to return to work after dropping Blake off, so I decided to head to the gym for a workout instead. I only have a few hours left before I need to collect him anyway, and then we'll head to Bridge. Bridge is the soup kitchen I run for the homeless when I'm not working my regular job—*the paying one*—the one that feeds and clothes us both.

I text my assistant, Olivia, to let her know I won't be back today.

> Mason: I've decided to take the rest of the day off. I'll see you in the morning. Call my mobile if you need me.

> Olivia: All good here, Boss. How is Blake?

> **Mason:** Just a sprain, but he wanted to go back to day care to show off his bandage and sling.

> **Olivia:** Aww, bless him. I bought him a packet of jellybeans on my lunch break, I know how much he loves them.

She keeps a jar of them on her desk; it's the only way she can get Blake to come anywhere near her.

> **Mason:** That's sweet. Thank you. You know I'm going to eat all the red ones, right?

> **Olivia:** Is that where my red ones have gone? You arsehole … that's my favourite flavour!!!

> **Mason:** Mine too, and I don't think it's wise to call your boss an arsehole via text. I have it in writing now. If you ever try to sue me for unfair dismissal you won't have a leg to stand on.

> **Olivia:** Pfft. You'd never fire me, you'd be lost without me. But if you keep eating my red jellybeans I might quit.

> **Mason:** You'd never find a boss as awesome as me.

> **Olivia:** Hmm.

I probably should head home and continue packing, but it's the last thing I feel like doing. There's so much to do before our big move, but I have a few more weeks to get it finished. Working full-time, overseeing everything at

Bridge, and having my son living with me, doesn't leave much time for myself.

So, today I'm going to do something for *me* ... a work-out. I rarely get time to go to the gym anymore. If nothing else, it may help release some of this tension. It's not like I get to fuck the stress out of my system anymore. I haven't been with a woman since Blake moved in. This is my longest dry spell in history, but the mental health of my little boy is well worth the sacrifice.

After two hours of pumping weights and some cardio, I find my mood hasn't lifted; instead, I can now add exhaustion to the list. My mind kept going back to what the doctor said about Blake's old fractures. He's such a sweet kid, and it kills me to know he's been mistreated. It brings back a lot of bad memories from my own child-hood, which is something I try not to think about. It's too painful to relive.

Grabbing the towel that's slung around my neck, I wipe my face as I head towards the exit, only to be greeted by my best friend, Connor, as he pushes through the door. I haven't seen him in weeks, and his face lights up as soon as he notices me.

"Hey, man. I was thinking about you earlier. I was going to call you tonight," I say, extending my hand and wrapping it around his.

We've only been friends for a little over a year, but I feel like I've known him my entire life. We met when he first joined the gym, and needed someone to spot him on the bench press. That was when I was living my carefree party life—prior to Blake. Connor told me he was new in town, so I invited him out for a few drinks that night, and the rest is history.

He's a good bloke, and I soon found out our lifestyles were very similar ... he was just a big a man-whore as I was at the time. The only difference being, I didn't want to settle down because of my childhood traumas, and he was anti-relationships because he'd had his heart broken by what he claims to be the love of his life at the tender age of nineteen. I don't believe in that kind of stuff, but I never voiced it out loud.

Needless to say, we became good friends fast ... he was the ultimate wingman; but that all changed when my son came into my life. His help in gaining full custody of Blake only cemented our friendship.

"It's unusual to see you here this time of day," he says.

I lift one shoulder. "I had a shit day, so I needed to work off some steam."

"Is everything okay?"

"Yeah, I'm just stressed is all."

"Nothing a bit of action between the sheets wouldn't solve ... oh, that's right, I forgot you're a practicing monk now."

"Fuck off ... I'm just trying to be a responsible parent."

He chuckles, slapping my back. "You know I'm just messing with you. I love that you're putting Blake first, I admire you for that. You are a good dad, and he's lucky to have you."

"Thanks." There have been times I've worried if Blake really is better off with me, but after hearing what the doctor said today, I know he is. I love my kid and there's nothing I wouldn't do to see him happy.

Connor's life growing up was very different to mine. It wasn't perfect by any means, he lost his mum when he was around Blake's age, but he was lucky he had a great dad who always put him first. Years later, when his dad remarried, he not only gained a new mother, but a little sister too. I feel envious whenever he talks about them; I've always yearned for that perfect family unit.

I look down at my watch. "Are you heading out?" Connor asks.

"Yeah, I've got to pick up Blake soon."

"Want to catch up for a beer later? We could order pizza and watch the game at my place."

"I'd love to, but I've got a million things to do, my house isn't going to pack up itself. Maybe another time?"

Connor understands how hectic my life has become, especially now that I'm a dad. "Sure, no problem. Jacinta's living with me now ... you guys could've finally met."

"Wow, she's living with you, how did that come about?"

He shrugs. "I just missed her, so when I was home for Christmas, I talked her into coming back with me. Our parents are wanting to travel, so I hated the thought of her being in that big house on her own."

Although we've never met, a part of me feels like I already know her. He talks about her incessantly. It's obvious he adores her.

"Fair enough."

"How was your Christmas?"

"Quiet, just the two of us."

"I'm sure you would've made it special for Blake."

"I got him so many presents, the poor kid didn't know what to do. When I told him they were all his, he burst into tears."

"Fuck, man."

"I know. You know what he said?"

"What?"

"One of his mother's friends gave him a packet of biscuits once ... how sad is that?"

"I wish you would've let me put that woman behind bars, instead of paying her all that money. She should be locked up, not living the high life on your dime."

"The *high* life sums it up perfectly," I chuckle. "She deserves to be behind bars," *especially after what I learnt at the hospital today,* "but in the end, I got what I wanted, so I have no regrets."

"I may not like it, but I understand. Have you got five minutes to spot me before you go?"

"Sure."

"Shit," I grumble to myself when I exit the gym and see it's now bucketing down. I hate riding my bike in the rain. Not only is the road slick, but when you're travelling at speed, the water feels like needles pricking your skin. I'm going to need to head home and grab my car before I pick up Blake, I don't want him getting wet.

Eyeing my bike parked across the street, which is already saturated, I shove my hands into the pockets of my sweats as I stride towards the kerb. I only make it a few metres when I spot a red blur barrelling towards me. Her head is cast downwards, and I don't even get a chance to move out of the way before she careens straight into me.

"Oomph," I groan when the top of her head smashes into my sternum. The sheer force of our collision has her bouncing straight off me. I try to reach out and grab her before she falls, but my reflexes aren't quick enough.

"Shit," I say when she lands on her arse and the phone and keys that were in her hand go flying. "Are you okay?"

She tilts her head back, making eye contact with me, and the moment she does, all the air leaves my body. Her pretty, too-blue eyes widen for a second before narrowing into slits, and I can't help the smile that tugs at my lips. Not only is she drop-dead gorgeous, I can already tell she's got spunk. I like my women feisty.

I extend my hand to her, in an offer of help, but she immediately slaps it away, making me chuckle. I take a step forward, bending to scoop up her phone and keys, and by the time I'm standing back to full height, she's already on her feet. The first thing I notice is how tiny she is. She's at least a foot and a half shorter than my six feet, three inches; she has to tilt her head back to make eye contact.

That movement has her red hoodie sliding back off her head slightly, revealing some of her blonde hair. Fuck, she's stunning and exactly my type. I immediately rein in that thought, my sole focus right now is my son. Once upon a time I would've been all over this, but I'm not that man anymore.

"Here," I say, holding out her belongings.

"Thanks," she snaps, snatching them out of my hand. If it was anyone else, I'd consider that movement rude, but for some reason, her attitude turns me on. She looks down at her hand, and I find my eyes gravitating there as well. I inwardly cringe when I see her phone. "Great, you cracked my screen you ... you—" Her gaze briefly moves down the length of my body. "—big baboon."

I bark out a laugh. I'm not sure why, but that insult amuses me to no end. "Wow, you sure are a little spitfire ... and for the record, your cracked screen is in no way my fault."

"You ran into me!" she screeches.

"I'm pretty sure it was the other way around, sweetheart."

My amusement grows when her hands go straight to her hips and those plump lips of hers pucker. It's a mouth that's made for trouble. "Don't call me sweetheart, you condescending jerk."

"Condescending?" I ignore the part where she called me a jerk. "Correct me if I'm wrong, but isn't *sweetheart* a term of endearment?"

"Not when you say it all thug like."

"Thug like?"

"Yes, with all your tattoos and smug good looks," she says, motioning her hand up and down in front of me. "It screams thug."

"Now who's being condescending ... and may I add judgemental? If anyone is the bad guy in this situation, I'm pretty sure it's you, Red."

"Red?"

"Since you have failed to tell me you name—"

"Which I have no intention of doing," she says, cutting me off.

I arch an eyebrow before continuing. "Like I was saying, since I don't know your name, and I can't call you sweetheart, I'm going with red." I reach for the drawstring of her hoodie, and she flinches slightly when I do. Although it concerns me, because I've witnessed Blake do the same thing, it doesn't seem to perturb me. "You remind me of Little Red Riding Hood in this," I say, tugging on the string.

"That would make you the Big Bad Wolf then ... which seems fitting I might add."

I smirk at her smug smile because she just walked

43

right into that one. "Does that mean I get to eat you then?" I lick my lips as I take a step towards her.

When she gasps, I bark out a laugh. My laughter only grows when she stomps on my foot and growls, "You can eat a bag of dicks," before storming away.

I feel instantly disappointed, I was enjoying the back-and-forth we had going on.

Turning my head, my eyes take her in from behind as she heads towards the gym. Interesting, I've never seen her in there before, and she has the kind of face you don't forget in a hurry. Her tight little body is rocking those body-hugging jeans despite the round wet patch now covering her arse—it has my traitorous cock twitching in my pants. Damn this celibacy crusade I'm on.

"It was lovely meeting you, Red," I call out as she pushes through the gym door. *The highlight of my day actually.* When she flips me the bird over her shoulder, the smile on my face grows.

If I didn't have to go pick up my son, I'd most definitely follow her back in there for round two.

Chapter 5

Jacinta

U gh. Could that guy have been any more annoying? The hide of him ... I know exactly where he was going with that *'eat me'* comment, and he didn't mean with a knife and fork. I'm choosing to ignore the little flutter I got in my stomach when he said that though. I'm not interested in anything more from him, or any man for that matter. I'm quite happy living my drama-free, *safe*, single life.

The sheer size of that tattooed man mountain should've been enough to scare me off, but for some reason, I wasn't intimidated by him, or his appearance. I usually avoid confrontation, but that didn't deter me from taking him on head-to-head. Not only was that uncharacteristic of me, it was a foolish move on my part. He could've been a roid-rager for all I knew. He was pretty buffed and clearly just came from the gym.

The adrenaline coursing through my body has my hands shaking as I look down at my poor cracked screen and feel tears burn the back of my eyes. I only got this phone for Christmas a few weeks ago. As irritated as I am, a part of me feels ashamed for how I just acted. I'm not a

45

mean person by nature, but I was anything but cordial just now. I'm against violence in any form, yet that didn't stop me from stomping on his foot like some kind of deranged lunatic.

He was right when he said it was my fault, I wasn't looking where I was going. There was no way I was going to admit that to him though. I don't know why hot-looking guys bring out the worst in me, but they always have. My therapist thinks my bitchy side is a defence mechanism ... a way of pushing the opposite sex away before any kind of attraction can be formed. It makes sense, I guess. If I can turn them off with my bad attitude, it won't matter how visually appealing *I* may find them. Nobody wants to date someone who appears to be unhinged.

Sliding my phone in the front pocket of my hoodie, my gaze darts around the gym in search of my brother. I roll my eyes when I spot him across the room eyeing himself in the mirror as he does some very impressive bicep curls. Connor is gorgeous and he totally knows it.

My attention is focused on him as I cross the floor in his direction. All the testosterone in this room is making me feel uncomfortable. Connor is so focused on himself he's totally oblivious to my presence, but the moment someone whistles, his arm pauses mid-curl and his head snaps to the side as his gaze scans the room. As soon as he sees it's me who is gaining the attention, his chest puffs out and his eyes narrow. It has a smile tugging at my lips. Of course, it's okay for him to objectify women, but when it's someone else doing it to his little sister, it's suddenly an issue.

"Jaz," he says, placing down the dumbbell in his hand. His eyes scan my face, and he must be able to see I'm upset, because he adds, "Ignore those fuckers."

I flick my hand, because it's not like I haven't been

whistled at before. Although I feel uncomfortable being surrounded by all these men, that isn't the cause of my distress. "I'm not worried about them."

"Then why do you look like you're about to burst into tears?" I wasn't going to mention my unfortunate encounter outside, but I know Connor, he won't let it go. Sliding my hand into the pocket of my hoodie, I retrieve my phone, holding it out for him to see. "Shit, did you drop it?" I lift one shoulder instead of answering, because I don't want to lie to him, but my vague response only heightens his concern. "Did something happen, Jaz?"

I blow out a puff of air before replying. "Don't go all mumma-bear on me, okay, but some guy knocked me on my arse outside and I dropped it when I fell." I turn to show him the wet patch on the rear of my jeans.

"The fuck!" Rounding me, he takes a step towards the exit.

"Con," I quickly say, reaching for his arm. "Don't ... it wasn't his fault; I wasn't watching where I was going. Please."

As soon as I say please, he stops and takes a moment to run his hand through his hair before spinning around to face me. There's now a deep frown marring his forehead. "Are you hurt?"

"I'm fine."

"Did he at least apologise?"

"It was my fault."

"He didn't apologise?"

When he goes to turn around again, I'm forced to lie. "Yes, he did."

He takes my phone out of my hand and walks back towards the bench. "Take my phone with you to Brooke's," he says, picking it up and passing it to me. "I'll get your screen replaced on the way home."

"Thank you." There's no point arguing with him, he's stubborn like that. "Here are your keys."

"Do you know what time you'll be home tonight?"

"Not late."

"Are you going to be okay driving in the rain?"

"Yes, Dad," I say, rolling my eyes. "It was raining on the way here."

He chuckles before pulling me in for a quick hug and placing a chaste kiss on the top of my head. "It will be dark when you're coming home."

"I've driven in the dark plenty of times, stop worrying."

"I'm your big brother, it's my job to worry about you. If you need me to come get you later just call."

"I will."

Thanks to the GPS, I find my way to Brooke's house without any trouble. As soon as I drive through the large iron gates and pull into their driveway, Angel comes running out of the house.

Their new place is so grand and completely different to the stylish penthouse where they used to live. I still remember the first night I went there, I was completely blown away by it, being such a contrast to the tiny, run-down shack I'd grown up in. Back then, I didn't know that people lived like that. I was awestruck. This new house though, is on a completely different level, and although I've been living in my own mansion since Mum married Dad, I still find myself captivated by the grandeur of this place every time I visit. Logan spared no expense when he built this for his family.

"Aunty Jaz," Angel screams, launching herself into the car the moment I open the driver's side door.

"Look how much you've grown," I say, twisting in my seat when she throws her arms around my neck, hugging me tight. When she tilts her head back and gives me a toothy smile, I can see her new front teeth popping through. She still had her baby teeth last time I saw her.

"I've missed you."

"I've missed you too," I say.

Angel reaches for my hand when I exit the car. She's almost eight years old and it won't be long before she's towering over me ... which I shouldn't be surprised by, everyone is taller than me.

"Hey, Jaz," Brooke says, greeting me by the front door, CJ at her side. He's grown so much too and is starting big school in a few weeks. I can't believe how much he looks like Logan. Those mesmerising green eyes of his are going to get him in a lot of trouble with the ladies when he's older. "It's so good to see you."

"Same," I reply, giving her a one-arm hug and stroking my hand over CJ's hair with the other. "Hi, CJ."

"Hi, Aunty Jaz," he says in a cute, soft voice, before bowing his head. He's a lot more reserved than his big sister.

"I can't believe how big the kids have gotten."

"Time goes fast. You were only twelve when we first met ... look at you now, you are all grown up. I can't believe you're almost twenty-one."

"Yeah, it seems like a lifetime ago."

When I glance down at my feet, Brooke reaches out to rub my back. I no longer flinch when she touches me, which in itself is huge. My life is so different and I've come a long way since then, but there's still a huge part of me that's held captive to my past.

49

"Come in." Brooke steps to the side so I can enter.

"Mummy made cupcakes," Angel says, smiling up at me again.

"They've been busting for you to arrive so they can have one," Brooke adds.

When I enter their home, my eyes gravitate to the grand staircase that sits in the centre of the foyer. The house is three stories high, and the kids have their own wing on the second floor. Although I've been here before, my eyes are still everywhere as we walk towards the back of the house, where the expansive kitchen is situated. The view from here is no less spectacular. The penthouse they once lived in was situated in the heart of the city, with the iconic Harbour Bridge and the Opera House practically on their doorstep. You can still see them in the distance, but they now live across the bridge, on the northern side of the harbour.

The moment Brooke places the cupcake stand in the centre of the table, the kids both reach for one. "Angel," CJ whines, "I wanted that one."

"There's a dozen cakes and they're exactly the same," Brooke says, and from the corner of my eye, I see Angel poke out her tongue at her little brother.

"Mummy, Angel poked her tongue out at me." When I look over at CJ, I see his little bottom lip quivering and curled over into a pout. It tugs at my heart.

"Angel Maree Cavanagh," Brooke chastises. "Don't be mean to your brother."

"You hurt my heart, sissy," he says as his big green eyes fill with tears. It has me clutching my chest ... if he gave me a look like that, I'm pretty sure I'd hand over a vital organ if he needed one.

"If you two are going to fight over the cupcakes then you can go without."

Angel leans her body closer to mine and whispers, "Daddy says Mummy is a cupcake Nazi." I have to roll my lips to hide my smile.

When Angel's eyes move to her brother and she sees he's about to cry, she sighs in defeat. That little sad face would have anyone caving. "Here, CJ, you can have this one then."

CJ's pout is immediately replaced with a smile.

"Go out on the back deck and eat them," Brooke says. "And keep an eye on your brother, don't let him go near the water."

"Okay, Mummy."

Brooke rolls her eyes as she places a mug of coffee down in front of me. "Have kids they say ... they'll enrich your life they say." I laugh at her comment because I know she adores her kids; she's a great mum. "Ignore me, it's been a long month; I'll be glad when school starts back."

"Is CJ excited to be starting kindergarten?"

She lifts one shoulder. "He says he is, but I'm pretty sure there'll be a lot of tears on his first day, and not just from me ... he isn't as strong willed as his sister. He has a soft heart like his daddy."

"He is so sweet. His little face when Angel took the cupcake he wanted ... and when he said, '*You hurt my heart, sissy*'."

"I know right," Brooke says with a laugh. "God help the female population when he gets older ... they'll be like putty in his hands."

"Right."

She takes a seat at the table. "Anyway, what's with this big move of yours?"

"Connor offered, so I accepted. Our parents are talking about travelling, so it made sense."

51

She reaches out and places her hand on top of mine. "It's going to be great having you around again ... and I couldn't be happier for your mum. Jim is such a nice guy."

"He's the best."

"So, when are you going to start working for me?"

"You don't need to give me a job."

"I know, but I want you there. You'll be an asset. Are you still doing those pole dance classes, because I've always wanted to give that a go?"

"Yes. I'll need to find somewhere new here in Sydney."

Her eyes widen. "We could install some poles at the studio."

I'm in the kitchen helping Brooke put the finishing touches on dinner when I hear Angel squeal, "Daddy."

Although we can't see them from here, the kids are laughing and carrying on with their dad, and it makes my heart pang. They're so lucky to have such a doting and caring father. I used to dread mine coming home from work. I know I have that kind of dad now, but still ...

A few minutes later, the giggling moves down the hall, and when Logan enters the kitchen, Angel is on his back and CJ is hanging off the front of him. The three of them are smiling. It's such a beautiful sight. Like so many other times, it makes me wish that Jim was my real father. I'd be a different person if I had been born into his family and spent my formative years living in a happy and loving environment.

"Hey, Jaz," Logan says when I give him a quick wave. His eyes then gravitate to his wife. There is so much love reflecting in them, and again, it tugs at my heart. I'll never get to experience a love like that either. "Hi, babe."

Brooke immediately stops what she's doing and walks towards them, wrapping her arms around CJ's waist and placing him safely on the ground. "Okay you two monkeys, dinner is almost ready, go and wash your hands."

Angel slides down the rear of her father's body, and I feel my cheeks flush when Logan instantly reaches for his wife. He pulls her into his arms and meshes their lips together, like he'd die without her kiss. I feel like a voyeur standing here watching them, but these two have a kind of love that anyone would be envious of.

"Eww, you two are always kissing," Angel complains, making a gagging sound, which CJ mimics.

Brooke and Logan are so engrossed in each other, neither of them notices the entire room is watching their public display of affection. Together, they are like the air each other needs for survival.

"I missed you today," Logan murmurs, running his knuckles down the side of his wife's face. The look he gives her has my heart racing in my chest.

"I missed you too, Hot Stuff."

Gah. *These two.* This is relationship goals right here. Who wouldn't want a man that adored his children as much as he adored his wife?

Chapter 6

Mason

Blake and I end up at Bridge for dinner. It's not what you'd call gourmet food by any means, but it's a hearty meal—meat and three veg—and much better than feeding my son takeout every night. Unfortunately, I can't cook to save my life. I'm trying though; I need to learn now for his sake.

I've managed to master scrambled eggs on toast, pretty sad I know, but it's a start. I can also cook a mean two-minute noodles. Sure, it only involves adding the contents of the packet to a pot of boiling water, but Blake seems to love them. He also loves fruit so I fill him up on that between meals.

I appreciate my son isn't fussy. He'll eat anything you put in front of him. I guess growing up hungry will do that to you.

"Are you done, buddy?" I ask him, reaching across the table for his plate.

"Yeah, Dad."

"Come," I say, standing. "I've got some paperwork to do in the office. Do you think you'll be able to manage the X-Box controller with one arm?"

"I think so," he replies with a shrug. I ruffle his hair with my free hand as he follows me towards the kitchen. He loves playing video games. He'd never played before coming to live with me, but he picked it up quick ... he even kicks my arse.

The day he arrived on my doorstep, he was carrying a plastic shopping bag containing only a few items of ill-fitting clothing, two pairs of underwear, and a ratty old teddy bear. Nothing else, no toys, shoes, or pyjamas.

I immediately threw out the clothes. They were old, tattered, and far too small for him anyway. He now has a wardrobe full of things that actually fit him, as well as toys. The bear stayed because he loved it; I couldn't bring myself to throw it away. He doesn't play with it anymore, but it's there if he wants it.

The numerous cars, trucks, and Lego he now owns are more fun. He also has an artillery of Nerf guns and we have a blast building forts throughout the house and shooting each other with the foam bullets. He enjoys hiding behind furniture and ambushing me. I love seeing him carefree and happy. It's a vast difference to the confused and scared little boy I first met. I'm hoping in time, his traumatic past will become a distant memory.

Having him around is fun. I can't say I'm reliving my own childhood, more like I'm experiencing it for the first time, like Blake is.

I had an abundance of toys growing up, but I wasn't allowed to make noise or mess—it used to set my father off. Instead, I'd play quietly in my room so as not to rock the boat.

I sit at my desk, going over Bridge's books. Money is tight right now, and since I virtually gave my life savings to Annalise, I'm currently in the process of selling my house and downsizing. Although it was supposed to be our forever home, it's way too big for the two of us anyway. My intention is to invest the extra money I obtain from the sale, then what I earn from that will be directed back into Bridge. We receive government funding at the soup kitchen, but with the homeless population continually growing, it's not enough.

I donate a portion of my weekly pay cheque, and it helps, but I have Blake to consider now, so I'm mindful. As much as I hated to do it, selling my house was the best option I could come up with.

I promised Betty, the founder of Bridge, I'd keep this place running if anything ever happened to her—it's a promise I intend to keep. I know how important this place is and all the good it does for the less fortunate. I vowed to do whatever was needed to keep her dream alive. Bridge was her life's work ... it's now become mine.

Without our assistance, the homeless would be forced to beg for food, or worse, resort to eating scraps from the bin.

Bridge opens every evening to distribute a hot meal to all those in need. We don't discriminate ... everyone is welcome. We also provide them with wrapped sandwiches, a piece of fruit, and a bottle of water when they leave. It's not as much as we would like to give, but it helps get them through to the following night. During the hotter months we distribute extra water, and in winter, warm jackets and blankets. Betty's dream was to be able to provide three meals a day, as well as services to help these people get back on their feet and find work. Hopefully, one day, I can realise that dream for her.

I'm lucky I have a horde of volunteers on my side. I wouldn't be able to do this without them.

I met Betty when I was fourteen. I'd been living on the streets for close to a year by that point. When my mother left, I became my father's full-time punching bag ... so leaving was the safest option. Betty took me in and treated me like one of her own, so I owe her everything. I wouldn't be where I am today if it wasn't for her.

She had the biggest heart and devoted her entire adult life to helping others. She was eighty-three years old when she passed suddenly. Her loss was felt by many, especially me. I was naïve, I guess, and expected she would live forever. She was all the family I had left.

Blowing out a frustrated breath, I close the ledger I've been studying for the past hour and rub the back of my neck. Staring at the damn figures won't make the extra money needed magically appear. I fix my attention on Blake as he concentrates on the game he's playing. He is making the cutest faces, and even with a sprained wrist, he's managing. My heart is so full of love for him. I resent missing the first years of his life, but I'm thankful I have him now. I have a lifetime to make up for what we lost.

Leaning back in my chair, I stretch my arms above my head, and out of nowhere, the little spitfire I encountered outside the gym pops into my mind. I feel a smile spread across my face as I relive our encounter. Damn she was fine, and that mouth of hers ... it's a pity she hadn't been forthcoming with her name because I'll probably never see her again, which is a damn shame.

I let out a groan when my dick twitches behind the zipper of my trousers. Fuck, I really need to get laid.

"Are you almost done with your game, buddy? It's time to leave."

"I'm nearly done."

It's getting late; I need to get him home and bathed. We have an early start in the morning, and I've got more packing to do before I go to bed.

As we are leaving Bridge, Blake reaches for my hand. That feeling of his tiny fingers wrapped in mine will never get old. I know it's something that won't last, he'll outgrow it soon enough, so I'm going to enjoy it while I still can. I never held my own father's hand.

"Dad," Blake says, looking up at me.

"Yeah, buddy?"

"Do we really have to move?"

"Unfortunately, yes."

"Why?"

"I told you; we're downsizing. We're moving into that apartment we looked at ... the one in Connor's building. It will be fun living near Connor, yeah?"

"I guess," he says with a shrug. "But I like it where we are now."

I stop walking and crouch down so I'm eye level with him. The only stability this poor kid has had is with me. I hate upending his life like this, but I'm sure he'll get used to our new place soon enough.

"Listen, the only reason I'm selling this house is because Bridge needs more money so we can continue to feed all the people that come here. You want to help them, don't you?"

"Yeah."

"Good boy," I say, ruffling his hair. "We have more than we need, so sharing it with the less fortunate is the right thing to do. Our new place is still going to be great, don't worry about that."

Blake dips his face, staring down at his sneakers. "Are you still going to keep me? I don't want to go back to Annalise's ... I like being with you."

Fuck. That is the last thing I want him to worry about. "I like being with you too. You don't have to worry about that, okay?" I say, placing my hand under his chin and tilting his eyes back to mine. When I see them glistening with unshed tears, I wrap his tiny body in my arms. "You never have to go back there, I promise." I draw back, swiping my thumbs over his cheeks to remove his tears. It breaks my heart to see him cry. I don't want him to ever know the truth of what his mother did, so I go with the kid-friendly version. "You know how Uncle Connor works with the police?" He nods his head. "He got some special papers drawn up that said you were going to live with me permanently, and Annalise signed them. That means it's going to be you and me forever so I don't want you to ever have to worry about that, okay?"

"Okay."

"I love you, you're my son and I'll always look after you."

It has been a long time since I've uttered those three words. It feels foreign saying them now, but I need him to know.

His little arms slide around my neck, holding on tight. "I love you too, Dad."

Chapter 7

Jacinta

"Hey," I say as Connor reaches over me and plucks a meatball out of the sauce I'm stirring in the pot. "Dinner will be ready soon."

"I know, but I'm starved ... and I've missed your cooking. I've been living as a bachelor for the past year—eating out every night gets old fast." He plops the meatball into his mouth and moans. "Fuck that's good."

"Is that why you asked me to move here?" I ask, narrowing my eyes.

"What? No! Although I did notice you've done my washing ... and may I add that the place has never looked cleaner."

"Connor!" I screech, spinning around and poking him in the ribs.

"Joking, sis." Leaning in, he places a chaste kiss on my temple. "I missed having you around, the rest of the stuff is just an added bonus."

"You could always find yourself a wife and settle down."

"Good one, Jaz."

"Why does that seem so unattainable to you? You're a

great catch and I know for certain you'd make an amazing father."

"Why buy the cow when you can get the milk for free."

"Oh my God, Connor ... you pig."

He shakes his head and chuckles. "Again, I'm joking. I'm not opposed to settling down one day, but I'd have to find someone I'm willing to spend the rest of my life with first."

"Out of all the girls you dated over the years, I find it hard to believe that there wasn't at least one you could see a future with."

When he dips his head and sighs, I gasp. "Oh my God ... who?"

His gaze moves back to me and the sadness I now see in his eyes is unmissable; so much so I feel compelled to reach out and hug him. Has my brother had his heart broken in the past? I've been there through them all, and to my knowledge, he was the one that did all the damage. I can't tell you how many crying and pleading girls turned up at our doorstep over the years. Too many to count. Or has it happened since he moved here?

He opens his mouth like he's about to say something, when there's a loud knock at the door. "Hah. Saved by the bell."

"By the knock, you mean?"

When he turns and leaves the kitchen, I walk towards the doorway so I can see who's here. I've been living here for five days now, and this is the first time we've had a visitor.

My view is blocked by my brother's large frame, but I hear Connor say, "Ugh, speaking of the devil." We weren't talking about anyone in particular, so I have no idea what he means by that.

"Get out of my way, Connor Maloney ... I'm not here to see you."

My heart rate kicks up a notch as soon as I hear that voice. Once Connor is shoved to the side, I race across the room and into her open arms.

"Cassie! What are you doing here?"

"I heard someone was missing me."

"Well, it certainly wasn't me," Connor mumbles from behind us.

"Zip it, Maloney ... and be a good boy and bring in my bags."

"How much stuff did you bring?" he grumbles as he starts wheeling her multiple suitcases inside. I know my best friend; she doesn't know how to pack light. We once went on an overnight trip with our school and she brought ten outfits and eight pairs of shoes. Everyone else had an overnight bag or backpack at best—Cassie rocked up with a giant-arse Louis Vuitton suitcase. "Are you here for a visit, or are you moving the fuck in?"

"I haven't decided how long I'm going to grace you with my presence yet," she retorts.

I laugh into Cassie's chest ... these two. They have a constant love-hate relationship going on, but in recent years it's more of a hate one.

Once the last of her luggage is brought in, Connor closes the front door ... a little more abruptly than usual. "Call me when dinner is ready, Jaz," he says as he heads towards his bedroom.

"What are you doing here?" I ask. "I wasn't expecting you until next week."

"Life sucks in Melbourne without you."

"Cass."

"It's true, it's been really shitty. I feel lost without you there."

"Aww, babe. I'm sorry."

"Besides, I have your birthday celebrations to organise. It's hard to do that from so far away."

"I just want something small ... you know I'm not into all that fanfare."

"Hah, good one."

"Cass," I groan. I was hoping for something low-key, I hate being the centre of attention, but I know what Cassie is like. She turned twenty-one a few months ago, and her parents put on a huge black-tie event with hundreds of guests present ... a vast majority of them strangers. It wasn't because they cared either, it's all about keeping up the appearances. Cassie was still in her element.

"Don't *Cass* me, you only turn twenty-one once ... besides, you owe me for abandoning me."

"I didn't abandon you."

"Hmm," she huffs.

"Come," I say, hooking my arm through hers. I'll never win this argument, so I'm not about to try. "We made up the spare room for you, so you're welcome to stay as long as you want."

"Eep. We are going to have so much fun, Jazzie. Tomorrow, you are all mine. We have a lot of lost time to make up for."

"I've been gone less than a week."

"Which equates to a year in best friend time."

"Right," I say with a laugh. "Did you forget I have a job now?"

She shrugs. "I can come hang out with you there ... can't I? You said Brooke was your friend, I'm sure she wouldn't mind. We can go out afterwards."

"Maybe I could talk to Brooke about giving you some work. She's in the process of installing some poles at the studio ... I'm sure she'd love to have another teacher on board." I nudge her shoulder with mine as I speak. "You could earn some extra cash while you're here."

My idea makes her cringe. "Money is the last thing I need."

"So, you're saying no to paid work?"

"I'm lonely, not desperate."

"One day you're going to surprise me and start standing on your own two feet. The sooner you get out of this financial hold your parents have on you, the better off you'll be."

"Never going to happen, I like spending their money too much. Besides they owe me ... think of it as financial compensation."

"Financial compensation? For what, not really giving a shit?"

"Oh, Jaz, you have no idea. It goes way deeper ... way, way deeper."

My nose screws up in confusion ... I have no idea what she means by that statement.

I'm abruptly woken from my blissful slumber when a heavy weight plonks down on top of me. "Happy Birthday, Jazzie."

"Ugh ... Cass," I groan without opening my eyes. My parents flew in yesterday afternoon, so we ended up having dinner with them at the hotel they're staying at. Since Cassie informed them that we were going out tonight to celebrate my birthday, we're meeting up with them again today for lunch.

"Wake up sunshine and let the festivities begin."

"What time is it?"

"Just after seven."

"Ugh."

"Come on, we have a big day ahead."

"We're not meeting my parents until midday ... that's hours away."

"I know, which doesn't give us much time. After a gourmet breakfast, we are hitting the shops."

"A gourmet breakfast? Which I'll be cooking, I presume? It's not like you or Connor can cook."

Cassie gasps. "What kind of a friend do you think I am?"

"A very annoying one."

"I'm going to ignore that comment. I'd never let you cook on your birthday ... I'm going to Uber Eats us something spectacular. After breakfast we will hit the shops. We need to get you a new outfit for tonight. It's not every day a girl loses her 'V' card."

I reach for the pillow beside me and place it over my head. I was waiting for this. "I never agreed to that."

"Semantics, my friend ... cobwebs remember? It's my duty as a best friend to rectify that. Speaking of cobwebs ..." She jumps off the bed. "I'll be right back."

"Where are you going?"

"To get your presents, silly."

"Cassie," I call out as she dashes from my room. It's too early for this. *I'm tired,* and running on five hours sleep. We stayed up talking until 2 am this morning, and God only knows when I'll get home tonight ... or should I say tomorrow. When Cassie parties, she parties hard.

When my best friend returns—hands laden down with a number of gift bags—she plops down on the side of my bed with a bounce. "Happy Birthday, Jazzie," she says, extending both arms.

I begrudgingly pull myself up into a sitting position. "There are so many bags."

"I like spending my parents' money."

"You know it would mean a lot more to me if you used your own."

She rolls her eyes. "You're determined to move me into peasantsville aren't you?"

"Forging your own way in the world doesn't make you a peasant, Cass." It's not like she's afraid of hard work or lazy. She's been helping me at Brooke's dance school the past few days ... voluntarily of course, despite Brooke offering to pay her. "Are you going to tell me what you meant the other day when you said your parents' owed you?"

"Open this one first," she deflects, grabbing the smallest bag and placing it on my lap. Sighing, I pull out the tissue paper on top. She has never forced her way into my past, so I'm not about to do it to her. If she wants to talk about it, I'm here ... if she doesn't, I'm okay with that too.

"Oh my God," I screech when I pull out the contents. "You bought me a vibrator?"

"For the cobwebs," she replies with a shrug. "You're welcome."

We are both laughing when Connor appears in the doorway of my room, dressed in only a pair of boxer briefs. It's nothing I haven't seen before, but when my gaze flicks to Cassie, I find her biting the corner of her bottom lip as her eyes move down the length of his body. "Can you two keep it down ... you kept me up half the night with your giggling, for fuck's sake."

"You might want to put some clothes on, Maloney ... I can't take you seriously when you're dressed like that."

"You like what you see, Cass?" Connor asks, puffing out his chest.

Cassandra dips her face, but I don't miss the tinge of pink forming on her cheeks. I've never seen her blush before.

My eyes move back and forth between them, and when Cassie looks up, she juts out her chin, saying, "I've seen better."

"Considering the number of men who've been through you, that doesn't surprise me in the slightest." Although there is venom laced in his words, he actually looks hurt by Cassie's comment.

"What's wrong, Maloney ... are you jealous?"

"Sloppy seconds aren't my style." Ouch!

When we were younger, I used to worry about these two, but it was around the age of sixteen that Cassandra started to spiral, so any kind of feelings my brother may or may not have had for my best friend, quickly turned to disdain. He hated me hanging around with her after that.

A part of me was relieved because I've had countless girls try to friend me over the years, in an attempt to get closer to Connor. My brother has never been with anyone long term, so if they had hooked up, it could've ruined our friendship. We had made a pact early on, that she happily agreed to, that he was off-limits.

Connor walks further into the room, coming to a stop beside my bed. Resting both of his hands on the mattress, he leans in and places a kiss on the top of my head. "Happy Birthday, little sis."

"Thanks, Con."

"Gag," Cassie mumbles from beside us. Her comment is purely for Connor's benefit because I know she's envious of our relationship. She's voiced many times that she wishes she had a sibling of her own. Maybe then she wouldn't feel so alone.

"What's that?" Connor picks up the box sitting beside me, and when he flips it over and see's the image of a silicon dildo on the front, he quickly drops it back onto the bed. "You bought my sister a fake dick for her birthday?" he snaps, narrowing his eyes.

Cassandra fakes a yawn as she holds out her hand, staring down at her perfectly manicured fingernails, like she's bored with this conversation. "She's not a little girl anymore, Connor ... she's twenty-one."

"I don't care how old she is, the last thing she needs is to be influenced by the likes of you."

"What's that supposed to mean?" she retorts with a huff.

"From what I hear, you're rarely off your back."

"Right! Like your revolving door of women? That's a little hypocritical don't you think?"

He just shrugs his shoulders. "I just call it how I see it."

Abruptly standing, she storms towards the door. "Fuck you, Connor."

"Cass," I call out.

She holds up her hand without turning around. "It's okay, Jaz ... I just need a minute."

That escalated quickly. I tilt my head towards the ceiling and groan. I hate confrontation at the best of times, especially with two people I care so much about.

"That was mean," I say to Connor once she leaves.

"I'm sorry, okay. For some reason she presses all my buttons."

"She's had a shit life; I wish you could be more compassionate." He stands to his full height and turns without acknowledging what I said. "Where are you going?"

"To bleach my brain. The last thing I need is images of you with that thing," he says, pointing to the vibrator on my lap.

Chapter 8

Mason

"Do you want to take this?" I ask Blake, holding up the plush dinosaur. Although he's been discreet about it, I've found it buried under his sheets the past few weeks when I've gone in to make his bed in the mornings, so I know he's been sleeping with it.

His face flushes as he turns his head to stare at the wall. "Nah, I'm a big boy now, only babies sleep with toys."

"Since when? When I was your age, I had so many stuff toys in my bed there was hardly any room for me."

His wide eyes snap back to mine. "Really?"

"Yes, really."

"What if Braydon thinks it's dumb and teases me?"

"What if Braydon has his own stuffed animal he sleeps with?"

"What if he doesn't?"

"How about we put Rex in the bottom of your bag? Nobody has to know it's there. That way you have it with you just in case."

"Okay," he says as a smile tugs at his lips. "And how did you know his name was Rex?"

"Just a lucky guess," I reply. He saw this in the store after watching Toy Story and he gravitated straight for it. "Are you sure you're going to be okay staying over at Braydon's tonight? I can always drop you there in the morning before they leave for the zoo."

The bigger question is, am *I* going to be okay? I'm so torn about letting him go, but he seemed so excited when he was invited to sleep over. I bombarded Braydon's dad with so many questions before I eventually agreed, but I'm still struggling with letting Blake go. He's never spent a night away from me since coming to live here. On the plus side, Braydon's parents are divorced, so they'll be no women in the house to scare my kid.

"I want to stay there. We are going to have pizza for dinner."

I chuckle at his reply. Of course, food is a factor in his decision. "You're going to have the best time, are you excited to go to the zoo?"

He lifts one shoulder. "Dad," he says in a soft voice, dipping his face.

"Yeah, buddy?"

"Are the animals at the zoo going to try and eat me?"

I roll my lips to suppress my smile. "All the animals will be in enclosures ... you'll be safe."

"Okay."

"I've packed your Minecraft wallet in your bag ... there's one-hundred dollars inside. I don't expect Braydon's dad to pay for everything."

"A hundred dollars," he says, jumping up and down. "I'm rich."

I laugh as I stand, reaching for his backpack. "Come on, we need to get going ... you don't want to miss out on the pizza."

I'm still straddling my bike outside Braydon's house. I've been sitting here for the past ten minutes, unable to leave. Why is letting go so hard? It's surprising how fast this kid has become my world.

When my phone pings in my pocket I immediately pull it out. I told Braydon's dad to call me if there were any issues. I also told Blake if for any reason he wanted to come home, I'd come and get him.

Looking down at the screen, I see it's a message from Connor.

> Connor: I know you have Blake, but I'm heading to the Ivy tonight. My sister turned twenty-one today. Would be great if you could come and save me from being the third wheel.

I sit there for a few minutes and ponder his message. I haven't been out since Blake came to live with me, and God only knows when I'll get the opportunity again. If nothing else, it might help keep my mind occupied.

> Mason: You're in luck, Blake is doing a sleepover at his friends tonight.

> Connor: Wow. How do you feel about that?

> Mason: I'm in two minds. What time are you guys going?

Connor: I'm still waiting for the girls to get ready, so fuck knows. I'll message you when we're heading out.

Mason: Sounds good.

Connor: It will be like old times.

Mason: It's been months, not years you drama queen.

Connor: I can't even comprehend going months without any action. Does your dick still work? *Asking for a friend.

I bark out a laugh.

Mason: There's nothing wrong with my dick!

Connor: Since you are child free tonight, you might be able to test that theory out.

Mason: As I said ... my dick is fucking fine. Magnificent actually.

Connor: Have you been giving Mrs Palmer and her five daughters a workout ... doesn't the monastery frown on that?

Mason: I don't give a shit what the monastery thinks ... despite what you say, I have no ambitions of becoming a monk.

Connor: Could've fooled me. How long has it been since you got laid?

Mason: None of your business.

Connor: That long, huh?

Mason: Fuck off!

Connor: Someone's a little touchy …
must be all the built-up testosterone.
Hopefully you can get a release tonight,
God knows you need one. On that note,
it will be good to have my wingman back,
even if it's only temporarily.

Connor: You are welcome to come here
and hang with me while we wait for the
girls. We can have a few drinks to get the
party started.

Mason: I'm heading home to do a bit of
packing. I also need to shower and
change. Just let me know when you guys
are leaving.

Connor: Okay, will do. FYI, if my sister's
friend tries to hit on you tonight don't go
there, okay?

Mason: Is there a reason why?

Connor: Just don't.

Mason: Does that mean your sister is up
for grabs?

I'm smiling to myself as I type that. I know how protective he is of his little sister. I don't even know what she looks like, but even if she's hot, the bro-code would negate me ever going there.

> Connor: Stay the fuck away from my sister too!

That was way too easy.

Starting my bike, I begrudgingly pull away from the kerb, heading towards home. I know what girls are like when they're getting ready, it could be hours before I hear from Connor again. It will give me time to get some packing done while I wait.

Connor was right, his next text doesn't come through until 10 pm.

> Connor: I'm sorry it's so late. Fuck my life … this is why I prefer to be single. We are downstairs waiting for the uber now. You're still coming right? Or is your old man body already in bed?

> Mason: I'm only three years older than you, arsehole, and yes, I'm still coming. I'll jump in the shower now. I'll be there within the hour.

> Connor: Leave the tunic at home?

> Mason: Tunic?

> Connor: You know, your monk attire.

> Mason: Remind me again why we're friends?

> Connor: Because I'm awesome … and don't forget devilishly handsome.

Sliding my phone back into my pocket, I shake my head as I pack a few more things into the box sitting on the table, tape it up, and add it to the ever-growing pile stacked by the wall. I'll remember to thank the girls for taking so long to get ready when I get there. One, because I know it will piss Connor off, and two, because in the past four hours I made a huge dent in my packing.

I head to the laundry to grab a clean shirt and a pair of jeans out of the basket before taking the stairs two at a time. I run the iron over my clothes before laying them out on the bed. My business shirts and suits that I wear to work get dry-cleaned, but the rest of mine and Blake's clothes are washed and ironed by me.

My mum used to do all those things for me when I was younger, but when I started living with Betty that all changed. *"I'm giving you a roof over your head and three meals a day, but I'm not your keeper … if you want to live here, you'll need to pull your weight,"* was one of the first things she said to me. It was a small price to pay to be off the streets. It opened my eyes to all things I'd taken for granted when I was a kid. I felt guilty for never acknowledging all the things my mother did for me growing up … I guess, like my dad, I took advantage of her too. She was a good mum, and I hate that I never got the chance to tell her that she was appreciated … by me at least.

It is close to eleven by the time I arrive at the Ivy, and after doing a quick scan of the pool bar, I pull out my phone to text Connor, only to find I already have a message from him. It was sent twenty minutes ago.

Connor: I'm thinking of bailing. Jacinta's friend had a group of guys join us in the cabana she hired for tonight. I'm going to end up punching one of these fuckers if I hang around here too long.

Mason: I just arrived. Are you still here?

When I don't get an immediate reply, I decide to get a drink. I'm here now, I might as well hang around for a bit.

I'm standing in line with my hands shoved in my pockets, minding my own business, when someone bumps into me from behind, causing me to lose my balance and take a step forward, nudging the person in front of me.

"Watch it," the guy says, giving me a dirty look over his shoulder.

"Sorry."

"So you should be," he snaps, which pisses me off. But I ignore his comment because I'm not looking for trouble, I just want a drink. I'm too old for this shit.

I look behind me, ready to berate the person that caused this, only to be met by two large blue eyes ... eyes that have taunted me on more than one occasion over the past week.

"Red?"

When those baby blues narrow into slits, my frown is immediately replaced with a smile.

"Wolf," she growls.

My eyes scan over her face. *Fuck*, she's even more stunning than I remember. The first time we met she was fresh faced, but tonight she's wearing make-up, and I can't decide which version of her I like best. She's a natural beauty, and doesn't need that gunk on her face ... it does make her look a lot older though, and the dark shadow around her eyes really makes the blue pop. I also got a hint of blonde hair last time, since the majority of it was tucked into her red hood. Now it's on show in its full glory, and I'm already itching to run my fingers through it. An image of me tugging on those long strands flashes through my mind and my cock twitches.

"You obviously make it a habit of bumping into people," I state.

"It wasn't my fault."

"Oh, so we're going with that again, are we?"

When I hear a throat clear behind her, my gaze flicks in that direction and my eyes lock with a brunette. She's a stunner too, but I'm not interested in her; I'm far too captivated with the blonde beauty standing before me.

"Do you two know each other?" she asks as her eyes move between me and Red.

"Unfortunately," Red snaps before turning on her heels and storming away. My attention immediately gravitates in her direction, and again, the view from behind is just as spectacular as I remember; even more so in the tiny, white, body-hugging dress she's wearing. *Fuck me.* She may be short, but in that dress her legs look like they go on for days.

"How do you know my friend?" the brunette asks, placing her hands on her hips.

"We go way back," I tell her, dragging my attention away from Red moments before she disappears around the corner.

"Way back? Did you know her before she moved to Melbourne?"

"When did she move to Melbourne?" I ask.

"Seven years ago."

"Then no."

"How do you know her then?"

"I met her last week."

"That's not exactly way back. Where did you meet?"

"The gym."

"Now I know you're lying; she doesn't go to the gym."

That explains the jeans she was wearing that day. They weren't exactly workout clothes. "Technically, I ran into her outside the gym."

"Hmm. Do you have a job?"

"Yes. Why?"

"I'm asking the questions here, mister." I hold up my hands when she gives me attitude. Now I know where Red gets it from. "Is it a good job?"

"I'm vice president of a large company."

"Impressive. Are you married?"

"No."

"Do you have a girlfriend?"

"No."

Her eyes dart down to my forearms. "Have you ever been in prison?"

"Are you stereotyping me because I have tattoos?" Red did the same when we met.

"You can't answer a question with a question. Are. You. A. Jailbird?" She punctuates her words as she pokes my chest.

"No," I answer, gently guiding her hand away from my body.

"Are you in a gang?" *Again, with the stereotyping.*

"No," I snap as my irritation grows.

"Have you ever maimed or killed anyone?"

"I just told you I've never been in prison, so doesn't that negate that question?"

She lifts one shoulder, "Maybe you never got caught."

"I don't condone any kind of violence." *I had enough of that when I was a kid.*

"How would you rate yourself in bed? Ten being mind-blowing and one being absolutely pathetic."

"Wow, are you serious? Next, you'll be wanting to know how big my dick is."

"Actually, that was my next question," she says, giving me a toothy smile.

I arch a brow, is this chick for real? "I'm not answering that." I don't know why I'm answering any of her questions to be honest.

Her eyes gravitate down to my crotch. "You look like you're packing, so we'll just go with that."

I've met a lot of forward women in my time, but this one is on a whole other level. "How much have you had to drink tonight?"

"Enough," she replies with a shrug.

"Hmm."

"Would you help an old lady in need cross the street?"

"Of course."

"Have you ever kicked a puppy?"

I bark out a laugh. "No." The more this chick talks, the more unhinged she becomes.

"A kitten?"

"Never."

"If you saw a baby bird fall out of its nest, would you put it back?"

"Okay, on that note I'm out." I've reached my limit with this one. When I take a step to the side to leave, she reaches for my arm.

"Don't go," she pleads. "We're getting to the good part."

"There's a good part to this insanity?"

"Yes. Can I see your driver's licence?"

"Why?"

"Because tonight is your lucky night?"

"I'm flattered, honestly, but I'm not interested." This chick has either been smoking crack, or she's lost a few marbles. She might be hot, but I don't do crazy. "I'm here to meet up with a friend and he's waiting for me." I look down at my watch to drive my point home.

"Do you think I'm trying to hit on you?"

"You're not?"

"God no, I'm doing this for my bestie," she says, jutting her chin towards the corridor her friend disappeared down. "I saw the way you eye-fucked her when she walked away."

"I'm pretty sure your friend can't stand me."

"That's where you're wrong. We're BFFs ... I know her better than anyone."

"BFFs?"

"Best friends forever," she says, rolling her eyes.

I'm twenty-eight, not what I'd call old, but I don't understand why this generation choose to speak with acronyms instead of fucking words. "You may be best friends, but since she's never mentioned me to you, how do you know she's interested?"

She taps her pointer finger against the side of her head. "This isn't my first rodeo, handsome. When she thinks a guy is hot, she gets all bitchy."

Interesting. "And how do you know this?"

"BFFs remember ... keep up, hot guy."

"My bad," I reply, clicking my tongue.

"And besides, that might work in your favour."

"How so?" I ask.

"Who doesn't love a good hate fuck?"

81

I clear my throat. "If you say so."

"You've never had one?"

"I can't say I have."

"Well, tonight's your lucky night, hot tattooed guy. How much have you had to drink?"

"I'm completely sober," I answer, unlike her. "I only just got here." But I definitely need a stiff drink or two after this conversation. I don't like being grilled, especially by a peculiar stranger.

"Good to know, because no one wants to hook up with a whiskey dick."

"A whiskey what?"

"Dick. Alcohol-induced erectile disfunction ... it's a thing, trust me." She is the second person today to doubt my capabilities. A man puts himself on a self-imposed break from dating and suddenly he's impotent?

"I'll take your word for it."

"So, here is what's going to happen, you're going to show me your driver's licence for precautionary reasons, and then you're going to take my friend home and give her the best birthday 'D' in history."

"And what exactly is birthday 'D'?"

"Oh my God," she groans, tilting her face to the ceiling. "You are lucky you're good looking, because you're not very smart, are you? 'D' for dick."

This conversation is getting weirder by the second, and to be fair, I definitely feel like I've lost more than a few brain cells during this interrogation.

Clearing my throat, I cross my arms over my chest and rock back on my heals. "Just so we're clear, you're wanting me to take your friend home and give her some birthday dick?"

"You catch on fast, pretty boy."

She holds her hand out in front of her, palm facing up. "Licence," she says, wiggling her fingers.

"Why?"

"I need to see where you live."

"Again, why?"

"Because if my BFF comes back upset, maimed, or unsatisfied, I know where to find you."

"Unsatisfied?"

"You know ... if you fail to give her all the 'O's."

"And 'O' stands for?"

"Are you kidding me? Orgasms! Are you sure you're up for the task?"

"I am, if she is ... I've never forced myself onto anyone, and I'm not about to start now."

"Great answer, you've past the test" she says, clapping her hands and jumping up and down on the spot. "You're perfect for this mission."

Against my better judgment, I slide my hand into my back pocket and retrieve my wallet. When I hold my licence out to her, she plucks her phone from her cleavage and snaps a quick picture of it.

Once she's done, she reaches around behind me and smacks me on the arse. "Okay, you big sexy beast, we're done here, go get your girl."

I stand there for a moment in stunned silence as she turns to walk away. She only takes one step before she spins to face me again. "You do know what a clitoris is right?"

"Of course."

"And you know how to find it? Do I need to draw you a map?"

I'm not even going to dignify that question with an answer.

Chapter 9

Jacinta

I 've been locked inside the bathroom stall for the past ten minutes and Cassie still hasn't come to my rescue. Where is she? I thought my dramatic exit would've been enough of a red flag for her. I pull out my phone ready to text her, when it hits me. "Shit," I mumble, springing to my feet and reaching for the lock on the door.

Oh, hell no!

What was I thinking leaving that demon out there with Wolf?

Although I didn't use the facilities, I rush towards the sinks to wash my hands, because even if the Ivy is an upper-class establishment, public toilets are gross.

I use my elbow to push through the door and I only take a few steps into the corridor when I spot him. *Gah.* He's looking way too sexy as he leans against the wall with his arms crossed over his chest. When his predatory gaze moves to me, he takes me in from head to toe, and when his tongue runs over his bottom lip, my stomach does a stupid flip-flop. *I'm going to kill my best friend.*

I dip my face and focus on the floor as I keep moving forward, all the while praying I don't stumble again in these stupid sky-high, heels Cassie made me wear tonight. The last thing I need is to fall on my arse in front of him for a second time.

This is not my usual attire. Unlike my best friend, I prefer comfort over glamour. High heels and I don't mix well. I'm a jeans and boots kind of girl, paired with a cute top, but since Cassandra decided tonight was Operation Lose My 'V' night, she made me dress accordingly.

If Wolf tries to talk to me as I pass, I'll just ignore him. And after strangling my ex-BFF, I'm going to hightail it out of here—with my virginity still intact.

"Red," I hear as I get closer, but I keep my head down as I pick up the pace. My heart is hammering in my chest and when I'm almost at the end of the corridor, and home free, the worst thing imaginable happens ... two strong, tattooed arms wrap around my waist, lifting me off my feet. "Oh, no you don't," he growls, effortlessly swinging my body around until it's plastered against the wall. He doesn't let go until my feet are firmly planted on the ground, but once they are, he wastes no time using his arms to cage me in. I feel his warm breath caress my skin when he leans in and says, "I've let you run from me twice now ... I refuse to let it happen a third."

When my face remains downcast, he pulls back, gently placing his finger under my chin and raising my eyes to meet his. His rich, brown orbs are the colour of milk chocolate, and framed by thick dark lashes that any girl would be envious of.

Despite the ridiculous heels I'm wearing, he still towers over me. His gaze scans over every inch of my face, and when I hear his breath hitch in the back of his throat, I draw my bottom lip into my mouth, biting down.

"Do you have any idea how beautiful you are, Red?" he whispers. "I've thought about you over the past week."

He's thought about me? "Have you thought about me too?" He raises his hand as he speaks, using his thumb to drag my bottom lip from the confines of my teeth.

"No." But his full smile tells me he sees straight through my lie.

"I don't believe you."

"It's the truth ... oh, wait, there was that one time."

"I knew it," he says as his smile grows even bigger. *God he's gorgeous.*

"Yes, it was when I got my cracked phone screen replaced ... you know, the one that you broke?" Which is another lie, because it was Connor who took it to get fixed, not me. "I was wishing I had the foresight to take one of those shards of glass and stab you with it."

He throws back his head and bursts out laughing. "You kill me, Red."

"That would've been my intention."

He taps his closed fist against his rock-hard abs. "It would take more than a sliver of phone glass to break this muscle and reach a vital organ."

I lift one shoulder. "I would've given it my best shot."

"I don't doubt that for a second, but for your information, your mouth doesn't turn me off, quite the opposite actually."

I gasp when he uses his pelvis to press me further into the wall, and I feel his erection against my stomach. Knowing it's me that has done this to him has me throbbing between the legs. It's a feeling that is foreign to me, and for that reason alone, it scares me.

"I have to go." Placing my flattened palms on his chest, I shove him back and try to duck under his arm, but his reflexes are too quick.

"Not so fast." His hand slides around my waist, jerking my body back until it's flush with his. "I'm not finished with you yet." I have to tilt my head back even further being this close, and when I narrow my eyes, the corner of his mouth tugs into a sexy smirk. "I haven't wished you a happy birthday."

"How do you know it's my birthday?"

"Your friend told me?"

"Ugh. What else did she say to you?"

"She grilled me pretty hard actually."

"About what?"

"She wanted to know if I'd ever kicked a puppy, amongst other random things."

"She what?"

"True story. Is your friend a little ..." He raises his hand to the side of his head, moving his pointer finger around in a circular motion.

I roll my lips together to suppress my smile. "At times."

"I thought as much."

"What else did she ask you?"

"What didn't she ask me would be a better question. Apparently, I did good though because I somehow became the chosen one."

My heart drops into the pit of my stomach when he says that, because I have a feeling I know where this is heading ... my dreaded 'V' card. Despite that, I still find myself asking, "Chosen for what?"

"To deliver the birthday 'D'." As soon as those words are out of his mouth, I bury my face in his shirt and groan. I don't need a mirror to know my skin is flushed ... I'm absolutely mortified.

When I feel his chest vibrate with laughter, I find myself wishing the floor would open up and swallow me whole. God only knows what else Cassandra said to him.

When we get home tonight, I'm going to smother her with a pillow.

"Look at me, Red?"

"No." I suck in a sharp breath which has me inhaling a whiff of his cologne. Mm, he smells divine. I could drown in his scent.

"Did you just sniff me?"

"No, umm ... maybe."

I feel his laughter again as he gently cups either side of my face, drawing my attention back to him. "We don't have to do this if you don't want to, but if you plan on going ahead with the birthday 'D' celebrations, just know, it will be me ... *and only me*, dishing out the 'D' tonight." I have never liked being manhandled, or dictated to for that matter, but there is something about this guy that makes me want to submit. He arches an eyebrow. "Okay?"

"Okay."

"That's my girl," he murmurs with a triumphant smile as he slowly lowers his face until his lips meet mine.

My girl.

I've never wanted to be anyone's girl before, but maybe just for tonight I can be his.

A shiver dances down my spine the moment our mouths connect. My first reaction is to push him away, but when I place my hands on his shoulders, my fingers end up fisting in his shirt to hold him in place. He uses the weight of his body to press me against the wall, and when he deepens the kiss and groans into my mouth, it feels like molten lava is running through my veins. I'm surprised I haven't melted into a puddle by his feet.

This is not the first time I've made out with someone, but I've never been kissed so deeply ... *so completely*. It's like live wires shooting through my entire body and I feel it right down to the tips of my toes. He tastes like a combination of mint and pure sin. I already know if my time with him goes no further than this, I'll never forget this moment as long as I live.

I'm panting by the time we come up for air, and I'm already missing the feel of his lips on mine. His warm breath ghosts over my skin as he whispers, "Happy Birthday, Red."

"Thank you."

"Come home with me?"

"I—" Although this was Cassie's plan all along, deep down I had no intentions of going through with it, but for a split second I'm actually contemplating saying yes. "I can't."

"Why?"

"I'm here with my friend, I can't abandon her." I feel bad when I see the disappointment now marring his gorgeous face, but vetted or not, going home with a stranger goes against everything I believe in.

"Please." I desperately want to say yes, which in itself should scare me, but thankfully, I remain strong.

"I'm sorry."

"I'll order an Uber for your friend, and personally escort her to it myself."

His eyes are pleading as they stare down at me, and internally, I start to panic. When I hear the ding from my mobile from inside the tiny gold purse that is draped over my shoulder, I scramble for it. "That's probably her now, wondering where I am."

Wolf releases me, taking a step back to allow me to retrieve my phone, and I immediately feel the loss of his body against mine. When I look down at the screen, I see it is in fact a message from Cassandra, but my relief soon turns to despair.

> Cassie: Okay, baby girl, we're out. Me
> and the boys are going club hopping.
> Enjoy all the 'D' with that delicious hunk
> of a man. And don't worry, he's been
> completely vetted ... I even have a pic of
> his driver's licence on my phone. Oh, and
> he knows his way around a clitoris—
> unlike Phillippe—so don't be afraid to
> ride that gorgeous face of his. And you're
> welcome for all the 'O's. Love you and
> can't wait to get all the deets in the
> morning. Mwah.

I know for a fact she's done this on purpose. She has never deserted me like this before. Ugh, she's so dead. Once I've smothered her with a pillow, I'm going to revive her just so I can do it all over again.

When I hear the deep rumble of a throat clearing, my eyes dart from the screen to Wolf, and the shit-eating grin on his face tells me he read the message too.

"Looks like it's just you and me now, Red."

I'm not sure how long our silent standoff in the corridor at the club lasted, but the moment he leant forward and ran his nose up the side of my face, whispering, "I need you, Red," in my ear, before placing a soft, lingering kiss on my temple—which obviously sucked all the common sense from my brain—I was done for. The consequence being, I'm now seated on the back of Wolf's Harley Davidson, wearing a helmet which is way too big for my tiny head, as we weave in and out of the city traffic, and surprisingly, I'm smiling like a lunatic.

This is my first time on a motorbike, and I've got to say, it's thrilling. If Connor got wind of what I was doing right now, I won't need to murder Cassie when I get home tonight, because I'm pretty sure he'd beat me to it.

I can't believe I'm actually doing this. Wolf even gave me an out and offered to drop me home instead, but that only made me want to go through with this even more. Especially after he gave me another lingering kiss once we reached his bike ... that one was filled with so much promise it had my toes curling in my heels. After wrapping me in his leather jacket that he got out of one of the saddlebags on the side of his bike and strapping his helmet to my head, he tilted my face up towards his and devoured my mouth just like he'd done in the club.

This man can kiss.

My body is still humming as my parted legs frame his. My chest is pressed firmly against his back, and my arms are wrapped tightly around his middle ... I don't know what it is about this man, but I've never felt more alive than I do in this moment.

When we come to a stop at the red light, one of Wolf's arms drops from the handlebars, coming to rest on my bare leg. I bite my bottom lip to stifle my moan when his big, strong hand slowly moves up my outer thigh. My eyes flutter shut as I savour all these new feelings he's evoking within me.

"You okay back there, Red?" he asks. The nicknames we have for each other are ridiculous, but since this will only be a one-time thing, it's probably for the best.

"Uh huh."

"You still want to come back to my place?"

"Yes." My reply comes without hesitation as his grip on my leg tightens.

I love that he keeps giving me an out, but the truth is, I'm not ready for our time to end. Am I apprehensive about what's going to happen when we arrive there? Hell yes, but I'm more inquisitive than scared. If his mouth alone can evoke these kinds of feelings, I'm eager to see where things go from here. I've only had a small taste of this man, but I'm already craving more.

The ride back to his place doesn't take long, and I'm disappointed when it comes to an end. I absolutely loved being on the back of his bike. The way he effortlessly navigated his way through the city traffic, darting in and out of lanes with precision and ease.

Wolf slows as we drive down a beautiful tree-lined street before turning into a driveway and coming to a stop at a pair of large iron gates. After punching in a code, a beautiful Victorian mansion comes into view. I'm not sure what I was expecting—maybe a chic bachelor pad—but definitely not this. I have so many questions, but I'm figuring the less we know about each other, the better.

After pushing a fob on his keyring, the garage door opens and he manoeuvres us the short distance inside before shutting off the engine. When the door closes behind us, he flicks down the stand and steps off. For a brief moment we are bathed in darkness and my heart rate kicks up a notch.

I hear the clunk of his shoes against the concrete as he starts to move away from me. I'm still seated on the bike and my brain tells me to hop off and follow him, but I'm frozen in place. Reaching for the zipper of the heavy leather jacket I'm wearing, I drag it down. The noise is amplified in the dead silence. I remain completely still unsure of what to do next, but when light suddenly floods the space, I find myself squinting my eyes.

My head frantically darts around the room until I notice Wolf standing by the door with his back to me. Is it wrong that my focus immediately gravitates to his nice, round arse in those jeans?

He slowly turns around, so I quickly raise my gaze towards his face. Our eyes lock for a brief moment before his big brown orbs proceed to caress my body, starting at my head and working their way down. He pauses midway, and when his hand flies up to grasp the back of his neck before he tilts his head back and groans loudly, I look down. That's when I see my dress has risen up, showcasing my white lace underwear, so I scramble to pull it down.

"Don't," he says as he starts to stalk towards me, quickly closing the distance between us.

My heart is beating so fast now, I can hear it thumping in my ears. He runs his tongue over his bottom lip as he approaches, and when he comes to a stop beside the bike, I gulp in a sharp breath.

His large frame is looming over me as he fists a chunk of my long hair in his hand, gently angling my head back until our faces meet. "Do you have any idea how sinfully beautiful you look straddling my bike like this?"

I swallow thickly, shaking my head and before I get a chance to blink, he's throwing his leg over the bike and retaking his seat, only this time he's facing me.

His fingers dance along the outside of my legs, pushing my dress up to my waist as he goes. I've never felt so vulnerable and exposed, yet turned on at the same time. He dips his face again, eating me up with his eyes, and my body shivers with anticipation as I await his next move.

"Fuck." The way he practically growls his words is so damn sexy.

When his attention moves back to my face, the intensity of his stare has my skin prickling with goose bumps. I can literally see the heat burning in his eyes ... nobody has ever looked at me like that before.

I let out a little squeak when his strong hands tighten around my waist, and I'm effortlessly lifted off the seat and lowered back down onto his lap. Straight away I can feel he's hard because it's pressing right against my core ... *it feels too good.* So much so, I have this weird compulsion to grind myself against him. Thankfully for now, I manage to curb that thought. I'm in unfamiliar territory here, and I have no clue how to act.

He leans in, licking a path from the base of my neck, all the way up to my ear. This time, I'm powerless to stop the whimper that falls from my lips.

"Wrap your legs around me," he murmurs before sucking my earlobe into his mouth and gently biting on the flesh. I don't hesitate to do what he asks. A deep, sensuous rumble escapes from somewhere deep in his chest as he cups my arse in his hands and pulls me even closer. The pressure only making the dull throbbing ache between my legs intensify.

When he starts peppering kisses along my jawline as he rolls his hips forward, my body reacts of its own accord. My head is thrown backwards and I moan so loudly I swear it echoes off the walls. I should be embarrassed by my display, but I'm too invested in how he's making me feel to care. I've never self-gratified before, so this kind of pleasure is new to me. I'm now understanding all the hype. I can't believe I've gone twenty-one years without experiencing anything remotely close to this, and I have a feeling as the night wears on, things are only going to get more intense.

"Jesus, Red," he utters, holding me firmly in place as he rolls his hips for the second time. "I want you so bad. I've never craved anyone the way I do you."

The moment his lips find mine, things really heat up. Wolf grasps my sides, dragging my body back and forth along his length in slow calculated moves, and as amazing as it feels, I need more. What? I'm not sure, but I start jerking my own hips in a feverish manner as my fingers glide over his chest before sliding around his neck, deepening the kiss.

My body is climbing higher and higher with each move; I can't seem to get enough of this man. My best description for what I'm feeling would be euphoria. The kaleidoscope of sensations cascading over me are confusing—indescribable—but I like them. *I like them a lot*. I completely understand why my best friend is so hooked. Who wouldn't want to feel like this?

I'm now chasing that elusive 'O' as Wolf's hands slide under my dress, gliding up my body as he goes. He draws back, pulling out of the kiss so he can drag the fabric over my head. We are both panting as he drops it down onto the concrete below. He dips his face to take me in, I've never let a man see me in my underwear before, but the way he gobbles me up with his eyes takes away any self-consciousness I should be feeling.

"You're perfect," he whispers, leaning down to run his flattened tongue over the swell of my breast. "So damn beautiful." I'm not sure why, but his words manage to do something to me ... I swear I feel a little crack form in the walls I meticulously installed around my heart when I was a little girl.

He palms my other breast before tweaking my nipple through the lace with his forefinger and thumb. That movement elevates my arousal, sending shock waves straight to my clit. I start to rock faster against him as I clutch either side of his face so I can capture his lips again. I'm in sensory overload and I'm not sure how much more I can take.

And then it happens ... I reach the peak ... and oh my

God, the euphoria I was feeling moments ago has nothing on this. I abandon his lips as my body arches, riding out the glorious waves that are now coursing through me. The noises I'm making are completely foreign, but again, I don't care.

"Yes," Wolf growls. "Come for me, sweetheart." His hand slides into the front of my underwear, and when his fingertips circle my clit, it sets off another wave of pleasure. He doesn't stop until I'm completely drained. I lean in, resting my forehead against his chest as I try to catch my breath. His hand is still down my pants, and when he slides in a little further, he groans.

I have to bite my bottom lip to suppress my whimper when the tip of one of his fingers pushes inside me. I can feel my inner muscles clenching around him as I silently plea with him to go deeper.

"Fuck, you're soaked."

"What?" I gasp, drawing back so I can see his face.

"I love how wet you are for me," he says, smiling.

Those words quickly bring me out of my post-orgasmic haze and I feel my face heat with embarrassment. I hope he doesn't think it's pee. "I'm so sorry."

His eyebrows pinch into a frown "For what? And why is your face getting redder?"

I quickly dip my head, and whisper, "Kill me now."

Chapter 10

Mason

Things went from hot to weird in a millisecond. Red bows her head, so I gently grab a fist full of her hair, tilting her face back to mine. "What is going on?"

"I don't know ... is it normal?"

"Is what normal?"

"The umm ... wet thing? I've never experienced that before."

"You've never experienced what? Arousal or an 'O'?" *For fuck's sake, I'm now using acronyms.* I wait for a response from her, but when one doesn't come, my stomach drops. "Please don't tell me you're a virgin."

"Okay."

"Okay what?"

"I won't tell you."

Shit. I scramble off the bike and reach down to scoop up her dress, passing it to her. The grilling from her friend now makes sense. She was looking for someone to pop her bestie's cherry. As appealing as that prospect sounds, it unfortunately won't be me. Which is a shame, I've never wanted inside someone more than I do this chick.

"Get dressed," I say. "I'll take you home."

"Why? I don't want to go home."

"You don't have a choice ... I don't do virgins."

Her pretty mouth gapes open as she throws her dress to the ground and leaps off the bike. When she's standing in front of me, she raises both of her hands, shoving me hard in the chest. "You are going to finish what you started," she demands, and although this situation is completely fucked up, I find myself fighting a smile.

She is such a paradox ... somehow managing to push all my buttons and turn me on at the exact same time. I'd like nothing more than to bend her over my bike and shove my cock deep inside her, but again ... *I don't do virgins.* "Not happening, Red."

She puffs out a frustrated breath as her hands come to land on her hips. She looks like a fucking goddess standing there in her skimpy white G-string, with her more-than-ample tits spilling out of her lace bra. "You are going to have sex with me, Wolf ... I'm not leaving here until you do!"

"Well, you'll be waiting a long time, sweetheart, because it's never going to happen."

Her bravado drops, along with her face, and I feel like a prick. "Why are you being such an arsehole?" she says as her eyes fill with tears.

I intake a deep breath, filling my lungs. "I'm not," I reply, reaching up to skim my knuckles down the side of her face. "I'm trying to be the good guy here. Your first time should be with someone special, Red. That person is not me. I don't do relationships—"

"Or virgins apparently," she snaps, cutting me off.

"I fuck pretty women and move on to the next, you deserve better than that."

"Am I not pretty enough for you?"

"Jesus." I dip my face, pinching the bridge of my nose.

Does this woman not own a mirror? When my eyes eventually meet hers again, I find her bottom lip is quivering. "You are perfect ... fucking gorgeous, and I'd like nothing more than to take you upstairs and devour every inch of that luscious body of yours—"

"Let's go then," she says, taking a step forward and pressing herself against me.

"Stop making this harder than it is."

She reaches for the top button of my shirt, popping it through the buttonhole. "The only one being difficult here is you."

When she moves down to the next button, I try to grab hold of her wrist, but she slaps my hand away. "You should wait until the right man comes along ... someone that deserves a prize like you."

"I don't want to wait; I just want my 'V' card gone, I don't like being the laughing stock of all my friends. There's already talk of buying me a cat." I bite my knuckle between my teeth to hide my amusement. "See, even you think I'm ridiculous," she says, pointing at my face.

"Being a virgin is nothing to be ashamed of, Red. You should be proud; most women give it away far too easily these days."

"I don't know one other person my age that hasn't had sex."

"How old are you?"

"Twenty-one."

"That's not old, but you're way too young for me."

"Stop making excuses, you're being completely irrational," she says as she continues to undo the rest of my buttons. I know I should stop her before this goes any further, but it's like she has me under some kind of a spell.

99

"Irrational? Me? I think I'm being rather mature actually."

Her gaze snaps up to my face and her pretty eyes narrow. "If I didn't need to borrow your dick for the night, I'd totally junk punch you." I bark out a laugh. This woman amuses me to no end; I never know what's going to come out of that mouth of hers. "How old are you anyway? My guess is mid-twenties at best."

"I'm twenty-eight, almost twenty-nine."

"Pfft, that's nothing," she says, flicking her hand. "My dad is twelve years older than my mum. And my sperm donor was seventeen years older than her."

"You were conceived by a sperm donor?"

She winces at my question. "Well, technically my mum was married to him at the time ... but I hate him, so I'd rather not talk about it if that's okay with you."

"You brought him up."

"Only to prove a point."

"For the record, I hate my old man too."

A small smile tugs at her lips. "We have something in common then."

"I'm still not having sex with you, Red."

My words have her ramping things up, as she reaches behind herself and unclasps her bra. I watch on mesmerised as she seductively pushes the straps down her arms, and I can't hold back my groan the moment her perky, flawless tits spring free. My cock is so hard I'm surprised it doesn't burst through the zipper of my pants.

"Red," I warn, sliding my hands into the pockets of my jeans so I'm not tempted to reach out and touch her ... because I'm aching to.

"The day I met you, you asked if you could eat me ... now's your chance, Wolf."

She opens her arms wide, offering herself to me, and I

100

almost blow my load at the sight. It has nothing to do with my self-imposed hiatus, and everything to do with her. This woman is a walking wet dream. "And when I first met you, you told me to eat a bag of dicks," I retort, trying my best to remain strong. "Maybe I should stick my cock in your mouth so you stop talking."

She casually lifts one shoulder as her baby blues lock with mine. "I've never done that before, but I'm willing to give it a go. Will you teach me how?" How can this woman be so innocent, yet alluring in the same breath?

As soon as she bites down on her plump bottom lip my willpower slips a little further. This little temptress has no idea what she is doing to me, or maybe she does.

Her pretty eyes move away from my face, travelling down my body. My shirt is now completely open thanks to her, and I know I should put a stop to this, but the reckless side of me is eagerly awaiting her next move.

She leans in slightly, looking up at me briefly through her eyelashes, and I swear to fucking God if she so much as breathes on me, I'm going to cave.

I mimic her movements when her tongue darts out and runs along her bottom lip. *The things I want to do to this woman.*

I'm holding my breath as I wait to see if she has the guts to do something, and she doesn't disappoint. "Someone works out," she says, running the tip of her finger over my abs. That simple contact sends a shiver shooting up my spine. Closing the last of the distance between us, her flattened tongue comes in contact with my abdomen, and the little minx licks a path right up to my sternum. "Mm." The moment her hand palms my dick through my jeans, I snap. Before I even realise what I'm doing, I have her lifted off the ground and pushed up against the wall.

"You don't play fair, Red."

A triumphant smile tugs at her lips. "Does that mean we're going to have sex now?"

"Are you going to get all clingy if we do?"

"I don't do clingy."

"I'm not looking for a relationship, Red."

"Ditto."

"Will you hate me if I order you an Uber when it's over?"

She lifts her chin, "I'll order my own Uber ... and a part of me already hates you, so there's that."

That's not the answer I was expecting, but I'll take it.

Reaching my room, she squeals when I drop her down onto the mattress with a bounce. My eyes are glued to her luscious tits as they jiggle from the impact. This woman has no idea what I'm about to do to her. I may not be a hearts and flowers kind of guy, but I'm not a complete arsehole. This is her first time, so I plan to give her a night she'll remember. There won't be a round two, so I'm going to make the most of this time with her as well. I'm pretty sure she's not the only one about to have her world rocked.

I place my hands either side of her body, leaning down to hover over her. "Are you sure you want to do this?"

"I'm here, aren't I?"

"Are you going to regret not saving your virginity for someone special? Because I mean it when I say this is a one and done."

"No. I'm only here to lose my 'V' card, I don't want anything else from you."

"So, you're using me for sex?"

"Pretty much."

I can't help but smile when she says that. She's so damn adorable, it's a shame I can't keep her. "What's your real name?"

"You can keep calling me, Red." If she wants to maintain anonymity then I'm down with that, but I'd much rather hear her call out Mason when I make her come, rather than Wolf. She reaches up, placing her thumb against my bottom lip, dragging it down. "My, what big teeth you have."

Those words only manage to make my smile grow. I see where she's going with this, so I chomp them together a few times for added effect. "All the better to eat you with," I reply, my voice sounding deeper than normal.

I'm eager to get this started, but first I place my lips on hers, wanting to pay her mouth some attention before I move on to the rest of her body. By the time I eventually draw back, her lips are red and swollen from the ravaging they just received.

I nip along her jawline before travelling down to her neck. I continue south until my tongue is swirling around her hardened nipple before sucking it into my mouth. I palm her other breast so it doesn't feel left out. I've been dying to get my hands on these since she removed her bra. They're perfect, just like the rest of her ... so full, so soft, and most definitely real. I've had my fair share of plastic women in the past, so the fact that she is completely natural only makes her more appealing.

Red's fingers are lightly tugging on my hair as she whimpers and squirms underneath my touch, but I've barely even started. By the time I'm done with her, she'll be lucky if she can remember her own name ... *whatever that is*. And although I was hesitant to go forward with this, I like that she's experiencing it all for the first time with me.

I take my time with her, making sure no piece goes untouched. When I reach my final destination, I push off the bed and stand to full height. Her eyes move down my body as I shrug out of my shirt. "I love your tattoo's."

"Thank you."

"I never knew I was into that type of thing, but obviously I am." Why do I find her word vomit so cute? Maybe because there's something refreshing about her honesty.

I flex my muscles. "Am I doing it for you, Red?"

"Don't get ahead of yourself," she says, rolling her eyes.

"I know you think I'm hot, your friend told me."

"Ugh. Forget anything that traitor told you; she'll be deceased by morning."

I throw my head back and laugh. *This woman.*

Reaching down, I adjust my rock-hard cock in my jeans, and Red moans. "You like seeing me touch myself?" Her eyes narrow, but her pinkened cheeks tell me she does. "If you're a good girl, I might let you play with it later."

I roll my lips together to suppress my smile when she growls. "How kind of you," she retorts sarcastically.

"I'm a nice guy like that," I say with a chuckle.

"Hmm," is her only reply.

Leaning forward, I hook my thumbs into the waistband of her G-string, slowly sliding them down her legs. I lick my lips the moment her bare pussy comes into view, and once I have her underwear removed and bunched up in my hand, I bring them to my nose inhaling deeply.

"Oh, my God, did you just sniff them?" she screeches.

I shrug. "You sniffed me at the club, so it's only fair."

Her eyes are as big as saucers and her mouth gapes so wide, I can't help but laugh. Tossing her tiny piece of lace over my shoulder, I fall down to my knees. I wrap my hand around one of her ankles, bringing it towards my face. Her horror is soon forgotten when my tongue— mixed with some open-mouthed kisses—tracks a path up the inside of her leg. Her hands are now fisted in my sheets as I drape that leg over my shoulder and move to the other one, spreading her wide in the process. I intake a sharp breath when she's revealed in all her glory. It's such an exquisite sight I wish I could take a picture so I have something to remember her by.

She has the prettiest, untouched pussy, and there is something about that analogy that has me wanting to beat my own chest. It's a sobering thought. I'm suddenly glad that it's *me* in this moment, because I can't stomach the thought of it being anyone else.

Leaning in, an inch from my target, I give her a small taste of what's to come when I blow hot air over her clit. She doesn't disappoint with her reaction. Her back arches off the bed as she moans into the silence, and I love how responsive she is to my touch. The longer I drag this out, the sweeter that initial contact will be for us both.

I use two fingers to part her, blowing against her for a second time. "Stop teasing me, you brute."

"Those little whimpers tell me you're enjoying it, Red."

"I need more," she pants.

"Tell me what you need, sweetheart."

"Weren't you listening? I said more."

"I need your words, smart-arse."

"Your mouth."

105

"Where?"

Her little growl has my lips tugging up at the corners. "On me."

I place a soft kiss against her inner thigh. "Here?"

"No," she snaps. I know I'm being an arsehole, but I want to hear her say it.

"Here?" I ask, moving to the opposite thigh.

She pulls herself up onto her elbows. "Are you being serious right now?"

"Deadly."

"You know where I want your mouth."

I arch an eyebrow. "On your pussy?"

"Yes!"

"Then say it."

"Ugh." She tilts her head towards the ceiling in annoyance, but I don't miss the blush rising up her neck as she does. "Please put your mouth on my ..."

"Pussy."

"Uh huh."

"Say the word, Red."

She flops back down onto the mattress, using her forearms to cover her face. "Pussy," she whispers so softly I barely hear it, but I decide to take pity on her, giving her what she wants.

The moment my mouth comes into contact with her sensitive flesh, her body jolts. "You're going to need to keep still," I say, laying my palm against her abdomen to hold her in place.

"Oh, God," she cries when I swirl my tongue. I groan against her skin when she threads her fingers into my hair, tugging me closer. She tastes just as sweet as I knew she would.

I don't hold back, giving her everything I've got, and it doesn't take long before she's bucking off the bed. I'm desperate to be inside her, but I felt how tight she was downstairs, and if I don't prepare her properly, I'm going to hurt her, and that's the last thing I want.

I start by sliding the first finger in, just the tip, and when I think she's ready, I add another. I'm only part the way in and I can already feel the resistance. I keep a close eye on her as I start moving my fingers around in a circular motion, trying to stretch her as much as I can. Her moans and the way she keeps thrashing her head from side to side tells me she's enjoying it.

It doesn't take long before I have her coming undone. "Wolf," she cries, and the tight grip she now has on my hair is almost painful, but I don't stop until I've drained every ounce of pleasure from her body. The clenching of her muscles against my fingers makes my cock weep.

When she is completely satiated, I remove her legs from my shoulders and stand, wiping my mouth with the back of my hand. "Are you okay?"

A grin tugs at her lips as her eyelids flutter open. "Yes," she breathes. "I'm ... I feel like I'm floating. Like I've just had an out-of-body experience."

"Have you had enough? Or do you want more?" I ask, popping the button on my jeans.

"I want more," she replies without hesitation. "I want it all."

"Someone's a greedy girl?" I say, dragging down my zipper.

She traps her bottom lip between her teeth as she pushes herself into a sitting position. Her eyes track my movements as I hook my thumbs into the side of my boxer briefs, dragging them and my jeans down my legs.

When I stand to full height and my hardened cock bobs, her eyes slightly widen. "Wow," she whispers, scooting to the edge of the bed. "Can I touch it?"

I love how inquisitive she is. "I wouldn't do that if I was you. Things might be over before they've even started if you do."

She pouts. "But you said if I was a good girl, I could play with it. Haven't I been a good girl?"

"You've been a very good girl," I say, reaching out to drag my thumb across her plump bottom lip.

Her eyes lock with mine and when she beams with pride at my praise, my heartbeat kicks up a notch. This girl ticks all my boxes and it's a shame our time together is quickly coming to an end.

I intake a sharp breath when she reaches out and wraps her dainty hand around my dick. "Red," I warn, but the moment she strokes it, I throw my head back and groan.

"What's this liquid coming out of the tip?" she asks, running her thumb over the eye of my cock.

"Precum—" That's all I manage to get out before she leans in, lapping it up with her tongue, and my knees buckle beneath me. "Fuck, Red," I grunt, widening my stance and threading my fingers in her long hair.

She looks up at me through her lashes as her mouth parts, and I watch on in amazement as the head of my dick disappears between her lips. I almost blow my load at the sight. She is tiny all over, her mouth being no different. She only manages to take in an inch. Her movements are clunky and amateurish at best, but fuck it feels amazing.

She's still clutching the base of my dick, so I wrap my hand around hers, stroking back and forth, showing her how I like it. My hips jerk forward of their own accord, but only marginally. The last thing I want to do is choke her.

It's been a minute, possibly only seconds, and my

balls are already tightening. I'm going to embarrass myself here, but I'm powerless to stop it. In my defence, it's been a while. At least if I blow now, I should be able to last longer once I'm inside her. *One can only hope.*

She looks up at me confused when I hastily withdraw. I take a step forward—aiming for her chest—as I blow all over her spectacular tits. "Wow," she whispers as thick ropes of cum splatter against her porcelain skin, marking her.

My legs feel like jelly as I bend down to scoop my shirt up off the floor. "Let me clean you. Lay back."

"That was ... I have no words," she says in a breathy voice, and I realise something in that moment ... I like this woman way more than I'm comfortable with.

Once I've wiped all my cum from her skin, I throw my shirt on the floor and slide my hands under her arms, moving her to the middle of the mattress. I lean over and snag a condom from my bedside table before joining her on the bed.

My eyes scan her face as I hover over her. *She's so fucking beautiful.* I use the tips of my fingers to brush the hair from her forehead, and when she gives me a sweet smile, my chest tightens. I'm not usually this gentle or affectionate with the women I bed.

Red raises her hand, cupping the side of my face and something passes between us. I'm not sure what, but it has a knot forming in the pit of my stomach.

Leaning in, I place my lips against hers. I thought it would take some time before I was ready to go again, but as soon as our mouths connect, my dick starts to harden.

My hand moves between her legs when our kiss deepens. We continue to make out until our kiss goes from deep and passionate to wild and frenzied. When I have her worked up to a place where I think she's ready for me,

I draw back, pulling myself onto my knees. She watches on in fascination as I reach for the condom and place the foil packet between my teeth, tearing it open.

Once I've rolled the rubber down the length of my cock, she opens her legs for me and I settle in between them. "Last chance to pull out, Red."

She lifts her chin, like the spitfire she is. "Not going to happen, Wolf."

I chuckle to myself as I reach for my dick, and stroke it a few times. She whimpers as soon as I lean in and move it back and forth through her arousal. She's ripe and ready for me, but I'm nervous. If it was anyone but her, I'd be buried balls deep by now, but there's something different about this one. The first word that springs to mind is *special*, but I quickly dismiss that thought.

Her hand tenderly skims over my hair as she lifts her head from the pillow and places her lips against mine. Her kiss is soft and sweet, unlike anything we've shared thus far. I try my best to ignore all these crazy feelings she evokes inside me as I continue to run the head of my cock through her slick heat, skimming over her clit before sliding back down. On the third or fourth pass, I add some more pressure, pushing just the tip inside her. *Fuck, she's so tight.* I drop my head against her shoulder and groan.

I draw back and repeat my movements.

Up.

Down.

In.

Out.

It's like a form of torture, and each time I re-enter her, I go in a touch further. Every fibre of my being wants to drive in all the way home, but for once this isn't about me ... I'm putting her needs first.

Pulling out of the kiss, I stare down at her. The head of my dick is now lodged snuggly inside her, but I can't take this torment anymore, I need to be all in. "Are you okay?"

"I'm fine."

"Does it hurt?"

She scrunches up her cute little nose. "Not really. I mean, it stings a little, but it still feels good."

"Do you want me to keep going? I haven't broke through your hymen yet, so it's not too late to stop."

"No ... I want to keep going. I need my 'V' gone. You have to make me a woman, stat." My body shakes with laughter as I rest my head against her shoulder. "Why are you laughing at me?"

I roll my lips together in an attempt to pull myself together as I draw back. "I'm sorry, but I've seen you naked, Red, and with or without your virginity intact, you are all woman."

"Thank you ... I think."

"It was a compliment. I'm going to need to move though ... are you ready?"

"I'm ready," she says, quickly closing her eyes and screwing up her pretty face in preparation. I can't help it, I bark out a laugh. She's so damn sweet.

"Look at me, Red." She opens one eye. "Relax," I say, running my knuckles down the side of her face. "If you're all tensed up it's going to hurt more."

"Ah, okay." Her features relax instantly.

"Just focus on our kiss," I say, leaning in to place my lips on hers. "Leave the rest to me."

She threads her fingers into my hair. "Wolf?"

"Yes, Red."

"Thank you for being so sweet with me."

I deepen the kiss, ignoring what she said. Lines are

getting blurred, and that's not how this night was supposed to go.

When I think I have her distracted enough, I start to move again, gently rocking my hips.

In.

Out.

In.

Out.

In.

Out.

It's still just the tip, but with my next pass, I put more pressure behind my movements, breaking through the resistance until I'm balls deep. "Shit," she cries. I instantly feel like an arsehole because I know I hurt her, but on the flip side, she feels good. *So fucking good.*

I pause, giving her time to adjust. "I'm sorry."

"I'm okay."

"You sure?"

"Yes."

Nevertheless, I give her a moment before I draw back to the tip and slowly push back in. We both moan in unison. My brain is telling me to go faster, or maybe that's my dick talking, but I keep a leisurely pace. It's not until she wraps her legs around my waist—linking her ankles together at the base of my spine—and starts to buck against me, that I ramp up the speed.

"Fuck." In some ways it feels like the first time for me too, because I can't remember it ever feeling this good. Pulling out of the kiss, I reach for her hands, lacing my fingers through hers as I manoeuvre them above her head. Leaning my forehead against hers, I clench my eyes closed as I try to get my emotions in check. "What are you doing to me, Red?" I whisper.

I look down at the washcloth in my hand and when I see a streak of blood, my stomach churns. I noticed some on the condom when I removed it as well. I know it's normal for a woman to bleed her first time, but it does nothing to ease the guilt I'm now harbouring. There is no turning back, what's done is done, and I can only hope going forward she doesn't regret what we did tonight.

I toss the cloth in the sink and rest my clenched fist on top of the marble counter in my bathroom. Instead of looking at myself in the mirror, I bow my head. I'm conflicted. It's time for her to go, but I also know once she walks out that door, I'll never see her again.

That is where my problem lies. I can't have her hanging around once Blake gets back, he's scared of females, and I need to put him first because nobody else has done that in the past.

With my mind made up, I push off the counter and exit the bathroom. I find Red exactly where I left her. I'm filled with a myriad of emotions, and I hate how seeing her in my bed pleases me. I'd like to blame that voodoo pussy of hers, but I'm pretty sure it runs far deeper than that.

I'm still naked, so I stalk towards my dresser and pull out a pair of grey sweats, sliding into them. My eyes dart to the digital clock sitting on the bedside table, and I see it's just past 1.30 am. Out of my peripheral vision, I see Red sit up.

"I guess I should get going," she says. And those words set off a panic inside me, because the truth is I'm not ready for her to leave.

When my gaze darts to her, I notice the sheets pulled

113

up, covering her chest. My immediate thought is to walk over there and tug it down, because I don't want her hiding herself from me, but thankfully, I manage to rein that in. I have no right to tell her what to do.

Her eyes track down my body as I approach the bed, flickering from my abs to the outline of my dick protruding through the thin fabric of my sweats. When she nibbles on her bottom lip, I know she likes what she sees. Is she thinking about round two? Any other time, I'd be all over that—especially with her—but I saw her wince when I cleaned her up, so I know she's sore.

I slip back under the sheets, and prop my head up by resting my elbow on my pillow. This whole situation is weird because this is usually the time I lose interest and start to withdraw. I *never* do sleepovers, but there's a part of me that wants her to stay. Blake won't be home until later today. Braydon's dad said he'd drop him off on the way home from the zoo this afternoon. That means I have the entire day to myself.

Sure, I could do some more packing, but I'd rather spend it with her. I took her virginity for crying out loud, I can't just toss her out. We could go somewhere nice for breakfast when we wake ... followed by a leisurely ride on my bike to the Blue Mountains. It's been years since I've done that. That thought sets off another wave of alarm.

What's happening to me?

Red flips back the sheets, ready to rise, but my arm darts out, snagging her around the waist. Thankfully, she doesn't resist when I pull her closer. I'm by no means a cuddler, and the last thing I want to do is give her false hope, but she deserves more than a quick lay. Although there was nothing quick about what we did.

I wanted to give her a night to remember, but I

already know I won't be forgetting her in a hurry. She's well and truly left her mark.

"Don't go."

"But you said—"

"Ignore what I said. It's late and I'm tired, lay with me for a while."

"Umm ... okay."

I reach for the lamp beside the bed, flicking off the light. I'm choosing to ignore how satisfied I feel when she wraps her arms around my middle, rests her head on my chest, and snuggles into my warmth. I let out a contented sigh as my eyelids drift close. I'll worry about all these odd feelings I'm having later; for now, I'm just grateful she's still here.

I lift my head off the pillow and place a chaste kiss on top of her head. "Night, Red."

"Night, Wolf."

A smile tugs at my lips. *Fucking wolf.*

Chapter 11

Jacinta

Although it was a huge struggle to stay awake, I somehow managed it. I've never lain in a man's arms before, but I couldn't risk falling asleep and having a nightmare. I didn't want to do anything that would taint our time together. Wolf has no idea how much he gave me tonight, and I'm not just referring to the abundance of orgasms. Our time together is something I'll treasure forever. But alas, all good things must come to an end, and there was never a promise of tomorrow. He made that abundantly clear, but I'm okay with that. I'm not capable of more anyway.

My eyelids are getting heavier by the second, and it's only a matter of time before I start drifting off. "Wolf," I whisper into the darkness, but when I get no reply, I decide it's time to make my move.

I carefully untangle my arm from around his waist and lift the one he has draped over my shoulder. I gently lay his limb back down, across his chest ... he doesn't even stir. I shimmy towards the end of the bed, slipping over the side. That was way easier than I thought.

Crouching down, I blindly feel around the floor for

my underwear. I have no idea where they landed after he sniffed them. My face heats at the thought. I still can't believe he did that.

After a few minutes of searching, I give up, creeping towards the door. I guess I'll be going home commando. I pause before I exit, turning to face the bed. "Thank you," I whisper, blowing a kiss in his direction. "I'll never forget you, or what you gave me tonight." *Because I won't.* It feels like I walked in here a girl, and I'm leaving a woman.

It feels wrong parting ways like this, but I hate good-byes, and it will be less awkward this way. He was the one who said he was going to call me an Uber when we were done, so I was perplexed when he asked me to stay. Given my circumstances though, he was probably just being nice.

I feel like a thief in the night—a naked one—as I tiptoe down the long corridor. It's pitch-black and I can't see where I'm going, so I hug the wall. Thankfully, when I reach the end, there's a light on in the main room of the lower level, so I can safely navigate the stairs without breaking my neck.

I'm not sure if he lives here alone, so my heart is thumping furiously against my rib cage as I creep towards the bottom, with one hand covering my breasts, and the other sitting at the junction of my thighs. I don't even know how I'm going to get out of here … I wasn't paying attention to my surroundings when he carried me upstairs.

I was too focused on him.

When I reach the bottom floor, I stop and take in my surroundings. This room is beautiful with all its rich woodwork and ornate ceilings. Furniture-wise, it's sparse. There's a large chocolate-brown leather sectional, a coffee table, and gigantic flat-screen TV mounted above the fire-place, but not much else.

The wall of boxes—stacked three high—on the other side of the room tells me he's either in the process of moving in, or out.

I round the corner and see the large wooden door down the end of the corridor, I'm guessing it's my way out, but I need to retrieve my clothes and purse first.

After a few wrong turns, I eventually find the attached garage. I quickly put on my bra and slip my dress over my head before bending to scoop up my purse and shoes.

I spy Wolf's keys still in the ignition of his bike; I could use the fob to open the garage door but that might be too noisy, and how will I close it? Taking his keys or leaving them outside isn't an option.

Re-entering the house, I'm frazzled by the time I reach the front door. I pause once I'm clutching the knob. What if the door is alarmed? *Shit.* This place is a mansion, so it probably has the best security system money can buy.

I intake a large breath and hold it as I slowly turn the knob, cracking the door open slightly. It's only then I exhale. If he does have an alarm, it's obviously not set.

Once I'm safely out of the house, I feel immediate relief as I dash across the lawn, but that reprieve is short lived when a spotlight comes on, illuminating the entire front yard. *Busted.* Without thinking, I dive behind the nearest bush, grazing my knee on the grass in the process, but that's the least of my worries.

My breathing is erratic as I lie there and wait ... for what, I have no clue? Minutes pass, and when I don't hear any noise, or approaching footsteps, I peek out from behind my hiding spot. I'm expecting to see Wolf standing there in those ridiculously sexy grey sweats he was wearing when I snuck out, but I find nothing. The porch is empty, and the front door is still closed. I must've set off the sensor light during my escape.

Feeling silly, I collect my belongings that I dropped in my haste and rise to my feet. My nerves are shot as I hobble towards the front of the property. That's when I discover my next obstacle ... the wrought iron gates. *Fuck-ity-fuck.* I completely forgot about them, and I paid absolutely no attention to the code when Wolf punched it in.

The rest of the property is surrounded by eight-foot-high brick walls, which I have zero chance of scaling. I blow out a puff of air because I feel like giving up, but I made sure to lock the front door when I left, so I can't even slink back into the house and rejoin him in bed, pretending this nightmare never happened.

I approach the gates with scepticism. I pole dance for exercise, so I'm pretty good at climbing, but this is completely different. On the plus side, they don't have spears on the top. Wolf may be relieved to wake up later this morning to find me gone, but maybe not so much if he discovers me undie-less and mooning his neighbours as I bleed out from being impaled atop of his front gates. A shudder runs through me at the imagery that evokes.

Bending slightly, I slide my heels and bag between two of the bars, dropping them onto the concrete on the other side. I take a few deep breaths and rub my hands together as I formulate a plan. Luckily there is an intricate pattern lacing up the centre, towards the top, so all I need to do is pull myself up high enough and I should be able to use that as a footing so I can swing my leg over.

I crouch my body slightly before jumping as high as I can. The moment my hands wrap around one of the bars, I grip the lower part with my knees and feet, using them to help propel me higher.

When I'm near the top, I use my legs to hold me in place as I reach up to grasp the bar that runs along the highest point with my hands. Only then do I let my legs dangle. I'm now hanging limply as I raise my right foot and slide it into one of the iron scrolls that run parallel along the inner edge of each gate.

Using all my strength, I pull myself up until the upper half of my body has risen above the top of the gate. I'm not afraid of heights per se, but when I make the mistake of looking down, seeing how high up I actually am, my stomach lurches. An image of my lifeless body flashes through my mind. I'm spread-eagle and lying deceased on the driveway below, with a pixilated crotch—because my bare vagina is in no way PG for the front page of today's paper. Imagine the headlines, *Pants-less woman falls to her death during her early morning walk of shame*.

I may have an overexaggerated imagination, but given my dire predicament, that scenario is a distinct possibility.

Pushing the prospect of death from my mind, I fill my lungs with air and swing my leg over until I'm straddling the top of the gate. My hands are trembling, but this time I make sure not to look down. All I need to do now is swing my other leg over and start my descent. *Easy-peasy*. But when I try to do just that, I realise the hem of my dress is tangled up in one of the fancy scrolls. I tilt my head back and groan. Is God punishing me for giving up my virtue before marriage?

I fist a handful of material and start tugging. At this stage, I don't care if I rip it. I'll ride home in the Uber naked if need be, I just want to get out of here in one piece.

I yank a few more times before I finally hear the tear, but the force I used to free myself ends up putting me off balance. My heart drops as I start to go over the side. By some miracle, or maybe just quick reflexes, I manage to get a firm grip on the bar that runs horizontally along the top, which ultimately stops me from plunging to my death.

However, the jolt from the sudden drop almost rips my arms out of their sockets, and I'm left dangling about three feet from the ground, but I'm alive. My breathing is now erratic as I take a second to regain my composure. I let out a little yelp, combined with a silent prayer, as I let go and hope for the best. Thankfully, I land safely on the concrete below.

Without hesitation, I retrieve my bag and my shoes and start hobbling down the street with my dignity still intact ... *but just barely.*

I snuck out of one house, and now I'm sneaking back into another. Connor will lose his shit if he sees me coming home alone ... even more so when he takes in my appearance. My dishevelled hair, panda eyes, bloodied knee, and torn, grass-stained dress isn't a great look. To the unknowing eye, you'd think I'd been attacked.

I tiptoe across the main room, past the kitchen, and down the corridor that leads to the bedrooms. My stomach drops when I see light coming from underneath my door. Does my brother know I went home with a guy? Is he waiting to confront me? My poor heart can't take any more excitement today.

I pause for a moment before I reach for the handle. I open the door just enough to stick my head inside, only to find Cassie sitting cross-legged in the middle of my bed eating ice cream straight from the tub.

"What the hell, Cass," I angry whisper as I slip into the room and close the door behind me. The last thing I want to do is wake up Connor.

"Jaz! Thank God." She puts the ice cream tub to the side and leaps off the bed. After pulling me into a crushing hug, she bursts into tears.

"Oh, no. What happened?"

My first thought is something went awry with the guys we'd been with, but she then goes into a crazy rant. I'm not even sure if she takes a breath during her spiel.

"After I left you at the club, I suffered from a severe case of mummy guilt ... I mean, as much as I wanted you to hand over your 'V' card, I never really planned on making you go through with it, but then that sexy beast appeared and I could tell you were into him by the way you acted, and he was definitely into you. I started asking him all these ridiculous questions and the more he answered the more perfect he became. I'm not sure if it was the cocktails I'd consumed prior or just a moment of insanity, but I put a plan into action and there was no going back from there. I even left the club knowing full well you'd try to get out of it, hence why I fled, leaving you with no choice but to go with him.

"By the time we arrived at the other club, I was an emotional wreck. I was having serious doubts about leaving you, so I jumped in a cab and headed back to the Ivy, but when I got there you were gone. It's safe to say I was freaking the fuck out by then, so I ordered an Uber and came back here first, to see if you were home. When you weren't here, I was going to head to that ridiculously hot guy's house and save you, but that's when everything went to shit."

"Why, what happened when you got back here?" *Please don't mention my brother's name.*

122

"You weren't here that's what, and neither was Connor. I went to order another Uber to come find you, but that's when I realised that I'd left my phone on the back seat of the last one. Normally, I wouldn't have cared because I could've just bought a new one today, but all that hottie's info was on the one I'd lost.

"I didn't know what to do, so I ended up knocking on the neighbour's door and woke them up. They weren't very pleased with me by the way, but that's a whole other story. Thankfully, when I told them it was a matter of life or death and that you'd possibly been kidnapped and were in danger of being sex trafficked, they took pity on me and decided not to slam the door in my face."

"You woke up the neighbours in the middle of the night? Which ones?"

"Number nineteen."

"Shit, Cass. The sweet old couple?"

"Yeah. They ended up letting me use their landline to call the police."

My eyes widen. "You called the police?"

"I mean ... what else could I do, Jaz? I had no idea if you were okay."

"Maybe you should've thought of that before you ditched me."

"I know ... I'm sorry. The police were no help anyway. I didn't have a name or address, and I couldn't identify any distinctive tattoos from your kidnapper."

"I wasn't kidnapped."

"How was I supposed to know that? Anyway," she says, flicking her wrist, "I described him as best I could: Really tall ... over six foot, extremely good-looking, panty-melting smile, brown hair, brown eyes, rocking body, but the dispatcher said my description was too generalised and vague. Like please," she says, rolling her

123

eyes. "How many guys do you see in real life that are that hot?"

"Exactly," I say, agreeing with her, because she has a point.

"I even offered to sit down with a police sketch artist, but he just told me to call back in twenty-four hours if you still hadn't returned. Can you believe it? In twenty-four hours, you could've been smuggled across numerous state lines ... or decomposing in a ditch while wild animals picked away at your flesh." She bows her head. "I'm the worst BFF ever and I wouldn't blame you if you never spoke to me again. I mean, it's some ungodly hour in the morning, but I'll pack up my things and head to the airport right now if you want me gone."

"I had planned on coming home to smother you with a pillow."

She gasps, placing her hand on her chest. "Well, that's a little dramatic, but I suppose I deserve it."

"Relax, I'm not going to murder you."

"Thanks ... I guess."

"I actually should be the one saying thank you."

Her mouth gapes open when I say that. "Oh, my God ... did you go through with it?" When I nod my head and smile, she throws her hands in the air and squeals so loud my ears ring. "Did you have an 'O'?"

"Three."

"Jazzie," she says, pulling me into another crashing hug. "My little girl is all grown up."

Chapter 12

Mason

This morning I got up early, showered, and after dressing, I packed up the remainder of my clothes. Today is moving day, and I'm in two minds about it. Once I carry the two suitcases downstairs, and the box that contains the stuff that wouldn't fit in them, I grab my drill and head back up to my bedroom to pull apart my bed. I strip the sheets and drag the mattress into the hallway.

Connor will be here soon, so I'll get him to help me carry that, and the larger items of furniture downstairs. Blake's still asleep, so once I'm finished with my room, I'll move to his. As long as I have it all done before the moving van arrives at ten, I'm good.

I take the drawers out of my tallboy, stacking them in a pile, and as I move the base away from the wall, I see something white sitting on the floor. Bending down, I scoop it up and it takes a second to realise what it is, but once I do, the myriad of feelings that have been raging through me the past week come rushing back to the surface.

"Fucking, Red," I mumble under my breath as I make

a fist, scrunching her G-string in my hand. I'm still pissed at her; no matter how hard I've tried to shake it, I can't.

When I woke that morning and found her gone, I can't even put into words how I felt. On one hand it brought back memories from my teenage years—waking up to find my mother had vanished during the night—leaving me behind, *alone* with that monster. Of course, my dad blamed me. He said it was all my fault she was gone, and although I've never found out what happened to her, I have my suspicions. The woman I remember would never have abandoned me.

My situation with Red, however, was different. After searching the entire house and perimeter of the estate, my concern for her soon morphed into anger. I felt like a fool for wanting more, even if it was only going to be a few extra hours together. I'll admit, I was also perplexed how she'd gotten out, but I didn't have to wonder for long.

Those answers were quickly realised when I pulled up the app for my security cameras on my phone. And as mad as I was, I'll admit I laughed out loud a couple of times as I watched my very own version of Harry Houdini make her escape. It was amusing if nothing else.

Pulling out my phone, I click on the clip I saved. My lips curve up at the corners as I rewatch her duck and roll behind the bushes after setting off the sensor light. When she limps towards the gates, I still find myself impressed with the ease in which she scales to the top. Those gates are eight foot high, and if I didn't have the footage to prove it actually happened, I never would have believed it.

My smile grows as I watch her dress get snagged on the fence, and the tug-a-war that follows, which almost resulted in a catastrophe. The first time I watched this, my heart was in my throat, but despite the odds, she managed to hang on. I zoom in and the look of horror on her face is priceless. A part of me is proud of her, but the pissed-off side wonders if it was her karma for sneaking out the way she did. If she didn't want to stay, she only had to say so. I would've made sure she got home safe.

I bark out a laugh when she bends to collect her stuff from the ground—squares her shoulders and raises her chin in the air like the kick-arse she is—and hobbles away with one of her arse cheeks hanging out, thanks to the large tear in the side of her dress.

My phone dings as the video comes to an end and Connor's name pops up on the screen.

> Connor: I'm here. I brought coffee and donuts.

I smile as I shove Red's underwear into my pocket and type a reply. I'm grateful to have a friend like him. I didn't even have to ask for his help today, he volunteered. I'm sad that I have to let this place go, but the silver lining in all this is I'll be living close to him.

> Mason: Coming down now.

"This is the last box," Connor says, "where do you want it?"

"Just put it over there with the others," I reply, flicking my chin towards the far wall.

It's been a long day, but I can't believe it's finally done. I've officially ended another chapter in my life by moving out of the house that I called home for the past year. I can only hope Blake is happy here. He cried when we did the final walk-through, and I'll admit I struggled to keep it together when we backed out of the driveway for the last time.

That place symbolised so much when I first bought it, so it's sad to see it go. It was supposed to be our forever home, where I'd watch my son grow up, but in my heart, I know I'm doing the right thing. Too many people count on Bridge for their survival, so I refuse to let that place go under. We'll eventually find our groove here, and make lots of new memories.

"Are you going to stay for pizza?" I ask.

"Nah, Jaz is cooking. You guys should come over for a home-cooked meal."

I haven't had a home-cooked meal since Betty passed. "Maybe another time. I need to put the bed's together and get the TV hooked up."

"Do you want some help with that before I go?"

"I'm good. I appreciate all you did today."

"You'd do the same for me," he says, and he's right, I would. I've had plenty of friends over the years, but nobody like him. "Some of the guys are coming over tomorrow afternoon to watch the game ... you should come. It's been months since you've hung with us. Plus, my sister is looking forward to meeting you both."

I lift one shoulder. "You know how Blake is around chicks."

"Yeah, but Jaz is great. The absolute sweetest."

Although I've missed my time with the guys, Blake's already struggling with the move, so I don't want to do anything that will upset him further. "I'll think about it and let you know."

"Okay." He taps my back as he passes on his way to the door. "Let me know what you decide ... oh, and welcome to the building."

"Thanks, mate."

Once Connor leaves, I head off in search of Blake. I find him in his new room, unpacking some of his toys and lining them up on his shelves.

"You okay, bud?"

"Yeah, Dad," he says, glancing up from the box he's rummaging through.

"Do you need any help in here?"

"Nah."

"I'll set your bed up soon."

"Okay."

"Want to order a pizza for dinner?"

As soon as I mention food, he stops what he's doing and gives me his undivided attention. "Can we get pepperoni?"

"You can order whatever you like."

"I want garlic bread too."

"Okay."

"And some chicken wings."

I chuckle as I leave him. I've got some unpacking of my own to do.

As I enter the kitchen, there's a knock on the door. I cross the main room, heading in that direction. I have no idea who this could be.

When I open it, I find Connor standing there. He holds up two bags in one hand and a container balanced in the other. "Jaz went to the shops today to get every-thing she needs for the game tomorrow; she also got some things for you. Bread, milk, butter, juice, eggs, cheese, breakfast cereal, coffee, sugar, and some fruit and snacks ... stuff she said you might need. She also baked some cupcakes for Blake."

"Wow, seriously?"

"I told you she was the best. I've never mentioned this, but she had a really shitty childhood. The first time I met Blake, he reminded me so much of her. Between us, she still carries some of those scars from her past, so I know she'd never overstep the mark with him."

"Good to know ... tell her I said thank you for these."

"Will do."

He turns and starts walking down the corridor towards the lift. "Connor." He pauses when I call out his name, glancing over his shoulder. "What time do you want us to come over tomorrow?"

A smile tugs at his lips. "The game starts a three thirty, so any time before that."

My stomach is in knots as we ride down the lift to Connor's floor. I'm not nervous about meeting his sister, I'm just apprehensive about how Blake will react.

"Connor's sister is going to be there today," I say. It's the first time I have mentioned it because I wasn't sure if he would've wanted to come if he knew. "The one who made you the cupcakes."

"They were yum." He ate three of them last night on top of his pizza, garlic bread, and wings. It still astounds me how he can fit so much food into that tiny body of his.

"There should be plenty of food here today. Connor said his sister is a really good cook."

"Okay," is all he says, but I can sense his apprehension.

I crouch down to his height. "If you feel uncomfortable at any stage, just let me know and we can leave."

He bows his head and murmurs, "Okay, Dad."

I'm now having second thoughts about agreeing to this.

We exit the lift and walk down the corridor towards Connor's apartment in silence. Blake's been here countless times, but Connor lived alone then.

When we reach the door and Blake clutches my hand, I want to turn around and head back upstairs. "Are you sure you want to be here?"

I can already smell the delicious aromas coming from inside. "I'm hungry," Blake replies, making me chuckle.

Obviously, food comes before his fear of women.

I raise my hand and knock. "What smells so good?" I ask when Connor opens the door.

"Jaz is cooking up a storm." He leans in and gives me a one-armed hug before reaching down to bump fists with Blake. "She's been in the kitchen for hours. Wait 'til you taste her cooking, man, it's the best."

"I'm hungry," Blake repeats. He had two cheese sandwiches, an apple, and a couple more cupcakes for lunch, so I don't see how.

"Jaz," Connor calls out when we step inside the apartment. "Mason and Blake are here."

I've waited a long time to meet this elusive sister of his, and it will be good to finally put a face to the name, but when she exits the kitchen and comes into view, my heart drops into the pit of my stomach.

Red!

What are the fucking chances?

The colour drains from her face as soon as our eyes lock. Mine narrow instantly, despite the racing of my heart. She looks different, *breathtaking*, and I hate that this is my first thought. Today, her long blonde hair is pulled back into a high ponytail, and her face is free of make-up. Her pale-blue, knee-length sundress makes her eyes pop, and despite how sweet and innocent she

131

appears, I know better. *There is nothing innocent about this temptress.*

I have no idea how this is going to pan out, but I'm guessing not great. Connor is going to lose his shit when he finds out I deflowered his precious little sister, and I can only pray he has enough composure not to do it in front of my son.

"Jacinta," Connor says when she's standing in front of us, "this is my best friend, Mason Bradley."

Her tongue darts out, briefly running over her bottom lip as she extends her hand towards me. "It's nice to finally meet you ... Connor talks about you all the time."

So, she's going that route. I should be relieved, but I'm not ... I'm livid. She's going to pretend she doesn't know me? That my mouth and hands haven't touched every inch of her body. That a week ago my tongue and my cock weren't buried deep inside her?

Game on, Red!

Her hand remains lingering in the air, and when Connor's attention darts to me, I sigh as I'm left with no choice but to reciprocate her greeting. My fingers wrap around hers, and her eyes slightly widen when I squeeze tighter than I normally would. "It's nice to finally meet you too ... Jacinta."

When I don't immediately let go, she tugs her arm back, freeing her hand from my grip. I feel a pang of guilt when I noticed her clench and unclench her hand a few times. I hadn't meant to hurt her; I just wanted her to know I wasn't happy.

Did she pretend she didn't know me because she doesn't want Connor to find out what we did, or is there something more to it? Does she regret her time with me? The way she risked her life to get away has me leaning more in that direction.

"And who do we have here?" she asks, crouching down to Blake's level.

I roll my lips to hide my smile when he ducks behind my legs. *Hah!* Take that, Red; your voodoo pussy has no power over a five-year-old.

Connor cocks an eyebrow when I don't speak. "This is Blake, Mason's son," he answers.

Her eyes briefly flicker up to me before focusing back on my son. She's probably shocked I have a kid. There's a lot she could've learnt about me if only she'd stuck around to find out, instead of sneaking out in the dead of night.

"Hi, Blake." She gives him a blinding toothy smile, which makes her entire face light up, and my anger grows. *I never got one of them.* "I'm Connor's sister, Jacinta, but my friends call me Jaz or Jazzie." I'll make sure to call her Jacinta from now on, because we are definitely not friends. "Do you like chocolate chip cookies?" she asks in a sugary sweet voice, and my lips thin as I try in vain to rein in my fury. If anything is going to get my son onside it'll be food. I struggle to quell my displeasure when he nods his head. "I made some earlier, do you want to come in the kitchen with me and try one?"

My nostrils flare when Blake whispers, "Okay."

Red stands to full height and extends her hand to him, and the little traitor wastes no time wrapping his small fingers around hers. *Un-fucking-believable.*

Connor places his hand on my shoulder as the two of them leave the room. "You okay?" he asks.

"Peachy," I snap.

"You sure, you seem off? Angry."

I exhale a long breath. "I'm good, brother," I lie. "You got any beer?" Because I need something to take the edge off.

Chapter 13

Jacinta

M y heart is beating a million miles a minute as I leave the room hand in hand with Mason's son. *His son.* I can't believe Wolf has a kid. I rack my brain trying to recall every single detail Connor told me about his friend, but my mind is too scrambled to think clearly.

It's a miracle I got through that meeting without Connor picking up on my inner freakout. He's usually pretty attuned when it comes to me and seems to know when things are off. What are the chances of all the men in the club that night, it was my brother's best friend that I went home with?

I felt awful just now, pretending I'd never met him, but my brother can never find out I slept with his friend. Things won't end well if he does. I know how protective he is of me.

"Wow," Blake murmurs when we enter the kitchen and he sees all the trays lined up on the countertop, laden with food. "Did you cook all this?"

"I did."

"My dad can't cook."

"He can't? Who makes your dinner?"

"We eat at Bridge," he says.

"Bridge? Is that a restaurant?"

"No, it's where the homeless people eat."

My eyes widen with shock. *Mason takes his son to a soup kitchen to eat?* He's taking food away from the needy, which is shameful. After our night together, I'd put him on a pedestal, but that knowledge just knocked him straight off ... his ugly side is definitely starting to show now. I saw the mansion he was living in and the fancy car that was parked in his garage beside his bike. I also know his new apartment would've set him back an easy few million ... after all, my father bought the one Connor and I live in.

I try not to let my disappointment show in front of Blake. But this is the perfect ammo I need to remember next time his gorgeous face sends my heart into a flutter— he's actually a wolf in sheep's clothing. Which is ironic given our nicknames for each other.

I bend down to Blake's level and I feel compelled to reach out and sweep away the long piece of brown hair that's flopped down onto his forehead, but I don't. Damaged gravitates towards damaged, I can see it in his eyes ... eyes that are so much like his father's. When I was his age, I hated being touched by others.

"Would you like some milk with your cookies?"

"Yes please."

I pull out a stool at the breakfast bar and help him climb onto it. As I'm getting a plate out of the cupboard, the guys enter the kitchen. Connor heads straight for the fridge, and Mason won't even make eye contact with me, choosing to focus solely on his son.

After putting some cookies onto the plate and pouring

Blake a glass of milk, I place them down in front of him. "Do you want me to carry these out to the lounge room for you, buddy?" Mason asks.

"Can I stay in here with, Jazzie?"

A smile tugs at my lips. He called me Jazzie, that means he must've already decided we're friends.

Mason clears his throat. He's obviously not too happy about that. "You just want to be near all the food, don't you?"

I see where he went there. He wants me to know that's the only reason his son is in here with me. "And Jazzie too ... she's nice."

Hah! Take that, you homeless-food-stealing jerk. When Mason side-eyes me, I make sure to give him a smug smile. His displeasure is evident as he lifts the beer Connor handed him to his mouth, taking a big chug.

"I'll be out here if you need me," he says to his son.

"Okay, Dad," Blake replies with a mouth full of cookie.

When he turns and leaves the kitchen, Connor follows. "I told you he'd love Jaz," he says.

"Hmm," is Mason's only reply.

After Blake eats way too much food for a small boy, I bring out the trays of food for Connor and his mates, then we head to my room. We were going to watch a movie because he said the footy was boring—I have to agree—but he spotted my Nintendo Switch, so we ended up gaming instead. He told me he had an X-box at home, so he wasn't familiar with Super Mario Bros., but I quickly got him caught up. I was surprised how fast he mastered the game; his hand-eye coordination is incredible for someone so young.

We are sitting side by side on my bed with our legs crossed when Blake suddenly pauses the game and asks, "Jazzie, do you have a mum?" It takes me completely off guard.

Connor briefly touched on Blake's unfortunate situation prior to coming to live with his dad, so there's no way I'm going to ask him about his own mother, unless he brings it up. I don't know specifics, but I'm gathering given their current circumstances, it wasn't great.

"I do."

"Is she nice?"

"She's really nice," I reply.

"My mum isn't nice."

"I'm sorry to hear that," I say, reaching for him before thinking better of it. "My real dad was really mean when I was little, so I know what that feels like."

"Really? My dad is nice."

"Yes, he is," I say, although the jury is still out on that one.

Blake bows his little face. "She used to scream at me and hit me when she couldn't get her medicine." I wonder if by medicine he means drugs. "Did your dad ever hit you?"

"Yeah, sometimes," I say. I hate talking about this, but if I can help this little boy in some way, I'll answer any question he asks.

"Did he lock you in your room?"

"No, but whenever my dad would get angry, I'd lock myself in my bedroom so I was safe."

"Annalise used to lock me away all the time ... mostly

when she had parties." When I hear him sniffle, I gently run my hand over his back. "Sometimes she would leave me in the room for a really long time. When it got dark, I was scared. If I needed to go to the toilet, I'd have to do it in my pants because the door was locked. That used to make her really mad. She said I was a naughty boy and would smack me hard. I tried to hold it in, Jazzie, but my belly used to hurt when I did."

"Aww, sweetie. You had no choice ... you weren't being naughty; I hope you know that."

He shrugs his tiny shoulders. "She'd put me in a really cold shower to punish me. I wasn't allowed to come out until she said I could."

What a nasty bitch.

"You poor little thing," I say as tears cloud my own eyes. When he uses his shirt sleeve to wipe his face, I know he's crying too. My heart hurts for him. "Would it be okay if I hugged you?"

"Yeah," he answers, giving me a small smile.

"You are a good, sweet boy, don't let anyone tell you differently, okay? The things your mum did to you were wrong." I place a soft kiss on the top of his head before letting him go.

"Do you still see your dad?" he asks.

"No. He ended up going to jail for all the bad things he did."

His eyes widen. "I don't see my mum anymore ... do you think she's in jail with your dad?"

"I don't know." Because that's the truth. I vaguely remember Connor mentioning that she'd signed over her parental rights to Mason, but I have no clue what happened from there. "You'll need to ask your dad that."

"Okay, Jazzie," he says, picking up his remote and

starting a new game, completely oblivious to the fact that he just broke my heart in two.

"I'm going to go get a drink, do you want one?" I ask, scooting to the side of the bed. What I really need is a moment to collect myself.

"Yes please."

When I step out into the hallway, I wipe my eyes with the back of my hand. My heart hurts for that little boy, and I can only hope he got away from that woman young enough for it not to leave permanent damage.

As I round the corner to enter the kitchen, I pause when I see Mason bent over, grabbing something from the fridge. Is he making the most of the freebies while he's here?

His eyes narrow when he stands to full height and sees me standing in the doorway. "Where's my kid, Red?"

"In my room playing video games. And my name is Jacinta," I snap, moving further into the kitchen.

His arm comes out to stop me as I try to pass, and I intake a sharp breath when he leans in, because for a split second, I think he's going to kiss me. I hate that my body immediately reacts, zinging at the prospect. "I only know you as Red," he whispers, tugging on my ponytail. "You know, like the colour you stained my sheets when I stuffed your tight virgin pussy full of my big fat cock."

My face heats at the vulgarity of his words, and when I turn my head in his direction, I can tell by his smug look he was going for the shock factor—he succeeded. "You did not just say that to me."

A smile tugs at his lips as he straightens and cracks the top off his beer. "I believe I did. I've seen you in action, Red, and this sweet and innocent act of yours is a complete farce. And by the way, I have a video of your awkward and rather comical escape from my place."

139

"You're lying," I accuse, although I don't think he is. How else would he know it was awkward and comical?

He slides his phone out of his pocket, moving his finger over the screen. He holds it up in front of me, and I gasp when I see myself diving behind the bush. I reach out, trying to grab hold of his phone, but he must anticipate my move because his arm rises above his head, holding it out of my reach. "I'm thinking of uploading it to YouTube."

"You wouldn't dare," I screech.

"I most definitely would."

I take a step towards him, stomping down on his foot. "Delete it this instant!" I demand.

He barks out a laugh as he turns to exit the room. "Not a chance in hell."

"I've never made popcorn like this before," Blake says as I empty the last of the corn kernels into the pot and cover it with a lid. "Braydon's dad cooked it in a bag in the microwave when I stayed at his place."

"This is so much nicer than microwave popcorn. And you'll be able to see the kernels pop through the glass lid." I slide my hands under his arms, lifting him up to sit on the counter so he can get a better view.

"Nothing is happening," he says disappointed as he leans over to peer through the lid.

"Give it a few minutes, but don't touch the pot, it will get really hot and I don't want you to burn yourself."

"Okay, Jazzie."

Could this little boy get any sweeter? How his mother could mistreat him is beyond me.

As time passes and nothing happens, I see his disillusionment grow. I double-check that the stovetop is turned on, which it is, so I reach for the handle on the lid, lifting it. As I do the first kernel pops, flying up into the air and landing on the countertop.

Blake squeals with excitement. "It's working."

Before I get a chance to replace the lid, a few more pop in succession, with one piece hitting me square between the eyes. Blake throws back his head and bursts out laughing.

"You think that's funny? I almost lost an eye," I say grinning, which only seems to make him laugh harder. His shoulders bob up and down as his arms hug his middle.

When I bend down to collect the few pieces that landed on the floor, I notice Mason standing in the doorway watching us. There's a huge smile on his face as he observes his son, and you can clearly see the love there.

He's still smiling as his eyes move to me, and for a split second, I think he forgets he hates me, but his face quickly sobers when he remembers. "What's going on in here?"

"We're making popcorn for our movie," I reply.

"A piece hit Jazzie in the face, Dad. It was so funny."

"It's a shame I missed it," he replies. *Ugh.* I don't even know why he's so mad at me. Is he upset that I snuck out of his house? He was the one who reinforced we were a one and done, and made it perfectly clear he wanted me gone once we were finished.

Standing, I walk over to the bin and discard the pieces in my hand, before helping Blake off the counter. "Why don't you go wash your hands, the popcorn is almost ready?"

"Okay," he says, dashing from the room.

I turn my back on his father to grab a bowl, and the

last thing I expect is for him to come up behind me and cage me in with his arms. His close proximity has my traitorous body zinging back to life again.

He leans in and his warm breath against my skin makes it pebble with goose bumps. "Don't get too close to my son, Red. He may be young and impressionable, but he's a smart kid."

"What is that supposed to mean?" I say, turning to face him, which is a big mistake ... his face is now inches from mine.

"This Mother Teresa act you've got going on. It's only a matter of time before he sees through it, just like I did."

My eyes narrow into slits. The hide of this guy. "That is rich coming from you," I sneer.

"Be careful, princess, your crown is slipping. Unlike you, what you see with me, is what you get. I'm an open book. I've never claimed to be something I'm not."

"Really? Because I know all about the food you're stealing from the poor and misfortunate ... I can't even with that. You should be ashamed of yourself."

"What?"

"Blake told me you eat at a soup kitchen every night. Are you that tight you'd rather take food out of homeless people's mouths instead of buying your own? If you're incapable of cooking for your son, take him to a restaurant to eat. I saw where you lived, you're not poor."

Mason's eyebrows pinch together as his face turns red. I'm not sure if it's from anger or embarrassment. "Oh, you mean Bridge, the soup kitchen I run?" *What?* "And I gather you're referring to the place I was forced to sell—the only stable home my son's ever known—to downsize to a shitty apartment, so I could use the extra money the sale generated to keep Bridge's doors open."

"You run the kitchen?"

"I do ... so next time you decide to get up on your high horse and judge me, I suggest you get your facts straight first."

With that, he pushes off the counter and storms out of the kitchen, leaving me being the one who's embarrassed and ashamed.

Chapter 14

Jacinta

"So, what do you think?" Connor asks, popping his head into my room after everyone has left.

"About what?"

"Mason and Blake?"

"Blake is the sweetest, I adore him, but I can't really comment on Mason. All my time was spent with his son." I have plenty to say about his friend, but I'm definitely not going there with him.

"Mason's a great guy. We'll be seeing a lot more of them now that they're living in our building. I'm sure you two will become friends when you get a chance to know each other better." *Hah! And pigs might fly.* "He was so worried about bringing Blake here, because he's petrified of women, but I knew if there was anyone who that little boy could relate too, it would be you."

A lump rises to the back of my throat as my conversation with Blake flickers through my mind. I hate that his childhood even remotely resembled mine. "What happened to his mother?" I ask.

"No clue."

"She's not in jail?"

"If I had my way she would be."

"Ah, okay. Blake just mentioned he doesn't see her."

"It was one of the conditions of their settlement," he says. "Mason paid her a large sum of money to sign her rights over, and agree to no further contact."

"Wow. I can't believe a mother would freely give up her child like that. For money no less."

"She's a junkie, Jaz."

"That explains a lot."

"I'm going to jump in the shower and head to bed, I've got an early start in the morning," Connor says. "Good night, and thanks again for all the food you made for us."

"Night, Con."

I open my eyes, blinking a few times until my vision clears. When I look at the clock beside my bed I see it's just after eight. My mum has usually woken me up for school by now.

Throwing back the covers, I rise and head down the hallway towards the bathroom. After using the toilet, I move to the sink to wash my hands, and when I look in the mirror, I see how young I am. I part my lips and one of my two front teeth has only half-grown in.

Once I've dried my hands, I head towards the kitchen where I gather my mum will be, making my breakfast. But when I round the corner, I find the room empty. Panic immediately rises. "Mummy," I call out, but it sounds more like a squeak. I get that sinking feeling in my stomach when I get no reply.

Turning, I run down the hallway towards her room.

145

Her bedroom door is closed, and when I crack it open and peek inside, I see her lying on the bed.

"Mum."

"Yes, baby," she mumbles, and I feel immediate relief that she's still alive.

I move further into the room and when my eyes adjust to the semidarkness, I gasp. Her face is bruised and swollen and I can see dried blood in her blonde hair and on the pillowcase. "Mummy," I cry as my vision becomes blurry. It's rare that I see her in this condition. She usually cleans herself up, covering the bruises as best she can, before collecting me from my room.

"I'm okay, Jacinta," she says, trying to sit up, but when she groans in pain more tears fall. "I won't be able to walk you to school this morning, do you think you'll be okay to walk there on your own?"

I can count on one hand the times I've had to get myself to school, but I've never seen her this bad before and there's no way I'm leaving her here on her own.

Stepping closer to the bed, I rest my head on her chest and sob. "Why does he hurt you like this, Mummy?" I can't understand why. I've never seen bruises on the other mums at school.

She lifts her hand, gently stroking it through my hair. "I'll be okay, sweetie. Please don't worry about me." I always worry about her, how can I not? "Do you think you'll be able to make yourself some breakfast?"

"Yes, I will make you something too."

"I'm not very hungry, but I want you to eat. There's some cereal in the cupboard and milk in the fridge."

"Okay." I lean in and place a kiss on her battered face. She's a nice mummy and doesn't deserve the awful things my father does to her.

My mind is swimming as I head back to the kitchen. I

know if she stays in bed all day and is unable to do her chores, my father will be angry when he gets home. I need to stay here so I can help her. I don't want him to hurt her any more than he already has, and if I'm home, I can keep an eye on her as well.

Once my breakfast is finished, I rinse my plate and spoon in the sink and get dressed. Heading into the laundry, I grab a bucket and take it into the bathroom. Placing it in the bathtub, I add some warm water. I get a cake of soap and a clean washer, then carry it into my mum's room.

I put it down on the floor beside her bed. "If I help you, do you think you'll be able to sit up? I'm going to clean the blood off your face."

"Okay." I see her bottom lip quiver as I help her sit, and when she groans in pain, I have to fight back my own tears.

I clean her up as best I can, and by the time I'm finished, the water in the bucket is dark pink. With my help, I manage to strip her out of her nightdress, sliding a new one over her head. "Let me grab a clean pillowcase."

Dashing from the room, I get what I need. Once I've removed the bloodied one and replaced it, I help her lie back down. "Thank you," she whispers.

"What chores do you have to do today? I want to help you so you don't get in trouble when Dad gets home."

"You need to go to school."

"I'm staying here." I never disobey her and always do what she asks of me, but I'm not leaving her alone.

"I need to wash your fathers work shirt. He'll need it for tomorrow."

"Okay. How do I do that?"

"Place it in the machine, add a scoop of laundry powder, turn the dial to regular wash, and press start."

"Do you want me to wash these too?" I ask, holding up the bloodied pillowcase and night dress.

"You can just soak them in the bucket. I'll deal with them tomorrow."

While I wait for the machine to finish, I fill a glass with water and grab two Panadol from the bathroom cupboard. I help my mum into a sitting position again, place the pills in her mouth, and bring the glass of water to her lips. That's when I notice the tears running down her cheek.

"Don't cry, Mummy."

"You're such a good girl," she says, choking on a sob. "I don't know what I'd do without you. You make my life worth living."

"You're the best mummy in the world." I lean in, placing a kiss on her cheek.

"I hate this life for you," she cries.

"I hate it for you too."

"I wish I could get you away from here, but I don't know how. I have no money ... nowhere to go."

When the washing is finished, I get one of the kitchen chairs and drag it out the back door and down the three steps. Once I've positioned it at the clothesline, I run back inside to grab my father's work clothes and the pegs. I've never hung out washing before, but I've watched my mum do it enough to know how it's done.

Between chores, my day is spent lying beside my mum as she falls in and out of a restless sleep. My eyes remain focused on her chest, grateful it continues to rise and fall.

At lunchtime, I manage to get a few bites of a sandwich into her, and by late afternoon, my dread starts to grow. I know my father will be home soon.

"Mummy," I say, gently waking her. "What can I cook for dinner?"

"There are sausages and eggs in the fridge. Your dad likes to have some buttered bread on the side."

"Okay."

"Do you remember how to use the stovetop?"

"I think so."

"Don't turn the element on too high, or you might burn the food."

For the next half an hour, I go back and forth between the kitchen and my mum's room getting instructions. And when I hear that familiar BANG! my body immediately tenses.

My hands start to shake as I use the tongs to turn the sausages in the pan. The moment my father enters the kitchen and sees me standing on a chair by the stove, I can tell he's angry by the look on his face.

"Where's your fucking mother?" he screams.

"Sh-sh-she's in bed," I stutter, frozen in fear. "She was feeling sick, so I told her to lie down and I would cook dinner."

When he reaches for my arm and drags me off the chair, I'm so frightened of what he's going to do to me I wet my pants. I feel my face heat with embarrassment, because I've never done that before, but my father is so angry and focused on what he's doing that I don't think he even notices.

The way he drags me down the hallway hurts so bad, but I don't cry out, because when my mum does, he gets angrier. When we enter their bedroom, I can no longer hold back my tears. I don't want him to hurt her any more than he already has.

"Get up, you lazy fucking cunt!" he screams, letting me go and dragging her off the bed.

"Mummy," I cry out, and I feel the hand that's wrapped around mine tighten. It's followed by fingers

149

lightly skimming over my forehead. "Jaz." I open my eyes and find Connor sitting on the side of my bed. "Are you okay?" he asks.

"No ... no I'm not," I reply, choking on a sob.

"Come here," he says, opening his arms.

As I cry into his chest, I know exactly what triggered that memory ... my conversation with Blake.

150

Chapter 15

Mason

It's been a week since our big move, and I finally have everything unpacked ... our new place now looks like a home. I still miss my old house, but I think we'll be happy here.

I've seen Connor a few times, but I've avoided his apartment and his little sister like the plague. Blake has been pestering me about seeing her again, but I'm avoiding that as well. I don't like to deny my son of anything, but no good can come from hanging around that woman.

Well, that's my story and I'm sticking to it.

One blinding smile by that little temptress, and *boom,* she's got my kid under her spell too. He hasn't even turned six yet, and although impressionable, he's too young to be smitten by a girl.

I enter the kitchen and find Blake rinsing and packing his plate and cup from breakfast into the dishwasher. He's such a good boy and gives me no trouble. It's sad his mother couldn't see how wonderful he is, but that's her loss, I guess.

Today is his first day of kindergarten, and I'm not sure

how I feel about seeing him dressed in his school uniform. He looks so grown up. It's a reminder of how much of his life I missed out on before he came to live with me, but I'm grateful to have him now. It's nice to have some family again.

"Why don't you go brush your teeth before we leave, and I'll get your lunch out of the fridge and pack it into your bag."

"Okay, Dad."

He seems excited about today; me, not so much. This whole parent thing is still relatively new to me ... it's been a long time since I've had to worry about anyone other than myself.

I reach into the fridge and grab the sandwiches the girls made especially for him last night at Bridge, adding some fruit, snacks, and a bottle of water into the bag.

"You ready to leave?" I ask when he comes bounding back into the kitchen.

"Yes."

After locking the front door, we head down the corridor towards the lift. "How are you feeling? Are you nervous?"

"A little," he replies. "I hope Braydon is in my class."

"Even if he isn't, you'll still get to play with him at recess and lunch."

"I know."

"Listen," I say, "I called the school yesterday." I'm only telling him now, because I didn't want him to worry about it all night ... like I did. "Your new teacher is a lady, but the principal assured me that's she's really nice. Okay?"

"Do you think she'll be as nice as Jazzie?"

I roll my eyes. *Fucking Jazzie.* This kid has it bad. "I bet she's even nicer," I answer as we step into the lift.

"You know if you have any problems today, you can go to the office and they'll call me."

"Okay, Dad."

"Good boy," I say, ruffling his hair.

He's definitely taking this better than I am. I've been feeling sick in my stomach ever since I picked up his school uniform a few days ago. I'm not sure if I'm ready for this.

When the lift stops on the floor below ours, my first thought is I hope it's not Red waiting to get on. Fate being the bitch she is, I'm not surprised when the doors open and I find her standing there, looking like a fucking goddess. Her long hair is down today and draped over one shoulder. She's dressed in a tight, pink top that stops just above the waistband of her body-hugging white jeans. My eyes focus on the sliver of skin showing, and I remember all too well how soft it felt under my touch. She has a killer body, and unfortunately, my cock agrees.

"Jazzie," Blake screams with such enthusiasm it echoes in the tight space.

Leaping forward, he throws his arms around her legs, and I'm starting to wonder if she put some kind of potion in his food the other day. *It's concerning.* A simple offer of a cookie and he did a complete one-eighty. It makes me anxious about what might happen if some creep approaches him with sweets. Will he go? That thought sets off a panic inside me. I make a mental note to have the stranger danger talk with him tonight.

"Look how handsome you are in your little tie and jacket," Jacinta says to him, and I cock an eyebrow. *What about me?* I'm wearing a tie and jacket too, but I get no praise. When I clear my throat, her pretty blue eyes flicker in my direction before skimming the length of my

153

body. "You're a little overdressed for feeding the homeless don't you think?"

The fuck!

"I see you're jumping to conclusions again, Red."

She lifts one shoulder. "I'm just calling it like I see it."

"I actually have a nine-to-five office job smart-arse—on top of the hours I put in at Bridge—you know, hence the suit."

"Oh."

"Yes, oh."

I still can't figure out how this woman manages to push all my buttons and arouse me at the same time.

Red turns her attention back to my son. "You've had your hair cut? You look so cute."

I've had my hair cut too, but again, that goes unnoticed.

When Blake's cheeks turn pink, I clear my throat, tugging at the tie around my neck. "Dad made me get it cut for my first day of kindergarten."

"Wow, you're first day of big school. How exciting."

Blake tilts his head back, making eye contact with me. "Can Jazzie come and see my new school, Dad?"

"Maybe some other time, buddy," I say. "I'm sure she's busy today."

Her gaze flicks back to me and I discretely shake my head, letting her know I don't want her there. When she lifts her chin in defiance, my eyes narrow because I can already tell she's going to challenge me.

"Actually, I don't have any plans." My brow furrows when she gives me a smug look, and I detest that my dick is turned on by this side of her. "I'd actually love to tag along."

Blake seems completely oblivious to my displeasure

because he punches the air and murmurs, "Yes," under his breath.

I have a feeling this woman is going to be the death of me.

My hands are gripping the steering wheel so hard my knuckles have turned white. I can't even tell you why I'm so mad. Is it because Red decided to come with us just to piss me off, or is it because she chose to sit in the back seat with Blake rather than ride up front with me? Either way, by the time we arrive at the school, my blood pressure has risen to a dangerous level.

Thanks to our *tagalong*, we had to take the car instead of the bike. Which also means, I'm going to have to drop her back at the apartment building instead of heading straight to work. I should make her find her own way home.

I exit the vehicle, opening the driver's side back door first. Jacinta gives me a strange look as she unbuckles her seat belt and hops out. I may be pissed at her, but I'm not a complete arsehole. "Thank you," she says as I close the door behind her and walk around the back of the car to get Blake.

After I retrieve his bag from the boot, throwing it over my shoulder, the three of us head up the hill towards the school.

Blake moves between us as we approach the front gate, reaching for my hand first, then Jacinta's. We share a brief look before she turns her attention to my son. "Are you nervous?" she asks.

"A little," he replies.

She stops walking, crouching down to his height. "Don't be, okay? I know it's scary to do new things for the first time, but you're going to have the best day and make lots of new friends."

"Do you think so?"

"I know so," she answers with such confidence even I believe her.

"What if the kids don't like me?"

"Impossible. You're the sweetest, smartest, and cutest little boy I know. I bet the girls in your class are going to have cartoon hearts in their eyes when they see you."

When he gags, I chuckle. "Braydon says that girls stink."

"I'm a girl? Do you think I stink?"

He leans in and inhales through his nose, and her eyes briefly snap to me. Is she thinking about the time I sniffed her underwear? My dick twitches at the thought. When I see the blush climbing up her neck, I know she is.

"You smell nice," Blake says.

She smells better than nice, and I'm not referring to her perfume either. I still have her scrap of lace hidden in the back of my bedside drawer. Despite wanting to, I couldn't bring myself to throw it away.

Her face lights up as she gently brushes her hand over his hair, and something inside my chest cracks. She's really good with him, and I'm suddenly not so angry that she's here. I try to be present in my son's life and give him the love and stability he's been missing, but that gentle feminine touch—the one Red's showing him now—I'm not sure if I'm capable of that.

The sweet look she gives him as her hands move down to straighten his tie, has me wishing my own was crooked, just so I could get the same treatment. She's so focused on him she probably wouldn't notice anyway.

156

Standing to full height, she reaches for his hand again, and Blake rewards her with a full smile ... it appears he's the one with cartoon hearts in his eyes.

Who knew I'd be competing with my own son for her attention?

Jacinta's phone rings as we're waiting in the front quadrangle for the kindergarten teachers to come out of the classrooms and collect their students. My eyes are glued to her tight arse as she slides her hand into her back pocket to retrieve it. It's so round and peachy, and I remember all too well what it felt like in my hands.

She looks down at the screen and nibbles on her bottom lip. "Connor," she says, answering the call and side-eyeing me. "I'm sorry about your coffee, I got side-tracked." Every time she goes silent, I know he's speaking, but I can't hear what he's saying to her. "I ... umm ... I'm at Blake's school with Mason."

"You're with Mason!" I hear when she pulls the phone away from her ear. It was more like a yell, so I know he's not happy. "Put him on."

She gives me a sympathetic look when she passes the phone to me. "Connor," I say.

"Why are you hanging out with my little sister? I swear to God if you lay one finger—"

I cut him off before he can get the rest of his words out. I don't want to be put in a position where I have to lie to him, because I've already had more than my fingers on her. "I wouldn't exactly call it hanging out."

"What would you call it then?"

"We ran into your sister in the lift earlier and Blake

157

invited her." My gaze darts to Red, and she's now chewing nervously on her thumb nail. "If you want the honest truth, I didn't even want her to come with us."

When her eyes slightly narrow, a small smile tugs at my lips.

"What the fuck, man. Why are you being mean to my little sister?"

"Dude," I say. "Calm down."

"Calm down?" he bellows. "It's a little late for that don't you think? What has she ever done to you?"

I tilt my head back, staring up at the sky. What hasn't she done to me would be a better question? The list is extensive, but it's not like I can unload any of that on him. "I'm confused, are you mad that your sister is here with *me*, or because I didn't want her to come with us?"

"Both."

"On that note, I'm going to put you back on to your sister."

Without speaking another word, I pass Jacinta her phone and shove my hands into the pockets of my trousers. My mood has soured again ... or maybe I'm just struggling with the guilt that's been eating away at me ever since I found out who she was. I never would've touched her if I knew, but either way, I'm not doing this here.

"Are you okay, Dad?" Blake asks, looking up at me with concern.

"I'm great, buddy," I reply, forcing out a smile.

"I promise I'd tell you if he was being mean to me, Con," I hear Red say, and obviously she's lying through her teeth, because I'm definitely not proud of how I've acted towards her since we've reunited. "No nothing is going on between us." *Another lie.* "Look I've got to go;

Blake's teacher is coming." And that completes her hat trick of untruths.

She ends the call without waiting for his reply, and this time, I'm the one giving her the sympathetic look because now we're both entangled in this clusterfuck of deceit.

I'm feeling emotional when it's time to say our good-byes. "Are you sure you're going to be okay, bud?"

"Yeah, Dad," Blake replies.

"If you have any problems tell the teacher and ask them to call me."

"Okay."

After giving him a brief hug, I straighten. "I'll see you at three o'clock."

"Are you coming too, Jazzie?" he asks, looking up at her with hopeful eyes.

"No," I say, answering for her. "I have to go back to the office, so you'll be coming with me."

He dips his face. "But it's boring there."

"I've got to work, bud."

"I have no plans this afternoon," Red interjects. "I can pick him up and take him back to my place until you finish if you like?"

Given everything that's happened, I don't think it's a good idea, but when Blake holds his two hands in front of him, like he's praying, and says, "Please, Dad," I can't say no to him.

I exhale a long breath before responding, "Okay."

159

Chapter 16

Jacinta

We leave the school grounds in silence. Things are even more awkward between us since the phone call from Connor. It's the first time I've ever lied to my brother, and I feel awful for it, but there are things he's better off not knowing. The last thing I want is to come between his friendship with Mason.

"Can I trust you to look after my kid and not ditch him, like you did me?" Mason says.

"I would never, and I didn't ditch you."

"Really, I have video proof that you did."

"I told you to delete that."

"Not going to happen, Red."

"You know what, I'll just get an Uber home."

"Nope," he says, wrapping his fingers around my elbow when I turn to walk away. "I'll drop you off."

"I don't want to get in the car with you."

"You don't have a choice."

"Ugh. You're impossible."

"Right back at ya, sweetheart."

"Won't you get in trouble for being late for work?"

He cocks an eyebrow. "I'm the boss, so no. The only person I seem to be in trouble with, is your brother."

I bow my head. "I'm sorry about that ... and for intruding on your time with your son. I shouldn't have come."

"Then why did you?"

My eyes move back to him and I blow out a puff of air. I've told enough lies today, so I'm going with the truth. "Because I knew it would annoy you."

He chuckles at that. "You like pushing my buttons, don't you, Red?"

I lift one shoulder and grin. "Kind of."

"I'll admit, initially I wasn't happy about you coming, and not for the reason you might think, but you're good with him, he's seems very taken with you."

"As I am with him, he's a great kid. He's like my kindred spirit."

"How so?"

"The things he went through with his mother ... I didn't have a great childhood either," I admit.

"Connor told you about that?"

"No. Blake did."

Mason's eyes widen slightly. "He talked about her with you?"

"Briefly, yes."

"Wow. Okay. He never mentions her to me. I saw firsthand the state he was in when he came to live with me, but I can only surmise what he went through."

"He didn't say much, but he told me his mother used to lock him away in his room when she had parties. I'm presuming for a long time because he said he was scared when it got dark."

"Fuck," he says, running his fingers through his hair.

"That's not even the worse part."

"What else did he tell you?"

"When he was locked away, he had no access to a bathroom and would get punished for wetting his pants. He said she used to hit him and put him in a freezing cold shower as punishment."

"That bitch!"

"I know. He cried when he talked about it ... it broke my heart." I turn my face away from him when my eyes cloud with tears.

"Hey," he says, reaching out to place his hand on my arm.

"I'm okay," I reply, swiping my fingers under my eyes. "I hurt for him ... it brought back a lot of things from my childhood."

"For what it's worth, I'm sorry for what you went through."

"My poor mum received the brunt of it ..."

"Mine too."

My gaze snaps back to him. "Your dad was abusive?"

He clears his throat. "Yeah."

This time I reach out and place my hand on him. "I'm sorry."

"Thanks," he says, giving me a tight smile. "We're a sad and sorry bunch, aren't we?"

"What doesn't kill you makes you stronger, so they say."

"Right." We start walking again. "I've wanted to broach the subject with Blake, but I'm not sure how. I tried to get him into therapy, but that didn't work, he just clammed up. How did you get him to open up?"

"I didn't. He asked me if I had a mum and if she was nice, and the conversation stemmed from there."

"Fair enough. Fuck this parenting thing is hard. My greatest fear is that I'm going to do more damage to him."

"Don't be so hard on yourself, he seems happy and adjusted. From what I've seen you're a great father. Anyone can see you care about him. As people we make mistakes once in a while, but I'm sure there's nothing you could do that would be worse than where he's come from."

"Do you consider me a mistake, Red?"

"What?"

"Do you regret what we did? Me being your first?"

I feel my cheeks heat. I can't believe he brought that up. "Do I have to answer that?"

"Yes."

"Do I regret you being my first? No. Do I wish it wasn't with my brother's best friend? Yes." He nods his head, but says nothing further. We stop when we reach his car. "Are you sure about the lift, I honestly don't mind calling an Uber?"

"I'm driving you home, Red." I step towards the car and reach for the handle of the back door. "I don't think so," he says, sliding his arm around my waist and drawing my body into his. My back is now resting against his chest, and my breath hitches in my throat as his fingers lightly skim over the bare skin on my stomach. "I'm not your chauffeur ... you ride in the front with me."

I bite my bottom lip as his warm breath skates over my cheek. This man makes me feel things I shouldn't.

"Smile," I say to Blake as we take a seat in the food court.

After clicking the photo of him holding up his milk-shake, I attach it in a text message to Mason.

> Red: Blake is safe and well. He loved his first day at school ... I'm sure he'll fill you in when you see him tonight. We stopped off to get a milkshake on our way home, I hope that's okay with you.

Mason asked for my phone number when he dropped me off this morning, immediately citing it was because I was picking up his son, and for no other reason. I shouldn't have felt disappointed by that knowledge, but I did.

We both know nothing more can come of us, even something casual would lead to catastrophic consequences for his friendship with Connor. Neither of us want that, but if we can manage to stay somewhat amicable with each other, I'll get to keep Blake in my life.

> Wolf: Thanks, Red. I'll come get him around 5.30 if that's okay. Earlier if I can manage it.

> Red: Whenever is fine. I have no plans tonight.

> Wolf: You mean your crazy friend isn't going to take you out to find more 'D'?

I can't believe he just sent me that. Staying amicable with him isn't going to be easy.

> Red: Firstly, she's not crazy ... just a little eccentric. Secondly, she is back in Melbourne. Thirdly, that was a one-time thing. Fourthly, me and any future 'D' I may acquire is none of your business!

I have no plans for any future 'D', but he doesn't need to know that.

Wolf: Firstly, the jury is still out on that one. Secondly, good, she's a bad influence. Thirdly, I'm happy to hear that. Fourthly, there better not be any 'D' in your future, unless it's mine.

My mouth is gaped open as I type my reply.

Red: Been there done that. And like I stated in point number four … it's none of your business!!!

Wolf: I can easily make it my business.

Red: How?

Wolf: I can tell Connor what you're up to.

Red: You wouldn't dare.

Wolf: Try me, sweetheart!

Red: You suck!

Wolf: I believe you were the one that sucked, Red. My dick has very fond memories of sliding between those luscious lips of yours.

Why do his words have me throbbing between my legs?

Red: On that note, goodbye!

Blake is in the lounge room watching a kid's movie on Netflix, while I prep dinner. I want to have it ready so I

165

can feed him before Mason gets here. I even let him choose what he wanted because I had to grab stuff from the store while we were out anyway. That's where I was heading this morning when I ran into him and Mason. I was also supposed to bring Connor back a coffee, hence why he called while we were at the school. He was waiting for it.

Blake chose pizza—he pointed to the premade freezer ones, but I'm going to make them from scratch—and jelly-beans for dessert. It was an odd request, but I bought him a packet, and told him he couldn't have any until after dinner. He gave me a cute pout, but I managed to remain strong. I didn't want to do anything that may get me in trouble with his dad. I've enjoyed spending the afternoon with him, and hopefully Mason will let me do it again sometimes.

"Jazzie," Blake says, coming into the kitchen. "I'm hungry."

"The dough is just about ready to roll, you can help me if you like."

"Okay."

I'm wearing the only apron we have, so I duck into my room and grab one of my T-shirts for him to put on over his uniform.

Once I remove his jacket, hanging it over the back of the chair, I undo his tie and roll up his sleeves before slipping my tee over his head.

"Why do I gotta wear this?" he asks, scrunching up his face.

"To keep your uniform clean." I lead him towards the sink. "Come wash your hands."

"Okay, Jazzie."

He's such a good boy, and with every minute I spend with him, he steals another tiny piece of my heart. All the more reason to try and be friends with his father. I'd be crushed if I could no longer see him.

After dragging one of the dining chairs over, I lift him up so he is the right height. He watches me scrape the dough out of the bowl, and onto the floured countertop, dividing it in two.

"I'm going to teach you how to knead the dough first, then we'll roll it out and add the pizza toppings."

"What's knead mean?"

"It's like mixing with your hands." That's probably the easiest way to explain it without getting too technical.

I sprinkle some flour over the top of his ball of dough. "Hold your hands out like this. That's it, palms up." He giggles when I dust his hands with flour as well. "That's to help stop the dough sticking to your skin."

"It's all squishy," he says, poking his finger into his ball.

"It is. Watch me do mine first, then I'll help you with yours." He gives me his undivided attention. "Flatten your ball out a bit, then fold it in half." He copies what I do. "Now, using this part of your hand—" I point to the heal of my palm. "—push down," I say before rolling it through the dough.

I bend his fingers back slightly and guide his hand down to the dough. He laughs again as he mimics what I just did. "This is fun," he says.

"Now, turn your dough around, fold it in half again, then knead."

"You're doing yours so fast."

"I've had plenty of practice. The more you do it, the better you'll get."

When someone knocks on the door, I wipe my hands on my apron. "Keep going, I'll see who it is." I'm surprised to find Mason standing on the other side. "You're early."

"My four-thirty meeting cancelled, so I thought I'd come and get Blake."

"Oh."

I intake a sharp breath when he reaches out and lightly skims his thumb over my cheek. "You had flour on your face."

"Oh, we're making pizzas."

"No wonder my kid is obsessed with you." He follows me into the kitchen where we find Blake frowning with concentration as he works his dough. "Hey, buddy."

"Hi, Dad. We're making pizzas from scraff."

"I think you mean scratch."

"Huh?"

"The word is scratch."

"Like when you're itchy."

"Yes."

"That's weird."

"Sometimes the same words have different meanings. You'll learn all about that at school. How was your first day?"

"Good."

"Do you like your teacher?"

Blake shrugs. "She's okay, but you were wrong about her."

"How so?"

"She's not nicer than Jazzie."

Of course, he'd tell his son that.

Mason clears his throat as I move back to work my own dough. "I was just trying to ease his worry about his teacher."

Fold.

Turn.

Knead.

I continue, completely ignoring his rationalisation.

"The pizzas should be ready in half an hour," I say after a brief period of awkward silence. "All the prep is done. Can Blake stay or do you have to leave?"

"I was going to duck upstairs and have a quick shower and change." He clears his throat again. I'm not sure why I find that sexy. "You know, since I'm apparently over-dressed for feeding the homeless."

"Uh huh," I say, biting on my bottom lip to suppress my grin.

"Can he stay down here while I do that?"

I keep on kneading. "Sure."

Just as Mason turns to leave, Connor arrives. "What is going on here?"

Great.

"We're making pizza, Uncle Connor," Blake states, proudly.

My eyes dart to my brother, and his gaze moves from me to Mason. Mason holds his hands up defensively in front of him. "I just got here. Your sister picked Blake up from school."

"So, you're not only being mean to her, you're now using her as a babysitter?"

"I offered," I cut in.

"On that note I'm leaving." Mason stalks out of the kitchen with Connor's eyes fixed on him as he does.

"I'll be keeping my eye on you, Bradley."

"Good for you, Maloney."

Shit. I need to find a way to de-escalate this and quick. "What is your problem?" I say to Connor when I hear the front door slam.

"My problem? I'm just sticking up for you."

"Then don't. I'm not sure what's going on in that thick head of yours, but you need to apologise to your friend when he returns. You're acting like a dick."

Blake giggles. "Jazzie said dick."

"I'm going to get changed and head to the gym," Connor says, rising from his chair and collecting his plate. "I need a workout after all those carbs." He leans down and places a soft kiss on my hair as he passes.

I'm still mad at him, or maybe it's betrayal I'm feeling. He has no clue that his concerns hold merit. All those flirty touches and sexual innuendos Mason keeps throwing my way have me tied up in a bundle of knots.

My brother apologised to his best friend the moment he returned, but you could still cut the air with a knife during dinner. Is Mason feeling it too? Because there's no denying this tension between the two of us. Every time I'm in his presence, I'm left feeling all hot and bothered.

"We should get going too," Mason says, reaching for Blake's plate and placing it on top of his own. "I've got a lot of work to get through tonight."

"You're burning the candle both ends."

"Something like that," he chuckles as he stands.

My eyes move away from his face and down his inked arms. He's changed into a pale, mint-green polo and a pair of faded jeans that are ripped at the knees. His dark-brown hair is still wet from his shower, and don't even get me started on how good he smells.

I'm not sure what version I like best—the casually dressed wolf, or the man in a suit. Because holy hell, I almost swallowed my tongue when I got a look at him this morning when I stepped into the lift.

Maybe if he wasn't so good-looking, I wouldn't be struggling like I am. That and the fact that the more I get to know him, the more drawn in I become. A gorgeous, doting single father, who moonlights by feeding the homeless—what's not to like?

"You done?" he asks, reaching across the table for my plate.

My gaze is now fixated on his big, strong hands as they grip my plate, dwarfing it in the process. "Yes," I breathe, gulping air into my lungs as I try and get my radically beating heart under control, because I know full well what those hands feel like against my body.

"You okay?" he asks.

My eyes snap back to his, and that smug look on his face tells me he's aware that I'm having impure thoughts of him.

"Yes," I squeak as my face heats.

I move my focus to Blake as Mason rounds the table, heading towards the kitchen, because I refuse to notice how well his arse fills out those jeans.

"I had fun hanging out with you today."

"Can you pick me up from school again tomorrow?" Blake asks.

"I have to work tomorrow, sweetie."

"Oh."

When his disappointed little face dips down to the table, I reach for his hand. "I'll talk to your dad when I have my next day off and see what he says, okay?"

The moment Mason re-enters the room, Blake pounces. "Jazzie has to work tomorrow, but can she pick me up from school on her next day off?"

Mason's eyes dart from his son to me. "It depends, is she going to cook for us again?"

"Please say yes, Jazzie," Blake begs.

"You're holding your son ransom in exchange for a home-cooked meal?"

"I can't cook for shit, so I've got to get something out of the deal."

"A free babysitter isn't enough for you?"

"Right, you've got a point there," he says, chuckling.

"Is that a yes, Dad?"

"I guess it is." Blake beams as he slides off his chair and joins his father.

"Wait, Blake's jacket and tie." I cross the room and grab them before meeting them at the door.

"Thanks," Mason says, taking them from me and slinging them over his arm. "And thanks again for dinner, and getting Blake this afternoon. I owe you."

"You might not be thanking me once you receive my invoice," I reply teasingly.

"You just said it was free babysitting."

"I've changed my mind; it's going to cost you."

Leaning in slightly, with a sly grin curving his mouth, he murmurs, "I'll reimburse you with 'O's."

I was joking, of course, but now I'm considering sending him an invoice.

Chapter 17

Mason

I lean back in my chair and run my fingers through my hair. It's been a long fucking day. I love my job, but being second-in-charge of a large and constantly expanding company can be stressful at times. There are days I wish I was still busting my arse down on the factory floor, but I've worked hard to get to where I am now.

I was only fourteen when I first started working here. Betty helped get me this job, and I've slowly worked my way up to the top during that time. We build, distribute, and export high performance motors, which is very labour intensive, but the corporate side—which I'm now in charge of—although less physical, can be equally taxing. Most nights when I leave here, I'm mentally exhausted. I guess that's why I get paid the big bucks, which I can't complain about. It allows me to afford my current lifestyle.

Rob, the CEO and owner of this company, is in the process of semiretirement, so I'm practically running the place now. He trusts me to make all the decisions when he's not here. I've been with him for almost fifteen years, and starting at the bottom has afforded me a wealth of knowledge. I know the ins and outs of every department.

When my phone dings on my desk, I sit forward and turn it over to look at the screen. I smile when I see Red's name.

> Red: Just got back to your place. All good here. I bought Blake a packet of jellybeans on the way home. He's currently sitting at the table taking out all the red ones and putting them in his shirt pocket. When I asked him what he was doing, he said, "They are dad's favourite … I'm saving them for him." This little cutie-pie melts my damn heart.

The smile on my face grows when I read her message.

We've been living in the apartment for almost a month now and have settled into somewhat of a routine. Tuesday, Thursday, and Friday afternoons, Blake spends here with me at the office. Mondays and Wednesdays—Jacinta's days off—is his time with her. It's like this weird sort of shared custody, but I'm okay with it, I trust her with him. She's good for him, the soft to my hard, and Blake adores her.

She watches him at my place. At first it was because of Connor and his bad attitude, but even he seems to be okay with her spending time with us now. He'd soon put a stop to it if he knew the improper thoughts I'm having of his little sister.

On the days Blake's with her, I head straight to Bridge from here. By the time I get home, he's bathed, fed, and ready for bed. I even have a hot meal waiting for me. Seeing Red in my space, and doting on my son the way she does, only draws me in further. It's getting harder and harder to keep my hands to myself ... she's like forbidden fruit and I want to gobble her up.

Wolf: He gets his cuteness from his dad.

Red: Hah!

Wolf: You don't fool me, Red. I see those long lingering looks you give me when you think I'm preoccupied.

Red: They're not long lingering looks, I'm actually plotting your murder.

I chuckle as I write my reply. She may act indifferent, but I'm not blind. She feels the sexual tension between us. This constant back-and-forth banter we have going on is like never-ending foreplay, and it's only a matter of time before one of us snaps.

Wolf: Liar!

Red: True story. I have a list.

Wolf: I need to see this list.

Red: Not happening. I prefer the element of surprise.

Wolf: Come on, you show me yours and I'll show you mine.

Red: I believe we've already done that.

Wolf: I'm talking about our lists, Red. Get your mind out of the gutter.

Red: You have a list too?

175

> Wolf: Yes!

> Red: What kind of list *Insert narrowed eyes here*

I bark out a laugh. This woman amuses me to no end.

> Wolf: A list of all the ways I'm going to take you next time I have you in my bed.

I don't need to see her face to know she's blushing. I may have taken her innocence, but her sweetness goes bone deep.

> Red: Next time? You're getting a little ahead of yourself, Wolf.

Fucking wolf.

> Wolf: You and I both know it's only a matter of time, Red. The clock is ticking.

I'm not surprised when I don't get a reply. Little Miss Innocent—who's not really that innocent—would now be blushing as red as the hoodie she was wearing the first day I met her. I'm betting she's wet too.

I reach beneath the desk and palm my rock-hard cock through my trousers. Great, now I've got a boner, and I have a meeting to attend in ten minutes.

Rolling back my chair, I stand, stalking towards the bathroom in my office. I'm going to have to take care of this before I leave. I can't even tell you how many times I've had to bat one out to images of her sprawled out on my bed all ripe and ready for the taking.

I hadn't planned on getting home this late, but we had an incident at Bridge, so I had to wait for the police to arrive. By the time I walk through the front door of my apartment, I'm not surprised to find Jacinta and Blake crashed out in front of the television. They're wrapped up in blankets and look like a pair of burritos. Seeing the two of them together like this does something to me.

If you asked me what my life was like prior to Blake, I would've told you it was perfect—I was living my best life. Or so I thought. Within a few short weeks of caring for him, I had a complete turnaround. An epiphany you could say. I realised the carefree partying lifestyle, and moving from one bed to the next, had been a hollow and meaningless existence.

Despite what I thought, I hadn't been happy, not even close. The truth is I had been running. Running from a past I can never escape. What I can do though, is break the cycle and make sure my lineage going forward won't have to experience the toxic and messed-up childhood I had.

Getting used to being a parent, when I had no clue how to be one, was a big adjustment in the beginning, but my son changed me in ways I could never have imagined. He not only opened my eyes and my heart, he's also enriched my life on so many levels.

Up until this very moment, I believed he was all I'd ever need, but as I stand here now, staring down at the two of them together, I'm left wondering if there isn't more I'm missing out on. Is this what life would be like if I had someone else to share it all with? The highs, lows, and everything in between. A mother to my son ... a wife by my side. A real family unit.

As soon as that thought enters my mind, I tilt my head back and groan. It's that voodoo pussy of hers, I'm sure of it, it's fucking with my mind. That and this permanent hard-on I've been suffering since I met her.

Red is barely an adult, and way too young to be tied down to a life like this, she hasn't even lived yet. Besides, I swore to myself years ago I'd never get married, and I meant it. Nothing has changed.

Reaching down, I carefully try and lift Blake without waking Jacinta, but the moment I raise his head from her lap, her too-blue eyes spring open. "Hey," she whispers, and I love the throaty sound of her voice. It makes my cock instantly stir. Fuck, I have it bad.

"Hey, sorry I'm getting in so late. It's been one of those nights."

"Did something happen?"

"Let me put Blake to bed and we'll talk."

Once he's cradled safely in my arms, I stand to full height. I look down and smile at his sweet face as I head towards his room. I miss having him by my side when he's with Red, but I'm thankful he wasn't at Bridge tonight. He's finally found his feet, and I'd hate for something like a knife-wielding lunatic to cause him to regress.

After gently lying him down on his mattress and untangling him from his blanket, I cover him with his quilt, tucking him in until he's nice and snug. I switch on his night-light, because he's still afraid of the dark. I grab Rex off the shelf and place it beside him before leaning down to kiss his forehead. We usually read a book before bed, but I'll make up for it tomorrow night.

When I turn to leave the room, I'm surprised to find Red standing in the doorway, watching me. "You're a good dad," she says as I loosen my tie and stalk towards her.

I'm surprised she doesn't move out of my way as I approach. I come to a stop in front of her, and she tilts her

178

head back to look up at me. Does she have any idea how fucking beautiful she is?

"I try my best," I answer.

"He's lucky to have you."

"Is he?"

"Yes. Why were you late?"

"A guy came into Bridge wielding a knife."

"A knife?" she asks as her pretty eyes widen.

"He was trying to find the person who'd stolen his shoes."

"Oh my God. Did anyone get hurt?"

"No, I helped de-escalate the situation before it got out of hand."

"How?"

"I gave him fifty bucks to buy some new shoes, and a bag full of food before sending him on his way."

"You let him go?"

"Yes."

"But he had a knife. Someone could have got seriously hurt."

"He just wanted his shoes back."

"That's still a little extreme don't you think. He sounds dangerous."

"I know what it's like when you're living on the streets. Sometimes the clothes on your back are all you have."

"I guess you'd see a lot of things being in that environment."

"I've also lived it."

"You've been homeless?"

"Yes."

"When?"

"When I was thirteen."

"You lived on the street when you were thirteen?"

"For a year."

"A year?" she squeaks.

"It was safer than being at home."

"Because of your dad?"

"Yes."

"What about your mum?"

"She'd left by then."

"She left you behind?"

Fuck, those words cut me to the core, and not for the reason you may think. "That's a story for another day." Because the truth behind her departure is something I've never spoken about.

"I'm so sorry."

"Don't be. Things could have been worse." *I could've ended up like my mother.* "It brought Betty into my life."

"Betty?"

"The founder of Bridge."

"Oh."

"She helped me get my life back on track. I owe her so much ... Bridge was her dream, so when she passed, I had to keep it going. You know, for her."

"Betty died?"

"Yes. She had a massive heart attack." *Fuck, I miss her.* And I hate that she never got to meet Blake. She would've loved him so much. I lift my hand and click my fingers together. "She was here one minute, and gone the next."

I have to turn my face away when an image of her lifeless body lying on the kitchen floor flashes through my mind. I try not to think about that day; it was one of the worst days of my life, and that's saying something considering the things I've experienced.

"Oh, Mason," Red says, placing her hand on my arm.

My eyes snap back to hers. "You called me Mason."

"It's your name."

"I've never heard you use it before." I stare down at her, and the air crackles between us. So much so it has her retreating a step. I quickly close the distance again, which has her taking another step backwards. "I'm still going to call you Red," I admit.

"Of course, you are," she replies, narrowing her eyes.

The corners of my lips tug up; I love her sass.

I continue moving forward until she has nowhere left to go. Her back is now pressed against the wall in the hallway outside my son's room. My bedroom door is only a few metres away, and the thought has all the blood in my body rushing to my cock.

The things I want to do to her.

I place my flattened palms against the wall on either side of her head. "What are you doing?" she asks breathlessly.

"Trapping you."

She swallows thickly. "Why?"

"Because the wolf is hungry."

"I made you dinner, it's covered in the fridge."

"I'm not hungry for food, Red."

She draws the corner of her lip between her teeth and bites down. I use my thumb to free it, dragging her plump bottom lip down as I go. Fuck, I want to devour this woman.

"What are you hungry for?" she whispers.

"You!"

"We can't."

"Why?"

"Connor."

"We're both adults, Red. What you and I do behind closed doors is none of Connor's business."

181

"I washed Blake's uniform," she deflects. "It's hanging on the fold-out line in the laundry."

"Thank you. I need to pay you for your time."

She dips her head, but I don't miss the blush climbing her cheeks as she does. "I don't want your money, Mason."

I reach for her ponytail, twisting it around my wrist. When I tug on it slightly, bringing her gaze back to mine, I can see the heat in her eyes. The sexual tension that's been brewing between us over the past month has finally hit boiling point. She wants this just as much as I do.

"I wasn't offering you money ... I was planning on repaying you in a different way."

Leaning in, I lightly brush my lips with hers. Once, twice. I draw back slightly, but our mouths are so close we're sharing the same air.

"How?" she whispers.

"With 'O's, sweetheart."

As much as I need to fuck this woman out of my system, so I can get some control back, I wait for an answer because the decision is purely hers. I'd never force her into doing something she didn't want to do, no matter how desperate I am.

Instead of words, she releases a tiny whimper as her trembling hands move up to fist the lapels of my suit jacket, dragging me closer, and I have my answer. My cock rejoices because he knows exactly how this night is going to end.

Chapter 18

Jacinta

Mason's hands leave the wall and skate down my back until he's cupping my arse. "Fuck, Red," he groans as his fingers dig into my flesh, dragging my body against his. I can already feel his erection pressing into my stomach, and knowing it's me who's doing that to him only makes me crave him more.

With every passing day, my resistance has been slipping. The chemistry between us is off the charts. All his flirty comments and playful touches haven't been helping. Secretly, I've been obsessing about being with him like this again, but there was no way I was going to make the first move.

My only hope is that Connor doesn't find out what we're up to. Mason's right when he says what we do behind closed doors is none of my brother's business, but the last thing I want to do is to come between their friendship, and that's going to be the main issue here. Not that I'm hooking up with someone, but rather with whom.

When Mason's hands slide down further, and his fingers curl around my inner thighs, he effortlessly lifts me off the ground. "Wrap your legs around me, Red," he says against my mouth.

I do as he asks, binding my ankles together behind his back. Again, he manages to bring out my submissive side. I'm not sure if it's due to my inexperience or just my willingness to please him.

Turning, he carries me into his bedroom, kicking the door closed behind us with his foot. When I hear the click of the lock, my heart rate picks up. *This is really happening.*

He moves us over to the bed and bends to gently lay me down, hovering over me in the process. "I've been dreaming about this moment," he says, standing to full height. "Do you have any idea how many times I've jacked off to images of you laid out on my bed?"

My eyes widen. "You have?"

"Why do you sound so surprised?"

I use my arms to push myself up into a sitting position. "I don't want this to change things between us."

"What do you mean?" he asks.

"One night, that's it. And tomorrow we go back to hating each other."

He arches one of his eyebrows. "Are you worried I'm falling in love with you, Red?"

"No," I squeak as heat flushes my face. "I'm worried you won't let me spend time with your son."

A smile tugs at his lips as he bends down, invading my space. "Are you using me for my kid?"

"Never. I'm just taking what I'm owed."

"The 'O's?"

"Yes," I pant. "All the 'O's."

"How many do I owe you?" he asks, resting his palms on the mattress and peppering kisses along my jawline.

"A lot."

He chuckles against my skin. "I best get started then."

"Before you do," I say, placing my hand on his chest, "I need your guarantee that on Mondays and Wednesdays Blake will still be mine."

"Yours?" he asks, drawing back to look at me. God, I could easily lose myself in his exquisite chocolate-coloured eyes. They're like a vortex into his soul, just like his son's.

Reaching up, I cup the side of his face with my hand. I know I have no claim over Blake, but I love being around him, spending time with him ... caring for him. That little boy has stolen my heart, and I can't lose him if things go pear-shaped.

"Promise me no matter what happens between us, you won't stop me from seeing him."

"I would never do that," he whispers, placing his lips against mine. "I'm glad he has someone like you in his corner."

I thread my fingers into Mason's hair when he guides me back down to the mattress, covering my body with his. The kiss he gives me is so different to the others, less frantic and hungry. It's sweet ... *almost loving.* I open my legs, letting him settle in between them, and the friction it provides has me moaning into his mouth.

"Fuck, Red," he groans, rolling his hips forward. "I've never craved anyone the way I do you."

Our sweet kiss soon turns smouldering, and Mason's hand moves in between us, as he rubs me through my tights. It's just what I need to send me over the edge. My back arches off the bed as I whimper into his mouth. I've thought about our last time together, remembering how good he made my body feel, but my imagination has nothing on the real thing.

"That's one," he says as he pulls away, moving onto

his knees and resting on his haunches. I immediately feel his loss. "I need you naked," he breathes. "Sit up."

Doing as he asks, he wastes no time sliding my top over my head and unclasping my bra. Both get tossed aside before he shrugs out of his suit jacket. When he moves to the buttons at the top of his dress shirt, I start at the bottom. He looks down at me with a devilish smile when our fingers meet in the middle.

Once we're both naked from the waist up, he lies me back down. He palms one of my breasts in his hand as his mouth moves to my neck. "I've missed your tits," he murmurs as he sucks one of my nipples into his mouth. "They're perfect, just like you."

The things he's saying to me make what we're doing sound more than a one and done, but I push that thought from my mind. I can only hope what we're about to do doesn't change things.

After lavishing the top half of my body with attention, he continues down south. Scooting off the end of the bed, his hands move to the waistband of my tights. His eyes remain locked with mine as he drags them down my legs. He moves to my underwear next, and once they're peeled from my body, he bunches them up and slides them into the pocket of his trousers. My eyes narrow. At least he didn't smell them this time.

"Why did you put them in your pocket?"

"If this is the last time I'm going to have you, I'm keeping them."

"Are you going to sniff them?"

He chuckles as he casually lifts one shoulder. "Maybe."

"In that case I want them back, I want no part of your depravity," I say holding out my hand.

"Not happening, Red. They are going into my collection."

"Collection?" I squeak, lifting up onto my elbows. "You do this with all your conquests?"

"Just you," he answers, grasping my ankles and spreading my legs wide. "How are you so flexible?"

"I'm a dancer."

"You dance?"

"Yes."

"Will you dance for me?"

"No!"

He barks out a laugh. "Can you do the splits?"

"Yes."

"Show me?" he demands, letting go of my ankles. Pointing my toes, I easily open my legs until I'm doing the splits. "Jesus, Red." He immediately falls to his knees, licking a path right up my middle. His palms come to rest on my inner thighs, holding me in this position. His eyes move up to meet mine as his tongue swirls around my clit. "Can I take a picture of you like this with my phone? It will be the perfect imagery for the next time I have to jack off."

"Definitely not." I can't see his mouth, but I feel his lips curl against my flesh.

"It was worth a try."

"You're depraved."

"Only with you."

He manoeuvres one of his thumbs to join his tongue, skimming it back and forth a few times before slipping it inside me. I tilt my head back and moan. I can already feel my second orgasm building.

Releasing his hold on my legs, he replaces his thumb with one of his thick fingers, followed closely by a second.

187

"Oh God," I whimper, moving my feet onto the bed and bucking my hips towards his face.

"Yes, fuck my fingers, Red."

He rotates his hand, scissoring his digits as he moves them in and out, stretching me, and it doesn't take long before I'm falling over the edge for a second time.

Mason doesn't stop until he's drained every ounce of pleasure from my body. "Two," he states when he draws back and wipes his mouth with the back of his hand. I slump back onto the bed in a sated bliss as I hear him unbuckling his belt. "I need to be inside you."

I watch as he swiftly stands and removes his trousers and boxer briefs, and I run my tongue over my bottom lip when his impressive erection springs free. He's like sculptured perfection.

Leaning in, he effortlessly moves me into the middle of the bed and crawls between my spread legs. Reaching over, he grabs a condom from his bedside drawer and wastes no time rolling it on.

I let out a contented sigh when his body covers mine; I love the feel of his heavy weight pinning me to the mattress. There's something comforting about it.

"You good?" he asks, gently sweeping a stray piece of hair from my forehead.

"I'm great."

"Are you ready for another 'O'?"

"You've already given me two."

"Last time we were together I believe I gave you three ... this time I'm striving for four."

"Overachiever."

"Nah, just good at what I do."

"And modest."

"Oh, sweetheart, my qualities are endless."

"You know what they say about people who blow their own trumpet?"

"It's only a matter of time before you start singing my praises too."

I roll my eyes as he slides the head of his dick back and forth through my arousal. "I hate you too much to ever do that."

His eyes slightly narrow before he gives me a dazzling smile. It's such a contradiction, I'm left feeling confused.

"Ditto, sweetheart," he grunts as he drives his hips forward and buries himself deep inside me in one swift motion. I intake a sharp breath as I'm unexpectedly stretched to capacity. *Did he just punish me for what I said?* Last time, he was a lot gentler with me. He rests his forehead against my shoulder and groans. "Shit, Red. I may dislike you, but I think I'm in love with your pussy." He draws back his hips slightly before surging back in. It burns, but nowhere near as much as it did the first time we had sex. "So tight ... so fucking good."

"You did that on purpose."

He lifts his head and stares down at me. "Did what on purpose?" he asks, but when I see him roll his lips together to hide his grin, I know I'm right.

"You bastard," I say, slapping his shoulder.

"I don't know what you're talking about," he replies, feigning innocence, but when he moves his head back down to rest on my shoulder, I feel his body shake with laughter.

"Get off me."

That sobers him immediately. "You're not serious?"

"Deadly."

His face drops. "Did I hurt you?"

"What do you think? You just rammed your giant man sausage inside me, I'm surprised I didn't split in two."

189

"Giant man sausage?" he says as his body starts to shake with laughter again. "You kill me, Red."

"Sometimes I'd like to," I retort, which only seems to amuse him further.

It takes a moment for him to get himself under control, but once he does, he says, "I'm sorry." His words are spoken with sincerity as he leans in and peppers kisses all over my face.

I place my hands on his shoulders, pushing him back. "Don't grovel, it doesn't suit you."

There's concern on his face as he stares down at me. "Did I really hurt you?"

"A little."

He starts to withdraw, but pauses before he's fully out. "Do you really want me to stop?"

"Yes, no ... maybe."

My indecisiveness has a small smile tugging at his lips. "Yes or no, Red?"

When I don't answer him straight away, he uses his arms to push himself up before dropping down onto the mattress beside me.

"I hadn't answered you yet," I say, turning my face towards him.

"You were taking too long."

"What if I wanted to keep going?"

"Have at it," he says, moving his hand down to wrap it around the base of his dick. I watch on in fascination as he strokes it. "Or you can lay there and watch me finish myself off ... totally your call."

"I like seeing you do that, but I'm feeling a little left out."

He chuckles before saying, "Jump on then."

My eyes widen. "What?"

"Ride me, Red. That way you can retain the control."

190

"I don't know how."

"Straddle my lap and I'll teach you."

When he taps his free hand against his thigh, I throw one of my legs over him. He grips my hips as his eyes rake down my body. "If you were my girl, I think I'd have to throw all your clothes away. This body should be illegal," he says, gliding his hands up my sides.

"Good thing I'm not your girl then."

He reaches for my ponytail, giving it a light tug. "That's enough of your sass, now kiss me." I lean down and fuse our lips. His hands make their way back to my hips, and when he drags my body down slightly, I can feel the head of his dick pressing against my opening. "Sink down whenever you're ready, babe."

Babe?

I shouldn't like hearing him call me that, but I do.

Raising my upper body into a sitting position, I place my flattened palms on his chest. My attention is firmly on him as I gradually begin to lower myself. I instantly feel the burn as I'm again, stretched to the limit, but the pleasure far outweighs any pain I'm feeling. He's so big, but thankfully, he put the time into prepping me. There's no way he'd fit if he didn't. Despite my own body wanting to react, I remain focused on him as his eyes roll back in his head. A smile tugs at my lips when he groans loudly as I slowly bury him further inside me. There is something empowering about knowing it's me that's making him feel this way.

Mason lies perfectly still until I'm fully seated, giving me a chance to adjust. Only when he thinks I'm ready does he coax me to move by lifting my hips slightly, then dragging them back down. It feels different in this position, but equally incredible.

Following his lead, I start to roll my hips, grinding my

clit against his pelvic bone with every pass. "Yes, that's it, Red ... fuck yes, just like that."

The more I move, the better it feels, to the point where I can no longer seem to get enough. Like the experienced lover Mason is, he predicts this. His hands leave my hips, one moving up to tweak my nipple between his fingers, and the other circling my clit with his thumb. When his hips buck up, perfectly syncing with mine, I fall over the edge. This orgasm is more intense than any of the others, and I throw my head back and moan. By the time I ride the last wave, I'm seeing stars.

"That was so damn hot," he growls, lifting my body off his.

For a moment I think we're done, but he flips me onto my stomach, then drags me onto my knees. He places his hand on the back of my head, pushing it down into the pillow as he swiftly enters me again from behind.

"When I deliver number four, I want to hear you scream my name," he demands.

I doubt he can achieve this ... I'm not even sure if my body can take another one.

He fists my ponytail, lifting my face from the pillow so I can breathe, but my chin and upper body remain pinned to the mattress by his clenched fist that rests between my shoulder blades. His other hand moves back to my hip, and he grips me so hard as he pounds into me I'm worried he may leave bruises. But this ... the way he's taking me—*owning my body*—may be rough, but I love it. I love it so much that I push my hips back to meet him with every thrust. I can feel his balls slapping against my clit every time he drives home, and if he keeps this up, he may just get me to number four.

Everything about this moment does it for me. The grunting noises he's making, the way he possessively takes my body, and how he moves inside me. I thought our first time was perfect, but this is so much more it scares me. Am I going to be able to walk away unaffected after this? I'm not sure if that's possible.

His hand on my hip slides down between my legs. "I need you to come, babe, I don't think I can hold back much longer ... you feel too good." When my inner muscles start to clamp around him, he stills.

"Wolf," I cry out. I'm not sure if that's the name he wanted me to scream, but that's all I'm giving him.

His movements become jerky, and I can tell he's coming by the ferocity of his groans. My only wish is I could see his face as he does.

When he releases me and withdraws, I flop down onto the mattress. I'm completely spent, but in the best possible way.

I watch him remove the condom, tying the end in a knot and dropping it on the bedside table beside the empty foil packet. "When I get feeling in my legs again, I'll put it in the bin," he says, lying down beside me and pulling me into his arms. He places a soft kiss on my temple, and it's such a tender move I feel tears sting the back of my eyes. "Are you okay? I didn't hurt you again, did I?"

"No."

"I don't know what it is about you, but you bring out the beast in me."

"It must be all those wolf genes."

"Fucking wolf," he chuckles. "And by the way, that's not the name I was wanting to hear screamed."

I bite my bottom lip as my eyes meet his, because I gathered that. "You seem to bring out my rebellious side."

He smiles, leaning in to place his lips on mine. "Don't ever change, I like you just the way you are."

Ditto.

I exit the bathroom once I've cleaned myself up and redressed, and Mason's eyes track my movements as I cross the room. When I spot his boxer briefs lying on the floor near his trousers at the end of the bed, I bend down and scoop them up.

"What are you doing?" he asks as I bunch them into a ball and shove them down my top.

"My trophy," I say, giving him a sweet smile. "It's only fair that I get one too."

He arches an eyebrow. "Who's depraved now?"

"Unlike you, I'm not going to sniff them."

He laughs as he rises from the bed and walks towards his dresser, retrieving and sliding into a pair of sweats. They sit low on his hips, showcasing his perfect 'V'. I bite my bottom lip as my eyes scan over his defined abs. *What is he doing to me?* He just gave me four orgasms and I'm already wanting more.

"Like what you see, Red?" he asks, closing the distance between us.

I bow my head, embarrassed that I just openly ogled him. "I've seen better," I lie.

He gently clasps my chin between his forefinger and thumb, raising my face back to his. "When?" I just shrug because I don't have an answer for that. "Have you been with other men since me?"

"No."

"Good, keep it that way," he says, releasing me. "Come, I'll walk you out."

When I was still lying with him in the bed, he invited

me to stay over, but I said I couldn't. I wanted to, but I think a clean break is best. The lines between us are already blurred, and the more we're together like this, the harder it will be not to catch feelings. I already like this man way more than I should.

We both stop and turn to face each other when we reach the front door. There's a brief awkward silence as we stand there and stare. "You sure you can't stay?" he asks, raising his hand to tenderly skim his knuckle down the side of my face.

"Positive," I answer, even though I'd love nothing more than to spend the night safe and snug wrapped in his arms.

"I guess I'll see you Wednesday then."

"You will."

Neither of us make a move, and I can tell by the way he's looking down at me that he wants to kiss me, but what we just did won't be happening again, so one of us needs to set some boundaries.

With that thought in mind, I take a step back and reach for the doorknob. "I should get going."

"Good night, Red," he says, grasping the edge of the door to hold it open.

"Night," I reply, ducking under his outstretched arm.

I can feel his eyes on me as I walk down the corridor towards the lift, but I don't turn around. My gaze remains forward even when I stop to press the button and wait.

When the doors finally open, I hear him call my name, "Hey, Red." I turn my head in his direction and find him leaning against the doorjamb shirtless and looking all sexy. "Dream of me."

That's a given.

I narrow my eyes. "Not a chance in hell," I say, stepping into the lift. I can still hear him laughing as the doors close behind me.

After pressing the number for my floor, I wrap my arms around myself. My heart feels heavy knowing I'm going to have to go back to pretending I hate him tomorrow.

Chapter 19

Jacinta

"The room turned out great, didn't it?" Brooke asks as we do a walk-through to take in the finished product. "I'm so happy with it."

"It looks amazing. I can't wait to get classes underway." We already have a list of women eager to start.

Brooke ended up turning one of the rooms at the back of the studio into the pole room. It's a large space behind the stage area that was previously used to store all the chairs and concert props. Logan, had a few large containers craned in and placed in the rear of the building to store all that stuff in.

Although the classes are mainly for fitness, Brooke still thought it was more practical to give us our own private space. She was also concerned that the smaller kids who attend her dance classes might hurt themselves by mucking around on the poles if they were in the main studio.

The room itself is huge, but the expansive cathedral ceilings make it seem much larger. Every inch has been painted a bright white, and the large wooden beams that run from one side of the wall to the other—installed to secure the metal poles—are stained a light oak to match the polished floorboards.

There's floor-to-ceiling mirrors spanning the length of one wall, and twelve poles in total—two rows of six, each elevated on a small stage.

"When can I start my private lessons?" Brooke asks. "Logan is already talking about installing a pole in our bedroom at home."

"Okay then," I reply as my face heats up.

"TMI?"

"Just a little," I answer, and we both laugh.

She slips her arm through mine as we leave the room. "So tell me, is there anyone special in your life? I mean, look at you you're gorgeous, you must have men falling at your feet."

I turn my face away from her. "Not really."

Pausing, she points her finger at me. "I know that look, Jacinta Maloney, are you keeping secrets from me?"

My eyes widen. "What?" Am I just a bad liar, or do all mothers come with a built-in lie detector? I can never get anything past Mum either.

"Spill."

"Well ... there's this one guy."

"Hah! I knew it. How long have you been seeing him?"

I dip my face. "I've known him for a few months, but we're not a couple."

"But you like him?"

I shrug. "It's complicated."

"He doesn't know you like him?"

"We've hooked up a few times, but that's it."

"Sweetie," she says, turning to face me. "You deserve better than a hookup."

198

"It was only ever meant to be a one-time thing ... I never thought I'd see him again."

"But you did?"

"Yes, he recently turned up at my apartment."

She gasps. "He found out where you lived?"

I wince. "No. He's Connor's best friend."

"Blake's dad?"

"Uh huh."

"Oh shit."

Oh shit is right. It's been two weeks since we last hooked up, and whenever I'm in his presence, I want to climb him like a tree, and when I'm not, I can't stop thinking about him.

"Hi, Jacinta."

"Hi ... umm?"

"Marissa ... I mean, Candy," the girl standing in front of me says, as she holds out her hand for me to shake. "Marissa is my birth name, but Candy is going to be my stage name. Cool huh."

"Stage name?"

"I'm going to be a stripper," she says, bouncing on her feet with excitement.

"I see."

"I've been a topless waitress for a year now, and the tips are great, but I know I can make a lot more money if I'm up on the stage." My eyes subconsciously flicker down to her large breasts before moving back to her pretty face. She definitely has the goods to be in that kind of industry. "Rocco, my boss ... the guy that owns the strip club, thinks I've got what it takes to work the stage.

Well, I will once I can master that damn thing without breaking my neck." She juts her chin in the direction of the poles.

"It takes a bit of time, but I'm sure you'll get there."

"Your pole skills are amazing," she says. "I was in awe watching you today."

"Thanks."

"Have you ever thought of stripping? You'd clean up if you did ... I can put in a good word for you with Rocco if you want."

"I appreciate the offer, but I enjoy working here."

"Fair enough. If you ever change your mind, I'm your girl."

My lips curve into a smile, I like her enthusiasm. She reminds me a lot of Cassie. "Thanks. I'll keep that in mind," I say, even though I know I'd never take her up on that offer. I have nothing against strippers, it's just not something I'd ever feel comfortable doing.

"I was wondering if you do private lessons?"

"I'll need to talk to my boss, but I'm sure that can be arranged."

"You're the best," she says, throwing her arms around me and pulling me into a crushing hug. "I'm so excited to work with you."

I close my bedroom door and hold my phone up to my face as I take a seat on the side of my bed. "She said she could get me a job as a stripper," I whisper down the line, which of course has Cassie howling with laughter. "Hey, it's not unrealistic. I know how to work a pole."

"Jaz," she says, looking into the camera with a straight

face. "Come on. You and I both know you'd never get up on stage and strip for a room full of men."

"I've performed on plenty of stages before."

"Dancing to a room full of parents ... completely different."

"Some of them were men."

"You were wearing clothes, and the majority were only in attendance because their wives made them come."

"Ugh."

"You know I'm right."

"Whatever. So how are things going down in Melbourne?" I ask, changing the subject.

"Don't ask."

"Are you still working the campaign trail with your dad?"

"I'm in the pits of hell. The moment the cameras are off they immediately dismiss me. I feel so used."

"Ah, babe, I'm sorry they treat you that way."

"I'm sick of being poked and prodded. My mum even gave me a list to study, things I can and can't say in public. Like I don't know how to act like a lady when needed? Sheesh. I mean, at least they're giving me attention for once, but still ..." I hate the way they treat her. Can't they see how much she yearns for their love? "Look what she had me wearing today." She walks over to her dresser and holds up a strand of pearls, which in turn has me laughing. "It's not funny. It's not the type of pearl necklace I'm used to."

"Eww."

"My mum said it would pair perfectly with the beige, cashmere cardigan she bought me. Beige, Jaz."

"There's nothing wrong with the colour beige."

"Right. Tell me one woman that willingly wears beige?"

"Terri and Bindi Irwin."

"I'm pretty sure that's khaki."

"It's beige-ish."

"Irrelevant. They wrestle crocodiles for a living, I don't."

"I think they're more into animal conservation now."

She purses her lips. "Remind me again why we're friends?"

"Because you love me."

She blows out a puff of air. "Unfortunately, I do, and I miss you terribly. The moment my parents loosen the puppet strings, I'm on the first flight back to Sydney."

"Hopefully you can make it for Connor's birthday next weekend. I don't want to go out with all the guys on my own."

"Is that sexy hunk of man beef going to be there?"

"Probably. I think he's going to ask Braydon's dad if Blake can spend the night there."

"Oh, so he'll be going back to an empty apartment all alone at the end of the evening?"

"I swear to God if you meddle again, I'll definitely smother you with a pillow this time." The cunning smile she gives me has me narrowing my eyes. "I mean it, Cass."

She looks over her shoulder and calls out, "Coming, Mother."

"You lying cow. Your mum did not call out to you."

"Got to go, biatch. Love you."

"Cassie!"

"Mwah, mwah," is the last thing I hear before she disconnects our video call.

I flop back onto the mattress and groan as I plot her murder in my head.

Chapter 20

Mason

I study Connor across the table as his eyes keep flicking towards the dance floor, where his sister and her best friend are dancing up a storm. If I'm not mistaken, that's longing I see in his eyes, and it's not the first time tonight I've noticed. I'm guessing it's the same way I've been looking at his sister for the past few weeks. Red and her voodoo pussy are under my skin, and no matter how hard I try, I can't seem to get them out.

"How long have Jacinta and Cassandra been friends?" I ask.

"Since they were twelve, why?"

Interesting, the timeline fits. "Just curious." I place my elbows on the table, leaning forward in my seat. "Tell me about this chick that broke your heart when you were nineteen?"

"What?" he answers as his gaze snaps back to mine. "How do you know about that?"

"You told me one night when you were drunk ... and if my memory serves me correct, you even cried into your beer like a little girl." I totally added that last part in.

"Fuck off I did. I was drunk, so naturally I wouldn't

have been making much sense ... and I've never cried into my beer, arsehole."

"You sure about that?"

"What's your problem anyway?"

"Is it her?" I ask, flicking my chin towards the dance floor.

"My sister? Are you kidding me right now ... that's sick."

"You and I both know I'm not talking about Jacinta, Connor. Her friend ... Cassandra?"

"Pfft. No! I think your limp monk dick is starting to eat away at your brain cells because it's starved of nourishment."

I shake my head and chuckle. "My dick is plenty nourished, cocksucker." *Thanks to your sister.*

His eyes are trained away from me, staring somewhere over my shoulder, as he takes a huge gulp of his beer. He looks as guilty as sin, and I'm pretty sure that's a stalling tactic.

"Speaking of cocksuckers," he says, slamming the bottle down onto the table, "I think that's exactly what the birthday boy needs." His eyes scan the room before he rises from his chair. "And I think I just found the perfect person to give it to me."

If that wasn't deflection, I don't know what is. I'm even more confident now that it was Cassandra ... his sister's best friend. An interesting turn of events, and information I'm going to store away, just in case he ever gets wind of what's been going on between me and Jacinta.

My eyes follow him as he walks over to a group of ladies standing nearby. They immediately welcome him into their fold, which doesn't surprise me. I've seen him in action; he has charisma in spades. I roll my eyes when one of the girls laughs at something he said and he slides his hand around her waist, drawing her closer. Sitting back from the outside looking in, I can't believe that was once my life. Sure, it was fun while it lasted, but I don't miss that lifestyle one bit. I now know that the grass is truly greener on the other side.

I've been sitting here by myself for almost an hour. Connor's two mates that came out with us tonight were doing shots at the bar with some chicks ... they've since disappeared. Connor is now the meat between a two-woman sandwich on the dance floor as they grind them-selves against him. And I swear to God, if one more dude puts his grubby hands on my girl, I'm going to lose my shit. I can't believe I gave up a night with my son for this.

I'm halfway through my third beer, that's now gone flat and warm. I hadn't planned on drinking much anyway. I have to get Blake first thing in the morning, and I don't want to be hungover.

My attention is so hyper focused on Red, and the hypnotic sway of her hips, I don't even notice Connor approach the table. "We're going to head out," he says, with his arms slung over the shoulders of both girls he was dancing with. "You want to join us?"

"I'll pass."

"Come on man, it'll be like old times."

"Not interested," I say.

Connor turns his attention to one of the girls. "He's a practicing monk."

Any other time, I'd refute that, but not in this

instance. "Eww, really?" the girl on the right says, screwing up her face.

"Yes, really," I state. "Refraining from any kind of sexual pleasure is a requirement of the monkhood."

The girl on the left looks me up and down. "What a waste. The good-looking ones are either married, gay or monks apparently."

The look of shock on Connor's face is priceless. "Hey, what am I, chopped liver?"

I can't help it, I crack up.

I reluctantly give the girls another hour, because Red looks like she's enjoying herself out there on the dance floor. She's also got the moves going on, so that may have something to do with it. I keep having to slide my hand under the table to adjust my cock in my jeans, because it's so hard for her, it aches.

A guy joined their circle of two about twenty minutes ago, but he seems to have eyes for Cassandra, so I let him stay, but when some other douche slides up behind Red and puts his filthy hands on her hips, I draw the line.

I slam down my beer and rise from my seat. As I'm storming towards the dance floor, I see Jacinta elbow him in the ribs, telling him to fuck off. *That's my feisty girl.* He doesn't seem to get the message, because by the time I reach them, he's still standing there.

"I believe she said fuck off."

He immediately holds his hands up in front of him. "Sorry, I didn't know she was taken." With that, he turns and walks away.

"What are you doing?" Jacinta snaps.

"I don't like people touching what's mine." Her mouth gapes open, but I'm surprised she doesn't refute what I said. "Connor has left, so I'm in charge of taking you girls home ... lets go."

"I think I'll hang around a bit," Cassandra says. "Josh and I were just starting to get to know each other."

"My name is Jordon," he grumbles, making me laugh.

"I got the J right, sheesh."

"Hmm," he responds, shoving his hands into the pockets of his jeans, clearly unimpressed.

"You can escort Jacinta home. I'm sure she'd love to go for another ride on your—"

Red leaps forward and places her hand over Cassandra's mouth. "I swear if you say what I think you're going to say I'll kill you right here ... I don't care if there's two thousand eyewitnesses, I'd happily do time for your murder." A few seconds later, she pulls her hand away, wiping it down the side of her dress. "Eww, did you just lick my hand?"

"You were smudging my lipstick," Cassandra retorts, placing her hands on her hips.

"That's gross."

"I was going to say bike ... you totally overreacted."

"You were not."

"Prove it."

"You were a hundred percent going to say ride on his dick!"

I bite my knuckle between my teeth to hide my amusement.

"Well, it's not like you haven't ridden it."

Jacinta gasps. "I told you that in confidence."

"Yeah, me and the other two thousand people in this club." Cassandra moves her hand around the room, gesturing to the rest of the patrons, before placing it over her heart feigning hurt. "I thought I was special."

This chick is certifiably nuts, but I'll be damned if I don't like her. "I can't even with you right now, Cassandra Lewis."

"Right back at ya, Jacinta Maloney. Come on, Jack, let's dance."

"It's Jordon."

"Whatever."

With that, Cassandra turns and storms away with Jordon tailing behind her.

"Can you believe her?" Jacinta says, looking up at me.

I shrug my shoulders. "She may have been going to say bike."

"Ugh. Not you too."

"It's a possibility."

"You really believe that?"

No, I bet my life on it she was going to say ride my dick. "You've ridden on both my bike and my dick, so who knows."

"You're impossible," she snaps, stomping down on my foot.

When she turns to walk away, I quickly slide my arm around her waist, pulling her back into my front. "Let me go," she says, thrashing around.

"Never," I reply, tightening my grip. Using my free hand, I sweep her hair out of the way and move my mouth down to her ear. "I'm happy to take you on a ride on my bike, or my dick if you prefer. Your choice, Red."

She looks at me over her shoulder with narrowed eyes. "Did you forget we travelled here in an Uber? Your bike isn't even outside."

"Oh, right," I say as a huge smile breaks out onto my face. "I guess my dick wins by default."

When we slide into the back of the Uber, Jacinta scoots right over, far away from me. So of course, I move into the middle, making sure our sides are touching. I see her staring at me out of my peripheral vision, but I keep my attention trained forward.

I wait until the driver pulls out into the traffic before I make my move. My hand lifts and comes to rest on her knee as my fingers curl around her leg.

"What are you doing?" Jacinta whispers.

"Something I've been aching to do since I saw you walk out of your room in this dress." I swear I almost swallowed my fucking tongue. Thankfully, I was sitting on the edge of their lounge with my legs spread and my arms resting on my knees, so I was able to hide my boner. Connor was too engrossed in Red's friend to notice me eye-fucking his little sister. It was my first sign that something was going on between them.

My hand makes a path up her inner thigh, sliding under her dress. "Mason."

"Shh," I say. "Just sit back and enjoy."

I hear her intake a sharp breath when I slide my pinkie finger inside her underwear, skimming it back and forth over her soft flesh. A growl vibrates in the back of my throat when she parts her legs slightly, giving me better access. Could this woman be any more perfect?

I continue to rub against her clit, and when I slide my finger through her slick heat, pushing it inside her, she leans her head back into the seat and whimpers. She's so wet for me, my cock is throbbing.

Fuck, the things I want to do to this woman.

I lean my face towards her. "When we get back to the apartment complex, you're coming home with me."

"Okay," she squeaks.

I abruptly remove my hand from under her dress, and her wide, confused eyes snap to mine. Despite what she may be thinking, I'm not done with her yet. Not even close. I lean forward in my seat, shrugging out of my jacket. I give her a sly grin when I place it over her lap. My other hand disappears underneath. Widening her legs, I push her underwear to the side, sliding two of my fingers deep inside her, using my thumb to rub her clit.

She whimpers again when I suck her earlobe into my mouth. "I own this pussy," I whisper. "It's mine."

When I draw back, her hooded, too-blue eyes lock with mine, and when I feel her inner muscles start to clench, I almost blow in my pants. Leaning in, I kiss her, swallowing her moans as she comes all over my fingers.

I don't stop until she's completely spent, and when I finally remove my hand, I lift it to my mouth. Her wide eyes watch on as I lick the two fingers that were just inside her. "Delicious."

Chapter 21

Jacinta

By some miracle, we manage to keep our hands to ourselves as we travel in the lift to Mason's floor. The moment we enter his apartment though, he pounces. After kicking the front door closed with his foot, he pushes me up against it.

"I need to be inside you."

"Here?" I ask as he pops the button on his jeans.

"Right here. I can't wait another second. My cock has missed your pussy, Red." He leans his forehead against mine. "And I've missed you." Apart from tonight, I've only seen him on the days I've had Blake, and even then, I hightailed it out of his apartment the moment he stepped through the door. It was safer that way. He's even come down to our floor a few times, so I hid in my room like a coward. "I don't like it when you avoid me."

"I'm sorry," I say, reaching up to cup the side of his face, because there is no point denying it.

"Don't do it again. I need you in my life as much as Blake does."

Those words have tears stinging the back of my eyes, because I need them both too. "Okay."

"I mean it."

"I know."

"I'm going to take Blake out for breakfast when I pick him up in the morning, I want you to come with us."

I part my lips to reply, but he places his mouth over mine before I have a chance to get the words out. Did he do that on purpose? Was he worried I'd say no? I want to spend time with them as well. Tomorrow is Saturday, and I don't have work, but it's also the week-end, which means Connor will be home. I'm not sure how I'm going to manage it without lying, but I'll think of something.

Mason's hands move to my hips, hiking up my dress. When he lifts me off the ground, I wrap my legs around his waist. He doesn't need to instruct me this time, I'm learning. He uses the back of the door and his upper body to hold me in place, as he moves my underwear to the side.

"I'm going to fuck you hard and fast against the door, and then I'm going to take you into my room and devour every inch of you."

"Umm ... okay. I have no complaints about that."

He rests his head on my shoulder and I can feel him shaking with laughter. "You are too adorable for your own good, Red."

This time when he slides inside me, he does it slowly and with care, which I appreciate. I may no longer be a virgin, but I'm tiny in comparison to him.

"Fuck," he groans, seeking out my lips. "Will I ever get my fill of you?"

I hope not, is my first thought, but I don't voice that out loud.

True to his word, after giving my body a moment to adjust, he lets loose. Drawing all the way to the tip, before hastily thrusting back in ... over and over again. I can't even put into words how good he feels.

We're both still fully clothed, and the only sounds echoing off the walls are Mason's feral grunts as he viciously impales me. And dear God, I can't get enough of this man. Seeing him lose control like this, is a total turn-on.

Our kiss is as wild as the sex, and I'm pretty sure I'm going to have friction burns on my back by the time this is over, but I really don't care.

I'm completely blindsided when my orgasm hits me from nowhere, and it's the most intense one yet. I tug on Mason's hair and moan so loudly he stills. Ripping his mouth from mine, he throws back his head. "That's it, babe ... milk my cock." When his hips start jerking forward, pushing me further into the door, he lets out one almighty roar. As soon as his release is over, he rests his forehead against mine. "Are you okay?"

"Yes," I pant.

"That was ... animalistic."

"It's those wolf genes playing havoc again."

His shoulders bob with laughter. "You say the most random shit."

"Yet you keep coming back for more."

"What can I say, I'm hooked ... maybe obsessed would be a better word."

"You're obsessed with me, or my ..."

"Your what?" he asks, grinning.

"Umm ..." He cocks an eyebrow as he waits for my answer. Shit, he's going to make me say it again. I lean in, placing my hand beside his ear. "My pussy," I whisper.

He barks out a laugh. "You kill me, Red. There's nobody here but us, why did you have to whisper it?"

"I ... umm." I feel my face heat.

"I love this," he says, lightly skimming the tip of his finger over my pinkened cheek. His eyes lock with mine, "Christ, I think I may even love you."

"What?" I screech.

"I mean ... shit, you've frazzled my brain. I like you, like really like you. But love? I've never loved anyone before, so I don't even know what that feels like. I mean I loved my mum, Betty and of course Blake." A huge smile breaks out onto my face. He's rambling, and it's the sweetest thing I've ever seen. "But I've never loved anyone romantically. I don't know what it is with you, but I'm hooked. I've tried to convince myself that it's your voodoo pussy messing with my head, or possibly my monk dick."

"Monk dick?"

"That's what your brother calls me now because I've been celibate since I got Blake."

"Because you haven't had time for extracurricular activities?"

"No, because I wanted to set a better example for my son. You're the first woman I've been with in over a year." *Wow.* "Ignore me," he says, turning his face away. "I think I'm having a mental breakdown."

"Hey," I say, cupping his face and bringing it back to mine. "You're not having a mental breakdown; you're just feeling things that are new and confusing. I've been feeling them too."

"You have?"

"Yes, and for the record I really like you too."

"I thought you hated me?"

"Well, I like you more than I don't," I say, grinning.

"I'm happy to hear that," he replies, tenderly tucking my hair behind my ear. "I know I'm completely messing up, but what I'm trying to say is that I want to see you all the time, not just on the days you have Blake. The last few weeks have been hell. I could tell you were avoiding me and it was driving me nuts. I even fabricated excuses to go to your apartment, in a hope of catching a glimpse. Fuck, I sound like a chick."

I dip my face. "It was a struggle to be in the same room and not be able to touch you."

"So, you want to see more of me too?"

"Yes."

"I know it's going to affect my relationship with Connor—he's my best friend—the only true friend I've had if I'm honest, so that's going to suck, but you're worth it."

"Don't worry about Connor. I'll talk to him."

I untangle my legs from his waist, and lower myself to my feet. That's when I feel something running down my inner thigh. I look down, and Mason follows my line of sight. "Fuck," he mumbles. "I didn't wrap it. Shit, Jacinta, I'm so sorry." That's the first time he's ever called me by my real name. He takes a step backwards, clutching his head in his hands. "This is what I mean, I can't think straight when I'm around you."

"It's okay," I say, trying to ease his panic. "I'm on birth control, and I'm guessing since you have a monk dick I don't have to worry about an STD."

"Monk dick," he chuckles, stepping in and effortlessly scooping me into my arms, bridal style. "Let's get you in the shower and cleaned up, so I can dirty you up again."

I like the sound of that.

The way he takes me again in the shower is different

215

to all the other times. He's so loving and gentle that my head is spinning by the time we get out. Being with him on a more permanent basis goes against everything I believe in, but I want this. *I want him.* He's everything I never knew I needed, and I only have to look at how he is with his son to know he's nothing like the monster I grew up with.

"Here," he says, getting one of his T-shirts out of his drawer and passing it to me. "You can sleep in this."

As soon as he says that, the panic sets in. "I can't stay."

"What?"

"I ... umm—" I turn my face away as heat flames my cheeks.

Mason steps up to me, sliding his arms around my waist. "If you're worried about Connor, don't be. He left with two women tonight. I doubt he's even home. Tomorrow morning, we can face him together."

"It's not Connor I'm worried about."

"Then why won't you stay?"

"I have nightmares."

"Is that why you always run off?" I nod. "Babe, they're just dreams."

"Mine aren't. They're really bad. Connor says I scream in my sleep."

"And you think that would bother me?"

"I don't want you to see me like that. It's humiliating."

"Red," he says, cupping my face with his hands. "You're staying. I don't care if you have a nightmare. Everybody dreams." He takes his T-shirt out of my hands, slipping it over my head. "Come." He leads me towards the bed, and when he pulls back the covers, I reluctantly climb in. Once he slides in beside me, he pulls me into his arms, wrapping me up tight. "You are safe here with me."

I nestle into his warmth and close my eyes, silently

praying that tonight my past doesn't come back to haunt me.

My eyes spring open as I sit up in bed; it's dark, but when I take in my surroundings, the street light outside my bedroom window illuminates the space enough that I recognise my childhood bedroom—the one I lived in before I moved to Melbourne. Being back here instantly fills me with dread and has my heart rate kicking up a notch. I look down and see Annabelle, my baby doll, lying beside me, so I reach for her, cradling her to my chest for comfort.

Glancing over at the clock beside my bed, I see it's 1.52 am. At first, I'm not sure what woke me, but then I hear it.

"Please don't hurt me," my mum pleads.

"Shut your fucking mouth." Whack. *"I said get on your knees. Get on your fucking knees!" my father bellows.* Whack, whack.

A few seconds later I hear a loud thud, and I can only assume that my father managed to knock her off her feet. Although these are sounds I'm familiar with, the ferocity of her situation still makes me feel sick to my stomach.

Throwing back my covers, I tiptoe towards my bedroom door. Opening it slightly, I peek through the tiny gap, and see my parents down the end of the hallway. My mum is on her hands and knees, and her nightdress is pulled up around her waist. My dad is positioned behind her, his trousers are down, and I can see his bare backside.

He's ramming himself into the back of her, really hard. Every time he makes contact, her body jerks forward and her head hits the adjoining wall. I don't know what he's doing to her, but I can tell by her cries it hurts. I clutch my doll tighter to my chest as tears fill my eyes.

"You like it when I fuck you hard?" He grabs hold of a

chunk of her long blonde hair, yanking her head back so violently I gasp. "Answer me you fucking whore!"

A tortured whimper is her only reply.

My gaze moves to Mum's face and I notice one of her eyes are swollen shut, and there's blood dripping from her nose. Drip, drip, drip. I watch the droplets fall, collecting into a small puddle on the floor by her hand. My heart hurts, I hate seeing her like this. I sniffle, swiping the back of my hand over my cheek to catch the tears.

Poor Mummy, I wish I was big enough to stop him.

He continues bumping into her, over and over and over again. I want to scream out, "Stop hurting her," but I don't.

His movements suddenly slow, and when he jerks his hips forward, he throws his head back and makes a funny sound. I secretly hope those are the sounds of death, but my hopes are dashed when he abruptly stands a few seconds later, pulling up his pants and buckling his belt.

My mum falls into a heap on the floor, sobbing; I hate seeing her cry. I want to give her a hug, but I'm not allowed to leave my room when my dad is like this.

He stands there for a moment, staring down at her, and I flinch when he draws back his foot and kicks her in the stomach. "Useless fucking bitch," he spits before turning and walking away.

"Jacinta ... babe, wake up." I bolt up in bed, and I can feel the warm tears trickling down my face. "You were thrashing around in your sleep," Mason says, wrapping me securely in his arms.

"He was raping her," I whisper, choking on a sob.

"Who?"

"My dad. He was raping my mum."

"Ah, babe," he says, tightening his embrace. "It was just a bad dream."

218

"No, it wasn't." I turn my face towards him. "When we first got away from him—and the nightmares started— they centred around him finding us, but as the years went by, they started to change. Lately, they've become more vivid ... so detailed, I think they're suppressed memories coming back to the surface."

Mason places his lips on the side of my head. "I'm sorry."

"This is why I didn't want to stay tonight," I say, burying my face in my hands. "I'm so embarrassed."

"Hey." He pries my fingers away. "You suffered a lot of trauma when you were a kid, you have nothing to be embarrassed about. None of this is your fault. If anyone can understand that, it's me. I have nightmares too sometimes."

My eyes widen. "You do?"

"Yeah, mine are always about the night before my mum left."

"Did something happen that night?"

"Fuck," he utters, tilting back his head to stare up at the ceiling. "I've never talked about that night with anyone."

I reach out, stroking my hand down the side of his face. "You don't have to talk about it if it makes you feel uncomfortable."

His haunted eyes move back to mine. "I think my dad killed her."

Chapter 22

Mason

J acinta gasps at my confession. "What?"

The fact that I'm even talking about this with her, speaks volumes. This is something I thought I'd take with me to the grave.

"The night before she disappeared something happened," I say as I'm immediately transported back.

I'm just drifting off to sleep when I hear a high-pitched scream followed by a loud thud. Leaping out of bed, I open my bedroom door and sprint down the corridor. As I approach the landing, I see my father standing at the top of the stairs, staring down below.

My eyes immediately follow his line of sight, and that's when I see her—my mother—lying at the base, in the foyer. Her body is twisted in a funny position, and there's a pool of blood near her head.

"What did you do?" I scream as fear grips me.

My father's gaze snaps in my direction. "Get back to your room!" And although I'm petrified of this man, my legs don't seem to move.

"Mum," I call out, and when there's no response, my pleading eyes move back to him. "Is she okay?"

"I told you to get back to your room," he bellows.

As soon as he starts to advance on me, I snap out of my daze and retreat a few steps. Turning, I race down the hallway that leads to my bedroom. I can hear the thud, thud, thud of his heavy footsteps as he chases after me. Or maybe that's the erratic beating of my heart.

Once I'm back in my room, I quickly close the door, clicking the lock. Turning I lean my back against it, trying to get air into my lungs. I jump when I hear him bang on the other side. "If you come out of that room, I'll beat your arse so bad, you won't be able to walk for a week. You hear me boy?"

I hate that man with every fibre of my being.

When his footsteps move away, I head towards my wardrobe. Shoving my hanging clothes to one side, I ball up my fist, smashing it straight through the gyprock. The hole it leaves matches all the others. I do this often, it's my way of releasing the frustration inside me. It also helps that I imagine it's my father's face when I do it. I'm only twelve and yet to have a growth spurt, but when I do, he better watch out.

"Oh, my God," Jacinta utters. "Was your mum okay?"

"I don't know. When I woke the next morning, he told me she'd left and it was all my fault because she didn't want to be my mother anymore. I never saw her again."

"Oh, Mason," she says, wrapping me in her arms. When I hear her sniffle, I know she's crying. It has me swallowing back the lump in my throat. "Did you go to the police?"

"How could I? I was a twelve-year-old kid, and I had zero proof that anything untoward had happened. Besides, my father is a Supreme Court judge. He has friends in high places."

I've gone over that night, and the following day, in my

head a million times. Sometimes I wonder if it was all a bad dream, but in my heart, I know what I saw. It hasn't stopped me from looking for her though. I'm always searching … even all these years later.

I walked out of that house not long after my thirteenth birthday and vowed never to return. *I haven't looked back.* As daunting, and sometimes terrifying, as it was being so young and all alone on the streets, I felt safer than I ever did under his roof.

I have so many questions, and can only hope that one day I'll get the answers I'm craving.

"Are you sure you want to do this right now?" Jacinta asks as we step onto the lift, hand in hand.

"Yes. I'm tired of hiding. He deserves to know what's been going on."

Neither of us slept well. It's not how I wanted to spend our first full night together, but maybe now she'll understand that I'm just as fucked up and damaged inside as she is. We're both held captive by our pasts, but together, maybe our two halves will make a whole. I can only hope.

I didn't even get my first ever morning glory, because her phone started blowing up. First it was Connor, then a message came through from Cassandra. I read the exchange over her shoulder.

Cassie: SOS baby girl, the jig is up. Connor busted me sneaking into the apartment five minutes ago, and when he asked where you were, I told him in bed. Of course, I presumed it wasn't yours, but he didn't ask for specifics, so technically it wasn't a lie. How was I to know he'd already checked in your room? How fast can you get down here? I can totally change my story and say you're downstairs paying the cab driver. That's plausible right?

Jazzie: It's okay, Mason and I were going to talk to Connor today anyway. We're coming down now.

Cassie: Oh boy, well I'm going to go and hide in my room. You know how much I hate confrontation.

Jazzie: Chicken!

Cassie: That's me. Chirp, chirp.

Jazzie: That's not the sound a chicken makes.

Cassie: And how would I know that? Just because I sometimes wear beige doesn't make me an Irwin.

The last part of their message exchange got weird, but it is Cassandra we're talking about, but it was soon forgotten when Connor started calling my phone. Jacinta begged me to ignore it, but I knew it was only a matter of time before he came banging on my door. He entrusted me to get them home safely last night. So here we are, on our way to her apartment to face the music ... or possibly the firing squad.

"We could lie and say nothing happened," she says.

"No, I want this out in the open, so I'm free to be with you wherever and whenever I want. Besides, we live in the same building, so there's no plausible reason for you to just stay over?"

"I could say I went home with a stranger. That puts you in the clear."

I growl at her answer, because even hypothetically, that pisses me off. "Not happening, Red. We are in this together. There's no way I'm letting you face this on your own."

"That's sweet."

"I'm glad you're finally seeing the real me."

"Don't get ahead of yourself, stud-muffin."

"Again, with the compliments. I could get used to this nicer version of you."

"I'm always nice," she says, playfully elbowing me.

I lean down and place my lips on her hair. "You have your moments."

"Are we going to tell Blake too?"

"I think we should hold off on that for now. He's young and fragile, I want to be sure it's going to work before we say something to him."

She dips her face, staring down at her feet. "If you're already having doubts, maybe we should wait and see how things go before we tell Connor too."

"Hey," I say, pulling her into my arms. "I'm not having doubts. I want this. You still want to be with me right?"

"Yes."

"Blake adores you, and I know he'd be thrilled with the news, but just having you in our lives more, is enough for now. It would break his heart if it didn't work out. I'm not implying it won't," I quickly add, "but this relationship thing is new to us both. Trust me when I say I'm all in, but let's just see how things pan out before we shout it from the rooftops."

"From the rooftops," she says, grinning.

"Yes."

"I look forward to seeing that."

I chuckle, because I was figuratively speaking, but if seeing me scream it from the top of our apartment complex, when the time's right is what she wants, then she'll get it.

Her hand is shaking in mine by the time we reach her apartment. "Do you want to head back to my place and let me handle this?" I ask.

"No, like you said, we're in this together, I'm just worried about hurting him. What if he gets violent with you?"

"Then I'll deal with it."

"Mason," she says, turning to face me. "He's my brother, and I love him. Please don't hurt him."

"That's not what I meant. I'm against violence in any form, but if he feels the need to lash out, then I'll cop it on the chin like a man."

"He better not hit you," she grumbles.

"Babe, it's nothing I can't handle or probably deserve."

"You didn't even know who I was the first time we had sex."

"But I did the second, third and fourth time."

I hear her intake a sharp breath as she fishes in her tiny bag for her keys. Once she has them in her hand, she looks up at me. "Are you ready?"

"As I'll ever be."

225

The last thing I want is to lose my best friend over this, but if it comes down to a choice, I'm choosing her. This is the first time in my life that I've ever contemplated exploring a relationship with someone. From the moment I met her, I knew she was different, and the more I've gotten to know her, the more captivated I've become. The fact that she loves and adores my son is just an added bonus. The key component here is *her* and the way she makes me feel. It may be foreign, but I like it.

Jacinta walks through the door first, and I hear Connor's voice straight away, "Jaz, thank fuck, I've been going out of my mind ..." His words die off the moment I enter behind her. "Why are you here with my sister?" he asks as his eyes move from her to me. The moment the penny drops, he lunges in my direction. "You fucking bastard."

He draws back his fist, but Red jumps in front of him before he gets a chance to swing. "Connor wait ... let me explain," she says, placing her flattened palms on his chest and shoving him backwards.

"Explain what exactly? That someone I thought I could trust took advantage of you?"

"Nobody took advantage of anyone," she says.

His angry eyes move to me. "She's my little sister."

"That's irrelevant," Jacinta snaps.

"There's a thing called the bro-code. Sisters are at the top of that list."

I'm pretty sure chicks have the same code, and I'm guessing brothers are on their list too.

"I wouldn't go there if I was you," I say, shoving my hands into my pockets. Maybe I should out him while we're at it, but that's only going to escalate things. And I have no proof, I'm only acting on a hunch. What am I going to say? *By the way, Red, your brother is secretly in love with your best friend ... he has been for years.* I could be completely off the mark here, but my gut tells me I'm not.

"Fuck you," he spits, charging in my direction.

"Connor, stop!" Jacinta screams. Ignoring her, he keeps advancing. "If you lay one finger on him, we're going to have issues."

That stops him in his tracks. "*We* are going to have issues?"

"Yes."

"I'm defending your honour here."

"Well don't."

He turns his attention back to me. "Get the fuck out of my house."

"If he goes, so do I," Jacinta threatens.

"You wouldn't dare."

"Watch me," she says, lifting her chin in defiance.

"I'll tell Mum and Dad."

By some miracle, I manage to hold back my laugh; he did not just say that. "What are you five?"

Jacinta gives me a look that clearly says, '*You're not helping*', before focusing back on her brother. "Tell them," she snaps, placing her hand on her hips. "I'm twenty-one, Connor. I'm not a little kid."

"I can't believe this."

"I met him before we even knew who each other were."

"When?"

"Remember when I told you someone ran into me outside the gym and broke my phone?"

"I believe it was you that ran into me," I interject.

This time when she looks at me, her eyes are narrowed. I turn my face away and roll my lips together.

"That was you?" Connor asks.

227

I hold up my hands in front of me. "Like I said, she ran into me."

"Oh, my God," Jacinta says, stomping down on my foot. "Can you just be quiet and let me explain?" I clear my throat and move my attention to the floor. "The night of my twenty-first, was the second time—I ran into him at the Ivy. Again, I had no idea who he was. That was the first night we slept together."

Oh, fuck. She had to go there.

"I'm going to kill you," Connor declares, and this time, he's so quick I don't even see it coming. His fist connects with my jaw, almost knocking me off my feet.

"I can't believe you did that," Jacinta cries. "Oh, my God. Mason, are you okay?"

"I'm fine," I reply when she reaches up to smooth her hand down the side of my face. There are tears brimming in her eyes as she does. I've experienced way worse than this in my life. I remember the day I left my childhood home for the last time, my father had beaten me so bad I was pissing blood for almost a week, so a right hook to the jaw is nothing.

"Fuck this," Connor spits as he turns and stalks from the room. A few seconds later Jacinta jumps when he slams his bedroom door closed.

"I'm so sorry," she says.

"Don't be." I completely understand why he's pissed with me. I probably deserved more than I got.

"Do you still want me to come to breakfast with you and Blake? I'll understand if you don't."

"Go get changed," I tell her.

I'm not going to let Connor stop me from spending time with her. Hopefully, he'll come around eventually; if he doesn't, that's his loss.

Chapter 23

Jacinta

I had the best day with the boys, despite how shitty things started off. After we picked up Blake, we had a late breakfast. From there we spent a few hours at Timezone in Haymarket, playing arcade games. It was so much fun. It was the first time I've been to a place like that. I didn't go out much when I was a little girl.

On our way home, we called past the store and got some groceries. It was kind of weird, because it felt so normal ... so natural, like we were a real family. A lady in the checkout line even told me how cute my little boy was. I know he's not mine, but I felt proud when she said that.

When we arrived back at the apartment building, I cooked us all a nice dinner, and then we watched a movie. Mason asked me to hang around until Blake went to bed, but I didn't. I needed to get home and try and sort out this clusterfuck with my brother. The events of this morning lingered in the back of my mind all day. We've always been close, and never fought, so I hate that things are strained between us. Connor's always been protective of me, but I still feel like he crossed a line today.

I also had to go home because Cassie's still there and it would be rude of me to leave her in that apartment alone any longer than I already have. I did invite her to come with us this morning, but she said she was tired and was going to spend the day in bed.

My stomach is in knots as I step off the lift and walk towards my apartment. My phone dings in my pocket before I reach the front door.

> Wolf: I miss you already. If things go south with Connor, come back here. You can bring Cassandra. x

I clutch my phone to my chest and sigh. Things have gone from zero to a hundred in a blink of an eye, but I'm excited to see where this leads.

> Red: I'll let you know how I go. xx

As soon as I enter the apartment, I find Connor sitting on the couch. When our eyes meet, he leaps to his feet. "Can we talk, Jaz?" I can tell by the tortured look on his face that he's just as traumatised by this situation as I am. I kick off my shoes and walk straight towards him, sliding my arms around his waist. Am I still mad that he hit Mason? Of course, but I also understand why he did it. "I'm so sorry," he says, wrapping me up in his arms and resting his chin on the top of my head.

"It's Mason who deserves an apology."

"I know."

"You overreacted."

"I've had all day to think about what happened, and you're right. I was blindsided this morning, seeing you two together was the last thing I expected."

"I really like him, Con."

230

"I can tell he likes you too."

"If we're going to be together, you need to make things right with him."

"I will."

"Thank you."

"Are we good?" he asks.

"Yes."

"I'm always going to protect you, Jaz ... that will never change. You're my baby sister."

"I'm twenty-one."

"Irrelevant. I know you're all grown up now, and I suppose I'm lucky I haven't had to worry about this kind of thing with you until now. Imagine if Cass had an older brother ... he'd probably be serving life in prison by now, for murder."

We both laugh at that. "Totally."

"All I want is you to be happy, Jaz ... I hope you know that. And if it's with him, then I'll deal, as long as he treats you right. If he doesn't, then him and I are going to have a problem."

"He treats me right."

"Good."

"Has Cass come out of her room today?"

"Yeah. Her and I actually had a big talk after you and Mason left."

I draw back, looking up at him. "You guys had an actual adult conversation?"

"I never said that," he chuckles. "She came out guns a blazing ... completely ripped me a new one."

"That sounds more like it."

"What she said helped, it got me thinking. Like me, she just wants your happiness, at least we have that in common."

"I'm glad."

"Is Mason home?"

"Yeah."

Connor places a kiss on the top of my head. "I'm going to go up and see him."

"Are you going to be nice? I don't want you two fighting in front of Blake."

"I'll be nice."

"Promise."

"I promise."

"Yes!" we cheer in unison when Candy perfects the current move she's been learning. She's come a long way since she first started lessons. In the beginning, she was so uncoordinated I worried she'd never get there, but her hard work and persistence is starting to pay off.

Cassie holds up her hand, giving Candy a high-five. She's been coming to work with me each day and helping me out with my lessons. Brooke doesn't seem to mind her being here, and even offered her some part-time work if she was interested. She thanked her, but politely declined, which I can't seem to wrap my head around. Her excuse is this stupid peasant thing, but I know it runs far deeper than that.

While she refuses to work for money, she's far from lazy, the complete opposite actually. Her room is kept immaculate, she constantly helps me around the apartment, and works her arse off when she's here at the studio. She's quite the conundrum.

"What made you want to strip?" Cassie asks, because she has zero filter.

232

"The money. It's not something I ever saw myself doing, but when my son was born—"

"You have a kid?"

"Yes, a little boy." And I can tell by the way her face lights up that she adores him. "He's just turned three."

"So, you need more money for him?"

She lifts one shoulder. "I used to be a checkout chick at Woolies, and I managed to get by, but when Kyle turned two, he was diagnosed with autism."

"I'm sorry," Cassie says, placing her hand on Candy's arm.

"He's currently none verbal, so the therapy he needs is expensive. I want to give him the best chance possible to live a relatively normal life," she says, and when tears rise to her eyes, my heart goes out to her.

"That's commendable. You're a good mum."

"I try."

"I'm proud of you for doing what you need to do for your son."

"Thanks," she says, giving Cassie a sad smile. "My parents don't think so. They stopped talking to me when I started waitressing at the strip club."

"Ugh. Fuckers. They sound like my parents. Who suck donkey's balls by the way."

"I wish they understood why I'm doing it."

"Who looks after Kyle when you're at work?"

"My neighbour, she's been a godsend."

"You're going to be up on stage and raking in the big bucks before you know it."

"Actually, Rocco has given me a spot next Monday night, it's a slow night, and I was telling him how well my classes were going."

"Oh, I want to come and watch you," Cassie says.

"I'd love that."

233

"You'll come too right, Jaz?" Cassie asks, turning her attention to me.

"I have Blake on Mondays."

"I don't go on stage until nine."

"Well, then yes. I'd love to come."

"You're going where?" Mason asks.

"To a strip club?"

His eyes narrow. "A male one?"

"No, a female one. One of my students is performing tonight."

"Your student? When you told me you taught dance, I imagined little kids in tutus."

"I teach them too. I do a range of different classes. Hip-hop, ballet, tap, and pole ... just to name a few. Brooke knew I was taking pole classes when I lived in Melbourne, so when I moved to Sydney, she thought it would be fun to start lessons at her studio."

"Fun?"

"Yes, it's good fun ... and great exercise."

"So, let me get this straight, you pole dance?"

"Yes, I've been doing it for years."

"Why am I only hearing about this now?"

"I don't know."

"What exactly do you do on these poles?"

"The usual stuff."

"Elaborate ... more importantly, when can I come and watch you perform?"

I smile when he pulls my body into his. "Get your mind out of the gutter, Mr Bradley."

"Oh, it's one hundred percent in the gutter, Miss Maloney."

"I can tell, you have that look."

"What look?"

"That look you get."

"Hmm, I have a look?"

"You most definitely have a look."

"So when can I see you in action?"

"You'll have to come to the studio for that."

"If I install a pole in our bedroom, will you give me a private show?"

"Our bedroom?"

"Yes ... well it will be when you move in."

I gasp. "I'm not moving in with you."

"Not straight away, but one day you will."

"Will I now?"

"You better believe it, sweetheart."

Trying to get some grownup time together has been a struggle. With our jobs, and Bridge, it doesn't leave a lot of free time. I've snuck over a few nights after Blake's gone to bed, and Mason steals kisses or cheeky butt grabs whenever his son's back is turned, or he's out of the room, but since we have to keep things PG in front of him—because we've yet to tell him that we're a couple—it's been tough.

There's been plenty of flirty and dare I say dirty texts during the day and late-night phone calls, which usually ends with Mason begging me to come over and ride his big man sausage—because he's never going to let me live that one down—or to sit on his face. He's relentless, but I don't mind. Our busy lives are actually forcing us to take things slow. I don't want to fall too fast too soon and end up with a broken heart. But he makes me happy—happier than I ever thought possible.

Mason's hands move down to my arse, squeezing tight. "I need you, Red. It's been days, I'm desperate for your pussy," he informs me, peppering kisses along my jawline.

"Don't you have an early meeting you need to get to?" I say, untangling myself from his arms. I want him too, but Blake is brushing his teeth and could walk in any minute. "I also need to get your son to school."

"What are your plans for later today?" he asks, following me into the kitchen.

"I don't have any. I'm heading to the shops to grab some groceries for my apartment, and stuff for dinner for you and Blake. After that I'm coming home. I have washing to do."

"My meeting should be done by ten. I'll meet you back here at eleven."

"Why?"

"You know exactly why," he says, slapping my arse. I yelp and turn to face him as he slides his hand into the back pocket of his trousers and retrieves his wallet. "Here. Take my card."

"What for?"

"To pay for the food."

"I don't need your money; I have a job."

"You've been cooking for us for weeks, it's only fair I pay for the ingredients."

"Put your card away," I say, pushing his hand down.

"Take it," he growls.

"On second thoughts, there's this cute little boutique that just opened up." I'm grinning as I pluck it out of his fingers.

I'm joking of course, but I like teasing him. "Do they sell sexy stripper clothes there?"

"Why?" I ask, narrowing my eyes.

"You're going to need something scandalous to wear when I get my private performance."

"I wasn't planning on wearing clothes," I say, winking and sliding his credit card into the top pocket of his suit jacket.

"You wench."

"Brooke pays me well, and I have no other expenses. I don't pay rent, and I also have an unlimited credit card that my dad gave me."

"Your dad?" I hear, and when I spin around, I see Blake's wide eyes looking up at me. "The mean one?"

"No, sweetie," I answer, bending down to his height. "The mean one is in jail; I'm talking about my new one."

"You have a new one?"

"Yes, and he's really nice."

"Can I meet him?"

Of course, Connor let the cat out of the bag with our parents, and now my mum is bugging me to meet Mason and Blake, but I'm not sure if I'm ready for that step yet. I have no clue what the 'meet the parents' protocol is, but I'm thinking it's a little soon for that.

"He lives in Melbourne with my mum."

"Will I get a new nice mum one day, Jazzie?"

"Maybe. Any mum would be lucky to have you as their little boy."

I straighten his tie and kiss his cheek before I stand. As I walk towards the fridge to grab their lunches, I notice Mason giving me a strange look. It's not one I've seen before, so it's impossible to decipher what it means.

By the time I pack Blake's lunch into his bag, and hand Mason his, he's still got the same weird look on his face. "What?" I ask, frowning.

"You."

"Me what?"

"It's going to be you, Red," is all he says as he turns and exits the kitchen, leaving me standing there with my mouth gaping open.

Was he implying that I'm going to be Blake's nice new mum?

Chapter 24

Mason

"Olivia," I say, taking a seat on the corner of her desk in reception when I arrive back at the office. "Can I ask you a question?"

"Sure, what's up?"

"How did you know that Paul was the one?"

"Paul, as in my husband Paul?"

"Of course, your husband Paul. What *other* Paul would I be referring to?"

"Just making sure," she says, grinning.

"You like busting my balls, don't you?"

"It's my favourite part of the day."

"I'll remember that when I'm considering your Christmas bonus this year."

"Isn't Rob the one who pays my bonus?"

"Yes, on my recommendation."

"Oh, you'll be recommending me for one."

"You sound very sure of yourself?" I ask, reaching for her jellybean jar, and searching inside for a red one.

She arches one of her perfectly sculptured eyebrows. "I don't think Rob would be impressed if he knew you were disappearing during the day when you're supposed to be working."

"I told you I had a meeting."

"No, you told me if Rob asks where you are, to tell him you're in a meeting. A meeting that wasn't in my diary."

"Doesn't mean I didn't have one."

"I can guarantee wherever you went was not work related."

"What makes you say that?"

She holds up one of her hands, ticking off each point with her fingers as she goes. "You left here all grumpy, and came back wearing a goofy smile—"

"Means nothing," I say, cutting her off and popping a red jellybean into my mouth.

"I'm not finished. Your tie is inside out, and your shirt buttons are all askew. Neither were like that this morning."

I look down and see she's right. "Shit."

"So where did you go?"

"To visit my girlfriend."

Her eyes widen. "Your girlfriend? Since when?"

"We've been together about a month."

"Wow."

"I know."

"Being a father has really changed you for the good."

"It has."

"Does this girlfriend of yours have anything to do with your question about me and Paul?"

I exhale a long breath. "I really like her, Liv, but this is all new to me."

"Do you love her?"

I lift one shoulder. "Maybe."

"Maybe? What kind of answer is that?"

"I've never been in love before, so I'm not sure what that feels like."

"Okay. Let's ask Google."

"Google? You're joking right?"

"It's the best I've got."

"Why don't you just answer my question?"

"Because I can't give you a definitive answer."

"Why not?"

"Because I was only eleven when Paul moved in across the street. I was immediately smitten, but he was fourteen, and didn't know I existed."

"How old were you when he finally noticed?"

"Nineteen."

"Wow."

"I know right. For years I used to sit at my window, watching his comings and goings, all the while pining for him."

"So, you were a crazy stalker?"

She laughs. "Kind of."

"What happened to change things when you were nineteen?"

"He'd broken up with his girlfriend of two years, and moved home. My parents were away at the time, so I hatched a devious plan."

"Which was?"

"I put on my sluttiest dress and walked across the street and knocked on his door."

"You basically entrapped him?"

"I wouldn't exactly call it entrapment." She lets out a small laugh before continuing her story. "I did lie to him though. I told him my parents were away and I was locked out of the house, and being the lovely person I'd always imagined him to be, he invited me in, we got talking, and the rest is history."

241

"Does he know that you used to stalk him?"

"Of course. We've been together fifteen years now. I didn't tell him right off the bat ... I waited until we were married and I was pregnant with Emmy-Lou."

I bark out a laugh. "Wise move."

She starts typing on her keyboard, saying the words out loud as she does. "Ways to tell if you're in love with someone?" She pauses for a moment, reading her computer screen. "Hmm, here we go. They have a questionnaire."

"This is ridiculous."

"Do you want to know, or not?"

"Fine."

"Question one: Do you think of her regularly?"

"Yes."

"Do you feel safe with her?"

"Of course. I wouldn't have her around my son if I didn't."

"Is life with her more exciting?"

"One hundred percent."

"Do you want to spend more time with her."

"I snuck out in the middle of the work day to see her, so that's a given."

"Do you get jealous of other people in her life?"

I look down at my lap. "Not people in her life per se, but when we went clubbing for her brother's birthday, I wanted to take out any guy that looked at her sideways ... and don't even get me started on the handsy fuckers that constantly approached her on the dance floor."

"That would be a yes," Olivia says, giving me the side-eye. "You sound like you've got it bad."

I clear my throat, because I can't even deny it. I'm glad I didn't mention the hickey I branded Jacinta with earlier today—marking my territory for her little strip club outing tonight—which is something I've never done, or wanted to do before. I chuckle at the absurdity. *I'm such an idiot.* Is this the kind of shit I've got to look forward to being in a relationship?

"That's rich coming from the creepy stalker lady."

"Huh," she says, clearly not impressed.

"Next question."

"No need, I've heard enough. Congratulations, Boss, you're in love."

"I am?"

"According to Google you are." With that, she reaches across her desk and snatches the jar of jellybeans from my hand. "Now scoot, I have work to do."

I shake my head as I stand and head towards my office, unravelling my inside-out tie as I do.

Fucking Google.

It's 10.30 pm, and instead of being in bed, I'm pinging off the walls. I've managed to refrain from texting Red. I have absolutely no problem with her being out with her friends, it's their location I'm not comfortable with. I've been to enough strip clubs in my life to know what goes on there and the type of riffraff those places attract.

By the time eleven o'clock rolls around, I lose my battle.

> Wolf: How's your night going?

Minutes pass before I get a reply.

> Red: It was great. Candy killed it. I'm so proud of her. The club was a real eye opener, but I had the best time.

I tilt my head back and groan. That's not what I wanted to hear.

> Wolf: Are you still at the club?

I'm asking because for a brief moment, I'm actually contemplating waking up Blake so we can go get her.

> Red: No. We just got in an uber. Cass wanted to stay, but I have work tomorrow.

> Wolf: Spend the night here?

> Wolf: Please!

> Red: I'd love to, but I'm really tired.

> Wolf: You do realise spending the night involves sleep, right?

> Red: And knowing you the way I do, I'm guessing other stuff as well.

> Wolf: Babe, I just want to hold you. If you're tired, we'll sleep. I got my fill of you earlier today.

> Red: About that ... I wasn't impressed when I saw the giant love bite on my neck. Lucky Cass has skills in covering them up.

Wolf: You weren't supposed to cover it.

Red: What was I supposed to do? Leave it? Shout to the world, look what I got up to earlier today?

Wolf: Yes!

Red: Okay, caveman.

Wolf: I wanted those sleazebags at the club to know you were taken.

Red: Or easy. Did you ever think it may scream that? Like hey, look at me, I'm a hoe, do you want to take me for a ride?

I bark out a laugh.

Wolf: No, I didn't.

Red: Exactly!

Wolf: When you get here, I'll make it up to you.

Red: I thought I was going straight to sleep when I got there.

Wolf: You are.

Red: Then how are you going to make it up to me?

Wolf: I'll think of something.

Red: You better think quick, we're almost at the apartment building.

245

Wolf: Does that mean you're staying over?

Red: It does.

And just like that, the pressure that's been weighing on my chest for the past few hours dissipates.

I'm standing at the door waiting, and the second Red steps off the lift and my eyes take her in, I groan. *Fuck she's a stunner*, and I know wholeheartedly I'm one lucky bastard to be able to call her mine.

Her long blonde hair is slicked back and pulled into a high ponytail. The off-the-shoulder black sparkly top she's wearing is paired with a pair of skin tight leather pants that has my cock literally weeping. Her sky-high heels complete her ensemble, the colour matching perfectly with her ruby-red lips. I'm regretting agreeing to no sex tonight, because I'm already wanting to devour every inch of her.

Those ever-present butterflies I seem to get whenever I'm in her presence, take flight as she approaches and her plump, red lips curve into a smile. These feelings she evokes are as equally terrifying as they are exhilarating. Nobody has ever come close to making me feel the things she does.

"Hey, you," I say. The second she's in reach, I extend my arms and slide them around her tiny waist, pulling her into me.

"Hey."

"I can't even put into words how edible you look in

246

this outfit," I tell her, joining our lips and sliding my hands down to grope her arse.

"Is that a dagger in your pocket, Mr Bradley? Or are you just pleased to see me?"

"I'm definitely pleased to see you, Miss Maloney," I chuckle, because that's the God's honest truth.

"If I come inside, are you going to behave yourself?"

My lips move down to her neck. "I'll admit, it's going to be a struggle, but I promise I'll behave."

Bending my knees slightly, I effortlessly lift her into my arms, carrying her inside my apartment. After kicking the front door closed with my foot, I head towards my room.

Sitting her on the edge of the bed, I lift one of her legs, removing her high heel. I use my thumbs to massage the ball of her foot. "What are you doing?" she asks.

"Making it up to you." She leans back on her elbows and moans. "You'll need to quit making those sexy little noises, babe."

"Why?" she asks, biting down on her bottom lip.

I lean in, dragging it free. "You'll need to stop doing that too."

"Why?"

"Because you know what they do to me, and I'm trying really hard not to break my promise."

"My bad," she says, grinning.

"Are you doing it on purpose?"

"No, it's just my body's natural reaction to your hands touching me."

I arch a brow. "So, what you're really saying is that I do it for you?"

"You definitely do it for me, Wolf." *I'll be damned if she doesn't do it for me too.*

Once I'm finished with her feet, I lean in and pop the

button on her leather pants. When she gives me a dubious look, like I'm going back on my word, I clarify, "I'm just getting you comfortable, and ready for bed."

By the time she's down to her skimpy black underwear, I'm struggling to keep my composure. My cock is so hard it's tenting my sweats. "You're giving me that look again."

"What look?"

"That wolfish one."

I chuckle at her reply. "Wolfish one?"

"Yes, that *I want to gobble you up look*."

"Am I that transparent?"

"Uh huh."

I reach for the T-shirt I placed on the bed before she got here, sliding it over her head. "I'm going to need you to remove your own bra ... I'm not sure if I can be trusted to do it." I retreat a step when she reaches under the tee, unclasping the back, and sliding the straps through the armholes. I'm forced to take another when I notice her hardened nipples poking through my shirt. I clear my throat. "There's a clean washer beside the sink in the bathroom, so you can remove your make-up."

"Thanks," she says, rising from the bed and heading in that direction.

I palm my cock through my sweats as my eyes hone in on the hypnotic sway of her hips. Why does this woman have me constantly battling my self-control?

By the time she exits the bathroom, I'm already in bed waiting. She flicks off the light and slips in beside me. I immediately pull her into my arms, my front to her back ... the big spoon to her little. "Night, Red," I say, placing a kiss on her hair.

"Night, Wolf," she replies over a yawn, and my lips curve up.

The arm around her waist, slips lower. "What are you doing?"

"This is the last part of me making it up to you."

"I thought—"

"Shh. Just lie there and enjoy it. It will help you sleep." She whimpers as soon as my fingers slide down the front of her underwear, circling her clit. My movements are slow and precise. My cock is now rock-hard again and pressing into her butt cheek.

"Let me fix this for you," she says, reaching around.

I draw my lower body back, out of her reach. "Don't, babe."

"Why?"

"It's part of my punishment."

"For marking me?"

"Yes. Like you said, I was acting like a caveman."

"Aww, don't be so hard on yourself. Although misguided, I understand where you were coming from. If you were going to a strip club without me, I'd probably do the same ... or worse."

"Worse?"

"Yes, like make you wear a T-shirt that says, *'Back off bitches, he's taken'*.

"I like being taken by you," I admit, sucking her earlobe into my mouth.

"And I don't mind being marked by you ... next time do it somewhere less obvious."

"Fuck, you're perfect," I say, moving my hand down and sliding a finger deep inside her. "Google was right."

"Google?"

"Long story."

Chapter 25

Jacinta

"Have you given any more thought to your birthday party, buddy?" Mason asks Blake.

The three of us are sitting down to a family dinner. We try to do this at least a couple of nights a week. With our conflicting busy schedules, it's usually just one of us eating with Blake, so it's nice when we can all be together.

"I want pizza."

"Of course, you do," Mason chuckles. "Anything else?"

He lifts one shoulder. "Can we go to Timezone again?"

"You can go anywhere you want. Who do you want to invite?"

"Jazzie," he says, giving me a bashful smile.

I reach across the table, placing my hand on top of his. "I would love to come to your birthday party."

"Anyone else?" Mason asks. "Braydon?"

"Yes, and Uncle Connor."

"What about the other kids in your class?"

"Can I invite some of them?"

"You can invite all of them if you want," Mason answers.

His eyes widen. "The whole class?"

"If you want."

"Okay, but I don't want Tristan to come ... he's a butthead."

His father laughs, but it brings out my mumma-bear. "Why? Is he mean to you?"

He bows his head, looking down at the table. "Sometimes."

My eyes dart to Mason, finding his fork paused midway to his mouth. He's frowning and his lips are now a thin line.

"How?" I ask.

"Today he threw my hat in the girls' toilets and teased me when I went in to get it. He told everyone in my class I was a little girl."

"That little shit," I mumble under my breath. "Is that the first time he's been mean to you?"

"No, yesterday he put grass and dirt in my water bottle and pulled on my tie until it nearly choked me."

I gasp. "Did you tell your teacher?"

"Yes," he says as his bottom lip quivers.

"And what did she say?"

"Tristan told her I was lying, and she said I shouldn't tell stories." When tears rise to his eyes, I see red, literally. "I wasn't lying, Jazzie."

That bitch.

I purse my lips. "Right," I say, dropping my fork onto the table. "First thing tomorrow morning, I'm going to march down to that school and have a word with your teacher." He gives me a small smile as a solitary tear rolls down his cheek. Seeing him upset like this breaks my heart; this little boy has been through enough. Reaching

251

over, I swipe his tear away. "You should've told us sooner."

"I thought you wouldn't believe me either."

"Sweetie, we'll always believe you. We need to know if something bad happens, so we can fix it."

"Okay."

When another tear falls, I scoot my chair back. "Come here." Blake slides off his seat and walks straight into my open arms. I hug him tight, kissing the top of his head. "Don't cry, your dad and I will sort it out tomorrow."

When my eyes move to Mason, I find him smiling. "Why are you looking at me like that?" I ask.

"No reason," he replies as he goes back to eating his dinner.

"You don't have anything to say about this?"

"I have plenty to say, but it looks like you've got it covered."

Mason sits down on the edge of my bed while I add Blake's latest present to the ever-growing pile in the bottom of my wardrobe. After visiting with his teacher, we went to the shops to grab a few things, and Mason saw something he thought his son would love. He's been leaving all his purchases here so Blake won't find them. Their apartment is a lot smaller than the mansion they once lived in so hiding spots are limited.

"Did I tell you how kick-arse you were this morning?"

I roll my eyes. "Numerous times."

"For someone so tiny, you can be awfully intimidating when you're mad."

I shrug. "I'm just protective of the people I care about."

"And I love that about you," he says, reaching out and pulling me down onto his lap. "My son is lucky to have someone like you in his corner, Red. His poor teacher was close to tears by the time you were finished with her."

"Hah! When we learnt that bully had been terrorising some of the other kids as well, and why his bad behaviour was being ignored, she's lucky I didn't give her an upper cut." Turns out this kid's mother works at the school, and Blake's teacher and her are friends.

Mason throws back his head and laughs. "Your feisty side turns me on." He juts his pelvis forward, letting me feel his hardening dick, so I slap his arm and rise off his lap.

"That little shit is a bully, plain and simple, and her ignorance makes her just as bad."

"Well, now you've involved the principal hopefully it will stop."

"Do you think we should change schools?"

"Why?"

"I'm just worried that now we've made waves there might be some blowback for Blake, he's under their care for six hours a day, five days a week."

"Babe," Mason says, standing and sliding his arms around my waist from behind. "We can't keep moving schools every time something bad happens."

"Maybe we should get him a phone then, so he can call one of us during the day if something happens."

"Jacinta, he's five. I'm not getting him a phone." When I blow out a puff of air, Mason slides his hand under my top, palming my breast. "You worry too much; it sounds like you need a distraction."

"Let me guess, that distraction is you?" He chuckles

253

as his fingers slip under the fabric, tweaking my nipple between his forefinger and thumb. When I rest my head against his chest and moan, his lips move down to my neck. "Don't you have to go to work?"

"I'll be quick." His free hand slides down the front of my tights, and when he feels that I'm already slick and ready for him, I'm abruptly spun around and lifted onto the edge of the bed. "On your knees," he orders.

Once I've done what I'm asked, he tugs my tights and underwear down and moves to free himself from his trousers.

"Hey!" I shriek when his free hand comes down to connect with my left butt cheek.

"This arse," he groans, slipping his fingers between my legs, and the slap is soon forgotten.

Mason spends the next five minutes working me over, to the point I'm withering with need. "Stop teasing me and put it in."

"Someone sounds a little needy?" he says, chuckling.

"You said you'd be quick ... *you lied.*"

"Are you desperate for me, Red?"

He removes his hand and replaces his fingers with the tip of his dick, running it back and forth ... again, without entering me. He's doing it purposely now. "Don't push me, Wolf," I growl.

"You never disappoint," he says, laughing.

"The only one disappointing here, is you."

"Is that—" His own words are cut off by his long, drawn-out groan as he *finally* slides inside me.

"Yes!" Arching my back, I push my body towards his because I want it all. Every delicious inch.

"Fuck, Red," he mumbles, grasping hold of my hips. He slowly withdraws right to the tip, and when he drives straight back in, we both moan in unison.

He does this a few more times before he completely lets loose. The room is suddenly filled with our cries of pleasure mixed with the sound of our bodies slapping together as he pistons into me at a frantic pace. One of his hands leaves my hip, moving back between my legs. It only takes a few skilful swipes of his fingers to send me over the edge.

He stills for a moment, grating out the word, "Fuck." I'm still coming when his hips start to jerk forward, and he releases himself inside me with a loud and powerful roar. And all I can think is, thank God Connor isn't home.

It's birthday eve, and I think I'm just as excited as Blake. We've been doing a daily countdown for the past week. I've bought some balloons and a happy 6th birthday sign to decorate the lounge room tonight once he's gone to bed. I hope it's a nice surprise for him when he gets up tomorrow morning.

The party is all organised for this coming weekend; I'm making up lolly bags for all the kids to take home, and I have a huge jar full of jellybeans for the guessing competition. I had to put that together at my apartment, so Mason didn't steal all the red ones. All I need to do now is order the cake, which I plan on doing after picking Blake up today.

All has been good at school since I approached his teacher, and she's been awfully sweet to me on the days I go there. I'd like to think it's because she's seen the error of her ways, but I'm leaning more towards the principal's involvement. Tristan even apologised, and Blake ended up inviting him to the party, which I'm happy about. I'd hate if the entire class was invited somewhere and Blake was the only one left out. It was the right thing to do.

"Jazzie," Blake yells when he spots me waiting outside his classroom with the other parents. I love the way his little face lights up whenever he sees me; it's a look I'll never tire of. I bend down and open my arms, which he runs straight in to. "I drew you a picture today."

When I release him, he drops his backpack on the ground, unzipping it. He's beaming when he holds it up to me. "Wow."

"It's you, me and dad."

"I can see that." There are three stick figures on the page; I'm presuming the one with the long yellow hair is me. We all have circles for hands, and three tiny lines for fingers. It's the sweetest thing ever, but what has me choking back the tears is what he's written underneath. The letters may be askew, and the 'F' is back-to-front, but it's still legible. *My Family.* "I love it so much," I say, leaning down to place a kiss on top of his head. "Thank you. I'm going to put it on the fridge as soon as we get home."

His little hand is wrapped in mine as he happily chats about his day on the way to the car. It's kind of scary how fast things have transitioned. In a matter of months, that's exactly what we've become ... *somewhat of a family*. We're even planning to fly down to Melbourne in the school holidays so the boys can meet my parents. Flights are already booked. A part of me worries that things are moving too fast, but I also feel like I'm exactly where I need to be. There's no set protocol ... sometimes people just fit.

Once Blake is strapped into the back seat, I round the vehicle and climb into the driver's side. Before I pull into traffic, I glance at Blake in the rearview mirror. "Have you decided what kind of cake you want for your party?"

"A dinosaur one."

"We're going to head to the bakery now so you can pick out your cake."

"I want it to look like my Rex."

"I think I have a picture of you and Rex on my phone, so we can show them."

"Okay."

"Are you excited about your party?"

He lifts one shoulder, looking down at his lap. "I don't know, I've never been to a party before."

"Ah, sweetie." I turn in my seat, reaching into the back to place my hand on his leg. I know exactly how he feels, I was thirteen when I attended my first birthday party ... *it was my own.* "You're going to have the best day."

His big brown eyes move back to mine, and he gives me a small smile. I swear this kid melts my heart ... he has the sweetest little face, with cheeks I just want to squish.

"Are you hungry?" I ask Blake, which is a silly question ... when isn't he hungry? "Would you like a milkshake before we leave?"

"Can I get a donut too?"

"A milkshake and a donut?"

"Please."

"Of course."

"Thanks, Jazzie."

The cake is ordered, and I even got some individual boxed cupcakes for the kids to take home, with dinosaur toppers on them. Since this is his first ever party, I want it to be special ... one that he'll remember. We've received an RSVP from all but two of the kids in his class, so there'll be almost thirty people attending.

I spy some decorative place cards in a window display as we pass a stationery shop, "I just want to duck in here and grab something," I tell Blake.

He has his donut in one hand and the milkshake in the other. When we enter the store, the lady behind the counter looks from me to Blake. "We don't allow food and drink in here," she says.

I almost walk back out, but I really want those place cards. They'll look cute on the table with the lolly bags and cupcakes. Plus, it will allow Blake to choose who he wants to sit near him. I can also place Tristan at the far end of the table. Although he's had no more trouble with that kid, I don't want to take any chances.

"Stand at the entrance," I tell him. I'll have a constant view of him from there. "I'll only be a minute."

"Okay, Jazzie," he mumbles, through a mouthful of donut.

I head straight for the sales desk, letting the staff member know what I'm after. My attention is constantly moving back to the door as I do. My eyes are on Blake when she returns. "We have two different types," she says, holding out the dinosaur place cards.

"These ones." I point to the green T-Rex, they're perfect.

"There's twelve in each pack, how many were you after?"

"Three packets will do." I turn my head towards the exit, and my heart drops when I see Blake is no longer standing there. "I'll be right back," I tell her. My immediate concern only escalates as I approach and see his spilt milkshake on the ground, and his half-eaten donut a few feet away. "Blake," I scream as I run out of the store, with my heart hammering in my chest. This is so unlike him. Coming to an abrupt stop, I look to the right and see nothing, but when I turn my head to the left my stomach drops. "Hey!"

A blonde lady has him by the arm, dragging him along the tiled floor. "Jazzie!"

"Stop!" I call out, breaking into a sprint. Blake starts to thrash around in her grip when he sees me chasing them, which is stopping her from making a hasty getaway. Adrenaline is coursing through my veins. I catch up to them, bend and wrap my arms around his tiny waist, lifting him off the floor. Although I have him in my grasp, his upper body is still tilted in her direction because she's yet to release him. "Let go," I shriek.

"He's my fucking son, you let go."

It takes a second for her words to sink in. *Her son?* My eyes dart down to Blake, and the terror I see on his little face tells me what she's saying is true. *Shit.*

One of my arms keeps a tight grip around his middle, while I use the other hand to try and pry her fingers from him. "Save me, Jazzie," he cries, choking on a sob.

I'm trying, sweetie.

When I finally manage to free him, I bring his body protectively against mine, wrapping my free hand around the back of his head. The blonde reaches for my hair, tugging hard. "Give him back."

She can rip my hair from its roots as far as I'm concerned, there's no way I'm letting him go. Especially for her, she's hurt this little boy enough. Her other hand comes out, clawing at my face. There's nothing I can do to stave off her attack, because keeping Blake safe in my arms is my only concern.

"Jazzie." Blake is openly sobbing now, and I can feel his small body trembling beneath my hands.

"I'm okay, sweetie ... everything is okay. I won't let her take you away."

Thankfully, security shows up, pulling this psycho away from me. "She has my child," she screams.

"He's not her child," I retort. She may have given birth to him, but she doesn't deserve that title.

"Yes, he is, you lying cunt."

"Is this your mummy?" the security guard asks Blake, pointing to the blonde. I hold my breath as I wait for him to answer, because if he says yes, she may be able to leave with him and for now, there'll be nothing I can do to stop her.

I can feel the trickles of blood from her attack on my face, running down my neck, but I ignore it. That is the least of my worries right now.

Relief floods through me when he shakes his head no, before burying his face in my chest. He's still in my arms because I'm afraid to let him go.

"She tried to take this lady's kid," a bystander adds. "I saw her dragging him away."

"That's true," another voice says from behind me, and when I turn around, I find the sales assistant from the stationery shop standing there. "I didn't see her take him, but the boy was definitely with this lady. They were in my shop a few minutes ago."

"Come with me," the guard says, pulling her off to the side. She's thrashing around in his arms, but she is no match for his weight or height. He pulls out his two-way, "I need assistance on level two ... we have an attempted kidnapping."

260

Chapter 26

Mason

I shove my key into the door, rushing inside. Connor called me when Jacinta and Blake were at the police station giving their statements and gave me a brief rundown on what had happened. I can't believe Annalise would try something like this. What was her motive? She didn't want him a year ago. Is she after more money?

This time, I'll definitely be pressing charges. I'm not giving that woman a chance to try something like this again.

"Red," I call out when I don't find either of them in the main room or the kitchen.

"We're in the bathroom."

I'm not sure what I'm expecting to see when I round the corner, but it's definitely not the deep, red scratches down the side of Jacinta's beautiful face. The sight only fuels my anger. Connor told me they were shaken, but okay ... there was no mention of injuries.

"Babe," I say, opening my arms, and when she walks straight into them, I wrap her up tight. My eyes flicker to Blake in the bath. "You okay, bud?" He nods his head and goes back to playing with his toys. I scan the top half of his body, because it's the only part visible, and when I see the finger mark bruises on his upper arm, my blood pressure rises to a dangerous level. It's been many years since I felt this angry. My gaze moves back to Red. "What happened?"

She flicks her head towards the hallway, silently letting me know she doesn't want to rehash it in front of Blake. Glancing over her shoulder, she says, "I'm going to talk to your dad ... we'll be just outside the door, okay?"

"Okay, Jazzie."

At a glance, he seems like he's doing really well considering what happened. I follow Red out. "How is he holding up?" I ask.

She lifts one shoulder. "Overall, pretty good, but he's been very clingy since it happened." She continues down the hallway before she stops and faces me; I presume so Blake can't hear what she says. I ghost my knuckle over her cheek. "How are you? Did she do this?" I ask, gesturing to her face.

"Yes," she says, nodding. "I was too busy shielding Blake to defend myself."

"Babe," I say, when I see her bottom lip quiver.

"She must've been watching us ... waiting for the right moment to pounce."

I still can't wrap my head around how this happened. "Start from the beginning."

"After I picked Blake up from school, we headed to the shops. I needed to order his birthday cake for the weekend, and I wanted him to choose it. He picked a dinosaur one," she tells me as a small smile tugs at her lips. "One that looks like his Rex plushie." I nod, because I don't give two fucks about the cake right now. "Before we left, I went and bought him a milkshake and donut, and as we were heading towards the carpark, we passed a stationery shop that had these cute place settings in the window display. They were perfect, and it would mean Blake could choose who he wanted to sit near ... I could also sit Tristan as far away from him as possible."

"Red," I say softly, reaching out to stroke my fingers over her hair. I love how thoughtful she is, but again that's not the information I want to hear.

"When we entered the store, the sales assistant said they had a no food or drink policy ... I almost walked back out." She dips her face, looking down at her feet. "I wish I had."

"You left him outside?" I ask, all the while hoping that's not what she's implying.

"No. I got him to stand in the doorway—I could see him the entire time. The counter was only a few metres away ..."

Her words drift off, and it's what she's not saying that concerns me most. "And?"

When her eyes meet mine again, they're brimming with tears. "I only looked away for a second." And there it is.

I swear I almost pop an artery when that knowledge sinks in. My brow furrows. "Keep going," I say, trying my best to remain calm.

"The sales assistant came back with two different dinosaur place cards, I glanced down, pointed to the one I wanted and when I looked back up, he was gone."

I fist my hair in my hands, tugging on the strands. I can't believe what I'm hearing. "I trusted him with you, Red!"

"I'm sorry."

"You're sorry?"

"Yes."

I am beyond mad, and if I was thinking with a level

263

head, I'd realise that this was just one of those unfortunate circumstances—that this woman cares for my son and would never intentionally put him in harm's way—but unfortunately, my rage is blurring the rational side of my brain.

Something inside me snaps, and old habits die hard. Before I even register what I'm doing, my hand balls into a fist and careens straight through the gyprock. Even though it's a good few feet away from Jacinta, when I pull my arm back, I find her crouched down beside me, cradling her head in her hands, shielding herself from me. It's only then I realise I've fucked up.

"Babe," I say, reaching for her, but when she flinches, I take a step back. Does she not realise that I'd never hurt her? That I'm not my father, or hers for that matter? My outburst is purely a coping mechanism I've developed over the years ... a way to expel all the fury swirling around inside me.

She springs to her feet, so I reach for her again. "Don't."

"Red," I plead, when she turns and starts walking towards the front door. "Please, I'm sorry."

When she holds up her hand, I see how much it is shaking and I hate that I'm the person responsible for that. She's had a harrowing day, with the wounds on her face to prove it. "I need to go." Her voice wobbles as she says that.

I'm such an arsehole.

"Please, let me explain."

Ignoring my pleas, she opens the door and walks over the threshold. I move towards it just as she breaks into a run. Everything in me wants to go after her, but I can't leave Blake here alone in the bathtub.

"Jacinta," I call out as she frantically presses the button to summon the lift. She won't even look at me.

Fuck.

What have I done?

Once she disappears inside the lift and the doors close, I pull out my phone. I need her to know the truth if nothing else.

> Wolf: Babe, please believe me when I say you were not, nor will you ever be in danger around me. I'd never lay a hand on you. NEVER! I was simply releasing my frustration out on the wall … it's what I've always done. It's how I coped growing up with my abusive father. Are there better ways to do this? I'm sure there are plenty, but I've yet to find something that works for me like this does. This is in no way an excuse for my behaviour just now, but I just wanted you to know I'm not my father. I adore you, Red.

Instead of adore, I want to write I love you, but there is no way I'm saying that to her for the first time via a text. And under these circumstances it would seem more like a copout instead of the truth.

When I press send, I hear a ding coming from behind me. Turning around, I notice Jacinta's handbag still sitting on the dining table. She was in such a hurry to get away from me she didn't even take her things.

I blow out a long, frustrated breath as I slide my phone into my jacket pocket and head towards the bathroom.

Entering, I crouch down beside the bath. "You okay, buddy?"

"Where's Jazzie?"

"She had to leave."

He dips his face. "She didn't say goodbye to me."

"She told me to say goodbye to you," I lie. "Are you alright after everything that happened today? I'm sorry I wasn't there, but I'll make sure Annalise doesn't come anywhere near you again."

He looks up, his eyes meeting mine. "Jazzie saved me, Dad. She came running after us and wrapped me in her arms like this," he says, moving one of his arms to curl around his middle and the other around his head. "Annalise was pulling her hair and scratching her face trying to get me back, but Jazzie wouldn't let me go."

"I'm glad she was there for you." I reach out, ruffling his hair. "You are safe now; you know that right?"

He nods. "I wish Jazzie was my mum."

Out of the mouths of babes.

"So do I," I whisper under my breath, but I'm pretty sure my actions just now ruined his chances of that ever happening.

After Blake is out of the bath, I get him dressed in his pyjamas and order us a pizza for dinner. I don't eat any, my stomach is too tied up in knots. Since Red's phone is still here, I can't even contact her, and I'm not about to drag Blake down there, especially since she'll more than likely slam the door in my face.

He's been really quiet all evening, and doesn't say much when I try to talk to him. All I can do is keep an eye on him and constantly reassure him that he's safe here ... I won't let anything happen to him.

It's just after eight when there's a knock at the door. I lift Blake's sleeping head off my lap, where he was lying wrapped in a blanket in front of the television. This is how he usually lies with Jacinta. I would've carried him to bed by now, but after everything that happened today, I just wanted to keep him close.

Standing, I run my flattened palms down the front of my sweats. I'm equally nervous and optimistic. Is it her? *Fuck I hope so.*

The moment I open the front door, I immediately deflate when I find Connor standing there. "I want to punch you in the face again," is the first thing he says, "but Jaz made me promise not to."

That immediately gets my back up, I'm in no mood for his attitude right now. "Hello to you too."

"What the fuck, man. You know what her life used to be like. Why would you do that in front of her?"

I step out into the hallway, closing the door behind me, so Blake doesn't wake. "Because unfortunately my childhood was just the same as hers."

"What?" he says, frowning.

"I grew up with an abusive father, and when he wasn't hitting my mother, he was beating on me. This is no excuse, but it's all I've ever known. I wasn't big, or strong enough to fight back ... or to protect my mum, so I used to lock myself in the wardrobe and punch holes in the wall. It was how I coped. I haven't done that since I was a teenager, but I also haven't been as fucked up as I was earlier today."

"Why have you never mentioned this before?"

"Because it's a part of my life that I don't like to talk about. I've touched on it briefly with Jacinta though."

"Wow," he says, shaking his head. "I had no idea, I'm sorry."

"You have nothing to be sorry about, it's my piece of shit father that should be sorry, but knowing him like I do, I doubt he even cares."

"Is this why you ended up on the streets?"

I turn my head and stare off down the hallway as images of my broken mother lying at the bottom of the staircase flashes through my mind. A lump forms in the back of my throat, so instead of answering, I just nod my head once.

"Shit, man."

"How's Jacinta?" I ask, turning my attention back to him.

"A mess. She sobbed in my arms for about an hour. I've never seen her so broken."

"Fuck," I groan, tilting my head back. "You know I'd never hurt her right? I may occasionally put my fist through a wall, but I'd never physically hurt someone, especially her."

"Is that why you never hit me back when I found out about you two?"

"No, I let you have that one because in a way I deserved it."

"Damn straight you did," he says, chuckling.

"Besides, a fairy tap on the chin is nothing compared to the floggings I've received in the past."

"It was more than a fairy tap," he grumbles, and this time I laugh. I'll admit my jaw ached for a few days afterwards.

There's a brief silence, before I speak again. "I love her, Connor."

"You do?" he asks, his eyes widening.

"With everything I have."

"Does she know that?"

"No. I haven't told her yet. I was worried it was too

soon, and it may freak her out." Now I'm concerned I'll never get the chance to tell her how I feel.

"Fuck ... I mean I could see she was different to all the others, but love? I didn't see that one coming so soon."

"When the heart knows, it just knows, I guess."

He dips his head, shoving his hands into his pocket. "Ain't that the truth." And it makes me wonder if he's thinking about the girl who broke his heart when he was younger.

"Do you think she'd let me talk to her? Let me explain?"

"Eventually maybe, but not tonight. She's locked herself in her room."

I blow out a frustrated breath. "Fair enough."

"I'm actually here to collect her bag."

"Right," I say, opening the door and entering my apartment. Connor follows close behind me.

His gaze moves to Blake, who's still fast asleep on the lounge. "How is he?"

"Quiet, but okay." I think I'll put him in bed with me tonight, just in case.

"The way he clung to my sister like she was his life-line at the police station, tugged at my heart. She adores him you know, and she'd never purposely put him in harm's way."

"I know. Is there any news on Annalise?"

"We are holding her overnight. She'll go in front of the magistrate tomorrow morning. She's been charged with attempted kidnapping, two counts of assault—on Jaz and the security guard—and possession. We found drugs on her."

"Why doesn't that surprise me? Do you think she'll serve time for this?"

"Absolutely. At least a few years, I'm going to push for

269

the maximum. She hasn't been keeping the best company, and as a result has racked up a pretty extensive rap sheet. Maybe prison will help straighten her out. If nothing else, at least Blake will be safe with her off the streets."

"Do you know why she did this? She was happy to see the back of him when she handed him over to me."

"Nope. Probably an attempt to extort more money from you."

I hand Jacinta's bag to him. "Surely she hasn't blown through all that money already."

"No clue, but I'll look into it and see what I can find out."

"Thanks."

He lifts his arm, tapping me on the back. "Don't worry, mate, everything will work out in the long run."

"Hmm." I'm not sure if he's referring to the Annalise situation or Jacinta, but I'm not asking for clarification. I can only hope that in time Red will forgive me for what I did. "Will you tell your sister I'm sorry?"

"I will. Just give her some time."

Once he's gone, I walk over to Blake, scooping him into my arms. The movement has him stirring. "Is Jazzie here?" he asks.

"No, buddy. I'm just carrying you to bed. Do you want to sleep with me tonight?"

"Okay," he answers, rubbing his eyes. "Will I see Jazzie tomorrow for my birthday?"

My heart sinks. With all the chaos today, I completely forgot about that, and all his presents are downstairs in her apartment. *Fuck.* He was living with me when he turned five, but I didn't even know it was his birthday. I only found out it had passed when I applied for his birth certificate. I wanted to make this one special for him, but now he's going to wake up tomorrow with nothing to open.

I look over at the clock beside the bed; it's just after 6 am. I barely slept a wink last night because my mind wouldn't stop turning. Is this what heartbreak feels like? If it is, it can go fuck itself ... with a cactus. I'd like to think we can get past this, but my gut tells me there's a possibility we won't.

Flicking back the covers, I rise from the bed and head into the bathroom. At least Blake slept soundly last night.

After I piss, I wash my hands and splash water onto my face. I glance into the mirror and see the dark circles under my eyes. I racked my brain last night for ways I can make things better between me and Red, but I don't know if I can. She doesn't know how I truly feel inside, and the possibility of potential violence is what kept her single for so long. What I did last night would be a huge red flag to anyone, except me, because I know in my heart I'd never lay a finger on her. It goes against everything I believe in.

I wipe my face with a towel and head out to the kitchen to make myself a coffee. I'm probably going to need more than one to get me through the day.

When I reach the end of the hallway, I come to an abrupt halt. It's the last thing I'm expecting to see, but knowing Red the way I do, I shouldn't be surprised.

The dining table is full of giftbags of all shapes and sizes. There's multicoloured helium balloons and a giant silver number six in the middle of them. A happy 6th birthday sign hangs from the wall behind it. The sight chokes me up. I have no idea how she pulled this off, or when; she must've snuck into the house while we were sleeping. I'm surprised I never heard her with how little I actually slept.

After what I did last night, this just speaks volumes about her and her kind and beautiful heart. My boy hit the jackpot having someone like her in his life, and I had to go and fuck it up for us both.

My heart sinks when I approach the table and see a lone key sitting there. It's the one I gave her for my apartment. Things are worse than I thought. The fact that she's returning this means it's truly over ... for both Blake and I. Was this her final goodbye?

I slide the key off the table and into the pocket of my sweats. My heart's heavy as I head towards the kitchen, and it's the first time since I was a kid that I feel like I'm on the verge of tears.

When I open the fridge to retrieve the milk, I almost break when I see the double stacked tray of cupcakes sitting inside—a little number six on each one. There's a Post-it Note stuck to the top.

For Blake to take to school today.

"Fuck, Red," I whisper, rubbing the heal of my palm over the ache that's formed in my chest. Did she stay up all night making these?

I don't know how I'm going to do it, but I need to make things right between us.

I lean against the counter once I've made my coffee, taking a small sip. Before I can talk myself out of it, I reach for my phone.

> Wolf: I can't even put into words how appreciative I am for what you have done for Blake. He's going to be so happy when he wakes. Thank you.

There is so much more I want to add, but I'd rather

272

say those things to her in person. I'm not expecting a reply, but one comes through.

> Red: You're welcome. I already had everything here anyway. Wish him a happy birthday from me.

> Wolf: Do you want to come up and watch him open his presents when he wakes?

I hold my breath as I wait for her answer.

> Red: I'm sorry, I can't.

She can't, or doesn't want to?

> Wolf: Okay. I got your key … does that mean you can no longer watch Blake on Monday's and Wednesday's?

> Red: You still want me to?

> Wolf: Of course. He loves those days with you.

> Red: I just thought after yesterday …

> Wolf: Babe. Fuck, I don't want you to ever think that. You mean the world to us, I'm so sorry for the way I acted yesterday, my actions had more to do with me, not you. And I'd hate for you to think I don't trust you around my son, because I do. He's lucky to have someone like you in his life … we both are.

I stand there waiting for her reply, but it never comes.

273

Chapter 27

Mason

Saturday couldn't have rolled around fast enough. The last two days have been hell without Red. After ghosting my last text Thursday morning, I finally got a message back from her later that day.

> Red: Would it be okay if I had a quick facetime with Blake?

Even though it wasn't what I was expecting, of course, I let her. I even stood off to the side, creeping in the background, so I could get a glimpse of her beautiful face. Like me, she looked tired; it made me wonder if she was struggling with her sleep too. She had some light make-up on to cover the scratches on her face, but they were still visible. She smiled throughout their entire exchange, but the sadness in her baby blues was unmissable.

It hurt my fucking heart to see her, not knowing if things will ever be right between us again. Even now as I pull up to Timezone with my son on the back of my bike, my stomach is in knots. Connor told me him and Red were going to be here, and that they'd be picking up the birthday cake on the way. I only hope she gives me a chance to talk to her. Nothing deep obviously—it's Blake's birthday party—but I'll take any glimmer of hope she's willing to offer.

I don't want to lose her over this.

It took me twenty-eight years to find her, so I'm not walking away without a fight. I'll wait for-fucking-ever if need be, as long as we're back together in the end. Hopefully it doesn't take that long. It's only been a few days, and I already miss her like crazy.

We secured a back room for the party, so we head that way after entering the building. Jacinta organised all the finer details, but I do know once the kids have eaten, they'll get preloaded cards so they can play the arcade games.

We're early, so I'm not expecting anyone else to be here yet. You can imagine my surprise when we enter the party room and I find Red darting around getting everything set up for Blake's arrival. My heart starts to hammer in my chest as soon as I see her. She looks stunning like always.

"Jazzie!" Blake squeals, dropping my hand and running straight for her.

She crouches down and catches him when he leaps into her arms. The genuine happiness I see on her face warms my heart. Will I get the same look when her attention turns to me? She wraps him tight, peppering kisses all over his face. *Fuck, I want some of those kisses too.*

"I've missed you," she says. "Are you excited about your party today?"

Has she missed me too?

"Yeah."

"I'm glad you're here, I need your help with the place cards."

She still hasn't looked my way, keeping her attention

solely on my son. It hurts. "What are place cards?" he asks.

"Little cards with names on them. You'll get to choose where you want to sit, and who you want to sit near."

"I want to sit between you and Dad." Blake's eyes widen when he spies the giant jar of jellybeans in the middle of the table. "Are they mine?"

"It's a jellybean guessing competition. You have to guess how many are in there, and the person who gets the closest wins." Jacinta holds up a lined A4 piece of paper. "When your friends arrive, you can write your name and the amount you think is in there, on here."

"I don't know how many," Blake says frowning. "I can only count to twenty."

Jacinta laughs. "Maybe your dad can help you with your guess." I may have got a mention, but there's still no personal acknowledgment from her. *Look at me, Red,* I silently plead.

Connor comes towards me, holding out his hand. "Hey."

"Hey," I reply, wrapping my fingers around his. "I didn't expect to see you guys here already."

"We've been here for about an hour, setting everything up."

My gaze moves to the long table in the centre of the room and see the entire length is decorated with colourful bouquets of helium balloons. I step closer, observing the dinosaur-themed plates, cups, and serviettes. There's a small gift bag sitting in front of each setting and a box that looks like it contains a cupcake. They're tied with a green ribbon and have a tiny card that says, *Thank you* on it. Her attention to detail is incredible, and I never would've thought to do any of this.

"The table looks great," I say as she and Blake sort through the place cards.

Her pretty eyes dart to me, but the happiness I saw when she greeted Blake is no longer present. "Thanks," she replies with a sparse smile before looking away. *Shit*, things between us are worse than I feared, and that thought makes my stomach churn.

Connor obviously notices too, because his hand clasps my shoulder, giving it a slight squeeze. "Give her time … it's been a tough couple of days."

It hasn't exactly been a walk in the park for me either. I can't concentrate at work, and I've barely slept or eaten.

I was in no way prepared for what it would be like with thirty excited, sugar-fuelled, five-and six-year-old's crammed into such a small space. If I'd known, I would've packed some earplugs. We're only an hour in and my ears are already ringing.

It's a small price to pay to see my son in his element. He hasn't stopped smiling and laughing. As for Red, I've tried everything throughout the day to strike up a conversation with her, but she's shut me down with one-word answers.

"Are you having a good time?"

"Yes."

"The kids look like they're enjoying themselves."

"Uh huh."

Basically, she's been avoiding me like the plague, but I like a challenge, so I'm not giving up.

"You look beautiful today."

277

That one only got me a small nod, but it felt like a minor win when her cheeks pinkened.

Helping her clear the table after the kids finish eating, I ask, "Are you going to give me a rematch at air hockey, since you cheated last time we were here?"

Her eyes narrow, and a smile tugs at my lips. "I did not cheat. I beat you fair and square."

If small talk and compliments won't work, I'll take the old route. Any attention she gives me is better than none. "I beg to differ. You purposely wore that low-cut top to distract me."

She gasps. "I did not."

"Prove it. I demand a rematch."

She snatches the paper plates out of my hand, stomping down on my toe. "Fine."

"What do I get if I win?"

"Bragging rights."

"Nah, I want a kiss."

"Not happening."

"We'll see," I chuckle, because if I win, that's exactly what I'm going to demand. "What do you want if you win?" I ask.

"For you to leave me alone," she answers, twisting the dagger she lodged in my chest earlier this week. I try my hardest to act unaffected by that comment, because in a way, I deserve it.

Leaning in, I inhale deeply through my nose, basking in her sweet scent. "I'm a wolf, Red, my genes won't allow it," I murmur low enough that only she can hear. She swallows thickly, so I know my words affect her. "It's what I do, sweetheart, I seek out my prey and hunt it down. You can run all you want, but in the end, I'll catch you, and when I do, I'm going to gobble you up ... Every. Delicious. Inch."

278

She slowly turns her face towards mine, we're so close we are practically sharing the same air. I'd only have to move a few inches forward and our lips would be touching. Everything in me wants to do just that, but if I'm playing the long game, I need to bide my time.

Retreating a fraction, I give her a cheeky wink, and chomp my teeth together for added clout. Turning, I shove my hands into the pockets of my jeans and walk away, and I can feel her eyes on me as I do.

I didn't get my rematch, because neither of us anticipated the enormity of what it would take to keep an eye on almost thirty kids once they were let loose inside the gaming arcade. What the fuck were we thinking? Jacinta and I divided and conquered as best we could, while Connor stood guard at the front entrance so none of the kids could escape. It was both a miracle and a relief when we made it back to the party room for cake with everyone accounted for.

Blake and his classmates had the best time, but honestly, my nerves are frazzled. I'm in need of a stiff drink, or seven, and a long nap.

When the staff member brings out the cake Jacinta ordered, I'm so impressed by it that I pull out my phone and snap a picture. She told me Blake wanted a dinosaur cake, but I wasn't expecting this. It's a tall, large circular cake, but the fondant icing on top, looks like it's been torn and folded back. Coming out of the centre is the open-mouthed head of a green T-rex, with large white teeth and clawed hands.

"Wow," Blake says, staring down at it in awe.

There is a scroll across the front that says, 'Happy Birthday Blake', and three candles down each side. Jacinta walks over to her handbag, digs inside, and pulls out some matches. She has thought of everything, and today wouldn't have been half as great if it wasn't for her and those special touches she added.

Once the candles are lit, everyone starts to sing happy birthday. The beaming smile on my son's face, and the glistening in his eyes as he looks around the room at everyone, chokes me up inside. It's the simple things that seem to mean so much to him. I tuck that image away in my head as I try to swallow the lump that has now formed in the back of my throat. I'm so humbled by this little guy, and so grateful I get to call him mine.

As soon as Red starts to cut the cake, the kids start crowding her, "Can I have the eye ... I want a claw ... Can I have a tooth in my piece?" Like the trooper she is, she tries her best to accommodate everyone.

When the cake has been eaten, I'm thankful the day is almost over. The last thing I need is a bunch of sugar-laden kids in my care.

"Do you want to find out who the winner of the jelly-bean competition is?"

"Yes," the kids scream.

Jacinta picks up the piece of paper with their guesses on it, and when my gaze darts to my son, I find his eyes clenched closed and the middle and forefinger on both hands crossed. A smile tugs at my lips. Fuck, I love this little guy. Red had the parents help the kids with their guesses when they dropped them off.

"There's one thousand, one hundred and fifty-two jellybeans in the jar." I already know my son has lost because our guess was five hundred. "Bianca, it looks like you're the winner," Red says.

Blake's shoulders immediately slump, and his crestfallen face tugs at my heart. I see Jacinta walk over to him and gently rub his back; she noticed too. It seems like we weren't the only ones, because when Bianca gets up to collect her prize, she walks straight over to Blake and hands the jar to him.

"You can have these," she says.

"Really?"

"Yes."

The smile he gives her in return is blinding, and I know in the coming years I'm in trouble. That thought is cemented when she leans in and places a kiss on his cheek and his face flushes bright red. I can't help it; I bark out a laugh.

My eyes dart to Jacinta and not only is there an adoring look on her face as she watches them, the piece of paper in her hand is now clutched to her chest. I'm not sure if she feels the weight of my stare, but when her attention flickers to me and she finds me watching, she quickly looks away. Does that discourage me? No, because the flush that's now creeping up her neck says way more.

She can fight this all she wants, but she's still mine.

Once the kids are all collected and it's time to go home, I breathe a sigh of relief. "Where are you parked?" Connor asks as he starts to load his arms with presents.

I'm such an amateur. I didn't even think about how I was going to transport everything home.

"We came on my bike."

Connor rolls his eyes. "Lucky Jacinta and I brought our cars."

When everything is loaded, I shake Connor's hand and thank him before he climbs in his vehicle. Jacinta gives Blake a hug, telling him she'll see him on Monday.

I'd like a hug too, but I'm pretty sure I'm not going to get one.

"Thank you for everything you did today, you made a little boy very happy," I say. "I owe you big time for this."

"You owe me nothing," she replies, raising her chin. That movement always follows with sass, and she doesn't disappoint. "I did it for Blake, not you."

To anyone else those words would sound harsh ... nasty even, but her fight—as opposed to her silence—actually gives me hope. This back-and-forth has always been like foreplay for us. I arch an eyebrow, rubbing my hands together.

Bring it on, Red.

The thrill of the chase will be worth it in the end, and when I get her in my bed again, I'll do whatever it takes to keep her there this time.

Chapter 28

Jacinta

I'm a bundle of nerves when Monday morning rolls around. Instead of going to Mason's apartment to collect Blake for school, he's going to bring him here on his way to work.

Apart from a quick text last night, saying he'll be dropping him off around 7.30 am, I haven't heard from Mason since we left Timezone, which I'm thankful for. Avoidance is best. Saturday was so hard, and if it wasn't for Blake, I would've ditched the party altogether. Being around Mason, or having any kind of contact with him, while I'm trying to unpack all these feelings swirling around inside hasn't helped. It's only confused me more.

Do I miss him with every fibre of my being? Absolutely. Am I able to move past his violent outburst? I'm not so sure. It goes against everything I believe in. I know he hit the wall and not me, but it was a side of him I'd never seen before. A side I didn't like one bit. That one action transported me back to my old life, growing up with my abusive father—a place I swore I'd never find myself again.

Did my father start off this way before progressing? I

have no clue. It's a topic I doubt I'll ever broach with my mum. She's happy in her new life, so drudging up her past and forcing her to relive that nightmare is something I don't want for her … for either of us.

I feel like I'm at a crossroads. Do I trust that this is as far as he'll ever take it? Or do I run like hell while I still have the chance? Either way, it's a decision I don't intend to take lightly.

After brushing my teeth, I run my fingers through my hair. I left it down today. The scratches on my face have now scabbed over, and the sight of them makes me sick to my stomach. It's a reminder of everything that went wrong that day. The domino effect that led me to where I am now.

Rummaging through my make-up bag, I take out my mascara and lip gloss. I don't bother with foundation; it doesn't cover the marks on my face very well anyway. I don't need to worry about being interrogated by the parents at school this morning, because that already happened at the party.

My stomach churns when the knock on the door finally comes. Connor has already left; he has court today and needed to leave early. If he was here, I'd ask him to answer it. I know that's the coward's way, but I feel weak around Mason and too easily drawn in by his good looks and charisma. Even though I'm seriously contemplating walking away, he still makes me feel giddy inside whenever I see him.

Hence why my bitchy side keeps rearing its ugly head … she's my defensive armour. It's always worked as a deterrent in the past, but not with Wolf and his beasty tendencies. It's almost like that side of me is an aphrodisiac for him.

I run my shaky hands down the front of my tights as

I approach the door, sucking in a deep breath as I reach for the knob. The moment I open it, Blake jumps forward, wrapping his arms around my middle, but my focus is on his dad. Our eyes are locked, and those all too familiar butterflies in my stomach—that only he can bring—take flight. It's funny what a difference a few days can make. This time last week I would've been leaping into his arms like it was the most natural thing in the world, but now, I'm not sure how to act around him.

"Hey," he utters with a look that says so much. *I miss you ... please come back to me ... I'm sorry.* It's enough to cause a lump in my throat.

Be strong, Jacinta, I remind myself. "Has he eaten? Do I need to pack a lunch for him?"

He exhales a long breath, and the sadness that washes over him hurts my heart. "No. He's eaten, and I've packed his lunch. The girls at Bridge made him some sandwiches last night."

"Okay. We'll be coming straight back here after school, so you don't need to worry."

His lips thin. "I'm not worried, Red. I know you'll look after him."

Blake's arms are still wrapped around me. "Say goodbye to your dad."

This whole situation feels awkward and bizarre ... like we share custody and we're doing a weird and uncomfortable swap over.

"Bye, Dad."

It's only then that Mason's attention is torn away from me. "Bye, buddy," he says, forcing out a smile. "I'll see you tonight."

God, I hate this. Everything in me wants to reach out and hug him. This sad and tortured side is too much. It's exactly why I need to stay away. It is clouding my judgment.

"Okay."

When Blake lets me go and moves inside my apartment, Mason passes me his backpack. "If you need me, you have my number." I nod my head and take a step back. "Goodbye, Red." Why do those words set off a panic inside me?

"Bye."

The dejected look he gives me before he turns and walks away has tears stinging the back of my eyes. The last thing I want to do is hurt him, but my future is on the line here, and if something positive can come from what my mother went through, it's that I don't make the same mistakes she did.

After I dropped Blake off at school, I came straight home and FaceTimed Cassie, bursting into tears the moment her face popped up on the screen. So, it didn't really surprise me when she turned up at my doorstep late this afternoon. She's awesome like that, and will be the perfect buffer when Mason arrives later to collect his son.

Blake is still a little wary with her, but the fact she's my best friend helps. It also didn't hurt that she arrived with half a suitcase full of birthday gifts for him.

"Do you like your presents?" Cassie asks. He's sitting on the floor surrounded by toys, designer clothes, and some new video games she heard him mention on her last visit.

"Yes," he answers, bowing his head. "Thank you."

"Does this mean I get an invite to your birthday party next year?"

When he shrugs, I laugh. I hope I'm around for his next birthday; a lot can happen in a year. What if we can't work through this? What if there's another woman in the picture by then? That thought makes my stomach sink.

"You okay?" Cassie asks.

"Yeah," I lie.

"Are you sure? Your face just dropped?"

"It's nothing," I answer, flicking my hand. She frowns, I can tell she doesn't believe me, but thankfully, she lets it go. I'm getting way ahead of myself anyway. It's only been five days.

By the time Mason arrives, Blake has already eaten dinner. I couldn't bath him like I usually do, because I didn't have his pyjamas here. I need to ask Mason to pack them next time. It's a long day for him, with work and Bridge, so the less he has to do when he gets home, the better.

"Cassandra," Mason says, when she answers the door. "I wasn't expecting to see you."

"I flew here earlier today ... my BFF needed me."

I want to facepalm when she says that. His eyes immediately dart to me before he replies, "That was nice of you."

"You know me," she says, "I'm always looking out for my girl."

"She's lucky to have you."

"I'm lucky to have *her*."

Mason dips his head, shoves his hands into his trouser pockets, and stares down at his feet. "Yeah," is all he says. Did he feel lucky to have me to?

Cassie glances at me over her shoulder. "Now that daddio's here to pick up his cute little mini-me, you

287

should probably jump in the shower and get ready ... it's getting late."

"You guys going somewhere?" he asks.

"Yes, we're going out drinking and dancing ... nothing like a few *cock*tails to lift a girl's spirit."

The way she says cocktails implies so much. *What the hell.* By the time Mason's gaze snaps to me, he's frowning. He's gone from looking miserable to livid. Does he think we're going out looking to pick up? Because that's the last thing on my mind. Despite our situation, my heart's still his.

"Right, well I'd hate to hold you both up. Blake you ready? Grab your bag."

I stand, suddenly feeling panicky. "I've got some left-overs from dinner if you're hungry."

"No thanks."

Umm ... okay then.

While Blake grabs his backpack, I get the bag that contains all his presents from Cassie. "These are Blake's too," I say, holding out the bag.

"Cassie bought me presents," Blake informs him.

"That was nice of her, I hope you said thank you." He's trying to act normal in front of his son, but I can see straight through him. He's majorly pissed. I would be too if I thought he was going out looking for my replacement. Having Cassie here was supposed make things easier, not worse. "Enjoy your night, ladies," he clips on his way out the door.

"Cassie," I snap as soon as we're alone. "What the hell was that?"

"What?" she gasps, feigning innocence.

"You know exactly what you did. We're not even going out for drinks."

"He doesn't have to know that," she retorts, placing her hand on her hip. "I'm just keeping him on his toes."

"Or widening the already unsurmountable gap between us."

She rolls her eyes. "You're so dramatic."

There has been radio silence from Mason since Monday night. It's now Wednesday, and I'm supposed to take Blake to school this morning, so when 8 am comes and goes with no word, I start to worry.

> Red: Hey, just checking you're still dropping Blake off this morning?

Twenty minutes pass and I get no reply, so I decide to call him ... it goes straight to voicemail. I'm about to hang up, but think better of it because I'm worried something may have happened, or possibly Blake is sick. I don't even want to entertain the idea it has something to do with what Cassandra said the other night. "Hi, Mason, it's Jacinta. You didn't drop Blake off this morning, is everything okay? Let me know either way when you get this."

When I end the call, I search for Connor's number in my phone. He answers on the second ring. "Hey, Jaz ... is everything okay?"

"Have you heard from Mason? He didn't drop Blake off this morning."

"Shit," he says. "I was supposed to tell you that Blake wasn't going to school today. Sorry, I forgot."

"Is he sick or something?"

"No, he and Mason have gone away for a few days."

289

Why that news makes my stomach recoil, I can't say. "I didn't know they were planning a trip."

"They weren't. It was a last-minute thing. Mason just said with everything that's gone on lately, he just needed to get away for a few days."

"Do you know where they went?"

"Up north somewhere."

"Oh."

"Are you alright, you sound upset?"

"I'm fine," I lie. "I was just worried one of them might be sick ... I'm glad they're not."

"I've got to go, Jaz, I'm expected in court in a few minutes. I'll talk to you tonight when I get home."

"Okay, bye."

The moment I end the call, I drop my phone onto the bed and bury my face in my hands and cry. Things are worse than I thought, but the truth is, I only have myself to blame.

Chapter 29

Mason

I hold out my arms in front of me when I enter the pool. "Jump."

"I'm scared, Dad."

"I'll catch you."

"But I can't swim."

Of course, he can't swim; why did I not consider that? His mother was lucky to feed him, so the idea that she would take him to swimming lessons is laughable.

I wade through the water and move to the edge, place my hands on the side and push up, lifting my body out of the pool. "Come," I say, guiding him back to the sun lounge where our towels are.

"Are we not going in the pool now?" he asks, looking up at me.

"We are, but we're going to the store in the hotel lobby first to see if they have any floaties I can buy."

"But floaties are for babies," he whines.

"I'll see if they have something cool you can wear."

"Okay."

I really didn't want to pull him out of school for the rest of the week, it's only his first term there, but I couldn't handle being in our apartment building, either running into Red or constantly worrying about what she's up to, or who she is with. The fact that she was going out drinking and dancing with Cassandra less than a week after our breakup really fucked with my head.

I'd been hoping we'd be close to getting back together by now, but I guess that's not the case. Not if she's out living it up already while I sit at home pining for her and feeling sorry for myself.

I needed to get away and regroup. If I'm going to be doing life without her going forward, I need to accept that. I may not like it, but if she no longer wants to be with me, there's not much I can do about it. Am I heartbroken? One hundred percent. It hurts more than I ever thought possible. And that says a lot considering the shit I've lived through. Will I get over her? I have no fucking clue, but if that's what is in my cards, I'll keep moving forward and hope in time it won't hurt so much.

I haven't completely given up. I'm willing to fight for her, but if I'm the only one fighting, it's kind of pointless. The only way to find happiness is to stop worrying about the things that are beyond reach. If fate wants us together, it will happen. If not, then I'll deal with it the best I can.

It's going to suck since we live in the same building; it's inevitable that I'll run into her from time to time, but there's not much I can do about that either. I'm not about to uproot my son again. I'm now thankful we never told him about us, the last thing I'd ever want to do is break his heart as well.

"What about these?" I ask, pointing to some pink Barbie arm floats.

"Daaaad!"

I chuckle, ruffling his hair. "I'm kidding, bud."

I keep walking past all the baby floaties hanging along

the far wall, and stop when I reach the kids life vests. These are more like it. My boy may only be six, but I'm not about to force him into wearing something that's going to ruin his street cred.

"What about these ones?"

He lifts one shoulder. "I guess."

"Blue?"

"Yeah."

I start looking through the rack, until I find one that looks like it might fit. Removing it from the hanger, I crouch down, unzip it, and try it for size.

"I'm going to give you some swimming lessons when we get back in the pool, and this will help you keep afloat until you can swim on your own."

"So, I don't get drowd."

"Drowned? No, I'd never let that happen."

I don't have my wallet on me, so I charge the vest to our room and we head back to the pool area. When I jump back in, I move away from the edge and hold my arms out again. I know he has issues with water, so I want to show him there's nothing to be afraid of. I've got him.

As soon as Red told me about how his mother used to put him in cold showers as punishment, I knew. He's never wanted to shower at home, always opting for a bath. The first day he came to me and I ran him one, I watched him swirl his hand around in the water before he got in ... *"It's warm," he'd said, surprised.* I thought it was a weird thing for him to say at the time, but I completely understand that statement now.

It wasn't until after we'd checked in here that I realised there wasn't a bath in our room, so I guess we'll be tackling his fear of showers while we're here. This mini holiday is going to be new beginnings for both of us.

293

"Come on, buddy, jump," I encourage. "I promise I'll catch you."

Blake tentatively walks to the edge, and this time he doesn't hesitate. I love that he trusts me. I hope things will always stay that way; I'd hate to let him down like I did Jacinta.

His head goes underwater for a split second, but my hands are on him in an instant, and the initial shock on his face when he breaks the surface, is immediately replaced with a smile. "You did it, I'm proud of you."

Moving him around to my back, he wraps his arms around my neck. I can hear him laughing in my ear as I start to breaststroke through the water. Hopefully, I'll have him swimming by the time we leave here. Either way, I'll be getting him regular lessons as soon as we return to Sydney. I want him to be a strong and confident swimmer. I don't want to be worrying about him when he's older and starts going to the beach with his friends.

It is close to lunch time when we get back to the room. "We're going to have a quick shower and then go get something to eat," I tell Blake.

"A shower?"

I see his eyes slightly widen, but I pretend not to notice. "They don't have baths here," I say as he follows me into the bathroom. I reach into the shower stall and turn on the taps. "Is this warm enough for you?" His shoulders visibly relax when he feels the water isn't cold. I leave my swimming shorts on, and climb in. "Strip down and I'll quickly wash your hair for you." His movements are tentative, but he does as I ask. When his hair is washed, I squeeze body wash into his hands, and step out, grabbing a towel. "Wash yourself and I'll grab you some clean clothes."

"Okay, Dad."

That was way easier than I thought. I lift our suitcase onto the bed and open it. Once I have clothes for him and myself, I pick up the remote and turn on the TV. Blake can watch television while I shower. Placing the remote back on the coffee table, I head towards the bathroom, but just as I'm about to enter, I hear something that has me pausing in my tracks.

"Breaking news, earlier today the Honourable Supreme Court Judge, Warren Bradley, was found deceased at his premises in Chatswood." That's a name I hadn't planned, or ever wanted, to hear again. I glance at the screen over my shoulder just as an image of an older version of the man I remember dressed in his judge's robe fills the screen. The sight of my father still affects me after all these years, and not in a good way. My stomach recoils as the clothes I'm holding drop to the carpet by my feet. "Police attended his home to do a welfare check after he had been uncontactable by his staff for a number of days. They are not treating his death as suspicious."

Am I sad he's gone? Not one fucking bit, but any hopes I had of finding out the truth about my mother just died right alongside him.

"I'm finished, Dad."

"Coming, buddy," I say as I bend down to scoop up the clothes I dropped.

I'm sitting in a restaurant while Blake eats his lunch,

when Connor's message comes through. I locked myself in the bathroom and called him as soon as Blake was dressed and preoccupied in front of the television. I'm not even sure why, but I needed to know more and since he works for the police department, I knew he could get some information.

> Connor: I just spoke with one of the officers that attended the scene. Looks like he passed sometime over the weekend. They found him in his bed, they're presuming he died in his sleep. The autopsy will confirm that I suppose.

> Mason: Thanks mate.

> Connor: For what it's worth, I'm sorry.

> Mason: Don't be. I hope he rots in hell.

Harsh I know but that's how I feel. My mother deserved so much more than what she got from him. Sliding my phone back into my pocket, I reach for my coffee and take a sip. I couldn't stomach any food.

I've decided to head back to Sydney this afternoon. I'm not even sure why, but it feels like something I need to do.

"Listen, bud," I say, "we're going to have to cut the holiday short and head back to Sydney."

I watch as he dips his cheeseburger into the glob of sauce on the side of his plate and takes a bite. "Why?"

"Something has come up and I need to get back to deal with it. I promise I'll bring you back here in the school holidays though."

"But we are going on a plane to see Jazzi's mum in the school holidays."

Fuck. I completely forgot we'd booked that. He's going to be crushed when I have to tell him we're no longer going, but I'll save that conversation for another day. I've got enough on my mind right now.

"When you're finished eating, we'll head upstairs and pack."

After dropping Blake off at school, I swing past Connor's office to pick him up. He pulled some strings and got permission to take me to the house. Technically it's not a crime scene, but given my father's high profile, and the circumstances in which he was found, they are treating it as one until they hear back from the coroner.

My stomach churns as we drive down the street where I used to live. So much has changed, but other parts look exactly the same.

I pull up behind the patrol car that is parked by the kerb and see the police tape that's been strung along the front of the property. Leaning forward in my seat, I glance past Connor and out the passenger side window. "It looks a lot smaller than I remember."

"It's a fucking mansion," Connor replies.

"I know, but I guess when you're a kid your perception of things are different."

"When was the last time you were here?"

"Sixteen years ago."

"Wow. So, you and your mum got away then?"

"My mum disappeared when I was twelve ... I ran away when I was thirteen."

"What do you mean disappeared? She left you here with him?"

"I don't know what happened to her. She was here one day and gone the next."

"You are my best friend, how come there's so much I don't know about your past?"

"One, because I don't like talking about it, and two, we're not chicks."

"What's that supposed to mean?"

"Men don't sit around talking about feelings."

"I told you my mum died when I was a kid."

"Of cancer, not at the hands of your father."

I see his attention snap to me in my peripheral vision. "You think your dad killed your mum?"

I shrug. "I don't know. Stuff happened the night before she disappeared ... it's a possibility."

"What kind of stuff?"

I remove my seat belt and reach for the door handle. "You're acting like a chick, Maloney."

"I am not," he whines as he exits the car and jogs to catch up to me as I duck under the police tape and stalk down the driveway. I don't want to be back here; so much fucked-up shit is running through my head already as we approach the house. "Did you ever report it?"

"I was twelve ... my father was a well-respected judge with friends in high places. You of all people should understand that."

"Enough said." He falls into step beside me. "We might find some evidence when we're in there," he states, flicking his head towards the house. That's the law in him speaking ... I seriously doubt my father was stupid enough not to cover his tracks. If by chance there is anything, I know exactly where to look. His office. It was always locked, and somewhere my mother and I were never allowed to enter.

Connor shakes hands with the officer who's standing

by the front door when we climb the stairs that lead to the porch. "Are we right to go in?" he asks.

"You'll need to put on these," the officer replies, reaching into the box near his feet and pulling out two pairs of blue booties. It makes me seethe inside. I hate that my father is getting any kind of special treatment just because he died. That motherfucker doesn't deserve it.

After sliding the stupid booties over my shoes, I push through the front door and I pause as soon as we enter the house. My gaze moves around the foyer, and my first thought is nothing has changed since I left. I close my eyes and dip my head as a multitude of images plays out in my head, like a fast forward snapshot of my life.

"You okay?" Connor asks, placing his hand on my shoulder. "We can walk straight back out if you're not ready."

I don't think I'll ever be ready to face the hell that I lived through in this house, but if I leave now, I know I'll never return. "I'm fine," I answer, releasing the breath I'd been holding. "I want to go to my father's office first. I want to know what's in there."

"Lead the way."

I take a few steps forward, pausing briefly to take in the mahogany staircase. My eyes move down to the base, specifically to the rug that's now lying there. I head straight for it, lifting one corner, and bile rises to my throat the moment I do. You can clearly see the dark stain embedded into the hardwood floors, and that sight conjures up the image of my mother's twisted body lying right there before me.

Quickly dropping the rug, I take a few hasty steps backwards. My reaction is enough to alert Connor. He mimics me by looking under the rug.

"Is there a way to test if that stain is blood?" I ask.

299

"It looks like it's been there for a while. Besides, your father wasn't found down here; he was upstairs in his bed."

"I'm not enquiring about that cunt. I don't give two fucks about when or how he died ... I'm just glad he did."

"Dude, that's a bit harsh."

"Harsh, are you fucking kidding me?" I yell. "That man would sometimes beat me so bad I'd piss blood for days? I was a kid, Connor, a defenceless fucking kid. And don't even get me started on the things he did to my poor mum. The Honourable Warren Bradley ... what a joke. He should've been in prison, not presiding in court. The man people saw outside of these four walls was a carefully constructed illusion. The real Warren Bradley was a malicious, spiteful, evil monster. The devil personified."

He bows his head. "I'm sorry."

Tearing the rug from his grip, I point to the stain, "I'm pretty sure this is my mother's blood. The last memory I have of her is lying right here, in this spot, in a crumpled mess ... it happened the night before she vanished. That bastard pushed her down the stairs." I point to the landing above us. "He was standing at the top just looking down at her. Not rendering her aid ... not calling for help. I heard her scream ... it still fucking haunts me. When I came out of my room and asked if she was okay, he chased me back in there and threatened to kick my arse if I came out."

"Shit," I hear him mumble. I drop the rug and storm down the long corridor that runs parallel to the staircase. "Where are you going?"

"To look for answers."

I'm expecting to find the office door locked, but surprisingly, it isn't. I guess being here on his own meant it wasn't necessary. It's the first time I've ever stepped foot in this room, yet I don't even stop to take any of it in; the anger that rages inside me—something only that man can fuel—has me wanting to smash this place to pieces.

My gaze quickly scans the room, and when I see a wooden filing cabinet in the back corner, I head straight for it. As I slide open the top drawer, I hear Connor enter. "Check the desk," I tell him.

"What am I looking for?"

"I have no clue. Anything incriminating."

My fingers skim through each folder, utilities, insurance, registration, bank statements ... nothing out of the ordinary. "This drawer is locked," Connor says. "Do you know where I'd find the key?"

I stop what I'm doing, glancing over my shoulder. "No clue."

"Can you remember where he used to leave his house or car keys, it may be with them?"

I rack my brain for a second, it's been so long since I've even thought of this place or that man. As I open my mouth to speak, a memory starts to play out in my head ...

"Oh, my poor baby," my mother whispers, leaning forward to blow air over my grazed knee. When her brown eyes move up to my face, I see tears glistening in them.

It's been almost seventeen years since I lost her, and I'd forgotten just how beautiful she was. Her dark-brown hair is pulled back into a low bun at the nape of her neck and tiny round pearl earrings sit in each lobe. They match the one hanging from the pendant on the gold chain around her neck.

Over time, her features have faded and blurred in my mind, but this image of her is so clear ... so vivid, I almost feel like I can reach out and touch her. Christ, I'd give anything to be able to hug her one more time, or tell her how much I love and miss her ... to apologise for not being able to protect her.

I inhale a deep breath through my nose. She always used to smell so good, like the flowers in her garden.

Her hand skims lovingly down the side of my face, as her thumb gently swipes under my eye, catching the tear that just fell.

My eyelids drift shut, as I saviour the memory of her touch.

"Don't cry, baby, mummy will make it all better for you." She leans in, placing her lips on my forehead. "Let me get a Band-Aid, but I have to be quick, your father will be home any minute and I need to be at the door waiting to greet him when he arrives."

She used to do that every night, not by choice, I'm sure.

I watch her scurry across the kitchen, and the skirt of the lemon dress she's wearing sways with each step. She pushes up onto her toes, hastily grabbing a large cane basket out of one of the upper cabinets. There's a sweet smile on her face as she makes her way back to me. She places the basket on the counter beside me. I look down at my injured knee, and notice my small hand resting on my thigh.

It's not much bigger than Blake's, so I must be young.

She squeezes a small amount of cream onto her finger, lightly dabbing it on my injury. I intake a sharp breath because it stings.

Her hand shakes, and I focus on the dark bruise that circles her wrist. "I'm sorry, baby boy," she whispers. "This will help make it better and stop it from getting infected."

I watch on as my mother wipes her finger on the apron that's tied around her waist and rummages through the basket for the box of Band-Aids, but before she has a chance to find them, the front door slams closed. Her body instantly stiffens and panic sets in on her pretty face. It's a look I'm familiar with, and I hate seeing her like this.

"Rebecca," my father screams from down the hall, and she quickly slides her trembling hands under my arms, lifting me off the counter before turning and dashing from the room.

I follow, but instead of going towards the front door, I slink back into the darkened hallway. I can feel my little heart beating out of my chest as I hide in the shadows.

"What have I told you about not being here to greet me when I return, you ungrateful, selfish woman. I've been out working all day, and this is how you treat me? This is the thanks I get?"

His arm rises, and I can see he's still holding his keys in his hand as it connects with the side of my mum's face. She whimpers and the force behind his hit almost knocks her off her feet. I can feel the warm tears running down my cheeks as I watch on. I feel helpless, and wish I was bigger so I could protect her from him.

My father calmly places the briefcase he's holding by his feet, shrugs out of his jacket, and tosses it in her direction. She quickly scurries to pick it up, and when she turns to hang it in the hall closet, I can see the trickle of blood running down the side of her face. The keys must have cut her. I hate him. I hate him so much.

He opens the side drawer on the hall table, dropping the keys inside. Bending slightly, he picks up his briefcase. "My dinner better be ready," he barks.

"I just need to dish it up, Warren" she replies, and I can hear the fear in her voice.

"Hurry up, I'm starving."

When he starts walking in my direction, heading

303

towards his office, I quickly duck into the half bath off the hallway and slide my small body behind the opened door.

My eyelids flutter open, and I find Connor watching me with a strange look on his face. "He used to keep his keys in the side drawer of the hall table by the front door," I say.

He nods once, and as soon as he leaves the room, I tilt my head back, digging the heal of my palms into my eye sockets. I shouldn't have come back here; the sensory overload this place brings with it is way too fucking much.

A minute later, he returns jiggling a set of keys in his hand. "You were right."

Of course I was; that scene that just played out in my head was way too detailed not to be real, and my father may have been an abusive piece of shit, but he was also a creature of habit.

I watch as Connor tries the keys he's holding, and on his third attempt, he finds one that fits. "Bingo," he says, sliding it open. He pulls out the large yellow envelope that's sitting on top. "This one has your name on it."

Closing the distance between us, I take it out of his hand. I'm not sure what I'm expecting to find inside, but I highly doubt it's a confession or an apology. And I'm right. Instead, I'm sickened by what I see inside. There is a stack of eight-by-ten photographs, all of me. The anger inside me grows as I flip through the pile. They are images of me living on the streets, and although I'm wearing the same clothes, because that's all I had, I can tell by the locations that they were taken over a series of days, because in the beginning, I moved around a lot. He must've had someone track me down and follow me.

My dark mattered hair is hanging in my face; it had been many months since I'd had my hair cut. The last time was prior to my mother's disappearance. I look so young, so frightened, so lost. Fuck, those first few days, weeks, and months on the streets were the hardest. I was starving, cold, and so damn scared.

Connor takes one of the images out of my hand. It's of me sitting by a brick wall, my eyes are wide, like I'm on guard. My knees are pulled up to my chest with my arms wrapped tightly around my legs, I have a black eye and I'm not wearing any shoes. I remember someone had beaten me and stole them right off my feet.

"Jesus Christ, Mason," he says as he stares down at the photograph. The compassion and pity I hear in his voice chokes me up. "You were so young."

"It was taken after I ran away ... when I was living on the streets. I can't believe he knew where I was and did nothing. Granted, I was probably safer out there, then being here with him, but this just shows how cold-hearted he was."

"Exactly ... what a cunt."

"Oh, so you agree with me now?"

"This," he says, holding up the picture in his hand and shaking his head. I watch as he swallows thickly, and when his eyes glisten, I have to look away. He steps forward, wrapping his arms around me and squeezing tight. "I'm so fucking sorry you had to go through this."

I clear my throat when I feel tears sting the back of my eyes. "You're acting like a chick again," I mumble, pushing out of his hold. I can't deal with his kindness or compassion right now. Losing Red, and now this ... it's all too much. I feel like I'm ready to break, and that's the last thing I want. I need to keep it together ... *I've got to stay strong for my son.*

Dropping the photos and the envelope onto the desk, I rummage through the drawer. My heart drops when I find a second yellow envelope, with *Rebecca* written at the top. Is she still alive? Did my father have her tracked down and photographed as well?

I flip open the lip and peer inside. I don't find any photos though, just paperwork. I pull it out and see a receipt sitting on top. It's for a slab of concrete. I glance up at the date, it was around the time of her disappearance. I flip to the next one and find the plans for a shed. I remember when that was built; he had it erected down in the rear of the backyard on top of the slab. In the bottom of the envelope lies a single key. Why would these items be in an envelope marked with her name? Then it dawns on me.

Fuck.

I fish out the key and rush from the room. "Where are you going?"

"The backyard," I answer.

I can feel my body trembling from the adrenaline as I storm across the grass. I stick the key into the lock when I reach the shed, turning it. There are no windows, so it's dark when I step inside. Pulling out my phone, I click on the torch, shining it around the space. It's completely empty.

"What did you expect to find in here?" Connor asks.

"The envelope that had my mother's name on it had the plans for this shed, and the receipt for the concrete slab inside it ... nothing else, apart from this key," I answer. "This was erected not long after she went missing."

It takes a second, but when his eyes widen, he realises. "Do you think she's buried under here?"

I don't even want to contemplate that, but it's definitely a possibility. I bend, placing my hands on my knees. I'm suddenly finding it hard to breathe. Although in my heart I've always believed there was more to her disappearance, there were times, especially when I was living on the streets, that I resented her for leaving me. For not taking me with her.

Connor takes a step away from me and pulls out his phone. "What are you doing?" I ask.

"Calling in a forensics team."

Chapter 30

Jacinta

I clutch the jar of red jellybeans in my hands to my chest as I step off the lift. I bought these when I found out about Mason's father's passing. I know they didn't have a great relationship, but I still felt like I needed to acknowledge it. Flowers just didn't seem like an appropriate thing to buy for such a manly man like Mason.

Blake is downstairs in our apartment with my brother and Cassie. Connor offered to pick him up from school. He gave me a brief rundown on what happened at Mason's father's house, and said he was pretty fucked up by the time they left. I felt compelled to come up here. Being alone is maybe what he wants, but I feel the need to check on him nevertheless.

When I reach his apartment, I come to a stop. Will he even want to see me?

Tucking the jar under my arm, I raise my hand and knock. A minute or so passes with no answer. I lift my arm for a second time, but think better of it. If he wants to be alone, I need to respect that.

I bend over, placing the jar by the door, but as I do, it

swings open. I tilt my head back and look up, seeing Mason smirking down at me.

My eyes dart down, and that's when I realise my face is only inches away from his crotch. "Did you come here to see me?" he asks. "Or to stare at my dick?"

I grab the jar and straighten. Everything in me wants to reply with something sarcastic, but I push that feeling down. He's going through a lot right now. Instead, I hold out the jar. "I just came up here to say sorry for your loss."

"My loss?" he quips. Now that I'm standing upright, I can smell the alcohol on his breath. "You really think that I—or this crazy fucking world we live in—is at a loss now that that motherfucker is dead?"

"I ... ah—"

"You disappoint me, Red. I thought you of all people would understand. We'd all be better off if people like your father ... *like mine*, no longer existed."

I glance down at my feet because he's one hundred percent right. "Yes, we would be," I whisper.

"Then why are you sorry?"

I lift one shoulder. "It just felt like the right thing to say. I'm sure in some way you're hurting."

He reaches out, gently tilting my face back to meet his. "Not because of him. I'm not sorry he's dead, I'm glad. Wouldn't you feel safer—*relieved even*—if you knew your father was no longer able to inflict pain on others?"

"Yes," I answer as tears sting the back of my eyes.

"Then for once we can actually agree on something."

"Is there anything I can do for you? Are you hungry? Can I make you something to eat?" Drinking on an empty stomach can't be good for him.

"I'm hungry, Red, but not for food." I have to look away when he says that, because the intensity of his stare tells me exactly what he's hungry for ... *me*. "I've missed

309

this," he mutters, skating his knuckle over my flushed cheek. "I've missed everything about you, Jacinta."

I've missed him too, so damn much, but I'm still apprehensive about us. His violent outburst is still weighing heavily on my mind. That side of him frightens me.

My eyes move back to his, and the smugness that was there a moment ago is now replaced with sorrow, and it pains me to see him like this. "Do you feel like some company?" I ask, because I don't want to leave him on his own. Especially if he's planning on drinking his troubles away.

"What kind of company are you offering?" I look away. "Right, I forgot, we can't do that since you've decided you no longer want me."

The venom in his voice has my gaze snapping back to him. "I never said that ... what I said was I needed space."

"From me?"

"You scared me when you put your fist through the wall."

"And you broke my heart when you deserted me."

"I never deserted you."

"Really? What would you call it then?"

I puff out a breath of air. "I'm sorry if you feel like I did."

He takes a step back. "If you'll excuse me, there's a bottle of Jack waiting for me. Oh, and thanks for the jellybeans."

He goes to close the door, so I quickly raise my arm, stopping it. "Please don't ride yourself off. Do you really want your son to see you like that?"

"No, I don't, but I need to do something to get all this messed up shit out of my head, and since I no longer have you to lose myself in, alcohol is the next best thing."

Before I even think it through, the words, "Let me help you with that," fall from my mouth.

He arches a brow. "Are you telling me you're willing to take one for the team, Red?"

"If that's what you need, then yes."

"Come on in then," he says without hesitation, and I may be making a huge mistake by doing this, but I care enough to do whatever is needed to ease his pain.

I tentatively follow him inside and stand back when he crosses the room and places the jar of jellybeans on the coffee table, then plonks himself down onto the lounge. The bottle of Jack Daniels sitting in front of him is already missing a third of its contents. There is no glass beside it, so I can only presume he's been drinking it straight from the bottle.

"How did you manage to get your hands on so many red jellybeans?" he asks, eyeing the jar.

"I cleaned out every Woolworths and Coles within a thirty-kilometre radius."

"What did you do with the other colours?"

"I have a lifetime supply in my apartment."

He nods his head. "I appreciate the effort you went to. Thank you."

"You're welcome."

There's a brief silence before he speaks again. "Are you just going to stand there all afternoon, or are you going to come over here and sit on my lap?" He sits up straighter in his seat, spreads his legs a little wider, and taps his open palm against his thick thigh. "Don't be shy, Red." I take a tentative step forward, followed closely by another one. Despite my reservations about us, I still hunger for this man. He lifts his hand, crooking his fore-finger. "Keep coming."

The second I'm within reach, he leans forward,

capturing me around the waist and dragging me down onto his lap.

"Hi," I squeak, because I don't know what else to say.

Mason shakes his head and chuckles. "You're still as adorable as ever, but I think we've already covered the pleasantries. Now I want to know what you're going to do to help me forget?"

"Any suggestions?"

He brings his face forward, and his eyes track the movement of his thumb as he drags down my bottom lip. "We could start with a kiss."

The air around us crackles as our gazes lock. Our mouths are mere inches apart, but neither of us make the move to join them. The anticipation of being with him like this again has all the nerve endings throughout my body pinging to life. Nobody can make me feel as alive as this man does.

My hand moves to affectionately skim over his hair. Despite him giving me his full attention, I can see how troubled and dejected he is by the things he learnt today.

"Kiss me, Red," he pleads, in a voice that feels like warm syrup running over my skin.

I inch my face forward, and by the time our lips connect, my eyelids have drifted closed. Mason's big, strong hands move from my waistline to cup my jaw, so he can tilt my head back sightly and deepen the kiss. This kiss is so profound, so sensual, I feel it right down to the tip of my toes.

I'm still sitting sideways on one of Mason's legs, but he effortlessly maneuverers me until I'm straddling his waist. His hands clutch my hips, dragging my lower body down to meet his, and I can feel his hardness through his jeans. I ache for this man.

He groans into my mouth when I grind myself against

him. Gripping my ponytail, he tugs my head back as his lips move to my neck. "Don't mark me."

Pausing for a moment, his eyes flicker up to my face. "Why? Because you're no longer mine?"

"No, because I have no intention of going out, or being with anyone else."

"And the other night?"

"We stayed home."

"Good," he growls as he runs his flattened tongue over my skin.

Although staying home was our intention all along, I'm not going to throw Cassie under the bus. Her objective may have been misguided, but the sentiment behind it wasn't.

The hand that's still on my waist moves in between us, slipping down the front of my tights. He scoots me a little further back on his lap to gain better access, and when his fingers slide into my underwear, I angle my head back and moan.

His fingertips move back and forth over my sensitive flesh, and it's only been a week without him, but I've missed these feelings he evokes in me.

My breath hitches in my throat when he slides a thick finger deep inside me. "That's it, babe," he utters when I roll my hips forward. "You're so tight, so wet ... I've missed your pussy." He withdraws his finger, and when he drives back in, I can feel he's added a second digit. The delicious feeling of being stretched wide has me whimpering. His mouth seeks out mine as his thumb moves to my clit, adding the perfect amount of pressure. When he pushes all the way in, knuckles deep, I jerk my pelvis forward, because like always, I can't seem to get enough of him. "Fuck my fingers, Red ... yes, just like that."

I'm seconds away from coming, but he suddenly withdraws, tugging my top over my head and tossing it aside. When he lifts me off his lap, I'm confused. He places me down beside him and abruptly stands, bending to reach for the waistband of my tights.

He hastily drags them down my legs, along with my underwear. When I'm stripped of everything but my bra, he stands to full height and takes me in. His tongue darts out and skims over his lips as he palms his cock through his jeans.

"I need to taste you," he growls.

Reaching for my ankles, he spreads my legs wide before dropping to his knees. My back arches off the cushion as soon as his mouth is on me. "Oh, God," I moan, threading my fingers into his hair when he pushes his tongue deep inside me, wiggling it around.

"I want to hear you scream my name when I make you come."

He moves back to my clit, swirling his tongue around in circles, and when I fall over the edge, I tug on his strands. "Mason!"

I feel his lips curve against my skin when I call out his name. He doesn't stop lapping me up until he's drained every ounce of pleasure from me. And when he's done, he places a soft kiss on my inner thigh.

"Good girl," he whispers against my skin. Straightening his body, he reaches for the neck of his shirt, whipping it over his head. His eyes are on me as he pops the button of his jeans. "I'm going to fuck you so hard, Red; you'll be lucky if you can walk by the time I'm through with you."

There's nothing about his words that frighten me. Even when he loses control of himself during sex, he never hurts me.

"I can take whatever you dish out," I say.

314

"I don't doubt that for a second, sweetheart," he retorts, dragging my body to the edge of the cushion. He tugs down the cup of my bra, leaning in to suck my hardened nipple into his mouth whilst dragging himself back and forth through my arousal. "You've been craving my humungous man sausage ... haven't you, Red?"

I narrow my eyes, because I know he's making fun of me now. "Not one bit."

"Liar."

"Don't get a head of yourself, Wolf, this doesn't mean anything. It's purely a distraction *for you* and nothing more."

A smile tugs at his mouth as he runs his flattened palms up the back of my legs, then hooks them behind my knees. He pushes them down towards my body and opens me up wide for him. "That's where you're wrong, babe." He glides the head of his cock inside me before driving all the way home. When his eyelids drift closed and he tilts back his head, a long, drawn-out groan falls from his lips. "This means everything," he growls, drawing back to the tip before thrusting back in. "Every. Fucking. Thing."

Chapter 31

Mason

The last few days have been an absolute shitshow. I'm physically and emotionally exhausted. I haven't heard from Jacinta since she let me use her body as a distraction, but I've been too preoccupied to let that worry me. I haven't gone back to work this week, but I've still been sending Blake to school. I don't want to be dragging him all over the place while I try and sift through this clusterfuck my father left behind. I want to shield him from all of it.

Connor has had the forensic team combing over the house for the past few days, and I've had to meet with the detectives a few times to give them detailed statements of what I remember about the night before my mother disappeared and his prior behaviour towards her. A firsthand glimpse at what the not-so-honourable Warren Bradley was like behind closed doors. It's forced me to relive so much of my past that I've kept buried, that by the time I lay my head on the pillow each night, I'm tempted to reach out to Red. She gave me a selfless gift the other day —although she did get two orgasms out of it—but I'm not about to take advantage of her like that. I can't continue to rely on her for a distraction—even if it means I get to spend time with her—because if she never comes back to me, I'm going to have to find other ways to cope moving forward.

Besides, it's only going to make it harder to get over her if I do. My time with her the other day was way too short and only made me miss her more. Every glance, every smile, every touch, every kind gesture, only amplifies the magnitude of my loss. It's another thing I can add to the growing list of why I hate my father. My coping mechanism to deal with him as a kid carried into my adulthood. It's what fucked up my relationship with Red.

I want her back full-time, not as a temporary stand-in. I love her, but I refuse to utter those words until she knows what she wants. It's not fair to put that on her if she's not sure about us.

"So, what's the plan from here?" I ask Connor as he takes a seat at my dining table.

"There's enough evidence to excavate the backyard."

"They're going to knock down the shed and pull up the slab?"

"Yes, with your permission of course."

"I don't give a fuck about that place; they can bull-doze the entire thing for all I care, I just want to find out what happened to my mum."

"I was able to track down his will," Connor says, pulling a manila envelope from his briefcase and sliding it across the table towards me.

"I'm not interested in that."

"He left everything to you ... the houses, his extensive share portfolio, the bank accounts, all of it."

"I don't want it."

"Half of what he owned rightfully belonged to your mother. His estate will go into probate, and if you decide you still don't want any of it, give it away. Think about what that kind of money could do for Bridge. You said yourself you're struggling to keep your head above water. We're talking multiple millions here, Mason. You could even donate some to a charity for battered women, in memory of your mum."

I lift one shoulder, because as of right now I want nothing from that man ... not a damn penny. But Connor's right; that kind of money could help a lot of people. It would be enough to help me fully realise Betty's dream, and I like the idea of doing something in my mother's name. I couldn't help her, but I might be able to help others in the same situation.

"I'll think about it."

"It's probably going to take a week or so to get everything organised, but do you want to be present for the dig when it happens?"

"Would you think I was a coward if I said no?"

"Of course not. If I was in your shoes, I doubt I'd want to be there either."

"Then no, I don't want to be present."

"I'll be there," he says, "and I'll make sure that if she's found, she'll be treated with the utmost respect."

My nostrils flare and my eyes burn as I push my chair back and stand. When I turn and leave the room, Connor lets me go. I'm not mad at him, not in the slightest. I'm grateful that I have someone like him in my corner. He's been amazing, but knowing that my mother may be lying underneath that slab of concrete is something I don't know how to deal with.

Blake's eyes move from me to Red. "Can I go back and finish watching my movie now?"

"Do you want seconds?" she asks.

Like always, she made us a beautiful dinner. Tonight, when she invited me to stay, I accepted. Although I still don't know where I stand with her, I like being around her. In a way, it feels like old times, and the fact that she even wants me here gives me hope.

"I need to leave room for my ice cream," Blake answers.

"Who said you're having ice cream?" I chime in.

"Jazzie."

My attention moves back to her; it gives me the perfect excuse to stare without looking like a creeper. I arch a brow. "Did she now?"

She looks gorgeous today. There's a light dusting of make-up on her face that only enhances her natural beauty. Her long hair is down, and she's wearing a sexy, little white sundress, which has large blue flowers printed on it ... it makes her pretty eyes pop. I want to eat her up.

"What?" she asks. "I always give him a small bowl of ice cream after dinner."

"Do I get one too?"

"If you behave yourself."

I push my plate away and rest my arms on the table. "Define what you mean by behave?" When she looks away and her cheeks pinken, I know exactly where her mind went. Leaning forward in my seat, I swipe my tongue along my bottom lip. "Are you going to answer me, Red?"

"I need to clear the table," she says, standing and lifting her plate.

I do the same and follow her into the kitchen. She heads straight for the sink, and I'm hot on her heels. Turning on the tap, she starts rinsing her dish. I slide my arm around her tiny waist, and I hear her breath hitch as I lean around her to hold my plate under the spray. She makes no attempt to free herself from my grip.

I dip my face until my mouth is level with her ear. "Are you sure you want me to behave?"

She nibbles on her bottom lip but doesn't answer. A smile tugs at my mouth. She doesn't need to say the words; I know the answer. If my son wasn't sitting in the other room, I'd lift her onto the countertop, spread her wide, and eat her for dessert.

When Blake enters the kitchen, I release my hold on her and take a step back. "Can I have my ice cream now, please?"

"Sure, sweetie," she says, and I don't miss the wobble in her voice. "Do you want chocolate topping and sprinkles?"

"Yes please."

I lean against the counter, cross my arms over my chest, and observe her every move. *The things I want to do to her in that dress.* She glances at me over her shoulder. "Do you want dessert?"

My eyes shamelessly run down the length of her tight body. "I think you know the answer to that one, Red."

I roll my lips together when she blushes again.

Blake is back on the lounge watching his show, and

Red and I are sitting at the table. I'm eating my ice cream while she sips on a cup of coffee. Her attention seems to be hyper focused on the spoon in my hand, especially every time it enters my mouth. She's trying to hide behind her mug, but I know what's going on here, so I make sure I put on a good show, running the silverware along the length of my tongue and occasionally licking my lips. I don't miss the way she squirms in her seat when I do. She's hot for me, there's no denying it. The sad part is, both of us will be left unsatisfied when this night is over.

"How have you been coping with everything?" she asks. "Connor told me they're going to start excavating."

I nod my head once and drop the spoon back into the bowl, pushing it away because my appetite is now lost. "Next week. I've been meaning to talk to you about that. I know we had plans to fly to Melbourne to see your parents, and given our current situation," I say, clearing my throat, "I'm presuming that's now off the table."

She places her mug down. "I was still planning on taking the trip, I haven't seen my parents in a few months."

"Would you mind if Blake and I tagged along? Just on the flight. I know you're still wanting space, so I'll book us a hotel. I don't want to be around here when ..." My words drift off, and when I bow my head, Jacinta reaches across the table and wraps her fingers around mine.

"I completely understand, and there's plenty of room at my parents' place, if you guys want to stay there."

"I appreciate it, but I think I'll book us into a hotel."

"Umm ... sure, okay." If I'm not mistaken, my rejection of her offer hurt her. It wasn't done maliciously; I simply don't want her to feel uncomfortable by having me around whilst she visits with her parents.

"I know the flights are already booked, but I'll go

ahead and make the other arrangements, and organise for an airport shuttle to pick us up from here."

She rises from her seat, picks up her mug and then reaches for my bowl. When she leaves the room without another word, it confirms my suspicions.

Chapter 32

Jacinta

I've been up since 4 am, because I couldn't sleep. I'm in two minds about this trip to Melbourne today. Of course, I'm excited to see my parents and Cassie, I'm also happy that Mason and Blake are coming with me, but I'm not sure how I'm going to explain their hotel stay to my mum. I haven't told her that we're taking a break, because I'm worried once she finds out why she'll tell me I did the right thing. *I'm not sure if I did.*

Does his fist going through the wall concern me? Yes. Do I think he'd ever direct that violence towards me? My gut tells me no, but that's not a guarantee. I want to be one hundred percent sure before I walk through that door again.

By the time eight o'clock rolls around, I'm a bundle of nerves. I've been sitting on the lounge dressed and ready for the past two hours with my suitcase beside me. Mason said the shuttle bus will be here to pick us up at quarter past, so I probably should start making my way downstairs.

Our flight doesn't leave until eleven. Mason wants to

323

have breakfast at the airport once we've checked in, but I'm not sure if I can stomach food right now.

Connor has already left for work, so I'm home alone. I stand and start wheeling my suitcase towards the front door just as someone knocks. I told Mason I'd meet them out the front of the building when he texted me the information, but when I open the door, I find him and Blake standing there.

"Jazzie," Blake shouts, rushing forward to hug my legs.

"Morning," I say, but my eyes are on his father. Why does he make my heart race whenever I'm in his presence?

His eyes rake down my body before coming back to rest on my face. "You look lovely." I'm wearing a pair of tight black jeans, a black top, and I paired it with knee-length tan boots and a matching suede jacket. "I'm a huge fan of those boots."

The heat in his eyes when he says that has a blush rising to my cheeks. "Thank you." I move my gaze away from his face, because he's far too handsome for his own good, and the intensity of his stare sometimes overwhelms me.

I use this time to take him in. He's wearing a light-blue, linen, button-up shirt with the sleeves rolled up to his elbows. He's left his shirt untucked over his white straight-legged jeans, and there's a pair of camel-coloured loafers on his feet. "You ... umm ... look nice too."

He chuckles at my statement because I think he relishes in making me feel uncomfortable.

"Do I look nice, Jazzie?" Blake asks.

I squat down in front of him. "Yes, you do. You're going to be the handsomest boy on the entire plane." The little smile that lights up his face warms my heart, and as

I'm standing to full height, I see his father roll his eyes. "Are we ready?"

"Just waiting on you," Mason says. I wheel my suitcase into the hallway and close the door behind me. "Are you moving back home?"

"What?"

"I'm just wondering since the suitcase you're bringing is nearly as tall as you. You do realise we're only going for a few days, right?"

I narrow my eyes. "I don't know if you've ever been to Melbourne before, but it's not uncommon to get four seasons in one day. A girl needs to be prepared."

That gains me another eye roll. "Chicks," he mumbles under his breath as he reaches for the handle of my suitcase.

"I can wheel my own luggage."

He just ignores me, moving forward with his in one hand and mine in the other.

"I have my own luggage, Jazzie," Blake says proudly as he drags his little suitcase along beside him. I smile down at him when his free hand reaches for mine.

Since it was Blake's first time on the plane, we gave him the window seat. That meant I was seated in the middle, surrounded by Wolf's intoxicating scent for the entire flight, with his arm constantly rubbing up against me. Occasionally his pinkie finger would brush mine, and the one time I needed to get up to use the bathroom, his hand skimmed over my arse ... upon the exit and return to my seat. Of course, he claimed it was an accident both times, but the cheeky smile he gave me when he apologised told me it most definitely wasn't.

Needless to say, by the time we land I'm a horny, hot mess.

Blake seemed to enjoy the flight, especially the takeoff and landing. He spent the majority of the time looking out the window and eating the abundance of snacks I packed for him. When we first got to the airport, he was a little overwhelmed by the amount of people and clung to Mason and I.

I'm sure he's still traumatised by the incident with his mother, although he never talks about it. His father and I have both told him he's safe now. Annalise is still locked up, awaiting trial. Connor told the judge she was a flight risk, and a danger to Blake, and thankfully, he agreed.

I told Mason not to organise a transfer from Melbourne to their hotel, because I know my parents would want to collect us. He's still adamant about staying somewhere else, but I know my mother, she won't stand for that. Hence why I talked him into meeting them before him and Blake leave the airport.

My parents are already waiting for us by the time we reach the baggage claim area. As we approach them, my mum lets go of my father's hand and rushes towards me. I release my hold on Blake, who is walking in the middle of his father and I, his little hands clutched in ours, and run into her open arms.

"I've missed you, sweetie," she says, wrapping me up tight.

"I've missed you too, Mumma."

"Oh, my gosh, my heart when the three of you were walking towards us hand in hand." She draws back and cups my face, "Love looks good on you, baby girl." Don't ask me why, but her words have tears rising to my eyes.

Love?

That's a word I've been fighting with for a while now, but she's right, *I do love him* ... I love them both, *so much*. My brain may have been toying with the idea, but my heart already knew the truth. That's why this decision has been so hard. If it was anyone else, I would've walked away and never looked back, but this is Mason Bradley we're talking about. His swoony—yet sometimes infuriating—arse is impossible not to love.

When the boys reach us, my mum wraps Mason in her arms and mouths to me, "Oh, gosh, he's gorgeous." I smile at that, because he most definitely is. She lets him go and takes a step back. "I'm Grace, Jacinta's mother, it's so lovely to meet you."

"Mason," he says, holding out his hand to her. "It's lovely to meet you too."

"So well mannered," she replies, "And handsome." Her attention moves to me. "You've done well, sweetie."

Well, this is awkward.

I catch Mason's side-eye, but ignore it. He obviously now realises I haven't told my mum what happened between us.

My father joins us, so I introduce him to Mason first. While they shake hands, my mum squats down in front of Blake. "And you must be Blake," she says. "I'm Jacinta's mum, my name is Grace, but you can call me Grandma if you like."

"Mum," I screech, and I hear Mason bark out a laugh beside me.

"I've never had a grandma before," Blake says, and here come the tears again.

"Well, you do now, sweet boy."

"I'm Jim," my dad says, extending his hand to Blake. "I'm Jacinta's dad."

327

"The nice one?"

"Yes, the nice one," he replies with a chuckle.

"I bet you guys are hungry," my mum says. "We've booked a table at your favourite restaurant for lunch, Jaz."

"Blake and I are actually heading to a hotel; we don't want to intrude."

"Nonsense, you're staying with us."

Blake tugs on his dad's jeans. "I want to have lunch with Grandma and Jazzie."

"Oh, I could just squish you," my mother says to Blake, hugging him. "You are the cutest thing ever."

Mason clears his throat before saying, "I guess we could do lunch, if it's alright with Jacinta."

I open my mouth to speak, but my mother gets in first. "You two are family now, and my daughter loves you, so of course it's alright."

"Kill me now," I mumble under my breath.

Mason, however, uses the opportunity to his advantage, throwing his arm over my shoulder and pulling my body against his. He even leans down and places a soft kiss on the top of my head. "The feeling is mutual, Grace, I can assure you."

Oh. My. God!

Did he just tell me he loved me—in a roundabout-way —for the first time? I mean, he did say it once after we had monkey sex against his front door, but I'm pretty sure that was his dick speaking, not him.

"Look at you two all loved up, you've made this mumma one very happy lady."

Mason's arm is still wrapped around my shoulder as we wait for the bags, and it's still there on the walk back to the car. He really is milking this for all that it's worth.

When we climb into the back seat, I again find myself squished in the middle of Mason and Blake.

Mason leans over, close to my ear. "So, when were you going to tell me you loved me, Red?" he whispers. "I'm a little hurt that I had to hear it for the first time from your mum."

I elbow him in the ribs, and when he chuckles, I feel his warm breath skate across my skin. "It is wishful thinking on her part, I never told her that."

"Or that we broke up apparently."

He reaches for my hand, lacing our fingers together. "What are you doing?" I growl.

"Keeping up appearances, babe." He pulls our adjoined hands towards his face, placing a lingering kiss on my knuckles. "I'd hate to disappoint your mum."

"You're enjoying this aren't you?"

"Abso-fucking-lutely."

Mason has spent the afternoon charming my mother, and she's fallen for it hook, line, and sinker.

"Dinner was delicious, Grace. Thank you." he says, leaning back in his chair and rubbing his stomach. He looks over at me and winks when I scowl. Ugh, he's such a suck, and already has my mum wrapped around his little finger.

"Yeah, it was really yummy, Grandma," Blake adds, and my scowl quickly turns into a smile. I can't even with this cutie-pie. "Thank you."

"You're both welcome." My mum leans towards Blake, who's sitting beside her, and places a kiss on his hair. "Do you think you have room in your belly for some cake, sweetie?"

His face lights up and my smile grows. "Is it chocolate cake?"

"It sure is."

"Yes," he says, doing a little fist pump. "I have room for a really big piece."

We all laugh at that. Mason aside, we've all had a really nice day. I've noticed Blake watching his father's over-the-top displays of affections towards me, but apart from a few grins here and there, he hasn't spoken up about it. I think he's secretly been wishing for this to happen.

It's great being home and spending time with my parents, and my mum hasn't stop smiling. She's always worried that her life with my sperm donor was the reason behind me never being in a relationship, but it had more to do with him than her.

She was trapped in a hopeless situation; I can't blame her for that. Unless you've lived it, it's hard to grasp why a woman would stay with an abuser. I know firsthand that walking away isn't that easy. My mother was absolutely petrified of him, and over the years, my father wore her down. Not only stripping her of all her self-worth and dignity, he alienated her and controlled her every move, including all the finances; she had nothing and nowhere else to go.

When it came down to it, being homeless and penniless with a small child to care for, must've seemed more dire than the horrendous situation she was living, and that makes me so sad. I can only imagine the hopelessness she felt during that time. She wanted more for me, *and herself*, but had no clue how to achieve it. Nobody deserves a life like that.

Standing, I take my plate to the sink. "I'm going to head upstairs and take a shower."

"Your dad put yours and Mason's bags in your room. I'm going to set Blake up in Connor's old room," my mum says.

"I'm not sharing a room with Mason."

"Sweetie," she says, "You're twenty-one years old, I was married with a child when I was your age."

"We're not married, Mum."

I swear I hear her mumble, "Not yet," under her breath. "Your father and I discussed this, and we're fine with it. I may be your mother, but I'm not a prude, I'm sure you've both—"

"Don't you dare finish that sentence," I screech.

"What I think your daughter is trying to say, Grace," Mason chimes in, "is thank you, and that we appreciate it. She has trouble sleeping without me beside her."

When my mouth gapes open, he smiles like a smug motherfucker. If I didn't have every eye in the room on me right now, I swear I'd kick him in the shins.

I'm already in bed by the time Mason comes up to my room. I quickly close my eyelids and pretend I'm asleep when he approaches the bed. When his footsteps cease, even though my eyes are closed, I can feel his stare. I left the lamp on, so I know he has a clear, unobstructed view of me from where he stands. It's kind of creepy, but sweet. I hold my breath when I feel his fingertips lightly brush the hair back from my forehead before tenderly running a path down the side of my face. It's such a loving move, and when I hear him sigh, a knot forms in the back of my throat.

Minutes pass, and it's not until he turns and enters

the bathroom, closing the door behind him, that I reopen them. Why was he watching me fake sleep?

When I hear the shower turn on, I groan, pulling the sheets up over my face, trying with all my might not to imagine him stripping down and slipping under the spray. I know exactly what his ripped body looks like glistening under the water. Ugh, of course my mind goes straight there.

Today has been a mixture of heaven and hell, and when Mason said he was going to keep up appearances in front of my mum, he wasn't lying. Any chance he got to have his hands or lips on me, he took it. It was like some kind of erotic torture, because I knew the moment we were behind closed doors, it would all stop. He was enjoying teasing me, and my traitorous body fell for each and every caress.

The moment the bathroom door opens, my eyes close again, but the one closest to the pillow cannot help taking a sneaky peek, and I'm not disappointed. He's completely naked as he strides towards the bed, and that huge cock of his is hanging heavy between those thick, muscly thighs. That ever-present ache between my legs intensifies, to the point I'm throbbing.

He reaches over to switch off the lamp, and although I hate the dark, I feel safe knowing he's beside me. I roll over, giving him my back when he slips between the sheets. "You better be wearing clothes."

"I think you know the answer to that since you were pretending to be asleep just now."

"I was asleep until your heavy elephant feet woke me up."

I feel the mattress shake with his laughter. "I'm pretty sure it was the sway of the elephant's trunk that had you

332

mesmerised since that seemed to be where your attention was focussed."

Busted.

"Trunk? Hah! I was actually squinting to try and find it ... it's the size of a slug at best."

He barks out a laugh. "You kill me, Red."

Scooting closer, he reaches for me, so I slap his hand away. "I swear to God, if I wasn't into anti-violence, I'd roll over right now and grab hold of your tiny man balls—"

"We both know they're not tiny."

"I wasn't finished."

"My bad."

"And crush them."

"Jesus," he groans, moving his lower body out of my reach. "Don't even joke about that kind of thing."

"Do you honestly think I'm joking?"

"Actually, no I don't, but since your anti-violence, I presume my boys are safe."

He moves his body closer and slides his arm around my waist, pulling my back into his front ... the big spoon to my little. I shouldn't like it as much as I do.

When his hand starts to travel south, and his fingers slip down the front of my sleep shorts, I'm torn. Do I remove it? Or part my legs to give him better access?

"What are you doing?" I grumble.

"You seem tense, babe, just relax and let me take care of you."

"I'm not having sex with you, Mason, my parents are down the hall."

"I don't want to have sex with you—well that's technically a lie, because I do, but I'm not going to. Our days of having casual sex are done."

"Why?" My question is followed by a whimper as the tip of his fingers circle my clit.

When they slide lower, he growls, sinking his teeth into my shoulder. "So, wet for me."

He pushes one of his digits deep inside me, and I unashamedly roll onto my back, spreading my legs wide. I've been dying for a release ever since we stepped off the plane. I was even tempted to touch myself in the shower, but I'm glad I didn't now. I could never pleasure myself the way he does.

He adds a second finger, and my hips buck off the bed. When he withdraws, coming back in with a third, I push my head back into the pillow and moan. "Fuck, Red," he pants, rocking his erection into my side.

Capturing my mouth with his, he drives his fingers in as far as my body will allow, swirling them around in a circle. I'm so stretched, so full, that I immediately come. I start to tremble as euphoria spreads throughout my entire being. The intensity of my orgasm has me feeling light-headed by the time I ride the last wave.

My inner muscles are still pulsing around his fingers as he draws back and looks down at me. "If you offer yourself to me again, be sure it's what you really want, because it will mean this standoff between us is done and dusted. Next time I have you, it will be for keeps. Understand?"

I nod my head, because I understand him loud and clear.

Chapter 33

Mason

It's day three of our stay in Melbourne, and I'm actually glad I came now. Jim and Grace are amazing and have been so accommodating to Blake and I. We already feel like part of the family.

Our mornings start with a hot breakfast cooked by Grace, and I clearly see where Red got her culinary skills from. Then we head out sightseeing for the day. We dine out for lunch and when we come back here, the girls make us an amazing dinner. I've never eaten so well.

At night, we head down to the media room to watch a movie, or play boardgames around the dining table, which is something I've never done before, sad but true. I love that Blake and I both get to experience this. It's the kind of family unit I've always yearned for, and hope to provide him one day.

I haven't heard from Connor since we arrived. I feel guilty not being there, but I'm thankful he's present on my behalf. When I told him we were heading to Melbourne, he said he'd keep me updated. No news is good news I suppose.

As for me and Red, I'm still all over her like a rash

when we have an audience, but at night when we head to bed, she stays on her side of the mattress, and I stay on mine. It's a struggle having her so close, and keeping my distance, but I want it all—a taste here and there is not enough anymore. She needs to be sure, because I can't go through this again ... it's been hell without her. I just hope she doesn't take too long, because my balls are bluer than her eyes.

It is late afternoon when we leave the zoo. Blake is walking ahead of us, holding Grace's and Jim's hands. He seems just as obsessed with Jacinta's mum as he is with her.

My hand drops from Red's shoulder, sliding down her back, until my fingers dip into the back pocket of her jeans. I give her arse a cheeky squeeze.

"Are you right there?" she grumbles.

"I'm peachy, thanks for asking."

"You do realise they are in front of us and can't see us, right?"

"But they could turn around at any moment," I retort. When she growls, I bark out a laugh. "You do realise your sass turns me on?"

"Because you're sick."

Leaning down, I place a kiss on the side of her head. She's right, I am sick ... *love sick* for her.

We arrive back at the house and once I've slid out of the vehicle, I hold my hand out for Red. I'm half waiting for her to slap it away, but she takes it gracefully, even thanking me.

I move around the back of the car to get Blake, but

Grace is already on it. Seeing her with my son makes me think of my own mother. I know she would've loved him, like she did me. It makes the disdain I hold for my father grow. He robbed us all of so much.

My mother used to dote on me whenever he wasn't around. Not so much when he was home, because it usually got her in trouble. *"He'll never become a man if you keep babying him,"* is one of the things he'd say often. I used to worry that becoming a man meant I'd be more like him, thankfully that wasn't the case.

As we're heading up the front stairs, my phone starts to ring in my pocket. I don't think much of it, because it could be Rob or Olivia, or someone from Bridge, but when I see Connor's name on the screen my heart sinks.

Jacinta pauses beside me as I stand there staring down at my phone. "Everything okay?" she asks, placing her hand on my back. When I hold up the phone, showing her the screen, she turns to her mother. "Can you and dad take Blake inside?"

I suck air into my lungs before answering the call. "Connor," I say once I've placed the phone to my ear.

"Hey, Mas," he replies and then the line goes quiet. I hold my breath as I wait for him to speak again. "We ... umm found her."

"You did?"

"Yeah."

"Where?"

"Exactly where you thought she'd be."

"Are you sure it's her?"

"The coroner will confirm it, but that could take weeks. Do you remember if she used to wear any jewellery?"

"Yeah, she did." I close my eyes and conjure up the image from when I was at the house with Connor.

"Pearl earrings and a pearl pendant on a gold chain. She also wore a solitary gold wedding band on her ring finger."

"Okay. We found the ring and the necklace with her remains, but the guys are still sifting through the soil, so they may also find the earrings."

I can't even describe the emotions that are running through me, but my despair must be evident because Red steps forward, rests her face on my chest, and wraps her arms around my waist.

"I'll organise a flight home," I say to Connor, my voice cracking as I speak.

"You don't need to rush home, we'll be here for a few more days, and as I said, the coroner could take weeks."

"I want to be there." The guilt I've been feeling since we found that envelope escalates tenfold. I never should've left. I should've spoken up all those years ago. My father got to continue on with his life, while my mother rotted in our backyard.

"Give me a call when you land then, and I'll come get you."

"Okay."

Once I've slid the phone into my back pocket, I fold Jacinta in my arms. "They found her."

"I heard. I'm so sorry, Mason."

"I'll need to organise a flight home."

It's most definitely not the outcome I wanted, but at least I now have answers. *My poor mum*; she deserved so much more than what she got.

I release my hold on Jacinta and take a step back, because I'm so overcome with the realisation of what I saw that night was true that I'm struggling to keep it together. I bend, resting my hands on my knees as I struggle to get air into my lungs.

338

"Can I come back with you?" she asks, rubbing her hand over my back.

"Yeah." I have a feeling I'm going to need her. I don't think I can get through this on my own. "I need to go and talk to Blake."

"Okay."

"I don't know what to tell him."

"Just go with the simplified truth ... he doesn't need to know all the gory details."

I stand tall, digging the heel of my palms into my sockets when my eyes start to glaze over. I don't want to break down in front of her. "I don't know if I can do it," I admit. I don't want to lose it in front of my kid either.

"Do you want me to talk to him?"

"Would you?"

"Of course. Stay out here if you want, or go up to my room, take as much time as you need."

I turn my face away from her and stare off into the distance, because if I look down at her sad eyes, I'm going to break. "Thanks, Red."

I wait until I'm alone before taking a seat on the top step. I bury my face in my hands when the first tears start to fall. "I'm sorry, Mum," I whisper. "I'm so sorry I let you down."

"Hey," I hear from behind me, but I don't turn around. "Jacinta told me the news and I wanted to make sure you were okay. Can I join you for a minute?" When I nod my head, Grace takes a seat beside me. "You didn't let her down, please don't ever think that."

"I should've done more."

"You were a kid, Mason. I'm sure Jacinta felt that way at times too, but there was nothing she could've done. What chance does a small child have against a fully grown man? I was in a situation just like your mum, and if

339

it wasn't for her dance teacher, Brooke, and her husband, chances are I would've ended up exactly the same way. I can assure you, I never would've had the guts or the means to do it on my own."

"He told me she left because of me ... he said it was all my fault."

"Unfortunately, that's what narcissistic people do, they blame others for their wrongdoings, always separating themselves from the culpability. I'm sure somewhere in their sick and twisted minds, they even believe their own bullshit. My ex-husband was a master at it. Even though in my heart I knew I wasn't the problem, he had a way of making me doubt myself. I used to think if I do better, he'll stop, but there was nothing I could've done. It wasn't until I was away from him that I realised that there is life after abuse.

"Reaching out for help seemed like an impossibility. Who do you trust when you can't even trust your own husband? The fear that came with speaking out was palpable. I used to worry what would happen if he found out. He used to threaten to kill me if I tried to leave, and there's no way I would've left Jacinta alone with that man. I'm sure your mother felt exactly the same way when it came to you. I could go on and on, but I'm sure you get my point. Over time, people like that wear you down until you're a shell of your former self. I can assure you your mother wanted better for herself—and especially for you —she just didn't know how to achieve it."

"She was a good mum," I say, swiping my fingers under my eyes.

Grace places her hand on my back, soothingly moving it back and forth. "I know she was, sweetie, she produced you."

A smile tugs at my lips. "Thanks, Grace."

"She wouldn't want you beating yourself up over this. You've found her, and you can finally lay those ghosts to rest. She's at peace now, Mason."

"You think so?"

"I know so." She taps my leg and stands. "Jim is on the phone organising flights, would you mind if I kept my grandson here for a couple more days?" I chuckle when she says that, but at the same time, I love that she did. "There's a lot going on back home, and I'm sure you'd rather shield Blake from it all. He'll be safe here, I promise."

"I'd appreciate it if he could stay. Thank you for everything you've done for him since we got here."

"You don't need to thank me. You've given me something I've always wished for."

I turn my face, gazing at her over my shoulder and see tears pooling in her eyes. "What's that? A grandson?"

"No, hope."

"Hope?"

"Yes ... hope for my little girl. The burden I've had to carry around for all these years, thinking my poor decisions had damaged her to the point she'd never find true happiness, like I have with Jim. That all lifted the moment I saw the three of you walking towards us hand in hand at the airport." She places her hand on my shoulder, giving it a slight squeeze. "I've never seen her so happy and content."

Christ, I was hoping I wouldn't have to go there, but I can't continue to lie to her now. "I need to tell you something."

"What is it?"

"Jacinta and I are actually on a break at the moment."

"You are?" she asks as her blue eyes—the ones just like

341

her daughters—widen. "You two certainly don't act like a couple no longer together."

"I may have taken advantage of the fact once I realised you didn't know."

"That was cunning of you."

"I know, but I miss her, and I want her back."

"May I ask why you're on a break?"

"Something happened with Blake and his biological mother when he was in Jacinta's care."

"Do you mean the time she tried to take him?"

"She told you about that?"

"No, actually it was Connor. When I called her, she said she didn't want to talk about it."

I bow my head. "I scared her."

"How?"

"When she told me what happened I lost my cool and put my fist through the wall." She remains silent, so I tentatively look over my shoulder again. She's watching me, but I can't read her face. "I'd never hurt her, Grace. Please believe me ... I'm not my father. *I love her.* I love everything about her, and she's so good with Blake ... she's helped him so much."

"Jacinta has a beautiful and kind heart."

"That she does."

She blows out a puff of air, and I'm expecting some kind of lecture, or for her to tell me I'm not the man she thought I was and to stay away from her daughter, but she does none of that. Instead, she tenderly skims her hand over the top of my hair. "I'm sure you two will work it out."

"I hope so."

"Just give her time, she's worth the wait." I nod, because the lump that's now risen to the back of my throat is hindering me from answering. "Jim and I will fly up to

Sydney in a few days with Blake, or sooner if you want him home before then." With that, she turns and leaves, and every part of my interaction with her just now has made me feel a little lighter.

I exhale a long breath as I tilt my head back, gazing up at the sky. "I hope you're at peace now, Mum."

Chapter 34

Jacinta

It's early when we arrive at Sydney airport and find Connor waiting for us by the kerb. Mason is again pushing my suitcase along with his. He didn't say much during the flight home, but his leg bounced for the majority of the time, so I know he's anxious about being back here. I don't blame him.

My dad couldn't get us on a flight until today, so we ended up staying another night in Melbourne. I went to bed before Mason because he opted to stay up and drink a few beers with my dad. When he finally came up to my room, the first thing he did was reach for me.

This time I didn't fight it. I rolled over, rested my head on his chest, and hugged him right back. No words were spoken, and I don't think he got a lot of sleep, but I was glad he wasn't alone, and I hope I was able to provide him with some comfort.

Connor moves to me first, briefly wrapping me in his arms and placing a chaste kiss on my temple. "Hey, sis."

"Hey. Thanks for coming to get us."

He releases me and walks towards his best friend, and the length and ferocity of their hug has tears rising to my eyes. "I'm so sorry, Mas," Connor says, tapping his back a couple of times.

"Thanks. I appreciate everything you did on my behalf while I was gone."

"Always, mate ... always."

I love that Mason has someone like Connor in his life, because I know how loyal and protective my brother is when it involves the people he cares about.

Connor opens the back door for me, and Mason slides into the passenger seat. There's been no more public displays of affection since we left Melbourne, and I miss it. I desperately want to reach out and comfort him. Hold his hand, rub his back, hug him. Let him know he has me too, but he has enough going on right now, so I'll bide my time.

When I was saying my goodbyes to my mother at the airport, she cupped my face, looked me in the eye, and said, *"Forgive him, baby girl. I believe him when he says he'll never hurt you. What you two have is special, anyone can see that. He loves you, and you love him, don't throw that away over one little incident."*

I'm not sure when they had that discussion, but obviously they did. Maybe it was when I was upstairs talking to Blake. All I told him was that his dad's mum has been missing for a long time, and that he just found out she'd passed away. He asked me a few questions, like was his mum nice, and even though I never knew her, of course I said yes. He also asked if his dad was sad, and again, I told him he was. When we went back downstairs, Mason was in the kitchen with my parents, and Blake ran straight to him. *"I love you, Dad,"* he'd said, hugging his leg.

"I love you too, buddy," Mason replied, choking up. It was a poignant moment to witness.

It's midmorning by the time we pull up outside the house. The three of us exit the car and stand on the sidewalk facing the property. There're numerous vehicles present and police tape strung around the perimeter of the yard. My eyes follow a man in a white hazmat suit as he carries a large brown paper bag towards a white van that is parked in the driveway. The sight makes my stomach recoil.

I gaze up at Mason and find him watching the man also. Without giving it any thought, I reach for his hand, wrapping it in mine. I can feel him trembling when I do. My heart hurts for him, because this was my greatest fear for my mother when I was a little girl.

Once the hazmat guy disappears down the side of the property towards the backyard, my gaze moves to the expansive two-story brick house in front of us. It's beautiful and vastly different to the one I grew up in, but it just goes to show that domestic violence is prevalent everywhere. Rich or poor, it doesn't discriminate against class.

This home, with its perfectly manicured lawn, gardens, and fairy tale-like appearance, is a total farce. From the outside looking in, you'd never guess the horrors that unfolded behind those doors.

"Do you want to go out back?" Connor asks.

"I don't think I'm ready for that yet," Mason answers, turning his head in Connor's direction. "I've been thinking about what you said concerning the will. I've decided I'm going to donate the entire estate to Bridge, and this place will be an extension of that. When the time is right, I'd like to make it a safe house. A place where

346

battered women and children can come to escape their abusers."

Oh, my heart.

That offer speaks volumes about the kind of person he is; he's going through so much and is still thinking of others. I lift my free hand and swipe it under my eyes to catch the tears that are now spilling down my cheeks. What a beautiful way to take a tragedy and turn it into a positive. I know how much that will help not only the victims of domestic violence, but their children who've been forced to grow up in situations like we did.

God, I love this man.

Two days have passed since our return to Sydney, and Mason and I are back at the airport, picking up Blake and my parents. Connor and I have done our best not to leave Mason on his own during the day, but at night he's been going back to his apartment alone.

He never ended up entering the property when we went there the other day; we just stood outside for a while, then left. He said when he's ready he'll go back, but I have no idea when that will be.

Tonight, we're all going to Brooke and Logan's for dinner, and Mason and Blake are invited. My parents wanted to visit them while they're here. Brooke's met Blake—I took him to the dance studio once—but not Mason.

"Dad," Blake screams as soon as he sees us. He barrels towards us, and Mason catches him in his arms when he leaps forward. "I missed you."

"I missed you too, bud." I love the dynamics between these two.

"Hey, Jazzie," he says when his father puts him down.

"Hey, cutie-pie. Did you have fun at Grandma and Jim's?"

"Yes. I got new toys," he replies, sliding off his backpack and dropping it to the ground so he can unzip it.

"Just what he needs," Mason mumbles under his breath, "more toys."

After I hug my parents, they move to Mason. My dad shakes his hand, and after my mother wraps him in her arms, she draws back and cups the side of his face. "How are you holding up, sweetie?"

"Good," he says, but by the pitch of his voice, and the way his Adam's apple bobs, I'd say he's trying to keep his emotions in check.

We spend the afternoon at my apartment, and when it's time to head to the Cavanagh's, we split into two cars. Since Connor is coming with us, we won't all fit in one. My parents opt to ride with him, and my mother practically shoves me into Mason's car. She's now on a mission to get us back together.

I think I'm ready to make that move too, but with everything else going on, I've yet to find the right time to broach the situation with him. I don't want him to think I'm doing it out of sympathy either, because I'm not.

"I feel awkward coming tonight," Mason says on the drive over. "I don't even know these people."

"They know all about you ... well Brooke does."

"Have you been talking about me, Red?"

"Brooke is my boss and she's also a good friend. They are the ones who saved Mum and I. They're great people, I think you'll really like them. Besides, my mum seems to have claimed you both as part of our family now, so you'll need to get used to being dragged along to gatherings when they are in town."

"How do you feel about that?"

"About what, having you around?"

"No, us being claimed as part of the Maloney clan?"

His eyes leave the road, darting to me. "I'm fine with it," I answer, because I am. He nods once, before focusing back on the road. "They have two kids, CJ, their youngest, is the same age as Blake."

"They know we're coming, right?"

"Of course, Brooke specifically asked for me to bring you two along."

"Does she know we've broken up, or am I going to have to keep up appearances?"

"I never told her."

"So, I'm expected to play happy families again tonight?"

I blow out a puff of air. "You're not expected to do anything, nor were you down in Melbourne. You chose that all on your own."

He shrugs. "Sometimes you've got to take an opportunity when it arises."

"I've been wanting to talk to you about us—"

He holds up his hand, cutting me off. "Not tonight, Red," he bites. "I've got enough shit going on in my life right now; I don't have room for any more drama."

Drama? Ugh. I cross my arms over my chest and abruptly turn my head towards the passenger side window.

Alrighty then, arsehole.

Chapter 35

Mason

I feel like a prick by the time we arrive at Jacinta's friend's house, and can I just say, *what a house.* I grew up around money, but this place is on a whole other level. This is stupid rich. I pray these people are nothing like the pretentious fuckers my father used to have my mother wait on when he'd invite them over for dinner.

I hadn't meant to snap at Red on the drive here, I just couldn't stomach whatever it was she had to say. It was either one of two things—we were done for good, or she was coming back to me out of pity ... neither is what I want. When, and if, that time comes, I want it to be out of love, nothing else. I need her to be with me for the same reasons I want her, because life without her in it, is unimaginable ... because she makes me happy. Not because she feels sorry for me for being the poor unfortunate son whose father brutally murdered his mother and buried her in the backyard.

Two weeks ago, she avoided me like the plague, and now she's making excuses to have me around. If that doesn't scream pity, I don't know what does.

I switch off the ignition and turn in my seat. I don't

even want to be here, but Grace can be awfully persistent when she wants to be.

"I'm sorry for snapping at you, Red," I say, when she removes her seat belt and reaches for the door handle.

Her shoulders slightly slump as she replies, "It's okay, Mason, I understand. You have a lot going on right now."

See ... that right there. This is what I'm talking about. Where is my fiery Red? The one that took no shit from me? I don't want her condoning my bad behaviour because she thinks I'm fragile; I want her calling me out on it, like she used to.

We all gather at the front door, and I hang back with Blake. I feel awkward being here now that Jacinta and I are no longer together ... like a stage five clinger that refuses to let go of the woman he loves, even when she doesn't love him back.

I'm expecting a butler or maid to answer the door, but the good-looking, casually dressed dude, with the jet-black hair and Colgate-worthy smile that greets us, doesn't look like the help.

I watch as he acknowledges each person, one by one. He shakes Jim's hand and tells him it's great to see him again. He kisses Grace and Jacinta on the cheek, and gets a growl from Connor when he ruffles his hair. I roll my lips at that one, because Connor is such a chick when it comes to his hair. They shake and exchange a few words, and then it's time for me to step forward.

"Mason," I say, extending my hand to him.

"Logan."

"This is my son, Blake."

"It's nice to meet you, Blake." When he holds out his hand, Blake shakes it, just like I taught him to. "Wow, that's a good strong handshake." Blake smiles, and I stand a little taller. "Angel, CJ," he calls out.

"Yes, Daddy," a little girl screeches as two kids come barrelling down the hallway.

"This is Blake," he says to them before turning his attention to my son. "These are my kids, Angel and CJ."

"Hi," Blake says bashfully.

"Do you want to come play with us?" CJ asks.

Blake looks up at me. "Can I, Dad?"

"Of course, bud."

When the three of them run off, Logan moves his attention back to me. "Come in," he says. We cross the expansive foyer and make our way down the long hallway, "So how do you fit in to this dynamic?"

"I'm Connor's best friend, and I dated Jacinta for a little while."

"Ah, the best friend's little sister, how did Connor take that? I know how protective he is of her."

"Not great at first, but he warmed to it after a while."

He chuckles. "Fair enough. Your breakup must have been amicable since you're still around?"

"I kind of messed things up between us, but I'm hoping she'll forgive me for that one day."

I'm usually a private person, so I have no clue why I'm opening up to a stranger. Maybe I've been hanging around Connor too much, and he's starting to rub off on me.

Logan reaches up, tapping me on the back. "The old unrequited love ... I've been there. It was like that for me when I first met Brooke, but look at us now. Take my advice, if Jacinta is really what you want, don't give up."

"I don't plan to."

"Persistence pays off in the end ... well it did for me. You're still here so count that as a positive." I dip my head, *I'm only here because they feel sorry for me.* "Come meet my beautiful wife and I'll grab you a beer. You drink beer, right? I have spirits if you prefer."

Beautiful wife. I love that he said that. This night is already turning out to be nothing like I expected, and I feel shitty for automatically judging them on the size of their house.

"Beer's fine, but I'm driving so I can only have one."

When we enter the kitchen, I see his wife is indeed beautiful, but she has nothing on my Red. I can tell by the way the women laugh and hug each other that they're close. I'm grateful Grace and Jacinta had people like this in their life to help; I only wish my mum had the same. Things may have turned out differently for her if she did.

I follow him towards the girls. He drapes his arm over his wife's shoulder, pulling her into his side and placing a chaste kiss on her temple. "Brooke, this is Mason. Mason, this is my wife, Brooke. He's Connor's best friend."

"And Jacinta's boyfriend," she says excitedly, and I see her husband grimace. "I've heard all about him." My eyes dart to Red, and her cheeks are now the same colour as her nickname. "It's so nice to finally meet you."

"Actually, they're not together anymore," Logan tells her.

"Oh no! How come?" she asks as her wide eyes move from me to Jacinta.

Thankfully, Grace steps forward and saves me from having to have that awkward conversation. "They're having a break, but I'm sure they'll work it out in time."

"I'm so sorry, Jaz," Brooke says, reaching for her hand and giving it a sympathetic squeeze. When Jacinta dips her face, I feel like a colossal arsehole for what I did.

353

"Would you ladies like a glass of wine?" Logan asks, and I'm grateful for the change of subject.

After a disastrous start, the evening continues to improve as the night wears on. Instead of the posh meal I was expecting, Brooke made a variety of salads, a hot creamy potato dish, and some cheesy macaroni—which Blake has already had three helpings of—and freshly baked, crusty bread.

Logan grilled seasoned steak, marinated chicken, and fish on the barbeque, well more like a chef-worthy outdoor kitchen. Despite their obvious wealth, I seriously misjudged these people. They are humble and very down to earth.

It is so beautiful here. The expansive back deck, where we are currently sitting, runs along the entire rear of the house. We're only metres from their own private beach, and the sound of waves crashing in the distance has a lulling effect on me. This is the most content I've felt in days.

"This fish is delicious," I say.

"I caught it myself," Logan replies.

"You did?"

"Yes, do you like to fish?"

"I've never done it, but I've always wanted to give it a go."

"Your father never took you when you were a kid?"

"No, he wasn't what you'd call an outdoorsy person." I leave it at that, there's no way I want to fall down that rabbit hole with these people.

"Mine either," he chuckles, "but occasionally we'd

fish when we were at the family cabin. I have a boat now; you should come out with me sometime."

"I'd like that, thanks."

"When he says boat, he's not talking about a small tinny either. It's massive," Connor chimes in.

"I took Connor out once," Logan says, and when I hear Connor groan from beside me, I know there's a story behind this. "Let's just say his regurgitated berley brought the fish that day."

"I was hungover," he grumbles in his own defence, and the entire table laughs.

"Sure you were," I tease.

"I'd like to see how well you do when you're out there bobbing around in those choppy seas."

"You should come out with us then," I challenge.

And when he replies with, "I think I'll pass," that earns another round of laughter.

"Do you work weekends?" Logan asks. "We could go out Saturday if you're free."

"No, just Monday to Friday, Saturday sounds good."

"He also runs a non-profit ... a soup kitchen for the homeless," Jacinta adds proudly.

"Oh wow," says Brooke. "What's it called?"

"Bridge."

"Is it in the city?"

"Yes, at The Rocks."

"Wow, that's not far from where we used to live," she says. "Do you get any government funding?"

"Some, but it's not enough. We rely mainly on donations."

Brooke's eyes move to her husband and when she arches a brow, he nods sitting forward in his seat, these two are so in sync they just had an entire conversation with only a few facial gestures. Seeing them together tonight makes me yearn for something like that with Red. The flirty touches whenever they're within reach, or the way their eyes always seem to gravitate towards each other when they're not. You can clearly see how much they love each other.

Is it even possible for two damaged and emotionally stunted people like Jacinta and I to find this kind of happiness?

"My company holds a charity ball once a year where all the proceeds go to a local non-profit," Logan says. "It's our way of giving back to the community. We charge an exorbitant amount of money per plate to attend, and we end the evening with an auction ... last year we raised over three hundred grand. We've been searching for a new beneficiary for this year, we could make it Bridge."

"Are you kidding me, you have no idea how far that kind of money could go."

"Well then that's settled. I'll let my PA Claire know, and she'll reach out to you with all the particulars."

"Wow, thank you."

When I feel Jacinta's hand willingly come to rest on my thigh under the table, I place mine on top of hers and lace our fingers together. That move, although small, means so much. It has nothing to do with keeping up appearances, because nobody can see it. I'm so glad I came now; I've enjoyed my time here and I feel like I've made new friends.

My eyes slowly move around the table. I've always been a bit of a loner, because I found it hard to trust people. Betty, Rob, and Connor were the only people I've ever let in. That is until Red. Since meeting her, I've changed, and I like the direction my life's taken. For both me and my son.

When my eyes move to Blake, I find him smiling as

his chin rests on his hands ... his focus is on Angel, and he's hanging on to every word she says. Are they cartoon hearts I see in his eyes? I smile at the thought; he's come so far in such a short time.

Our circle is expanding, and all we need now is for Red to come back to us—for the right reasons of course—and when she does, I'm going to marry her.

Chapter 36

Mason

I let go of Blake's hand so I can knock on the door. Connor answers a short time later. "I come bearing gifts," I say, holding up the small esky in my hand. "Freshly caught fish. Since I have no clue how to cook it, I thought Jacinta might do it for us."

I had the best time out on the water with Logan today. I really like him; he's a good bloke. Blake spent the day at their house, playing with his kids.

Connor cocks an eyebrow as his eyes scan over my face. "You're looking very healthy, sun-kissed and ... non-green."

I bark out a laugh. "That's because I handled those rough seas like a champ. Don't feel bad," I say, placing my hand on his shoulder. "We're not all cut out for those kinds of manly adventures."

"I was hungover when I went out with him," he growls.

"Right."

"I fuck—" His words die off as soon as he notices Blake standing beside me. "I was."

"So, you're sticking with that story?"

"Absolutely."

I chuckle again because we both know he's full of shit. "Is Jacinta home?"

"No, she got called into work?"

"Really? Brooke never mentioned that when we got back to the house."

He lifts one shoulder. "Some girl named Candy called an hour ago and begged her to fill in for her tonight. Her son was in the hospital or something along those lines."

"Candy the stripper?"

"What?"

"Her friend Candy is a stripper."

"You must have her mixed up with someone else, Jaz would never ..." He frowns, pulling out his phone. I get an uneasy feeling in the pit of my stomach as I watch him type out a message to her.

> Connor: When you said you were going into work, you meant the dance studio right?

I'm holding my breath as we stand there in silence, waiting to see if she replies. "She just read it," he says. "She's replying now."

When his phone pings, he holds the screen up for me to see her reply. It's one word.

> Jaz: No.

> Connor: Please don't tell me you are at the strip club?

> Jaz: Okay, I won't.

"Give me that," I snap, snatching his phone out of his

hand. Adrenaline is thundering through my body as I press call. "What the hell, Jacinta," I bark the moment she answers. I hear a little squeak on the other end and then the line goes dead. "She hung up on me." I press call again, but this time it goes straight to voicemail. "She's turned her phone off."

"What are we going to do?" Connor asks. "I can't go there ... she's my sister and seeing her ... you know ... I'd have to gouge out my eyes if I did."

"Can you watch Blake for me?"

"Yes."

I look down at my clothes. "I'm going to have to run upstairs and have a quick shower and change. I smell like fish guts, and I doubt they'll let me in dressed like this."

"Do you know which club she's at?" Connor asks.

"Shit, no. She went there with Cassandra one night to watch Candy perform, but I never asked the name of the place."

"Okay, you go shower and I'll call Cass and get the details for you while you're gone."

I'm seething by the time I make it back down to their apartment. "Here's where she is," Connor says, handing me a piece of paper. "Cass could only give me a name, so I googled the address for you."

"Thanks." I hand him the bag I'm holding and take the piece of paper.

"What's this?"

"Blake's pyjamas ... just in case I end up in jail for killing someone tonight."

"I hope you're not referring to Jaz?"

"Of course not, but rest assured I'm going to spank her arse when I get my hands on her though."

"Dude, fuck" he groans, throwing back his head. "Did you really have to go there? She's my sister remember. That's an image I do not need in my head."

"My bad."

I'm already punching the address into my GPS on my phone as I jog towards the lift. I have no clue what I'm going to do when I get there but dragging her off that stage isn't out of the question.

I have to circle the block a few times until I find a parking spot, but the second I do, I switch off the ignition and jump off my bike. It took me longer than expected to get here, the traffic in the city is always chaotic on Saturday nights. Especially in Kings Cross.

I'm clenching and unclenching my hands as I walk towards the entry. I need to calm the fuck down before I go inside. Losing my cool isn't going to help my plight with Red, but I'm already struggling. What the fuck was she thinking? This is no place for a girl like her.

"Hey," I say as I approach the guy at the front door.

"Hi."

"My girl is dancing here tonight, and I'm here to get her."

"Which one?" he asks.

"It's her first night." *And her last if I have a say in it.* "She's filling in for Candy."

"The blonde is your girl?" He lets out a long whistle and the caveman inside me wants to reach for his throat. "Nice."

"Can I go in?"

"You'll have to pay the cover charge first."

I pull out my wallet. "How much?"

"Depends on what you're after."

"I'm not after anything, like I said, I'm just here to collect my girl."

"It's five hundred to get in, or a grand if you want complimentary drinks and a lap dance."

"You're kidding right?"

"Nope. This is a high-class establishment. Our girls are the best of the best ... you won't find better."

I clear my throat and count to ten in my head. I'm struggling to keep my composure. I pull out my credit card and hand it to him. "I'm not after a lap dance," I say.

He chuckles. "Not when you can get a free one at home by blondie, right?" When he mumbles, "Lucky bastard," under his breath, I'm tempted to reach for him again.

He holds my card out to me once he's scanned it; I snatch it from between his fingers and stomp up the steps. I only make it halfway when I hear him on the phone. "Boss-man, there's a guy on his way up ... he's here to collect the new blonde, claims she is his girl. He looks pissed."

By the time I reach the top of the stairs, two burly security guards and a man in a three-piece suit are waiting to greet me. *Fuck.* The guy in the suit with the slicked-back black hair holds his hand out to me. Each finger is adorned with a large chunky gold ring. "Rocco," he says with a heavy Italian accent. "I hear you're looking for Jacinta."

"Where is she?"

"She's just about to go on."

"Not if I can help it," I snap, trying to push past him.

362

One of the security guys grabs hold of my arm, but when Rocco shakes his head, he lets me go. "I've got this," he says, slinking his arm over my shoulder. "Come, would you like a complimentary drink while you wait?"

"No. I just want to get Jacinta and leave."

"All in good time," he says. "I know this is hard for you ... and that your girl is only here because she's doing Candy a solid. Rest assured, I look after all my dancers, they're like family to me. Jacinta simply didn't want Candy to lose her job."

"If you indeed look after your girls, threatening one with her job because her son is in hospital is not only contradictive, but pretty underhanded."

He barks out a laugh. "You know about that part, huh? You've got me there," he says, holding his hands out in front of him. "At the end of the day I still have a business to run, and there was nobody else available to fill her slot." He leads me to a booth down near the stage and encourages me to take a seat. "Saturday nights are my busiest." He runs his thumb over the tip of his fingers as he seats himself beside me. "Tonight, is when the big bucks come into play, so I only have my best dancers perform."

"Yet you're going to let a newbie get up there?"

"Have you not seen her on a pole?"

"No, have you?" I snap, because the thought of his beady little eyes on her makes me livid.

"She's done wonders with my dancers, she's a great teacher, they can't talk highly enough about her. And as for your question, yes I have, but only briefly when she came in. I had to see for myself before I let her up there. And let me tell you ... if stripping was something she was interested in full-time, I'd snap her up in a heartbeat. She'd make me rich, or should I say richer." He laughs, and I shake my head in disgust. I go to stand, and he grabs my arm. "Sit. Are you going to behave, or do I need to call my guys over?" My nostrils flair as I huff out a breath. When I retake my seat, he grasps my shoulder, giving it a squeeze. "Smart man. One dance, and then she's all yours. Relax and enjoy."

"Forewarned, if one of these fuckers lays a hand on her—"

"Like I just told you, *relax*, there's no touching, unless they pay for it of course."

"I don't care how much they pay for the privilege; they touch her and they die."

He throws back his head and barks out a laugh, "I actually like you," he says once he pulls himself together, then I see him motion with two fingers and his goon moves over to stand beside our table. "I assure you she is safe up there, I'm even allowing her to leave her clothes on, which is a first for me."

"How noble of you," I spit.

"I did however, hand pick her outfit. I think her looks, sweet persona, and dance skills will be enough to keep my patrons happy."

A topless waitress appears beside our table, placing two tumblers with a small amount of amber liquid in each down in front of us. "Thank you, Catrina," Rocco says, lifting the glass to his mouth. I don't touch mine; I'm only here for one thing ... *to get my girl the fuck out of here.*

The cages either side of the stage, containing two scantily dressed women dancing, suddenly start to rise towards the roof and the lights turn off. "Okay ladies and gentlemen," booms a voice over the speakers, "Are you ready for the highlight of the evening?" The room erupts into cheers while the knots in my stomach tighten. "Our first act tonight is a newbie, please welcome on stage for her debut appearance, Sparkles."

Rocco nudges my side when they say her stage name. "I picked that, good one huh. I knew once she got out here, she'd shine."

Ignoring him, I keep my focus straight ahead. When a spotlight suddenly hits the stage and I see her, I almost swallow my tongue. "You call that an outfit?" I growl.

"Compared to what the others wear, yes."

Red stands front and centre, with her back leaning against the pole. Her arms are high above her head and her fingers are wrapped around the metal. Her head is tilted back, and her long blonde hair falls down around her waist and has soft waves in it. It must be teased out, or something, because it looks a lot puffier than usual. The barely there clothes she's wearing—if you can even call them that—are what has my blood pressure rising through the roof.

The teeny-tiny black leather shorts, that look more like skimpy underwear, are paired with black leather boots that go up past her knees, stopping mid-thigh. On top, she's wearing a black lace midriff bustier that is so tight her more than ample tits are spilling out, and the glittery stuff they've slapped all over her skin makes her glisten under the lights. As mad as I am, my dick instantly comes to life. She's sparkling just like her stage name, and as much as I hate this for her, she looks like a walking fucking wet dream.

I reach for my glass, gulping down the liquid in one go. It burns the shit out of my throat, but I barely feel it, because all the blood in my body is now rushing towards my dick.

She stays deathly still, despite all the cat calls and woof whistles that now fill the room, but the second the introduction of 'Take Me to Church' by Hozier starts, her legs spring outwards into a perfect split and her body swings in a full circle around the pole with ease. The room erupts again, but my focus remains on her; I'm mesmerised. I'll never be able to listen to this song again without getting hard.

Every move she makes is precise and graceful, and I'm glad I'm sitting down, because my boner is in danger of bursting straight through the denim of my jeans. I hate to say it, but she was born to perform on that stage.

Her eyes remain closed throughout her routine. Her make-up is heavy, and the long lashes they've stuck along the lids of her eyes rest against her cheeks. She looks like pure fucking sin.

Each transition she makes looks effortless, but I can only imagine the hours of training she put in to get to such a high standard. I've been to strip clubs before, and although there's a lot of skin on show and some of her moves are risqué and suggestive, to me, her performance seems more artistic than sleezy. I'm actually in awe of her dancing.

Her back is now to us, and half of her peachy, round arse is hanging out of those goddamn barely there shorts. I groan and palm myself through my jeans as she grabs hold of the pole and slowly slips down into the splits, rolling her hips forward once she's fully seated on the stage. That move has my mind going straight to the gutter. One day, I'm going to get her to recreate that exact move as she sinks down onto my cock.

"Fuck me dead," I hear Rocco mumble from beside me making the sign of the cross as he does, and it pisses me off. If I could tear my eyes away from Red, I'm sure I'd see dollar signs flashing in those greedy fucking eyes of his. I hate that I'm sharing this moment with a room full of sleazebags.

"Heads up," I say, leaning towards him while still watching my girl. "Not only is her father one of the country's most prominent lawyers, but her very overprotective brother is a police prosecutor right here in the CBD. I'd think very carefully about ever inviting her back ... I'd hate for the law to come crawling over this fine establishment of yours."

He has no response to that, but I'm confident I got the message across.

Red wraps her legs around the pole, using both her hands and knees to climb to the top. An image of her doing this exact movement as she scaled the eight-foot fence on our first night together has a smile bursting onto my face. I thought it was her inner ninja, but I was wrong; it was the stripper inside her that got her over that gate.

There's never a dull moment with her around, and it makes my heart pang with the realisation that she makes me happier than I ever thought possible.

The dickhead behind me starts to holler, "Marry me, Sparkles," when she flips herself upside down and does the splits again. I clench my fists together a few times, trying to rein in my irritation. *She's mine fucker, she'll never belong to you.* When I get her back, I'm installing one of these poles in our bedroom, so I can get an uninterrupted private showing whenever I like.

The song comes to an end, and the room goes crazy. I wish I had the foresight to film that because I want to watch it on loop again and again.

Rocco stands as Red makes her way off the stage. "Come," he says, "I'll take you to her."

We head to the far side of the room where one of the

security guys lifts a black curtain, revealing a long corridor. I see her just before she disappears into a side room.

"Red," I call out, and that has her freezing on the spot and spinning in my direction.

The second she sees me, her blue eyes almost pop out of her skull. "Mason," she gasps. I'm already shrugging out of my leather jacket as I stalk towards her. "What are you doing here?"

"I could ask you the same thing." I drape my jacket over her shoulders, bend slightly at the knees, lift her off the ground, and throw her over my shoulder. My hand immediately connects with her luscious arse, and the loud crack it makes against her skin vibrates off the walls.

"Ouch, what was that for?" I'm not even going to justify that question with an answer.

I hear Rocco bark out a laugh behind me. "You did good out there, Sparkles, real good, but it looks like it's time for you to head home."

"My stuff is still here, Mason" she whines as I turn and start moving down the corridor, towards the exit. "Please. I don't want to leave my purse and phone behind ... I need them."

"Hold on, I'll grab them for you," Rocco calls out to my retreating back.

Blowing out a frustrated breath, I pause. He returns a few minutes later with her bag in his hand. "Can you give Candy all the money I earnt tonight, Rocco; I want her to have it," Jacinta says, whilst still hanging upside down. And I love that her kind heart said that. I can't really be mad at her for what she did tonight; she was just helping out a friend in need.

"Sure thing, darlin', I'm sure she'd appreciate that."

The moment we descend the stairs and step out into the night, I look from left to right and spy an alleyway next to the club. I keep walking until we disappear into the shadows. Only then do I slide her body down mine until she's back on her feet.

"I can't believe you just did that," she shrieks.

"You have no place on that stage."

"What I do with my life is none of your business."

"Really," I growl, backing her into the wall. "So, you'd be okay if I went back upstairs and got one of the girls to give me a lap dance?"

She slings her bag over her shoulder before her hands move to her hips. "You wouldn't dare."

"Try me," I threaten. Her eyes lock with mine, challenging me, and although she still looks beautiful with all that gunk on her face, she's barely recognisable. "Better still, how about I call your parents and let them know what you've been up to tonight?" Her mouth gapes open, but no words come out. "That's what I thought."

"How did you know I was here?"

"Connor, so you're going to have to face him when you get home too."

Her eyes narrow. "I'm an adult, I can do what I like."

When she tries to duck under my arm, I capture her around the waist. "Not so fast, Red. I'm not finished with you yet."

"I've got nothing more to say to you."

"Tough, I have plenty to say to you."

She opens her mouth to respond, but I cover her lips with mine, swallowing whatever sass she was going to give me. Her hands fist in my shirt, and instead of pushing me away, she tugs me closer.

We are both breathless when we finally come up for air. "Are you coming home with me?" I ask.

"To the apartment building?"

"No, to my place." I move my hand up to cover her

369

mouth because I need her to hear me out first. "Remember our deal? No more casual sex, next time I have you it's for keeps, so think about that before you answer."

Once I remove my hand, I intake a sharp breath and hold it. The smile she gives me has my heart rate kicking up a notch. Is our break finally over? *Please let it be over.* I impatiently wait for her reply, and the next sentence out of her mouth is the last thing I'm expecting.

"I love you, Mason Bradley."

Chapter 37

Jacinta

"You love me?" Mason asks, frowning, and that's not the reaction I expected.

"That's what I said."

"Let's get something clear, is it a friendly kind of love? Or—"

"Love, Love," I say, cutting him off.

He lifts me off the ground, swinging me around in a circle. "You love, love me?"

"With my entire heart."

"I love, love you too, Jacinta Maloney," he says before his mouth bears down on me. When he draws back from the kiss, he places my feet back on the ground. "So, we're back together?"

I lift my hand, cupping the side of his face. "If you still want me?"

"I think you know I do ... I'll always want you."

"Are you going to hit any more walls?"

"I hope not, but please know even if I do, I'd *never* hit you."

"I believe you."

"I've actually been thinking of reaching out to a thera-

371

pist. I have a lot of fucked-up shit from my childhood to unpack."

"My mum and I had some extensive therapy when we first moved to Melbourne ... it helped. It made me see that I wasn't broken, just damaged. Our fathers may have not loved us the way a parent should, but we were lucky to have mothers that did."

"We were," he says, pulling my body against his and wrapping me tight. When he rests his chin on the top of my head and exhales a long breath, I know he's thinking about his mother.

I lay my cheek against his chest and listen to his rapidly beating heart. I hate that he's going through this, and I doubt he'll ever be able to accept what happened to her, but I hope in time it will get easier.

We stay like this for the longest time. It's nice to be in his arms again. His phone pings in his pocket, and when he lets me go, I instantly miss his warmth, so I wrap his jacket around my body.

"Connor," he says, looking down at the screen.

Connor: Did you find her?

Mason: Yes.

Connor: And?

Mason: She's with me now.

Connor: Good.

Mason: How's Blake?

Connor: He's asleep in front of the TV.

> **Mason:** Can he spend the night there? I'll come get him first thing in the morning.

> **Connor:** Why? Where are you going?

> **Mason:** I'm taking your sister back to my place.

> **Connor:** Why?

> **Mason:** To punish her. I can see a good spanking in her future.

"Oh, my God," I screech as I read over the thread. "Why would you tell him that?"

He chuckles. "Because it's fun."

> **Connor:** Dude! What the fuck?

> **Mason:** You asked. Did you want me to lie to you?

> **Connor:** YES!!!!

Mason throws back his head and laughs.

"You're so mean," I say.

"Your brother is too easy." He slides his phone into his back pocket and reaches for my hand. "Let's get you home before you get arrested for public indecency."

"I'm not naked ... I have clothes on."

"Hmm," is his only reply.

After Mason strapped his helmet onto my head, he

373

pulled me in for an earth-shattering kiss that I felt right down to the tips of my toes. When we arrive back at the parking garage at our building, he does the same thing but in reverse order.

"Don't you think we should take this upstairs?" I ask.

"I'm just making up for lost time, babe." He places his thumb on my bottom lip, dragging it down. "I've missed this mouth ... I've missed everything about you."

"I've missed you too, but I'm eager to see what my punishment's going to be."

"Is that so?" he says, chuckling.

"What do you have instore for me, Wolf?"

"For starters, I'm going to strip you of everything bar those boots. Then I'm going to put you over my knee and spank that luscious arse of yours."

I frown because I don't like the sound of that. "Why?"

"After your poor choices tonight, you need a deterrent."

"Is that so?" I say, placing my hands on my hips.

"I don't want you back on that stage unless you're teaching, from now on you'll only be dancing for me."

I narrow my eyes. "That's awfully possessive of you."

He lifts one shoulder. "It's my wolf genes, Red. I can't help it."

"Wouldn't your wolf genes rather eat me instead of spanking me?"

He laughs as he drapes his arm over my shoulder. "I can do both. Come on, let's get you upstairs."

When we reach his apartment, he leads me straight to his bedroom. He takes a seat on the edge of the mattress, manoeuvring me in between his spread legs. He unzips his leather jacket that I'm wearing, pushing it off my shoulders until it's pooling at my feet.

He blows out a whistle through his teeth as his eyes skate down my body. "This fucking outfit," he groans. "My dick sprang to life the moment I saw you on stage. I'm sure I wasn't the only one with a boner there tonight."

"Rocco picked it out," I say as my face flushes.

"Are you allowed to keep it?"

"I doubt it."

"I think you should, I'll send him a cheque to cover the damage."

"Why?"

"Because you're going to need to wear this outfit when the pole gets installed in this room."

My eyes widen. "You wouldn't."

"I most certainly would."

"You're serious?"

"As a heart attack. From now on, you only dance for me, Red." He ghosts his hands up the sides of my body. "Turn around." I hear a growl rumble in the back of his throat when I do. "This arse," he groans, bending down to bite the exposed fleshy part of my butt cheek before moving to unbutton the hooks and eyes of my corset. "Can you even breathe in this?"

"Barely."

Once I'm freed from my constraint, he tosses the corset to the ground and runs his tongue along the length of my spine as his hands scoot around to my front to palm my breasts. I angle my head back and whimper when he tweaks my nipples between his fingers.

"Turn and face me," he commands.

Mason's eyes remain locked with mine as he pops the button on my leather shorts, and slowly drags down the

375

zipper. He hooks his thumbs into the sides wiggling them and my G-string over my hips and down my thighs. "You might need to remove my boots first."

"The boots stay on," he grumbles. He manages to get them down to my ankles, and when I step out of them, they get tossed with the rest of my clothes. "Lay across my legs."

"You're seriously going to spank me?"

"Absolutely."

"But I don't want you to."

"Next time you decide it's a good idea to perform on stage in front of a room full of men dressed in next to nothing, you best remember this moment." He rests his open hand on his thigh, tapping it twice. Against my better judgment, and because he brings out my submissive side, I do as he asks. The moment he lays his hand on one of my cheeks, I tense. "Relax," he says, lightly rubbing his palm over my flesh.

"That's easy for you to say, you're not the one about to get hit."

"I'm going to spank you, not hit you, Red."

"There's a difference?"

"Yes, and if you relax you might even enjoy this."

"Hah!"

"Spread your legs a little."

Again, I follow his command. When his fingers dip in between my thighs, I whimper. He runs them back and forth before slapping the tips of his digits against my clit. The force of it has me moaning. Is this what he meant by a spanking? If it is, I can definitely get on board.

His hand moves back to my butt cheeks as he rubs and lightly squeezes. He continues to do this, moving between my legs and sliding his fingers through my arousal, tapping my clit, then returning to massage my arse. Within minutes he has me withering on his lap. I'm so turned-on and climbing higher with each pass.

"So wet for me," he groans, pushing a finger inside. I spread my legs a little wider because I need more. He withdraws, dragging the tip backwards and pausing at my puckered hole. He runs the tip of his digit around it, and I can't stop the moan that falls from my lips. "I'm going to take this arse one day."

"And pigs might fly."

I feel his body vibrate with laughter. "I can assure you, Red, when the time comes, you'll be begging for it." The way my body so easily submits to him, I don't doubt it, but I keep that thought to myself.

He returns to my clit, circling it a few times, and I'm about to burst at the seams. He taps it, draws his fingers back, and dips two inside me this time, crooking them to reach my G-spot. I cry out from the pleasure it brings, but just when I'm about to come, he withdraws. I feel like I'm embroiled in some kind of erotic torture. Every time I'm about to fall over the edge, he denies me. Is this what he meant when he talked about punishment?

This time when he moves to my back passage, he adds more pressure, but doesn't go any further. I'm not going to lie; it feels so good that a part of me wishes he would.

His attention returns to my cheeks, as he palms them in his big strong hands, and then *whack*, the bastard spanks me. The sting that follows makes me yelp. "Good girl," he coos as he soothes the area with his palm. "Your arse looks divine pinkened with my hand print."

"I wonder if I'll say something similar after I've blackened your eye with my fist?"

He barks out a laugh. "You kill me, Red."

"I'm contemplating it after that."

Whack. He smacks me again.

When I go to rise, he places his free hand in the centre of my back, halting me. "I'm not finished with you yet."

I part my lips to argue, but my words are replaced by a moan when he slides his fingers back inside me. This time he doesn't withdraw, and when my orgasm finally hits, the intensity has my back arching off his lap.

Mason waits until I've ridden my last wave before he lifts me up and places me on the bed beside him. I just lie there in a sated bliss. My eyes follow his movements as he grasps the neck of his tee, tearing it over his head.

Dropping to his knees, he fumbles with the buttons on his jeans, and as soon as he has them tugged down around his thighs, he lifts my legs, parts them, and moves in between. "Now I get to do what I've wanted since the second you walked on that stage."

He hooks my booted legs over each shoulder, pumps his dick a few times with his hand, and then drives himself inside me. We both moan in unison as he buries himself to the hilt.

The light is filtering in through the open blinds when I wake. I lift my head and find I'm lying on top of Mason. Sometime during the night, we both crashed from exhaustion. Every muscle in my body aches, and I'm still wearing my boots.

A smile tugs at my lips as I recall our marathon sex session and all the orgasms he gave me. The first time he took me was wild and frenzied, the second was different. He was gentle, loving, and whispered sweet nothings in my ear the entire time.

Leaning down, I place a soft kiss on his chest. "Morning," he rumbles in a deep baritone voice.

"Morning."

He lifts his head off the pillow and the moment he takes in my face, his body starts to shake with laughter. "What's so funny?"

Reaching up, he peels something off my cheek. I wince and heat floods my face when he holds up one of the fake eyelashes I'd been wearing. It must've come off during the night.

After placing it on his bedside table, he slides his hands under my arms and drags my body up until his lips cover mine. "I've missed waking up beside you."

"I've missed it too."

His hand comes up to caress the side of my face. "I love you, Red, and I'm going to dedicate the rest of my life to making you happy."

Tears burn the back of my eyes. "I love you too."

"I promise I'll never take advantage of your love, I'm going to cherish it ... and you."

"Can we tell Blake about us now?"

"Yes. We'll take him out for breakfast this morning. Come," he says, sitting up. "Let's get you in the shower and wash all this gunk off you. I'm going to need to change my sheets too, because they're covered in glitter."

I rise from the bed and he follows, slapping my arse on the way to the bathroom. I look over my shoulder and narrow my eyes. "Hey, I've already taken my punishment."

"And don't pretend you didn't enjoy it," he says, capturing me around the waist and lifting me off my feet, making me squeal.

"I still owe you a knuckle sandwich." He chuckles, placing me back down in front of the vanity. His hands move up to palm my breasts as he watches on in the mirror.

"You are too adorable for your own good, Jacinta Maloney."

"And you, Mason Bradley, are a brute."

He rests his chin on the top of my head and laughs. "You don't mean that."

"I don't," I admit as I lean in to remove the other fake lashes from my eyelid. I look like a hot mess, with panda eyes and blonde locks that now resemble a bird's nest. "I'm going to need to run a brush through my hair before I wash it. The girls teased the roots last night to give it more volume."

"Let me do it," he offers, opening the drawer and pulling out a brush. I'm grinning like a fool when he goes to work, gently running the brush through the ends. It's the sweetest thing ever. I wince when he moves up to the roots, and the brush gets caught on a knot. "Sorry, babe," he says, leaning in to place a soft kiss on the top of my head. That movement makes me all emotional. I believe him when he says he'd never intentionally hurt me, and I feel silly for walking away from him now. "How much product did they put in your hair?"

"About a can of hairspray."

"I don't doubt it."

When he's done, he leads me under the spray, steps in behind me, and reaches for the shampoo. I close my eyes, angle my head back, and moan as he massages it into my scalp.

"Keep making noises like that," he says, "and I'll have to dirty you up again once I've got you clean."

I glance over my shoulder at him and smile. "I'm okay with that."

Chapter 38

Mason

I place the bunch of white roses down beside my mother's gravestone. The lady at the florist told me they symbolise purity, youthfulness, and innocence. Everything she stood for. She was only thirty-four years old when my father took her life. Five years older than I am now.

It took three weeks for us to get confirmation from the coroner that the remains were indeed hers, and another week for me to organise her funeral. I opted for a private, small gravesite burial with only a handful of people in attendance—the ones that have welcomed me and my son into their lives with open arms. Jacinta, Connor, Grace, and Jim ... my new family. It was a sombre occasion, but with Red by my side, I managed to get through it.

I run my fingertips over her name:

Rebecca Anne Miller
Deeply loved and not forgotten.

There was no way I was going to put my father's last

name on her final resting place, so I chose to use her maiden name instead.

My mother is now at peace, and when her tragic story broke, my father's impeccable reputation was ruined. It was headline news, and although I hated that my family's dirty secrets were splashed on the front page of every paper, I was glad that the truth was out in the open and my father's true colours were revealed to the world. I finally feel like I'm able to move forward with my life and leave the past behind.

It's been two months since the funeral, and it's time for me to tackle the house. I'm going ahead with my plans to make it a safe place for battered women, with Grace's help. I'm grateful to have her on board, and she's just as eager as me to see this come to fruition.

Jacinta and I are on our way to the house now; her mother and Connor are meeting us there. Jim's volunteered to take Blake to his first football game, because I'm still trying to shelter him as much as I can. Maybe when he's older I'll tell him the whole story, but for now, the less he knows the better.

When Jacinta's phone pings, I push to my feet. "It's Mum," she says. "Dad just picked up Blake, so her and Connor are heading to the house now."

"We should head off then." I reach for her, drawing her close and placing a chaste kiss on her plump lips.

"Are you okay?" she asks.

"Yeah."

"If it gets too much for you today, just speak up."

"The sooner we can get it ready, the quicker Rebecca's Place can be up and running." That's what we've decided to call it.

Yesterday, I had a large skip bin delivered to the house. Most of the furniture will remain, but I will be replacing my father's bed and adding bunk beds into some of the spare rooms so we can accommodate more people. As for my father's personal belongings, I'm throwing it all away—every single item, valuable or not. I want him and every reminder permanently erased from this earth, along with his black soul.

The girls are upstairs packing my mother's belongings into boxes to be donated and putting aside anything they think I might want to keep. Connor is hauling out all my father's stuff and throwing it straight in the skip. I don't even want to go through any of it. I'm grateful that they are here to do the things I'm not sure I can. I'm currently downstairs going through the buffet and hutch in the formal lounge room.

I've already gone through the kitchen and dining room, emptying the fridge and pantry. I left all the China, pots, pans, and cooking utensils behind. The new tenants will need those. I make a list of anything I might need to add as I go.

Most of the things I've come across I don't remember, but I've found a few things that have sparked a memory or two. In one of the drawers of the buffet, I came across one of my old matchbox cars and a yo-yo. I stuffed them into the pocket of my jeans for Blake.

Once the drawers are emptied of any personal effects, I crouch down to open the cupboards below. I'm surprised when I discover a couple of board games stacked on the top shelf. That's something I don't recall doing with my parents; there were no games or fun to be had in this place. I push them to the side, they can stay.

383

The next thing I pick up is a photo album. When I take a seat on the floor and open it to the first page, an immediate lump rises to my throat. It's a picture of my mum on her wedding day. I gently run my hand over it. She looks so young, so beautiful ... *and happy*. If only she knew the hell that lay ahead of her.

My sadness turns to anger when I flip to the next page and see a photo of my parents together. It's funny how deceiving a picture can be. They look so in love, but we all know how that turned out. I place the album down beside me and stand, heading for the kitchen. I saw a pair of scissors in here earlier.

Once I retake my seat, I carefully take out each photograph with my father's image in it, and cut him out. They can go in the skip with the rest of his belongings.

Red enters the room and spots me sitting on the floor, so she comes and takes a seat beside me. "You okay?"

"Yes, just cutting my father out of these wedding pictures."

"Is that your mum?"

"Yeah, she's beautiful, isn't she?" I say, passing her the other half of the photo in my hand.

"She is ... you look so much like her."

I've always been grateful for that, because I didn't have to look in the mirror and see my old man reflecting back.

She passes me back the image and reaches for a wooden box beside her. "I found this in your mum's wardrobe and wanted to show you."

My hand slightly shakes as I take it from her; I'm nervous about what's inside. When I flip the lid, the first thing I see is a picture of me sitting on top. It's a photo of me on Santa's lap, and I'm not much older than Blake in

384

it. The resemblance is so uncanny, you could mistakenly think it was him.

I flip through the contents and find more photos, a few small dried flowers—that I'm presuming I must've picked for her—a vast variety of pictures I'd drawn for her when I was a kid, and some handmade cards. I pick up one that has a red heart drawn on the front and open it to see what's written inside. *You are the best mummy in the world, I love you. From Mason.* Tears cloud my eyes as I read it. She *was* the best mum, and I'm grateful that even though I don't remember ever saying those words to her, she knew.

It's late by the time we arrive back at the apartment building. We got through a big chunk of the cleanout today, but there's a lot more to do. I'm physically and emotionally spent but grateful I didn't have to go it alone.

Everyone heads to Connor and Jacinta's place, while I duck upstairs to take a shower and change. We're ordering in tonight.

I head straight to my bedroom and into my walk-in robe, sliding the album and the box I brought home with me up onto the shelf. It's jam-packed with parts of my childhood, and one day, when I'm ready, I'll sit down and go through it in its entirety. I'm touched that my mother kept everything I ever made for her.

Today I realised something; my lack of recollection from those earlier years has more to do with my childhood trauma than simply not remembering. There were good times with my mum, but I was so busy burying all the shit stuff with my dad—because it was far easier than dealing

385

or trying to understand it—that some of the happier times got lost amongst it all.

When I arrive back downstairs, I find my girl and Grace sitting at the table brainstorming. I love how passionate they are about this project. I gave Grace my list of things I thought we might need from the rooms I went through, only to find she has one of her own. I can tell this place means as much to them as it does to me.

"Dad," Blake yells when he sees me. He leaps off the lounge and runs in my direction, hugging my legs. I love this little guy and can't imagine my life without him.

"How was the footy?"

"Good, Grandpa Jim bought me a hotdog and a meat pie." I chuckle because of course food would be his highlight of the day.

"Grandpa Jim?" I ask, looking over at Jacinta's dad with a raised brow.

"I've been promoted," he replies with a shrug.

"You okay with that?"

"Absolutely."

This family has been a godsend. For the first time in years, I feel like I truly belong somewhere. Bending, I lift Blake into my arms. "So, who won the football game?"

"My team."

"Your team?" I ask, because I was unaware he had one.

"Yeah, the red ones?"

"Red ones?" I see my son needs a lesson on the names of each team, only an amateur would refer to them by the colour of their jersey.

"He said he was going for the blue team when the game started, but when the red team scored lots of goals, he switched sides," Jim pipes in with a laugh.

When the pizzas arrive, I help Red set the table and we all sit down to eat ... *like one big happy family.*

"What's the plan of attack for tomorrow?" Connor asks, and Grace moves down her list of things that need to be done, including who's going to watch Blake while we accomplish it.

I just sit there taking it all in, realising how lucky I am. I have the girl of my dreams—the love of my life—by my side, a best friend who is like a brother to me, and their parents who have accepted me and my son into the fold like we're one of their own.

Chapter 39

Jacinta

Mason does a double take when I exit the corridor and enter the main room of my apartment. I'm dressed in a sleek and sexy, yet sophisticated, silver ball gown, compliments of Cassie. I don't own any dresses like this, so she brought some of hers for me to choose from. She's here to get me ready for tonight, and to also help Connor look after Blake, since Mum and Dad are coming with us to the event. They've both been warned to be civil to each other in front of him, the last thing that boy needs is to be caught in the middle of one of their mud-slinging contests.

Tonight, we're attending Logan Cavanagh's fundraising ball, where Mason's charity will be the beneficiary. Since he's still waiting for probate to go through, he's going to use whatever money is raised this evening for Rebecca's Place, so we can start implementing things to get it off the ground.

My mum has been working tirelessly behind the scenes in preparation for the impending opening, because this cause is close to her heart. She knows firsthand the good it will do and the lives it could possibly save. It's not only going to be a safe place for the women to live, but there will be a team of people to help them get back on their feet and become self-sufficient again.

My mum had never held down a job prior to coming to Melbourne and subsequently had no clue how to manage her finances, because that was something my father had always controlled.

"Fuck, babe," Mason groans as I approach. His jaw is lax, and I can clearly see the heat burning in his eyes as he takes me in from head to toe. "You look …" His gaze moves back to mine, and the smile that curves his lips makes my heart beat a little faster. "like a goddess."

"You don't look so bad yourself," I reply, walking into his open arms. Mason Bradley is the definition of sexy, clothed or otherwise, but in a tux … Oh. My. God.

After placing a soft kiss on my temple, he leans down to run his nose along the length of my neck. "Mm, you smell amazing." His fingertips skate over my bare spine, setting my body alight, and they don't stop their descent until his hand is groping my arse. "As gorgeous as you look in this dress, Red, I'm already anticipating unwrapping you when we get home tonight," he whispers, and his warm breath against my skin makes it pebble with goose bumps.

I draw my face back to meet his, grasping the lapels of his tuxedo jacket. "Something to look forward to."

"On a scale of one to ten, how badly do you want to attend this function?"

I laugh. "You're the guest of honour, we can't bail."

"Am I going to have to walk around all night with a semi until we get home?"

"If the opportunity arises sometime throughout the night, I promise to take care of that for you."

He arches an eyebrow. "You've never been into PDA

in the past, what's changed? Is this glittery dress you're wearing bringing out your inner Sparkles?"

I narrow my eyes, and the smile on his face grows. "For that comment you can suffer for the rest of the night, Mr Bradley."

"Is that so?"

"Yes, I'm hereby reneging the promise I just made you."

Chuckling, he tugs my body closer. "You never disappoint, Red."

"Tonight, will be a first then."

"Challenge accepted."

"That's not a challenge, it's a fact."

His hands move down to cover my arse, squeezing both cheeks. "We'll see, Miss Maloney ... we'll see."

I've never attended one of Logan's functions before, but I was blown away when we first entered the grand ballroom he'd hired for tonight. My mum has always raved about the ones she's attended in Melbourne in the past. The attention to detail is meticulous, from the ambiance in the room and exquisite table settings, right down to the seven course a la carte meal on offer. It's first class all the way, but I guess when people are paying one thousand dollars a head to be here, you'd expect that.

We met my parents here since they're staying at Brooke and Logan's during this visit. We're seated at a table with the four of them, at the front of the room, along with a few other VIPs. My mum and Mason are both speaking prior to the auction. Neither of them is particularly keen on getting up and pouring their hearts out to a room full of strangers, but Logan said it will help boost the donations. These people may have money to burn, but still like to know where it's going.

When the last course is placed in front of us, Mason's leg starts bouncing under the table beside me. I reach for his knee, giving it a comforting squeeze. I know this isn't easy for him. He's a private person, and since my brother's close to his mother's case, Mason's identity has been shielded from the press up until now. They know there's an existence of a child, but no details. One of his father's colleagues came forward after his mother's murder made the news, and said Warren had told him years earlier that his son had gone to live with his mother. That started rumours of a second murder, but thankfully, because the police know the truth of his whereabouts, that notion was quickly squashed.

Logan gets up to say a few words first, then invites Mason and my mother to the podium. "Good luck," I whisper, then he leans in for a kiss before he stands. I have butterflies in my stomach for him ... for both of them.

Mason takes the microphone from Logan and introduces himself to the room. "Hi, my name is Mason, and I not only run a charity right here in the heart of Sydney, called Bridge, that helps feed our local homeless population, I'm also the founder of Rebecca's Place. Did you know that two-point-three million women, which is twenty-three percent of our population, and seven-point-three percent, which is roughly six-hundred-and-ninety-two thousand men, experienced intimate partner violence in Australia last year? Among the G20 nations, Australia ranks eighth when it comes to domestic violence against women, and on average, one woman a week is murdered by her current or former partner.

"You may have heard, or read about one such case

391

that was recently in the news. A former Supreme Court judge by the name of Warren Bradley, who tragically murdered his wife seventeen years ago ... her body was not discovered until after his death." His voice cracks as he speaks and tears sting the back of my eyes as I wring my hands together under the table, because I desperately want to go up there and give him a hug. He's only putting himself out there like this to help his cause. To save women like his mother, and mine.

"The not so honourable Judge Bradley, told the world that his wife had left him—that she'd disappeared in the dead of night—and everyone believed him. But the real truth is, he'd been abusing her and their young son for years. One day he took that abuse too far, which resulted in her untimely death. Because he was a coward, and not man enough to admit what he had done, he blamed his young son for her disappearance, telling him he was the reason she had left. Those words took a heavy toll on that child for many years to come.

"To cover up his crime, Judge Bradley buried her body under a slab of concrete in the backyard of his premises, and erected a shed on top." He looks up from the piece of paper in front of him and engages the room. "That woman's name was Rebecca, and she was my mother."

The entire room gasps when he says that. Mason bows his head and swallows thickly, and I can tell he's struggling to keep his emotions at bay.

My mum places one hand on his back and reaches for the microphone with the other. I know he had more to say, but the words he managed to get out were enough.

"Good evening, everyone," my mother says, and I feel incredibly proud as I watch her. She's come so far over the years, and no longer resembles the woman that was once afraid of her own shadow. "My name is Grace Maloney, and I'm a survivor of domestic violence. When I was eighteen years old, and fresh out of high school, I met my abuser ... he was much older than me, and my first serious boyfriend. I was young and impressionable, and completely smitten by his charm, charisma and the unwavering attention he bestowed on me. Yes, you heard me correctly, in the beginning he was wonderful, like a dream come true, because the truth is, most monsters don't show their hand straight away. It's part of their grooming ... a calculated plan, and how they draw you in." Mason shoves his hands into his pockets and dips his face, staring down at his feet. After seeing his parents wedding album, and how happy they seemed in those images, he knows his mother's story is eerily similar to my mum's.

"Back then, I had so many dreams and aspirations for my future, I wanted to go to university and earn a degree, but that all changed when I met him. I was young and in love ... completely under his spell. My parents didn't approve of our relationship from the very beginning, but he used that as a weapon to try and turn me against them. When they threatened to disown me if I didn't break it off with him, he persuaded me to carry on our relationship in secret, which I willingly agreed to. Four months later, I fell pregnant with my daughter, and he convinced me to run away with him, he said it was our only option, and that my family would make me terminate my pregnancy if they found out. I believed him, so I did as he asked and left my old life behind.

"I was completely unaware of what lay ahead, and once he had alienated me from my family and friends, our relationship started to change. I suddenly found myself at his mercy, and under his complete control. If I didn't follow his orders, I'd be punished for my disobedience. It

393

didn't take him long to earn my complete submission. My life depended on it. With a young baby to care for, I felt like I had no choice ... I was imprisoned by a man who was supposed to love and care for me. What else could I do? I had nowhere else to go, no skillset, no money ... and nobody to turn to for help.

"Over the years things progressed to a point that I no longer recognised the person I had become. I was conditioned to the abuse. People often say, why didn't she just leave, but I can assure you, it's not that easy when you are in a situation like I was. I was petrified of this man, but I was also completely dependent on him. Not only did he constantly threaten to kill me if I ever attempted to leave, he also said he'd take my daughter away from me. That was a fate far worse than the one I'd been living. My little girl was my pride and joy ... my sunshine and the *only* reason I chose to get out of bed each morning." Tears are now streaming down my face as Brooke's hand reaches for mine under the table.

My mum straightens her shoulders, and her eyes are glistening with unshed tears when her gaze meets mine. "It was easier for me to take the beatings if it ensured her safety." Mason wraps his arm around her shoulder as she continues to tell her story ... a story I've never heard before. "Every time I suffered at the hands of that man, the severity of my punishment would escalate. I knew it was only a matter of time before I became a statistic, like Rebecca, but I had no idea how to get myself and my daughter out of the situation we were in. There was nobody I could trust with my secret, or so I thought. I was living a nightmare, but I'm happy to say that I am standing here today because of one woman, her name is Brooke Cavanagh, and she was my daughter's dance teacher at the time." I look to Brooke and smile, as Logan leans in and places a kiss on the side of her head.

"You see, we had no landline at the house, again, it was part of my ex-husband's isolation and control, and unbeknownst to me, Brooke had noticed something was off, and gave my daughter a secret phone to use in case of an emergency. That day came when Jacinta, my twelve-year-old, found me unconscious on the kitchen floor with a fractured skull, missing teeth, and numerous broken bones. I'd been beaten until I was black and blue ... I was barely recognisable." She bows her head and swipes her fingers under her eyes to catch her tears. "I owe my life to my daughter who despite her own fear, was courageous enough to make that call, and to Brooke, who didn't hesitate to come to my aid."

Once my mother regains her composure, she raises her face and looks around the room, and I'm pretty sure there's not a dry eye in the house. "This is why Rebecca's Place is a cause close to my heart. This safe house will save lives, and give women in situations like I was, a fresh start, a chance for a future ... and hopefully a happy ending like the one I got."

When she places the microphone down, everyone in the entire room rises from their seats, giving Mason and my mother a standing ovation.

The night ends up being a huge success, and the auction raises over a half a million dollars.

Chapter 40

Mason

I lift my head off the pillow and place my lips on Red's bare shoulder, peppering kisses along her skin until my face is buried in the crook of her neck. It's the first time she's stayed over this week, and I've missed waking up with her in my arms. Her and Grace have been at the house for the past five days, until late, putting all the final touches on Rebecca's Place, ready for the grand opening today.

Jacinta's taken the week off work, and Cassandra is teaching her classes in her absence. Since there was so much work to do at the safe house, she wanted to be there to help her mum. It still feels odd referring to it as that, because it was the furthest thing from safe when I lived there.

Connor and I were there last weekend, putting all the new beds and bunks together. There were painters in earlier this week to give the place a fresh coat, and the girls have been busy shopping for new linen and things of that nature, as well as cleaning the house from top to bottom.

I'm yet to see the finished product. To say I'm apprehensive about it all would be an understatement. This place is a good thing, I know that, but it still hurts that my mother never got the chance that these women will.

"Mm," Jacinta hums. "Morning." She rolls over and rests her cheek on my chest. "How did you sleep?'

"Okay," I lie.

She lifts her head and her squinty eyes make contact with me. I love her sleepy face when she wakes. "Are you lying to me, Mason Bradley?"

"Maybe," I say, chuckling.

"It's going to be a success; Mum has a whole team of people ready to help these women get back on their feet."

"I know, and I'm grateful for everything she has done. It's just bittersweet. I wish my mum had that same opportunity."

"Aww," she says, reaching up to cup my face. "I know, I do too. Her memory will live on there, and I know she'd be so proud of you for doing this."

"You think?"

"Absolutely. I'm proud of you too."

"You are?"

"Of course! You have overcome so many things throughout your life, things that should have taken you out, but you continued to forge forward regardless. You could have easily taken a darker path, but you didn't. Instead, you let the things you went through make you a better person. You go to work every day and bust your arse to provide a good life for your son, and spend your nights making sure the less fortunate are fed. You silently battle things in your head that nobody else knows about, and lay in bed at night wondering if things will get better. Despite that, you continue to get up every morning and kick life's butt," she says, making me choke up. "You are a good man, Mason Bradley ... don't ever forget that."

I wrap my arms around her, squeezing her tight. How did I get so lucky? "Thank you."

"I meant every word."

When she leans up and places her lips on mine, my hand skims down her back and over her arse until my fingers are wrapped around her inner thigh, so I can drag her body over mine. "Do you know what would make my morning better?"

"What?" she asks as a smile curves her lips.

"If Sparkles took a ride on my pole."

"Ugh," she groans as I spread her legs to straddle my hips. "Am I ever going to live that night down?"

"No. The memory of you on stage that night is now sitting proudly at the top of my spank bank list."

"Eww."

I arch a brow. "Would you rather me imagine someone else when I'm—"

"No," she objects, cutting me off.

"There's no one else that could take your place, babe." And that is the God's honest truth. This woman does it for me on so many levels. "You are it for me."

"I feel the same," she says.

"We're going to have a great life together, Red. The kind of life we both wished for when we were kids."

"I love you," she says.

"I love you too, so fucking much." My fingers slide into her hair, pulling her lips back down to mine.

She moans into my mouth when my hands glide down to grasp her hips, dragging her clit back and forth over my hardened cock. I don't stop until I have her whimpering and withering on my lap.

When I can feel she's slick and ready, I lift her slightly so I can slide inside. She pulls out of the kiss, sits back, and rests her flattened palms on my chest, taking every last inch of me. My eyes roll back in my head and a long, drawn-out groan rumbles in the back of my throat when she starts grinding against me.

My fingers dig into her flesh as she starts to bounce up and down, and my trepidation about today is instantly forgotten. "Fuck, Sparkles," I growl as my hand slaps down against her arse. "Yes, that's a good little stripper ... ride my cock just like that."

She throws back her head and moans, and even though her movements don't slow, I know my words irritate her because she captures my nipple between her finger and thumb, pinching it.

My body shakes with laughter. "Ouch, what was that for?"

"You're being an arse—" Her words are cut short when I hold her in place and buck my hips off the bed, thrusting myself inside her over and over again. "Yes!" The ferocity of my movements has our bodies making a slapping sound every time we connect.

"You love my pole, don't you, Sparkles?"

"Mason ... oh, God I'm coming, don't stop."

I have no intentions of ever stopping when it comes to her—I want a lifetime with this woman. And when the time is right, I'm going to slip a ring on her finger to prove it.

We pull up outside the house, and the difference from my last visit here is astounding. There is now a six-foot-high, black wooden fence that runs the entire length of the premises, completely shielding the house from view.

The fence is set back a few feet from the sidewalk,

and a garden has been planted along the front. The white flowers and green shrubbery soften the harshness of the black, giving it great street appeal. In the centre there is an Asian inspired gate and pergola set back even further into the yard, clearly marking the entrance.

"Mum thought the fence would give the women privacy from the street and make them feel safer. There is a code and a camera installed at both entrances."

"I love it. Your mum has thought of everything."

"Wait until you see inside." My stomach churns and my grip on Red's hand tightens as we walk towards the gate. "The code is seven-two-three-three," Jacinta says, punching it in. "It spells safe."

When she hears the click, she pushes it open. The yard also looks different, with more colourful gardens added and wooden bench seats placed under the shade of the two large trees. A long brick path has been laid, leading towards the front door.

The house itself, although it's had a refresh, still looks the same. A knot forms in the back of my throat when we reach the door and I see the sign that now sits front and centre.

Welcome to Rebecca's Place.

When we enter, the first thing I smell is paint, the second is the large vase of white roses that sit on the side table in the foyer. Above the flowers is a huge black and white canvas, it's a picture of my mum. Underneath it are the words, *'Everybody's safe place should be their home'*. It chokes me up.

I clear my throat and move towards Grace, who stands at the bottom of the staircase with two ladies I've

400

never met. I hug her first. "Thank you for everything," I whisper.

She smiles when I draw back. "Thank you for allowing me to be part of it."

Grace introduces me to Carol and Dianne, two of the counsellors that will be here to help rehabilitate the women that come through our doors. "It's such a wonderful thing you're doing here, Mason," Carol says.

"Yes, this place is going to save so many lives," Dianne adds, who then informs me that she is a domestic violence survivor.

After a brief conversation, we walk through the house room by room. Each one is set up beautifully.

My hand remains clutched in Red's the entire time, and all the inspirational quotes that have been painted in fancy scroll on numerous walls throughout the house, have me struggling to keep my emotions at bay.

Together we can break the silence and bring a voice to domestic violence.

You are not the darkness you endured. You are the light that refused to surrender.

And here you are living despite it all.

From every wound there is a scar, and every scar tells a story. A story that says I survived.

At every given moment you have the power to say this is not how my story ends.

Don't judge yourself by what others did to you.

The enemy doesn't stand a chance when the victim chooses to survive.

Although they are hard for me to read, I agree it's a nice touch. They are empowering words and resonate with me on so many levels. I am a survivor too, after all.

Once the tour comes to an end, we gather in the kitchen and I find out that our first family, a woman and her two young children, will be moving in later this afternoon. It's all happening so fast, but I'm grateful that something good is coming out of my mother's tragedy. This place will ensure she is never forgotten.

"Do you want to come and see the backyard?" Jacinta asks, and my stomach drops, because I'm not sure if I can go out there. She must see the unease on my face because she tightens her grip on my hand. "Please. I think you'll like what we've done."

Against my better judgement, I nod my head and let her lead me out the back door. A large covered deck has been built along the back of the house. There is a comfy lounge area, and a long wooden table with chairs down both sides. I see a swing set and a cubby house just beyond it, but I can't bring myself to look any further, specifically where the shed once stood.

"It looks great out here," I say as I turn back towards the house.

"There's more." When she tries to pull me towards the stairs, I resist. She stops and turns to face me. "I know it's hard being out here, but I did something special for you where your mum was found. I want to show you, but if it's too much we can go back inside."

402

The hopefulness I see in her eyes has me caving straight away. "Okay, show me."

My focus remains on the grass as she leads me across the lawn. It's not until we stop walking that I eventually look up. "It's a memory garden," she says.

Tears instantly cloud my eyes when I see a circle of fragrant, colourful rose bushes surrounding a marble fountain, where a large white, winged angel stands in the centre. "Babe," I say, choking on the word. There is a plaque at the base that reads:

In memory of Rebecca Miller.
You will always be in my heart, because in there
you're still alive.

Fucking hell. I drop her hand and dig the heel of my palms into my eye sockets when the tears threaten to fall. Jacinta just wraps her arms around my waist, holding me tight. I actually love that she's done this for me. I'd much rather picture this than the fucked-up image I have swimming around in my head of my mother lying under that slab.

Once I regain my composure, I say, "Thank you."

"You're welcome. Mum has everything covered here, why don't we go get Blake and go somewhere nice for breakfast?"

There's no fanfare associated with today's opening, because this is, after all, a safe house, and its anonymity remains important.

I fold her in my arms, leaning down to place a kiss on the top of her head. "Have I told you how much I love you today?"

"Yes, but you can tell me again."

"You make me happy, Red. So, fucking happy."

"Ditto, Wolf," she says with a smile as she gets up on her toes to place her lips against mine.

"We are going to have the best life together, and give our kids everything we never had."

"Our kids?"

"One day I'm going to fill that luscious body of yours with all my babies."

Her eyes widen. "Umm ... okay."

I drape my arm over her shoulder as we walk back towards the house. "Think of all the street cred I'll get at the nursing home when I'm older."

"What?"

"Who else can say they knocked up a stripper named Sparkles?"

"You're such a dick," she says, laughing as she play-fully elbows me in the side.

"But I'm your dick, babe. You're very own walking, talking mobile pole that you can dance on any time you like."

"Geez, thanks."

"You're welcome."

Chapter 41

Jacinta

Rebecca's Place has been up and running for six months now and countless women and children have been through there. I've visited there a few times, and mum does too whenever she's in Sydney, but Mason hasn't been back. He trusts the people he has running it, and they are doing a marvellous job.

He still remains heavily involved in Bridge, and with the money he inherited, he's been able to expand. They now open for lunch and dinner, and he's got counsellors working with the people who want to get back on their feet. Helping them find jobs and accommodation.

I was surprised when he told me not everyone wants that. Some people actually choose to live on the streets, and are happier there.

"Babe, you got a sec?"

"Hold on," I answer, bending to get the party pies and sausage rolls out of the oven.

Mason is in the lounge room watching the football with Blake. He's trying to teach him about the teams, so he stops referring to them by their colours. He's not that keen; he said he'd rather go to the games with Grandpa

405

Jim because they have hot dogs and pies there, hence why I'm in the kitchen cooking him some snacks.

I transfer the pastries onto a large plate, and add a small bowl of sauce in the centre. When I enter the lounge room, the last thing I'm expecting to see is Mason down on one knee with his smiling son standing beside him.

"Dad wants you to marry us," Blake says.

"Dude, you were just supposed to stand there for moral support." Mason's eyes move back to me. "I guess the cat's out of the bag."

"I think that happened when I saw you on one knee holding out a ring."

"Right," he says, chuckling. "Will you marry us, Jacinta Maloney?"

A huge smile bursts onto my face as I place the plate in my hand on the table. I had a feeling this was coming because he's been saying things like, "when we get married" or "when you're my wife ..." So, I've been silently hoping it was only a matter of time before he popped the question.

I place my hands on my hips. "Are you asking me, or Sparkles?"

"Who's Sparkles?"

"You," he says, ignoring Blake's question. "But your alter ego is more than welcome to come along for the ride." When he wiggles his eyebrows, we both laugh, because his innuendo was loud and clear. Blake just looks back and forth between us like we've lost our minds. Mason stands, closing the distance between us. "I don't want anyone else to have your heart, to kiss your lips, or be the reason you smile."

"Am I allowed to make her smile, Dad?"

His lips curve up as he glances over his shoulder. "Yes, bud."

He brings his attention back to me. "What do you say, Red? Do you want to spend the rest of your life with me?"

I leap forward, throwing my arms around his neck. "With every fibre of my being."

He lifts me off my feet, spinning me in a circle. Once he places me back down, he slips the huge diamond onto my finger and then kisses me like his life depends on it.

When he draws back, I turn my attention to Blake and freeze when I find him down on one knee, like his dad just was. He's also holding a small jewellery box in his hand. "Will you be my new nice mum, Jazzie?"

Tears instantly rise to my eyes as I nod my head. "Hey, how come he gets your tears?" Mason gripes.

"Because he's cuter, and his proposal was more heartfelt."

His brow furrows, so I reach up and cup the side of his face. "I love you, and I'm looking forward to becoming Mrs Mason Bradley." My words have his frown turning into a smile.

"I can't wait for that day," he whispers, leaning in to kiss me once more.

"Dad," Blake whines.

"Sorry, buddy."

Moving over to Blake, I fall to my knees so I'm at his level. I take the box from his hand and see a gold, heart-shaped locket lying inside. It has *Mum* engraved on the front. "There is a picture of you and me inside," he says proudly.

"I love it," I say, closing the lid and holding the box to my chest. "And I love you. I'd be honoured to be your mum."

A huge smile lights up his face as he stands, throws

his arms around my neck, and then does something unex-
pected ... he bursts into tears.

This kid.

"Are you sure you can't stay the night?" Mason asks as
he says goodbye to me at the door.

"I can't, I've been here all day, and I promised Cassie.
I feel bad for her, she hasn't been the same since she had
that big fight with her mum."

"She went clubbing with the girls from dancing last
night, she can't be that upset."

"She was drowning her sorrows. You obviously don't
understand how women work."

He holds up his hands in front of him. "I never
claimed to, and I'm not sure I want to either." When I
narrow my eyes at him, he smiles. I swear he only says
some things to get a reaction from me. "Can you sneak up
here when she goes to bed? I need to make love to my
fiancée."

"You say that like it's been an eternity. We've been
engaged for two hours tops."

"That's at least two weeks in man years."

I poke his side, and he laughs. "I'll try, if not, I'll see
you tomorrow."

He kisses me one more time, and when I reach the
lift, he's still standing there watching me. He's in his usual
position, leaning up against the doorframe looking as sexy
as hell. After all this time, he still gives me butterflies.

When I step inside, I look down at my ring and smile.
I can't believe I'm going to marry him one day. Hopefully
sooner rather than later. I press the button for my floor

and reach for the locket around my neck, clutching it in my palm. I can't wait to share this news with my family.

I burst through the apartment door, but when I find the lounge room empty, as well as the kitchen, I set off down the hallway. I'm not even sure if Connor is home, but I know Cassie is.

I find my brother's bedroom door open, and empty, so I keep walking. Cass's door is closed, so I lightly rap on it twice before reaching for the knob. I freeze the moment I pop my head through the gap and see my best friend's naked back as she bounces up and down on top of some random guy.

Connor is going to lose his shit if he finds out about this. It was his only stipulation for her staying here.

As I go to retreat, I hear something that immediately has bile rising to the back of my throat. "Yes, Connor," she moans.

What the actual fuck?

"Are you kidding me?" I scream. *Please let it be a different Connor.* But the look of horror on Cassie's face when she glances at me over her shoulder tells me everything I need to know. "I can't believe you two."

"Fuck, Jaz, let me explain." Oh, that's definitely my brother's voice. Explain what exactly? That to get back at me for sleeping with your best friend, you thought you'd sleep with mine. This ... this is completely different. I didn't know who Mason was when we first got together, I never would've crossed that line if I did.

I slam the door and run back down the hallway. I stop when I reach the main room, clutching my head in my hands. This must be some kind of a bad dream; no way did I just witness my best friend riding my brother's dick. She swore to me she'd never do this ... that she wasn't like all those other girls that tried to befriend me over the years just to get their hands on Connor. And don't even get me started on him.

I feel so betrayed. Those two could have anyone they wanted, which they often do, so why would they do this to me?

Connor is the first to come out of the room; he's shirtless, but at least he managed to put his pants back on. "Jaz," he says, and I can hear the pleading tone in his voice. "It's not what you think."

"So, I didn't just witness my best friend bouncing on your dick?" He winces at my words but doesn't try to deny it. "You could have any girl you wanted, why would you choose her?"

He bows his head. "Because I love her, Jaz ... *I fucking love her*."

His words have me doing a double take. "You love her?"

"You still love me?" Cassie asks at the same time.

Still?

Connor looks over his shoulder at her, she's now standing in the hallway with a sheet wrapped around her traitorous body. "Yes," he answers.

"Since when?" I ask.

"Always," Connor answers.

"You've always loved her? Right, you act like you can barely stand to be in the same room as her most of the time."

"It's true, I do."

"So why now? Why are you suddenly acting on those feelings? Is this some kind of revenge because I'm with Mason?"

"No, that has nothing to do with it."

"Then why?"

He blows out a long breath, bowing his head. "Because I want her back."

"Back? This isn't the first time you've been together?"

"No."

My head spins as I try to make sense of it all. "When was the first time?"

"When we were younger."

"How young?" I ask as I feel my temper rising again.

He lifts one shoulder. "I was seventeen when we started seeing each other."

"Seventeen? So how old were you, Cassie? Fifteen?" She's staring at the floor and can't even make eye contact with me. "Was that before or after you said you weren't like the other girls? That you were my friend first and foremost, and you'd never betray me like that."

"After," she whispers.

"You know what?" I say, storming towards my room. "Fuck you, Connor." My shoulder bumps into Cassie's as I pass her. "And fuck you too, Cassandra Lewis."

I slam the door behind me and immediately burst into tears. I can't believe two of the most important people in my life—two people I trusted implicitly—have been lying to me ... for years. If they truly loved each other and wanted to be together, I would never stand in their way. This has more to do with their betrayal than anything else.

Heading straight for my wardrobe, I pull out my small suitcase, laying it on my bed. I open my drawers one at a time grabbing what I need. When I'm done, I zip it up and head back out the way I came. As I wheel it down the hallway, I pass Cassie sobbing in Connor's arms. It hurts to see her like that, but I'm too angry in this moment to care.

"Where are you going, Jaz?" he asks.

"Anywhere but here."

"Let's talk about this," he says, reaching for my arm.

"Don't touch me," I snarl.

I slam the front door on my way out and tears stream down my face as I power walk towards the lift. Only minutes ago, I felt like I was on top of the world, and now, I'm drowning in the depths of despair.

When Mason opens his door, I fall into his arms and sob. "Babe." He cups my jaw in his hands, and I can see the confusion and concern on his face when he tilts my head back. "What's going on?"

"Can I stay here for a while?"

"You can stay here forever if you want."

The way I'm feeling right now, I may take him up on that offer.

Chapter 42

Jacinta

"Hey, babe," Mason says, answering my call on the second ring.

"Hey."

"Is everything okay?"

"Yes, I just wanted to let you know that Blake arrived at school safely."

"Okay, thanks. I was going to call you to see how you're doing? You were quiet at breakfast."

I pause for a moment. "I'm getting there. I'm on my way to my apartment now to get some more of my things."

"Why don't you move it all upstairs ... permanently. I love having you living with us."

"That's a huge step."

"You're my fiancée ... it's only a matter of time before you become my wife, Jacinta. We'll be living under the same roof then; you won't have a choice."

"Okay, caveman."

"You may as well just move in now to save all the hassle down the track."

"You're very persistent when you want something, aren't you, Mr Bradley?"

"Do you know what I want?"

"What?"

"I want to go to bed with you every night, wake up with you in my arms every morning. Have your pretty face be the first thing I see when I get home from work in the evenings, or be able to snuggle with you on the couch once Blake goes to bed, just to name a few, my list is pretty long. I want all the perks associated with you, Red."

"You say the sweetest things sometimes."

"It's all true. Blake wants you with us too. Last night when I put him to bed, he asked me if you're going to be living with us forever."

"When I dropped him off at school this morning, he called me mum again."

"I love that he does that now."

"Me too."

"We're both lucky to have you in our life."

"I feel like the lucky one."

"You're the best thing that's ever happened to both of us, Jacinta Maloney."

"I love you," I say.

"Well, it's settled. On the weekend, I'm going to move the rest of your things upstairs."

I laugh. "Stop being so pushy."

"Just agree to my demands and I won't say another word."

"Fine, I'll move in."

"Good girl, now that we have our living arrangements out of the way, I need to talk to you about the wedding."

"The wedding? We've only been engaged for a few days."

"Way too long in my opinion. Let's organise something small, just with the people closest to us. How's next week sound?"

"Mason," I screech. "I need more than a week; I don't even have a dress yet."

"You best get on to that then."

"I'm not marrying you next week."

"All right, I'll give you one month ... that's reasonable."

"Ugh, you're insufferable."

"Do you have anywhere in mind?"

"When I showed Brooke my ring at work yesterday, she offered up her place. It would be nice to get married by the beach."

"That actually sounds perfect. I don't want a big fanfare."

"Me either."

"Tell her we gratefully accept and book it in for next month."

"Later in the year sounds more plausible." He clears his throat, not liking my suggestion, and I bite my bottom lip. I need to make things right with my brother and best friend first, because I couldn't imagine my wedding day without either of them present. "I'm at my apartment now, so I'll let you go, I'm sure you have work to do."

"I'll always make time for you, Red, I hope you know that."

"I do."

"I love you, sweetheart."

"I'll see you tonight."

"I look forward to it."

"Wait, before you hang up. Do you have any special requests for dinner?"

"Yes, you spread out on the table naked, but since

415

that's not an option because of our son, I'm easy. I love everything you cook for us."

Our son.

"I love that you said ours."

"You are part of our family now, babe, so get used to it."

I'm still smiling when I end the call and slide the phone into the back pocket of my jeans before fishing in my bag for my keys.

I'm apprehensive about being back here; I'm only coming now because I know Connor will be at work. As for Cassie, I have no clue if she stayed behind or went back to Melbourne, but if she's inside, I'll turn around and leave. I'm not ready to talk this out yet.

The apartment is empty when I enter, and I feel immediate relief. I spy numerous empty beer bottles sitting on the coffee table. Looks like someone has been having a party, more than likely a pity-party, and as much as that thought hurts my heart, I ignore those feelings and head straight for my room.

As soon as I enter the hallway, Connor's bedroom door opens, and I jump because I'm not expecting it. "Jaz." I turn on my heels and start heading towards the door. "Wait," he says, reaching for my arm. "Don't go."

I swing around to face him, and the first thing I notice is he looks like shit. "I have nothing to say to you."

"Please," he pleads.

"Is Cassandra in your room?"

"No, she flew back to Melbourne a few days ago. She is so broken, Jaz, I'm worried about her. I tried to get her to stay, but she wouldn't." Tears immediately burn the back of my eyes. I hate this situation so much, and I know Cassie only has us, so I can imagine how she's feeling

416

right now. "She has been trying to reach out to you to explain everything."

I dip my face, staring down at the wooden floors. "I'm not ready to talk about this yet, and it has nothing to do with you guys getting together. I'm struggling with the fact that two of the most important people in my life have been lying to me for years."

When my voice cracks, Connor reaches for me, folding me in his arms. I don't fight it. "Neither of us ever meant to hurt you."

"Well, you did."

"I know, and for that I'm sorry."

I unfold myself from his arms and take a step back. I feel like I'm ready to break. I can't deal with this right now. My phone starts ringing in my back pocket, but I don't answer it. I don't even look to see who it is. I just stand there, staring at my brother.

When the ringing stops, his phone starts. He pulls it out and looks down at the screen before turning it around and holding it up to me. Cassandra's name flashes on his screen.

I take another step back. "I have to go."

"Jaz, please." I turn towards the door and put one foot in front of the other. It's killing me to walk away, but it's what I need to do for *me* right now. When I reach for the doorknob, I hear Connor answer Cassie's call. "Cass," he says. "Can I call you back? Jacinta is here."

"Connor," she slurs over the speaker, and that has me pausing. Is she drunk? It's nine in the morning. "Can you tell Jazzie I love her ... I'm so sorry for everything."

"Cass, what's wrong? Why do you sound like that?"

"Con, I don't feel so good."

"Have you been drinking?"

"I—" That's all she says before we hear a loud thud.

417

"Cass ... Cass!" he screams into the phone. "Cass, are you still there."

I hold my breath as I wait for her reply. It never comes.

The panic-stricken look on my brother's face as he continues calling out her name has me instantly pulling out my phone. My hand trembles as I punch in my mother's number. "Mum," I say the second she answers.

"Hey, baby—"

"Mum, listen," I say, cutting her off. "Something is wrong with Cassie. She just called Connor and was slurring her words; I think she has passed out because we heard a thud and now, she's not responding ... you need to go over there and check on her."

"Oh, my goodness." I hear her relay the situation to my dad. "We are going there now."

"I'm going to hang up and call triple zero just in case. When you get to her house, if nobody answers the door there's a key lock box ... shit, I don't know the code."

"It's zero-five-zero-nine," Connor chimes in. "Cass's birthday."

I stare at him; how does he know that and I don't? "Did you hear that, Mum?"

"Yes. Zero-five-zero-nine. We're backing out of the driveway now."

"I'm going to hang up and call an ambulance, will you keep us informed?"

"Of course."

When I get off the phone from the dispatcher, I close the distance between me and my brother as he desperately continues to try and rouse Cassie, to no avail. I take the phone out of his hand and slide my arms around his waist. I'm in shock, and I hate that the last thing I said to

418

her was *"Fuck you, Cassandra Lewis."* I'll never forgive myself if I don't get the chance to rectify that.

It seems like an eternity passes before we get the call. "Mum." Connor is now clutching his head in his hands as he paces back and forth.

"Jacinta." She's crying and that has my heart sinking. "I'm here with her now. We found her in her bedroom. She's unresponsive, but she still has a pulse ... it's weak, but it's there. There's a half a bottle of Vodka and an empty sleeve of pills beside her," she says choking on a sob. "We can hear the sirens in the distance, so help is close. Your dad has gone downstairs to let them in."

Tears are streaming down my face as I try to make sense of it all. Cassie was a mess when she arrived here for her last visit because of her fight with her stupid bitch of a mother. She's always struggled with the way they treat her, but something was different this time. I haven't seen her this down in years. I should've known that our fallout might send her over the edge.

Why didn't I answer her calls?

The guilt that now consumes me is insurmountable. Connor turns and stalks towards his room. "Where are you going?" I ask him.

"Melbourne."

Finding Forgiveness

***Sometimes forgiveness is better than the
alternative ...***

Cassandra Lewis has owned my heart for as long as I can
remember. When I was nineteen years old, I told her I
loved her for the first time ... she said she loved me back,
but two days later, she ghosted me.

For years, I've tried to hate her, tried to move on, but
no matter how many women I bed, my thoughts always
lead back to her. It doesn't help when she's my little
sister's best friend—she's like a constant torture I can't
escape.

As soon as I graduated from college, I took a job in
another state. I told my family it was all that was available. *That was a lie.* The truth is I was running from the
woman who ripped my heart out and stomped on it like it
meant nothing.

When my sister crosses the border to move in with
me, the woman I can't seem to let go of is back. The push
and pull between us is stronger than ever, and it's only a
matter of time before we implode.

I've obsessed about Connor Maloney since I was thirteen years old. *Believe me, I'm not alone.* His good looks and charismatic personality made him very desirable. I stood on the sidelines for years as he moved from one girl to the next ... I was almost sixteen when he finally noticed me, and what a glorious day that was.

From the outside looking in, I had it all. Money, looks, talent, great friends, but what I lacked most in life was love. To my parents, I was a burden that stood in the way of their fancy jobs and lifestyle. I had an endless line of credit to placate me in lieu of their presence. Connor was the first person to show me what true love looked like, and consequently, I fell hard and fast.

Lying to my best friend was a heavy weight on my shoulders, but I was addicted to her big brother, and the way he made me feel, so I couldn't let him go. That is until my mother got involved and forced my hand. The sequence of events that followed my altercation with her, still haunt me to this day, but hurting him paled in comparison to the alternative.

All these years later, I can still see the longing in his eyes, but if he knew the truth of my betrayal, he'd hate me. How can I expect him to forgive me for what I did, when I can't even forgive myself?

Prologue

"I 'll see you at school tomorrow," Jacinta says, hugging me on their front porch. I've spent the weekend with my dream family, the Maloney's, and I always get an ache in my heart when I have to leave and go back to my real home, because I want to be here with these people, always. It's a place where I'm wanted, cared for, and loved.

The last two days have been extra special, because my best friend's brother, Connor—the love of my life—was home for the weekend from college. I miss not being able to see him every day; it's been really tough, even more so since Jacinta has no idea what we are doing behind her back. That is something I struggle with most.

Jacinta and I met when we were twelve and became besties straight away. That girl breathed life into my miserable existence, and for that, I'll forever cherish her and the bond we share. She makes my life worth living. That's why lying to her is so hard. I've seen firsthand how girls constantly use her to get close to her brother and how much it hurts her. Even though I've been pining for him from afar for years, I still swore to her I'd never be one of them, yet here I am, carrying on a secret relationship with him, without her knowledge.

In my defence, every girl with a heartbeat wants him, I can't help but be one of them.

I climb into the passenger seat of Connor's car, trying my best to act cool as his sister watches on from the porch, but inside, I'm absolutely giddy. It's been two weeks since I've been able to touch him, smell him, bask in his love. We still talk and text every day, but it's not the same as having him here in the flesh. He's nineteen—three years older than me—I have just over a year left before I graduate high school, so it's not like we can be together anytime soon.

My hands wring together in my lap as he reverses out the driveway, and the moment we pull out onto the street, he reaches for me, lacing his fingers through mine. I sigh when he pulls our conjoined hands up to his mouth, placing a kiss on my knuckles. "Fuck, I've missed you, Cass."

"I've missed you too, Con," I reply as tears sting the back of my eyes.

Connor has never held a relationship for long, he's had a plenitude of girls in the past, but they've always been short lived. For some reason, things seem different with me. It doesn't stop my inner panic every time I have to say goodbye though. I've lost countless hours of sleep since he's been gone—knowing he's surrounded by women his own age—and silently worrying that he'll lose interest in me, but that's yet to happen. Two nights ago, he even told me he loved me for the first time ... of course, I told him I loved him right back, because I do.

I loved this man long before he even knew I existed.

His grip on my hand tightens as he turns the corner, heading towards our secret spot ... the place he started

424

bringing me to last year when our friendship began to develop into something more.

It's a lookout that sits about halfway between his parents' house and mine. I was fifteen when he got his driver's licence and offered to start driving me home. Prior to that, Jim, his father, used to give me a lift.

Connor and I have always been kind of friends because Jacinta and him are super close, so being alone with him was awkward at first. *Exhilarating but weird.* It was nice to finally be the sole object of his attention, because that usually went to his sister.

In the beginning, he'd drop me off without many words exchanged between us, but when he started to notice I was often going home to an empty house, the questions began, which in turn led to an interrogation. Although my family dynamic is not something I like to talk about, I found myself gradually opening up to him.

Over time, as our interactions grew, so did our friendship. I became desperate for more from this man but never believed that was possible. Somewhere along the line, things gradually began to change ... I noticed he started looking at me differently, *staring may be a better word,* and he prolonged our time together. I've always loved being with Jacinta and her family, but my lift home at the end of the night was what I found myself looking forward to most.

On my birthday, as we sat in his car by the kerb in front of my house, I made a backhanded comment about how I was sweet sixteen and had never been kissed. To both my surprise and elation, he turned his body towards mine, leant forward in his seat, and whispered, *"Let me do something about that then."*

My heart was hammering in my chest when his fingers threaded into my hair, drawing me closer. The

425

instant our lips connected, I was a goner ... who am I kidding? I'd been dreaming about that very moment for as long as I could remember.

Over the weeks and months that followed, our make-out sessions became longer and hotter, but apart from some light petting, he never progressed any further from there. I was at the age of consent, but no matter how much I pressured him, he was hesitant to relent. He wanted it as much as I did—the ever-present tent in his sweats told me that—but despite it not being his first time, it was mine, and he said with our age difference he didn't feel like it was right. He wanted to wait until I was older. It was sweet of him, but unnecessary. I was all in.

I knew it was only a matter of time before we went all the way, and once that day finally came, there was no looking back. I've never felt so close, so connected, to another human being, but it hurt that I wasn't able to share any of this with my best friend, after all, it's what girls my age do.

The deeper I fell, the guiltier I felt. My betrayal towards Jacinta was profound, but my friendship with her was something I couldn't bear to lose. I was caught between a rock and a hard place, but keeping this secret felt like my only option.

"You're quiet tonight," Connor says as he pulls into a space at the lookout and switches off the engine. When my parents aren't there, which is often, we usually go back to my place, but my mother texted me earlier asking when I'd be home, so he brought me here instead.

I have so much to tell him, but I'm scared. I'm not sure how he's going to react to my news, and he has exams coming up, so I'm thinking it can wait. "It's hard when you're gone ... I die a little inside every time I have to say goodbye," I reply, because it may not be the real reason I'm quiet tonight, but my confession isn't a lie.

The sweet smile he gives me has me swooning in my seat. This man is seriously good-looking, and I'm so lucky that I get to call him mine. "Hey." He reaches across the centre console, wrapping me in his arms. "The holidays are coming up soon, and it will be just like old times, I'll be able to see you every day."

Not in the way I wish.

When Jacinta's around, I have to act like this man isn't the air that I breathe. It's a constant struggle not to reach out and touch him, hold him, mesh our mouths together, or ride the high that only he can give.

"Yeah," I say, dipping my head.

"Cass." He grasps my chin between his forefinger and thumb, gently tilting my face up to meet his. "What's going on? You're not having second thoughts about us, are you?"

"What? God no! I love you, Connor Maloney ... with everything I have." I lift one shoulder. "I'm tired of hiding though, every time I look Jacinta in the eye I feel like the worst person in the world. She deserves better."

"I know, me too. I'm thinking it's time we come clean."

"I can't lose her, Con."

"You won't, she loves you."

"She's not going to be happy about this."

"When she sees how much we love each other she will."

"You think?"

"Yeah, I do. We'll talk to her in the holidays, that way we won't have to hide our true feelings anymore."

"Okay." The thought still makes me sick to my stomach, but we've kept this secret too long.

"Now that we have that out of the way," he says, peppering kisses along my jawline, "let's make the most of this short time we have together before I have to head back to my dorm."

And that's exactly what we do. By the time he drops me off at home two hours later, I feel lightheaded, delirious, and thoroughly satisfied. Is it enough to last until he returns? Not even close; I'll be pining for him again by morning. But for tonight at least, I'll be falling asleep with a smile on my face.

There's a definite spring in my step as I bound along the path that leads to my front door. Although I'm petrified about the news I have to tell Connor, and our impending talk with Jacinta, I can't stop smiling.

I punch the code into the lock box by the front door that holds the key to get inside, but before I get the chance to retrieve it, the door swings open. "Who was that?"

"What?"

"Don't play coy with me, young lady, the person who dropped you off?"

"Connor, Jacinta's brother. He was home from college for the weekend, and offered to drop me off on his way back to campus."

My mother roughly grabs hold of my arm and drags me over the threshold. She may not be the most loving parent, and despite the venom she often spews in my direction, she's never once manhandled me like this before.

"Is it him?"

"Is who him?"

I don't even see it coming, but when her hand connects with the side of my face, the force almost knocks me off my feet. "Do you have any idea the scandal this will cause if it gets out? It could ruin your father's career."

428

My flattened palm is now resting against my stinging cheek as I try to make sense of what she is saying. Is she talking about Connor being older than me? "I don't know what you are talking about, and I can't believe you just hit me."

When she pulls out the white plastic stick from her pocket—the one that was hidden in my room—and waves it in my face, my heart sinks to the pit of my stomach.

Shit!

She wasn't supposed to find that.

Printed in Great Britain
by Amazon

28752437R00245